TIME *in* BETWEEN

LIBERTY VALLEY LOVE: BOOK 6

JOSIE MALONE

TIME IN BETWEEN
Copyright © 2022 by Josie Malone

ISBN: 978-1-955784-51-1

Published by Satin Romance
An Imprint of Melange Books, LLC
White Bear Lake, MN 55110
www.satinromance.com

Published in the United States of America.

Cover Design by Lynsee Lauritsen

For Karen Muir, author of The Daddy Coach, who listened and helped me with plotting questions even when my books had nothing to do with the contemporary romances she wrote. She always stepped up when she was needed regardless of the situation. Her bright smile and gentle hugs that warmed our hearts will be missed.

TIME IN BETWEEN – TRILUNON GLOSSARY

Amalodia – The largest continent in _Trilunon_ with a matriarchal society, its witch queen rules the entire realm with the support of the Mage Priests from _Ethlestia_ and the soldier-wizards of Warpathia.

Banexorting - A spell that transports someone or something thousands of miles including through Time.

Capostrol – The wizard-partner to a witch who serves as a _Vaslattel_, who is a secondary mate, subordinate to the other wives and any female servants in the household. Her children also reflect this lesser status.

Ceroymatand – Man in an arranged, marital match, but there isn't a soul-bond and in the higher classes, any children return to the woman's family if something happens to her. If she holds a higher rank, like that of a queen, he's considered a consort, not her equal.

Chapalmatand – a wizard who sacrifices his heart, mind and soul in an ancient rite binding himself to a witch – no, this doesn't kill him, but he swears to love and protect her beyond death in an eternal soul-matching ceremony.

Dracklegons – A cross between humans and dragons, these Mage-Priests are the dreaded enforcers of Trilunon laws burning criminals alive in the _Fires of Eternity_ since they prefer their "meat" roasted. This fatal punishment keeps convicted criminals from reincarnating.

Ethlestia – The smallest continent in _Trilunon_ where the Mage-Priests, _dracklegons_ rule and create the laws that the people of Trilunon follow.

Garungap – Foul, muddy sludge at the bottom of a sewer.

Hisprinarch – Oldest son and heir to the throne of *Warpathia*.

Hisprinling - The title for a second royal son who might ascend the throne of *Warpathia*.

Huspowner - How a woman refers to her chosen soul-match in *Warpathia*.

Laspowima – A female, eternal mate, or partner, usually a *Trilunon* witch who accepts a soul-bound wizard for an eternal life match where he agrees to "know all, accept all and love her unconditionally." She must be worthy of such a noble sacrifice.

Liminfovia - A *magick* place, between Time, Life and Death. People end up there when they anger witches. It may take days, weeks or even years to escape, or cross from one realm to another.

Majeenler – Title for the High Queen or Regent of *Trilunon*.

Relkinam – All members of an extended family.

Siblerbro – New brother after a soul-matching ceremony with a female relative, often a sister or cousin.

Talipenlace – An enchanted set of jewels created by a wizard and then he seals them with his heart, mind, blood, and soul in an eternal spell-casting before giving them to his mated witch.

Trecesalty – Three royal witch-queens born at the same time – (triplets), a rare occurrence in *Trilunon*, and one that unites all three continents since it's seen as a sign of immense favor by the *Goddess* and her consort, the *Horned God*. The three witch babies are blessed by the Mage-Priests and marriages are arranged for them while they are still in the nursery to gain support from everyone who lives on the three continents.

Triholath – A religious, holy day when the Sabbats or Fire Festivals fall on days when all three moons are present, and the three rings of the sun show in *Trilunon*. It often includes the Fires of Eternity.

Trilunon – A distant realm with three moons and a three-ringed sun, destroyed by the treachery of a demon prince who unleashed a *magick* curse that affected the air, soil, and water killing many of the inhabitants. The survivors managed to escape through a portal to this realm (Earth).

Vaslattel - A secondary mate, subordinate to the other wives and any female servants in the household. Her children also reflect this lesser status.

Vow-Shredders or Oath-breakers – Those who break their promises and dishonor their families, a heinous offense to the people of *Trilunon*. Punishment is a death sentence, one that prevents reincarnation.

Warpathia – One of the three continents in *Trilunon*, with a patriarchal society based on a military structure. All male citizens must serve in the armed forces.

PART I

"Learn to use your magick, or your magick will use you."

— ASTRA JAMISON, ATTORNEY AND
HEREDITARY WITCH

PROLOGUE
"MAGICK, MARRIAGE AND MONSTERS!"

Trilunon – 10 days before the New Year Triholath festivals

THE TENSE SILENCE IN THE STONE-WALLED BEDCHAMBER MOUNTED as her two sisters stared in shocked silence at Satiranika. She took a deep breath and studied them in the weak daylight filtering through the narrow slits of the barred windows. All three were tall with dark red hair. Born in the same hour nearly thirty years before, they were the *Trecesalty* and considered favored by the *Goddess*. She was the oldest, a former High Judge in the courts of *Amalodia*, their country. "Well, say something."

"What is there to say?" Katiranika, the youngest war-queen of their family, favored armor over the dark blue tunic, leggings, and riding boots she customarily wore. She pulled a decorative dagger from its sheath on her slender hip. "Our aunt, the regent of our land, steals the thrones left us by our mother instead of turning them over to us at the Winter Festivals this year. Now, we're denied the privilege of royal deaths at the sacred fires. Instead, our aunt orders us wed, gives us away like sex slaves from the marketplace, as if we really are the treasonous criminals, she labeled us. Who does that witch think she is?"

"The new High Queen of our realm." A tear trickled down Matiranika's pale, wasted cheek as she leaned against the pillows of the giant bed the three of them shared in their tower prison. Several blankets covered her, but she still shivered in one of the nightgowns she always wore. "Who would match with us? My *ceroymatand* died in the first wave of the plague. Yours would have taken you, but his *relkinam* refused you, Sati, saying you're too much like our sire who slew our mother. Our aunt delayed Kat's binding to Prince Hughondear of Warpathia."

"She claimed to fear my death from the disease that killed the women and girls in that region." Katiranika ran a careful finger along the edge of the blade, testing its sharpness. "Even she can't mean to give us to strangers from other worlds. It'd lead to more wars."

"It's not strangers." Satiranika picked up the goblet of wine on the table near the door, crossed the thickly carpeted floor, and carried the glass to her middle sister. "Drink your tonic or you won't live to the New Year. You'll be on a *Journey to Rebirth*, rather than joining us in the sacred fires or at a soul-binding ceremony or traveling with us since she's banished us to a distant realm."

Matiranika nodded agreement before sipping the restorative beverage. Her link to *Trilunon* poisoned her as much as the fire rain that fell from the smoky, gray skies. She barely managed to breathe the soot-laden air and rarely tasted the food delivered from the palace kitchens. "So, who are the men?"

"The Warpathians I sentenced to death before my arrest." Satiranika sat on the edge of the bed, holding the golden cup for her sister. "After the Priest-Mages of *Ethlestial* demanded we serve our sire's sentence when he fled the fires and our aunt refused, there aren't any other males for her to choose."

"What else did you learn?" Katiranika joined them on the bed, glaring across the room at the elaborate painting of their aunt on the wall. "Giving us to the felons in the dungeons couldn't have taken that long. How does she know they won't kill us when we're sent to this new world?"

"At first, she only said what I told you." Satiranika placed the goblet on the table next to the bed. "We talked of the Healers, Kat. They still don't have a way to cleanse the waters, air, or soil of this realm. The creatures here in *Amalodia* continue to die as do the people. Our aunt intends to have the Healers strip our powers before the soul-binding rites. Those in your army are to be sent with us to a new land far from our home here. She asked after Mati and wanted to know you controlled your temper."

"My temper!" Katiranika leaped to her feet. "I'll show that witch my temper." Whirling, she hurled a fireball at the painting. Ashes scattered on the carpet as the picture burned. "So much for her spying!"

Shaking her head, Satiranika waved her hand and put out the fire. "Cease, Kat. This chamber is smaller than either of our palaces, but at least we're together where she had us jailed. As for your other question about our mates, our aunt has decided they will serve as our *chapalmatands*."

"What does that mean?"

"Using a set of jewelry as tokens, they sacrifice their hearts, minds, souls along with their *magick* and powers. It doesn't kill them." Satiranika continued describing the ancient rite that would bind them and their newly matched mates. "We will wear the ornaments, the *talipenlace* sets for the rest of our lives and we will be bonded forever, through Time, Death and Rebirth."

"I won't." Katiranika lifted her chin, narrowing violet eyes. "I'll only be pushed so far. I will not be degraded or some man's property."

"Our aunt says that all three of us must wed on the same day, at the same hour or we lose our *magick*," Matiranika said. "She claims it's the law decreed by the Goddess."

"Our aunt doesn't know as much as she thinks." Satiranika gestured for her sisters to draw closer. "I'm the one who has always studied every canon and *Book of Shadows* in all of the libraries here, in *Warpathia* and in *Ethlestial*. We are supposed to choose the *talipenlace* sets that we wish to wear. We can refuse and insist our newly *Chosen* mates place the jewels on us. They will believe us obedient, as women were in their land before dying in the plague."

Katiranika rested a hand on the dagger hilt. "If I set myself afire at the ceremony, it will start a war. I'd rather be dead than linked to Hughondear."

"No, Kat." Matiranika held up her palm. "If harm comes to you, I feel it. Your death will bring about mine."

"And I will die without both of you." Satiranika caught both their hands and gripped tight. "Listen to me. Our aunt doesn't have to win. For the *talipenlace* jewels to affect us, we must wear them of our own free will. Otherwise, they become tokens of Power. They focus our *magick* but give us the talents of our new mates too."

Matiranika ran a hand through her thinning hair. "I might regain my health."

"That alone would make it worthwhile." Katiranika frowned thoughtfully. "Could we really trick them so easily? Afterward, we'll escape. I'll rally my soldiers and take back our thrones. Let our aunt go to the fires she loves so much."

"One problem at a time." Satiranika relaxed her grip on them. "I've never trusted our aunt with her love of the throne. Think. Who'd be forced to do the evil ritual to strip our *magick* and return all our powers to the High Queen?"

"Our oldest half-sib, the leader of the Healers who serve with Kat," Matiranika mused. "It'd slay Robin's heart. She cries when she comes to heal me now. She'll pretend to take our powers and lie to our aunt. We act as if we're without *magick* until we evade our enemies."

"A simple ploy," Katiranika said, "but those tend to be best in wars."

"Exactly." Satiranika stood and went to the table on the far side of the room to fill three glasses. "Thanks be to the Goddess that we've always treated our older sister with respect and kindness. She serves us willingly and with much love. She knows we are the royal *Three*."

"And the *Three* are the *Trecesalty*," Katiranika and Matiranika joined in the chant. "*Trilunon* is ours. We have the powers of the *Three*."

———

Rowindache studied the flame-haired woman seated at the table in the corner of their shared quarters. She'd changed from the traditional scarlet dress to a black tunic over leggings and low-heeled slippers. When they arrived here after the soul-binding ceremony, she'd performed a *Sex Magick* spell on him. He'd enjoyed every moment. It had not, however, given her the control she'd apparently hoped for when she pleasured him with her mouth. Afterwards, she'd served him tainted wine, unaware his healer talents made him immune to poison.

Her efforts to gain the upper hand amused him. He wondered how long it would take for her to accept their binding. For both of their sakes, he hoped not long. When he was called away to attend a grievously ill patient, he returned to find his new mate had abandoned him to visit a former lover. It'd taken Rowindache less than an hour to find them and retrieve her. In his land, he'd have had to kill the other man even if the knave laid all the blame on Satiranika, but things were different in *Amalodia* and to his mind, a change not for the better.

I'm not going to be shamed by her in Trilunon or at our home in the next realm. She is supposed to be a laspowima, my eternal mate, to be known, accepted, and worshipped by me alone. Instead, she dishonors me and our union. She did not come to our soul-matching with the same integrity that I did.

Rowindache filled two goblets with the wine he'd ordered and blessed to keep safe from her machinations. He wouldn't allow her to poison him a second time. He crossed the room and passed a glass to her. "Granted, we have shared much, but why did you choose me when you obviously didn't want me as a mate?"

"Your trial was not a sharing." Her tone was overly patient when she accepted the cup. "And I didn't choose you, *High Healer*. You chose me. Answer your own question. Or is that too difficult for you?"

The contempt sliced into him, but he didn't let it show. "You are mine, my sweet. What does that make you other than the witch I took to reclaim the morality and renowned reputation I earned as a *High Healer*? You impugned my honor at my trial. What true judge accepts false evidence?"

"Who is to say it was false?" She arched a red-gold brow, then raised the glass of wine to her lips. "You have no *relkinam*, no heritage, no real name. How could someone like you have any prestige? Impossible. Unconceivable."

He took a step forward, caught her chin in hard fingers and tilted it so their gazes met. "You will conceive and give me children, Satiranika. You will teach them that I am a fair, ethical man you admire and respect."

"You obviously drank too much at the ceremonies today." She laughed, dark blue eyes amused. "You may have brought me back to this mating chamber, but I'm not yours and I never will be."

"You are not fit to be a *laspowima* to me." He held her gaze a moment longer before releasing her and stepping away. "It'd ill serve you to be renounced and returned to your aunt for burning in the sacred fires."

"Do what you wish, *Warpathian*." She continued to drink the wine, seeming unperturbed by his low opinion of her. "I will do what suits me as always and being linked to you won't keep me away from whatever males or females I wish to bed."

"I'm not surprised by your antics. You think you're above everyone else."

"Only because I am. Respect your betters."

He refused to answer immediately. He finished his wine first. So, his new *Chosen* thought she could order their soul-binding the way she had his trial. She'd lie, cheat, flaunt her lovers in front of him, and expect him to tolerate what he considered to be wrong. It was time for her to learn to behave with honor and treat others with respect. She needed to be a good ruler, not a dictator, and he'd teach her that.

He glanced at the law scrolls and the texts on the table. "Study what it means to be a *vaslattel, Trecesalty*. You will beg for the chance to be my *laspowima* before our battle ends. I will send word to the law-givers of the change in your status in the morning."

She gasped. "I will not be a secondary mate to the likes of you or serve your other wives and any female servants in the household, nor will my children reflect this lesser status. My *relkinam* have ruled all of *Trilunon* for eons."

He grinned at her. "As you say, I do the choosing, *Vaslattel*. You refused."

Her hand clenched on the wine glass. She stormed to the table to flip through the law book on top of the stack, muttering insults. "*Garungap!*"

"Careful, *Vaslattel*." He headed over to the large bed, sat down and removed his boots. "Annoy me further and I will renounce you again. It takes three lifetimes and several sons to regain the status of a *vaslattel* once I claim you as a third-level mate. Learning *Warpathian* laws should occupy you until we arrive at our new home."

"And what will occupy you other than insulting me, Rowindache?"

He crossed to her, caught her hand, and drew her into his arms. "Discovering what you like when I take you to bed. After being with me, no one else will satisfy you for the rest of eternity."

———

In the Very Beginning...

Official Ethlestial Scroll given to the Bard for safekeeping

So, it came to pass the three moons of Trilunon aligned. The thrice-ringed sun shone bright on the *Triholath* when the *Trecesalty* were given away in soul-matching rites by their regent. Yet, their *chapalmatands* culled from the prisons of *Amalodia* were an insult to the three young queens, the long lineage of the Ranika *relkinam* and the Mother Goddess.

Following the ceremony, the *Trecesalty* were exiled from the realm which gave them life. Stripped of their magic, they were sent with their *chapalmatands* to die ignoble deaths on a world that denied sorcery and the true Mother Goddess. Thus did the usurper, Clympetranika declare herself to be High Queen, and steal the thrones of her own sister's daughters.

This was a plan long in the making for Clympetranika. It all began when she murdered her own sister. Afterwards, Clympetranika cast the blame on the innocent *ceroymatand*, Jarvesel. His only crime was to love the Most Serene, Most Gracious, Most Beautiful, Most Powerful of all Witches, Mother of the *Trecesalty*, the true High Queen, Dianaranika.

With her sister's death, Clympetranika stole the three royal babies from their nursery and spirited them away, declaring herself the Regent of Trilunon. When the innocent *ceroymatand*, Jarvesel attempted to reclaim his children so he could serve as their rightful Regent, the usurper had him jailed.

In a mock trial, he was sentenced to death, doomed to die in the fires of the next holy day. However, he managed to escape this punishment. Determined to save his daughters from those who would enslave them, he followed them in their disgrace to a new realm....

Enscribed by the Bard, Destynee LaFleur, for Jarvesel,
Rightful King of Ethlestial and True Ruler of all of Trilunon

1

Armstrong Horse Rescue, Washington ~ October 1st, 2018

ASTRA JAMISON GRIMACED AS SHE TURNED OFF THE WIDE PAVED driveway to a rutted, narrow gravel track. She didn't want to think about what this would do to the shocks of her new Lexus and flicked a sideways glance at her mother in the passenger seat. "Why am I driving you to see Nina Armstrong on my one day off this month? You could have come by yourself."

"I could, but you know the rules." There was a faint edge to the older woman's voice. "When it's witchy business, you get on your broomstick and ride where I send you. The *Lady* told me you were needed here and no, I don't know why yet. I'm your mother and I love you, Astra, even when you think you can block me. You're not that strong of a witch yet, my dear. You're too pale and under that heavy make-up, I see the shadows under your eyes. You're not sleeping. Why?"

"Because I'm a junior partner in a law firm and I work at least eighty hours a week, plus doing horse saving whenever Meteor gets a psychic 9-1-1 from an equine in trouble." Astra hoped the sarcasm would prove sufficient defense, but from the heavy sigh she heard, she tended to doubt it. She waved at her younger brother and Kyle Morgan, their time-traveling ranch-hand who'd accompanied the teenager here. She slowed the car and opened her window. "How's it going?"

"Good." Orion, a tall seventeen-year-old, sauntered toward the vehicle. "Why did you come, Astra? Venus said you intended to sleep late, clean your apartment and walk down to the Farmer's Market in search of fresh herbs."

"That was the plan all right, but Mom called."

Concern slid across her younger half-brother's handsome features. He stopped, stiffened and listened hard to something only he heard. Then, he shook his head, his sandy pony-tail flopping. "I've got nothing. What's wrong, Mom? What can I do?"

"I don't know yet." Their mother gave him an approving smile. "This may be a witch's duty, not a wizard's, but be prepared."

Orion nodded, then turned back to Astra. "The dreams are getting worse, aren't they? What you do comes back three-fold even if it takes years or centuries."

"I've done nothing evil. I only defend the innocent. Everyone knows there aren't any guilty people in prison."

"In this life, you may have chosen honor, but there were others when you opted for expediency. The *Guardian* opened the door when she passed through the *Time Portal*, the *Seer* guides the dying, and the *Bard* records the past. As you've been warned repeatedly in this life, your *mage* mate *is* coming soon, and *he'll* make you pay the price you've avoided all this time."

"Wizard's *magick*." Astra struggled to sound unconcerned, dismissive of the warning even if she'd suspected the same. "I ward myself and my sisters have 'white-lighted' me and mine."

"I will too," her mother said.

"It won't work." Through the car window, Orion rested a hand on Astra's shoulder. "You and my father set all this in motion long ago. Your loyalties belong to a larger destiny. My sisters face this danger on their own. If you continue on this path, Sister, regardless of your weapons, he'll force your return to morality."

Despite his words, Astra felt a wave of calm wash over her and knew Orion added his energy to keep the psychic barriers around her strong. "But you're with us?"

"Always." Orion leaned in to kiss her cheek. "I guard my sisters in all their battles as they protect me."

"Good to know." Astra smiled at him again before casting another sideways glance at their mother. Short and plump, Estelle Jamison stared back at her, calm and serene in faded jeans and a bright, red-flowered shirt that should have clashed with her graying auburn hair but didn't. Oddly, her blue eyes looked darker in the car. It must be the light or lack of it.

"Nina is riding in the corral. She's thinking about taking one of the horses out on the trails but doesn't want to go by herself. I don't recall her being so timid before," Orion said. "That killer who attacked her has a lot of evil coming back on him and his being from Corbettstown makes it worse. The village reeks of blood, death, and destruction on too many planes."

"Let it come," Estelle told him. "He's not the only one who answers to the *Rule of Three*. We do too."

"Yes, ma'am." Orion eyed Astra again, and she gave a small nod.

Her mother swore by the three-fold doctrine, but Astra was always willing to give justice a hand, especially when it came to wreaking vengeance for the innocent. Her clients might claim they were unjustly persecuted or prosecuted, but she read the truth behind their lies and saw to it that they paid for their crimes. The lucky ones ended up behind bars. The truly unrepentant lawbreakers found their way to Corbettstown and their doom as feed for a pack of rogue shapeshifters.

If the Goddess didn't like it, then it was time the *Lady* and *Lord* stepped up and stopped allowing evil to happen to those who couldn't or wouldn't defend themselves. Astra parked the car in front of the cabin, switched off the engine and paused to study the small log structure. "You did a warding. I see the dome of protection around Nina's home."

"Yes. She's safer here than in her mother's house with her step-father and stepsisters. The *Law of Contagion* permeates everything there."

"Are they truly evil?"

"No, simply weak with a yearning for power and pelf, for what they don't earn. They take advantage. No need to play *Hecate* yet, my dear, or turn them over to your demon father to use for blood sacrifices in one of his ceremonies. Your strengths are needed in other places."

"Is that your word or the *Lady's*?"

"Both."

"Good to know." Astra reached in the back seat for her black jacket. She shrugged into it, feeling the comfort of its power as she fastened the buttons. She wasn't a judge yet, but somehow her dark lawyer suit of black pants, sleeveless navy shell, and fitted black coat always made her feel as if she donned the robes of justice. Her sisters had their defenses. The law was hers.

Everett, Washington ~ October 31st, 2018

Hereditary witch, Venus Jamison, paced the hospital waiting room, clutching the medallion she'd worn day and night for the last seven years, the thin gold chain biting into the back of her neck. "Whatever I do comes back thrice-fold so I can't fight the Corbetts with their own weapons, but if it wasn't for the *Rule of Three*, I'd wreak vengeance."

"Stop it, Venus. As you know, whatever we do comes back on us three-fold. I've told you too many times we serve the Goddess and the Light. We won't be less than what we are. Your brother was drunk and had no business driving. I just pray he lives." Petite and plump, Elder Witch, Estelle Jamison slumped into a chair in the hospital waiting room. Gray-streaked red hair curled around her face, then fell halfway down her back. Dark blue eyes filled with tears. "How could Orion take such a risk? Why didn't he stay at his friend's and return home tomorrow or call one of us for a ride?"

"It's my fault, Mother." Venus hurried across the room, knelt in front of the chair and wrapped her arms around the older woman. "I should have read the omens better. I thought it'd be safe for him to hang out with his buddies at a Halloween party."

"I didn't know they drank. Orion loves flying. Why would he jeopardize his chances of attending the Air Force Academy?"

"He wouldn't."

Venus knew their age-old enemies practiced demonic rites. If she'd recognized the lack of warning as one in itself, she'd have kept Orion home on the ranch. However, she'd thought the people in Corbettstown were too busy dealing with the federal investigators and the county law enforcement officers after the disappearance of Nina Armstrong and her fiancé, Kyle Morgan in a blood-soaked cabin, on the outskirts of the town.

Everyone suspected the young couple must be dead either in an attack or in the fire set by the attempted murderer, although their bodies hadn't yet been discovered. Nor would they be. Early this morning, Venus and her sisters sent the pair to safety in Liberty Valley of yester-year, and no one would look for them in 1888. Meanwhile, having law enforcement hunt for Nina and Kyle should have distracted the town mayor and his pack enforcer, the police chief so they couldn't attack any of the Jamisons, or the members of their coven.

Despite what Detective Watkins told her, Venus knew her half-brother's accident wasn't the result of too much alcohol and teen hijinks. Orion never touched the wine they used during their own ceremonies—he drank fruit juice instead. He insisted nothing must affect his responses as a new pilot.

Footsteps on the tile floor alerted Venus. She glanced at the doorway in time to see her older sisters. The three of them were triplets, but not identical, despite their red-hair and blue eyes. She was taller than Meteor, her middle sister, but both of them were more curvaceous than their oldest sibling, Astra. Estelle never spoke of their father, claiming he had nothing to do with them. Still, Venus occasionally wondered what he was like. Had he been a wizard? Did any of their *magickal* talents derive from him?

Tonight, Meteor wore a lemon-yellow wig with purple streaks. Light blue eyes revealed a willingness to fight. Skin-tight black pants clung to her curves, and a matching crop-top revealed a gold ring in her navel. Knee-high, low-heeled boots completed the ensemble, undoubtedly part of the costume she needed to tend bar at one of the parties she and her college friends would be catering tonight.

Where was her sister's amulet? The pendant focused power and they'd need all they could summon even if it was near a *Sabbat* and the Lady and Lord would be listening. The answer came in the next moment. Meteor had the vintage necklace in her pocket. She usually opted for different weapons, saying a knife served her better than any gold baubles.

At first, she'd refused to accept the antique set of jewelry which her mother, head witch of the coven, gave to each of the triplets on their twenty-first birthdays, seven years ago. In rare attempts to placate Estelle and avoid her rages, Meteor occasionally wore the necklace, but not the bracelets or earrings, making up the *talipenlace* collection.

Talipenlace, Venus thought again. Where did the term originate? Why had that particular word come to mind tonight? Was she finally going to remember her past four lives? Her mother's best friend, another Elder Witch, a sister in spirit if not in blood, Diana Yarbro said the memories would come in dreams, fantasies or when Venus finally met her soul-mate. It hadn't happened yet.

Her oldest sister, Astra, claimed not to know much of her history either. Venus eyed the other woman, unsure whether to believe her. She must have driven straight to Everett from the law office in Seattle. Astra still wore navy blue slacks and a jacket that matched her cobalt eyes. She'd coiled her waist-length, strawberry blonde hair into a bun on the back of her head. Her appearance always gave the impression of a woman totally in control.

Other attorneys, judges, politicians and even the media consistently said Astra was on the fast track to success. She planned to be a judge before she turned thirty. She wouldn't stop until she was on the Supreme Court and it wasn't the one in Washington State. Under the collar of her cream blouse, Venus glimpsed a gold chain. So, Astra expected a *magickal* battle too and arrived prepared.

"All three of you are here? I didn't summon you." Estelle sighed and shook her head. "Why do I think Diana sent you to raise a ruckus? Tell me you don't plan to dance naked in the moonlight in the middle of town."

"Don't ill-speak Diana." Meteor sauntered forward. "She was more of a mother to us than you ever dreamed of being. You didn't have time for us until we came into our powers and joined your coven. She was the one who always listened to our dreams."

"You know we save our sky-clad forms for ceremonies." Astra ranged up beside Meteor. "Stay away from our grove on nights of the full moon and you can pretend we only do the *magick* you order. It's the same thing you do whenever there's a fight at hand."

Anger flickered in Estelle's eyes. "Watch your mouths. The two of you have no respect for your elders and betters most of the time."

"Make that the three of us, Mother." Venus greeted her sisters with quick hugs. Rebellion burned in her heart. She didn't want to be polite or courteous. She longed to return their enemies' evil, a triple 'whammy' as Meteor would say. Astra gave a little nod as if she heard the silent wish.

"Enough." It wasn't necessary for Astra to raise her voice. "We're not here to argue with you. We'll do sufficient of that during the next few days of *Samhain*. The doctor says you can see Orion now. Go to him. We'll stay with Venus."

"And that's all I want you to do." Estelle glanced at the doorway as a nurse arrived. "I'm coming." She paused and gazed at her daughters again. "Be good. I need your help, all your help. Don't do anything rash. Just help me and your brother."

"That woman!" Meteor barely waited until Estelle was out of earshot. "How does she do it? Call for our aid at the same moment she denies who and what we are?"

"Because she's a very smart witch," Astra said. "She always has been and we under-rate her talents. She'll do anything to protect our half-brother, her only son. Do you blame her?"

"Of course not." Meteor's faint smile didn't touch her eyes. "I'd do the same for my children. What happened, Venus? How did the Corbetts get past your protections on Orion and his car?"

"They didn't," Astra said. "If they had, Orion would have died in flames, not gone off the highway in a single car accident. This was brought about by the Corbetts."

The pronouncement in her sister's utterly calm voice eased the guilt in Venus' mind. "I knew they did it and that's not all. We need help on the ranch again. The last hand quit within hours. He hadn't even unpacked when the Corbett loggers frightened him away. Mother needs our help more than she knows or admits."

"What do you offer for payment?" Speculation glittered in Meteor's eyes. "They beat up the last three hands. The only one unafraid of them was Kyle Morgan and he's gone for good, back to his own time. He and Nina Armstrong will live out their lives where they're meant to be in 1888. The police are just as scared of the Corbetts as everyone else around here."

"We know they want the Rocking J," Astra said with obvious impatience. "We've fought this war too many times, in too many lives. The ranch is the last piece of sacred ground with its old-growth cedars and the grove. The county and state politicians are under the Corbett influence. What do you suggest, Meteor?"

"You already know." Meteor crossed to the windows, opened the blinds to reveal the full moon. "Undo what you did when he murdered me the first time."

"What are you talking about?" Venus demanded. "Who killed you? When? We can stop it."

"Not this man," Astra said. "He's killed her in each and every one of her past four incarnations. She and I blocked his memories to keep him from repeating his actions in this life. If he succeeds despite our efforts, she's vowed to be dead for eternity. She's refused to continue being his victim."

Venus took a step forward, leaned into Astra's embrace. "I didn't know any of this. Why haven't you told me before? How do we save our sister?"

"Undo what you did the first time you found me dead," Meteor repeated. "You meted out primitive justice on those who aided my killer and they escaped the consequences. Undo that. Then, we can start over."

"Three hundred years ago? In 1718?" Astra shook her head. "On this backward planet? These people opted for science over *magick*. They're barely civilized now and most still haven't any respect for the *Craft*. I won't return to those barbaric days or ask Venus to give up her children. There must be another choice."

"My babies gone? Torn from my heart and mind?" Venus shook her head. "No. It keeps Orion and other younglings in the coven from being born, too. They're all new witches and wizards who've hardly come into their powers."

"Well, you think of something else. I've got to admit it isn't my favorite option." Meteor shivered, although the room wasn't cold. "Having to forgive him for killing me four times is bad enough. No amount of *Sex Magick* makes up for it, not when I constantly have to watch for traps in and out of bed."

Venus grimaced, pulling free from Astra and crossing to the window to gaze out at the moon. Tonight, she felt closer to the Goddess than usual. What if she sought protection and aid from a new partner? It was the end of one year, the beginning of the next according to their witch's lore. She could seek something new, someone different.

If she traded her body to save the family again, so be it. She didn't have to love the man. She had a feeling she'd almost found true love once, then lost it for all time. She was twenty-eight years old in this particular life-cycle. She hadn't found her soul-mate yet. What were her chances? Slim to none. No man haunted her dreams or fantasies, regardless of what Aunt Diana said.

Venus swung around, facing her sisters. "Me. I'll trade me to protect Quaid, Fallyn and Orion from the Corbetts."

"And Edwin," Meteor said.

"Who?" Venus lifted her chin. "Who is Edwin?"

"Her oldest son." Astra closed her eyes for a moment. She opened them, waved her hand at the door, which swung closed without more human intervention. The lights flickered, then dimmed. "Fine, Meteor. It gives us the three younglings and a newly fledged wizard to protect. Let's do it."

"I've never met Edwin," Venus said, reaching for Meteor's hand. "Where is he? Why didn't you bring him to me before?"

"He's coming. You'll know him when he arrives. I want him safe from his father. If he doesn't kill him, he'll destroy Edwin's soul."

"I'll protect him too." Venus grasped her amulet with her free hand. The gold disk warmed until the engraved figure of a primitive warrior on a horse seemed to burn into her palm. She didn't loosen her grip. She felt Astra's arm steal around her waist.

Time to begin, Venus thought. "*On this night and in this hour, I call upon the Ancient Power, that which is mine by birth and blood, that which is known and understood. Lady and Lord, hear my plea. Send a man to fight beside me. A man who battles evil in each day and way, one who looks beyond what is easy to see, one who is right for me...*"

When they finished the spell, Meteor stepped away. "Well, that was heavy-duty and not what I expected, but it should work as well as the *Undoing* one I wanted. We didn't have to travel back to the start." She smiled, kissed Venus' cheek. "I'm going to the party up in Eagleville. It's a good night to hunt Corbetts and return their evil."

"How do you do it without breaking the *'Rule of Three'*?" Venus asked. "You only have this life left unless you change your mind and return to us for the rest of them."

"I simply send back their evil thrice-fold." Meteor giggled. "Try it sometime. It's better than sex. Blessed be, sisters."

Venus watched her vanish into the shadowy hall. "What else does she know that we don't?"

"Too much." Astra leaned against her. "It's because she linked with her soul-bound mate already, despite the fact she hates him. She knows all of our past, but it's forbidden for her to share it. At least, that's what Mother tells me. Does Aunt Diana ward Quaid and Fallyn tonight?"

"Yes, although Mom refers to it as baby-sitting." The heat from the medallion still warmed Venus' palm. "What do you think we did to those who killed her the first time?"

"It couldn't be more than they deserved. I passed judgement. You rendered it. Our spell-casting rebounds on us three-fold as well. The worst punishment we faced was when the Goddess separated us from each another."

"We've been linked since childhood this time around. Did we share any of our past lives with Meteor? Why would we allow anyone to hurt our sister over and over again? Do you know?"

"An interesting point. I'll scry for an answer for you. I have to go. I need to *Forecast* outcomes for my new clients before we cele-brate *Samhain*. I've healed Orion as much as I can. I'll white-light him too. Remember to set wards around him to keep the Corbetts away."

Venus nodded. "I will. Doesn't anyone wonder why you win so many cases?"

"Not when I only defend the desperate, not the innocent. Those who go free die on the streets or suffer severe consequences for their actions." Astra's confidence didn't waver. "I judge them fairly and they answer for their crimes either in Seattle or in Corbettstown."

"So, you're out for vengeance, too. Why haven't you and Meteor shared that before?"

"You're the *Maiden*. We keep you safe and pure to protect us. Tell Mother that our brother will be fine. Blessed be, sister mine."

"Blessed be." Venus drifted to the window after her elder sister left. Astra was right. Orion needed shielding while he recovered in the hospital. Although the oldest of the triplets had apparently departed, she still felt close by and Venus knew her sibling had opted to stay behind on the astral plane, if not the physical.

It was easy for a witch to create psychic barriers in a hospital. So much *Power* swirled in the halls. Venus would only use the positive energies, the love, warmth, concern, devotion, approval and selflessness. She blocked the negative ones pervading the huge building. Pain, blood, sorrow, grief, heartbreak, sadness, desolation, misery, and despair clouded the rooms, but she didn't have to surrender to the wretchedness.

Afterwards, she slowly relaxed her grip on the pendant. Why had the real name of the *talipenlace* come to her tonight? Did she and her sisters speak another language, one that only they knew? Where had they traveled from three hundred years ago? Another realm? Why didn't the idea shock her? How could it simply feel right?

Somehow, she knew they'd been sent here from a faraway place. Who traveled with them, other than Meteor's killer? And who was he? Would any of them recognize him?

2

Corbett's Town, Washington Territory ~ October 31ˢᵗ, 1888

SUNRISE PAINTED THE DARK SKY WITH FINGERS OF RED LIGHT. RAIN on the horizon, the last thing Hugh O'Connell wanted. Of course, it was cold enough to snow, but he hoped it didn't, since a long day of riding lay ahead. He intended to be in Junction City by nightfall. From there, they'd take the next steamboat to Snohomish City, and then he'd decide whether to return to Texas or head east to Montana.

He'd wanted to leave immediately after the funeral yesterday, but it wasn't possible when dusk fell early on these late fall days. He couldn't bear to be in the same place with the same people who killed the woman he loved without wreaking vengeance, but she hadn't wanted that. On her deathbed, she'd asked him to save her son, to take the seven-year-old to safety with her sisters if he couldn't raise him to be an honorable man. She'd said nobody would stop them because she'd told her husband's entire family that her former affianced, he, Hugh O'Connell, a drifting, forty-dollar-a-month cowhand was the father of young Edwin, not the rich timber baron she married. Still, she said it was wise to leave quickly before Tom Corbett returned from his business trip.

While the Corbett women and the minister chastised Mary for her supposed sins, she simply smiled at Hugh. She'd whispered that the greater crime would be to leave Edwin to his father. Tom Corbett beat her, threw her down the stairs in their fancy home and abandoned her to die in agony. When he left the house, her baby came two months early and Mary began to bleed. The doctor couldn't stop it. Hugh brought his best friend, Rowdy Tall-deer to see her because the older man was a skilled healer, but he finally agreed it was too late. Nothing he did would save her.

They'd overstayed their welcome in town. That was clear before three wanna-be toughs confronted the half-breed in the saloon last night after her burial. The fight ended with two men badly injured and unconscious, but the third died on the sawdust floor. The town marshal refused to arrest Rowdy, saying men who looked for trouble had no business calling on the law to handle what they couldn't and the mayor, the patriarch of the extended Corbett clan, agreed. Still, he advised them to leave as soon as possible. Had he wanted them somewhere secluded so there wouldn't be any witnesses to an ambush? Did he intend to kill all three of them, even a child?

Hugh turned in the saddle to check their back trail. A chill went through him. He hadn't seen anyone in hours but couldn't shake the feeling of pursuit. Who or what followed them? He glanced at Rowdy, a lean, dark-haired man in well-worn buckskins who led the way, Edwin's paint pony behind him. Did the older man sense it too? They weren't alone in the forest. Should they have waited until Hugh confronted Tom Corbett? Was he following them?

Anger swept through Hugh again. He eyed the towheaded boy who rode the brown and white pinto mare. Edwin must be safe before Hugh orphaned him for once and for all. Despite his puny size, the boy was a fair rider and he hadn't had a coughing spell in the past two days. That was lucky since Rowdy refused to give Edwin any of the bitter tonic the doctor provided to ease his breathing.

Rowdy said he didn't know what was in the medicine, but he didn't trust the man who'd moved Mary back to her bed before bandaging her broken bones. If she'd had appropriate care right away, the outcome would have been different. She'd probably have survived both the beating and being thrown down the long flight of stairs, although she could still have lost the baby boy who hadn't taken a single breath.

Hugh reined his buckskin stallion to a halt and listened. The breeze rustled evergreen boughs. A nearby creek chuckled over rocks. An indignant squirrel chattered. Something more sounded. What? A mist swirled past the giant cedars. Vapor cloaked the trees in soft, cool shrouds. Gray fog thickened, became a curtain separating him from Edwin and Rowdy. Hugh closed his eyes, strained to *Hear*. He used the same sense he'd gained over the last five years, the one that foretold danger or death. A whisper came on the wind, a woman's murmur, a sweet voice softer than the squirrel.

He struggled to *Hear*. He'd heard her before. She called him late at night while he watched herds of cattle. He saw her in the sunrise, listened to her chant spells, greet the dawn and honor sunset. She was the woman for him, but she wasn't Mary. He knew it now. Mary had been right when she'd said he was a brother to her, but the haunting voice was that of the woman who owned his soul. Where was she?

Then, he saw her! The dim shape of a woman floated in the air before him, shimmering in and out of view. Bronze-red hair, the color of autumn leaves, framed a lovely face. Violet-blue eyes as bright as a snow sky captured him, heart, mind, and soul. Why had she sent him away? No, it hadn't been a mere sending. She'd thrown him through *Time*, casting a *banexorting* curse intended to last forever. It almost had.

During their time in this realm, he'd been born four times, grown to lead an army into war after war, and died in battle over and over. In this fifth life, he'd opted to change things. He'd become a cowboy rather than running away as a child to enlist in the Union Army as a drummer during the War Between the States. By the time he was a man grown, he'd worked his way to being the foreman of a ranch in Texas. When he was twenty-eight, he finally found his best friend, Rowdy on a cattle drive, and the two of them had ridden together for the last seven years.

Hugh stared further into the trees. Why had he forgotten her? It must be part of the spell she cast so he'd leave her alone. Not again, not anymore. Did he see her by one of the giant cedars? Her name floated into his mind as she drifted closer. Katiranika. He urged the stallion forward. Mustard pranced, unsure of the new trail. If she hid in the mist, vanished again, how would he find her? He'd track her down, but how? He remembered what he'd told her three hundred years before. "You're mine, *Laspowima*. You'll always be mine."

Evergreens surrounded him, towered high in the air. The hair rose on the back of his neck. He gazed deeper into the grove. Trees in front of him appeared to move. He spurred the reluctant buckskin onto the new, rarely traveled path. She wouldn't have to wait for long. *I'm coming, Katiranika!*

———

Rowdy tasted snow on the wind. Should they camp early or push on to the next town? He heard the cry of an owl as it hunted and stiffened in the saddle. That wasn't a good omen. The birds sought prey at night, not in the middle of the afternoon. He looked over his shoulder, saw the small blond boy, but no sign of his saddle partner. "Where's Holt?"

Edwin blinked at the question, then swung his pony to stand across the trail. "Uncle Hugh? Where are you?" His voice carried in the sudden silence. He lowered it to almost a whisper. "He was right behind me, Rowdy. Honest."

"I believe you." Rowdy rode past the boy to retrace their steps. Hugh wouldn't leave the child he'd called his son for the past three days. The youngster always spoke with respect to Hugh but didn't admit their blood tie. Rowdy had to respect Edwin for honoring truth along with his mother's wishes.

"Stay behind me, boy." Rowdy drew his Winchester from the scabbard. "If this is a trap, you escape. This trail will take you to Burdette's town and the marshal's lady, the new *Guardian*. She will put you on the next steamboat to Snohomish City. The captain on the boat will look after you until your mama's sisters arrive. You'll know them by their jewelry. They'll protect and treat you well. They'll show themselves to you, but not to me or Hugh."

The owl screeched again. When the cry died, Edwin said, "Why haven't I met them before now? Mama only spoke of them a few times. She said they couldn't come to Corbett's Town, that there was too much evil and blood *magick* for two good witches to suffer silently. How will I know them?"

"Two women with hair like fire and *magick* in their bearing." Rowdy allowed the memory to seep into him like whisky. "Your mama's necklace, the one she gave you to wear will call to theirs."

"What do I tell them about you and Uncle Hugh?"

"We died well. We thought of them at the last. We'll find them in our next lives. They better be waitin' if they know what's good for them."

"Sounds kinda rude, Rowdy. I don't want them walloping me as soon as I meet them. Can I wait to say that part?"

The owl's cry came again and saved Rowdy from an answer. Three cries of an owl in daylight meant it wasn't the shapeshifting Corbetts or their *relkinam* on the prowl, hunting them. It was someone else, the *Trecesalty*, two of the three soul-bound witches perhaps. He'd take care. He wouldn't let his hopes lead them into danger. He replaced the rifle, rested a hand on the butt of his pistol. Slowly, he led the way down the trail, retracing their steps.

No tracks appeared for nearly a hundred yards. He reined his horse to a stop, isolated in *Time* for a long moment. The odor of ozone filled his nostrils and he glimpsed images from his past lives. He remembered removing armor when he tried to heal a warrior mortally wounded in battle. It wasn't the first time he'd seen the pictures in his mind. His memories of those bygone days had started to return after his thirtieth birthday, eight years before. He'd grown comfortable with the recollections, although thoughts of Satiranika, his soul-mated witch often aroused him as if he were a boy.

He hunkered down in his coat, cold biting at his face and nose. Steam rose from the horse's nostrils and the bay stallion tossed his head. Rowdy shuddered, dizzy before he managed to center himself. Then, he saw the imprint of the distinctive shoes worn by the buckskin. Hugh had ridden off the trail into a grove of cedars. Wisps of fog tangled in the giant evergreens.

"Stay close, Edwin."

"I will. It's downright spooky."

An eagle dove from the top of one of the cedars. The bird flew toward Rowdy. Its wings almost brushed the hat from his head. A long, black feather fluttered. It twisted, twirled in the air and then landed on his right hand.

He lifted his fingers from the gun, caught the gift. As soon as he touched the feather, he knew. Somehow, Mary, the second witch of the Trecesalty guided their journey. "Lead the way, Sister. We'll follow."

The bird circled above them, before it flew through the trees. He was grateful to have the chance to follow Hugh on one more adventure. Rowdy doubted things would be easy. His chosen bride tried to kill him more than once. Last night's ambush in the saloon hadn't ended as she would have planned. The shapeshifter pack should have ripped him to shreds, eating him alive and quarreling over his bones as they had before. The only reason they hadn't succeeded was because Hugh kept the fight fair, limiting it to the first three attackers.

As he and Edwin rode the new trail, Rowdy glanced behind them to see the trees shifting position. It wasn't the first time he'd seen them walking, expanding to fill the opening. As always, he struggled to control the wave of nausea that swept over him. He tightened his hold on the reins when the bay stumbled on the shifting ground, steadying the horse.

The giant trees stood as sentinels, witnesses, and the wind swirled. Remnants of dirt, pinecones, cedar needles, and broken branches covered the tracks, followed by snowflakes. In moments, no sign of the three who rode through the mists into *Liminfovia*, the *Time In Between*, remained.

———

Tom Corbett studied the tracks again. They stopped in the mud before a cluster of huge evergreens. The men who'd stolen his son disappeared with him several hours ago. Where had they gone? Had they hurt Edwin? What had they done with his boy?

"Let's ride." His uncle dismounted and came to stand next to him. "We can catch up with the others and make Junction City by dark. It's the nearest place to catch a steamboat. They know that too."

"I came through on yesterday's boat and it will be at least two weeks before it returns from Snohomish City. They're not in Burdette's town." Tom turned his anger on the older man. "What happened while I was away? How did my wife and baby die? How could you give away my son?"

"Like everyone told you, on her deathbed she swore you weren't his father. She claimed she'd been with Hugh O'Connell and he sired the boy. She passed him off as yours to get our money. What did you want me to do? Let her bring more shame on us?"

"Be serious." Tom laughed, but it wasn't a happy sound. "You called Creed a shame to us until you discovered he intended to use the church's power for your ends. We don't have a single person in the pack who hasn't committed at least one mortal sin except the children, and their innocence is always short-lived. You could have sent word to me in Portland by a raven or magick. You were the one who insisted I go to Oregon even when I told you Mary was too close to her time and I didn't want to leave her."

"She wasn't due for two months and you'd have been back before the birth. It was pack business, and I didn't dare send anyone less in stature to the meeting. Now, stop your whining. It doesn't become a Corbett."

Tom glared at the man, then scowled at the dirt and the tracks again, pushing his way past the branches into a grove of cedars. "I don't understand why she lied. She knows Edwin's always been sickly. He can't go a week without seeing Doc. I have to find my son. What if he has one of those times when he can't breathe? Why did Mary do this? She must have had a good reason. What could it be? You—"

A gun clicked and Tom swung around to stare at his uncle. "What are—"

Too late, Tom scrabbled for his pistol. A bullet slammed into his chest. His knees buckled. He tasted blood, the metallic silver of it, and knew. "You did it. You killed Mary and our little boy."

"And you." His uncle stood over him, rage in the pale gray eyes. "If you two would just stay dead, would stop finding each other in every new life, would stop breeding brats, I wouldn't have to do this time after time. Four damn lives. You never learn. It's your own fault."

"Next time—" Tom struggled to rise, to attack his murderer, but his legs wouldn't support him. "Next time, I'll kill you first."

"No, you won't." His uncle laughed, rage changing to amusement. "You always say that at the end, but I kill you the right way so you can't shape-change and heal. When you return, you won't have any memories of how this life ended. As for your little whore, she thinks you're the villain, not me. She won't forgive you again."

"Mary loves me. She'll always love me."

"Not anymore. Not after *you* killed her babies."

A second silver bullet struck his chest and Tom knew the next one, the last one, would tear his skull apart. In the final moments while he waited to die, he prayed Edwin was safe with Hugh O'Connell. *Take good care of my boy for his mama and me, please.*

———

Hugh eyed Edwin's sleeping form. How long would the boy keep them in this campsite? He'd dozed off in the saddle today. His horse slowed and walked easy in an effort to look after him. Obviously, he had his parents' *magick* with critters. Hugh turned, strode to where their horses grazed. He had to find his own woman before Katiranika vanished again.

"They're fine." Rowdy poked at the campfire with a branch, breaking up the coals. "Let them eat, Holt. We'll travel faster in the daylight. Decide how you'll protect us."

"Why should I when *She* called?"

"Their powers, like ours, are unleashed in this new realm." Rowdy added a small log to the fire. "We're together in *Liminfovia*. I've been here afore. Haven't you?"

Hugh considered the question. An eerie silence filled the woods around them. He hadn't heard birds or small creatures during their ride this afternoon. Yet, it wasn't the first time he'd felt the ominous quiet. "You're right, Rowdy. I'd forgotten. How many lives has it been since we were here?"

"Cogitate on it. Remember when we found Mary dead the first time? We'd just come through the portal to this realm. You refused *Warpathian* justice to Thojedescar although he begged for it."

"Guilt prompted his choices. He blamed himself for her death and couldn't face life without his soul-match."

"And he suicided afore we learned who murdered her." Rowdy shook his head. "Shape-changers—not one ever picks reason over feeling."

Hugh smiled at the old argument. He recalled triumphs on his home world and his downfall. Captured by the commander of another army, the Mother Goddess proved kind. He won Katiranika, the beautiful war-queen as a soul-match, an eternal life-mate, his *laspowima*. "If I'd bonded with her while we waited for the *dracklegons* to open the *Time-Gate*, would she have trusted me to seek justice? You taught me to be patient in battles, Rowdy, not to squander lives or energies."

"On our first night together, my own mate, Satiranika, attempted to control me with *Sex Magick*." Rowdy studied the flames. "When her spell failed, she seemed so frightened, it sickened me. I didn't treat her as an enemy. Instead, I promised to give her time to know me. Then, she served me poisoned wine and fled to her former lover. I insisted she honor her vows, but I never forced her to share my bed. She always came willingly."

"I never doubted my mate's terror. Her energies were so pure and she used a soldier's weapons, not guile or deceit. What of Thojedescar?"

"He and his mate loved one another. He called me to their cabin when she became ill at the sight and smell of certain foods. He feared her private *Healer* poisoned his queen."

"She expected his child then." Hugh glared into the darkness. "We'll find him and demand answers. Who killed her? Why? He must know by now, after he and Mary had so many lives together."

"One can only hope."

The buckskin stomped and whinnied at the edge of the clearing. Something or someone bothered the stallion. Hugh's hand went to his pistol as he headed toward the horses. Being left afoot was nigh on murder and a man could die here as well as anywhere else.

"Hello, the camp?" A man called. "Got room for company?"

Hugh paused, as a young dog frisked forward, tail wagging, obviously expecting to be petted. "Who wants to know?"

"Kyle Morgan."

Hugh ruffled the dog's fur, glancing toward the trail and the two riders. "Any relation to the marshal in Junction City?"

"My older brother." Kyle stopped his strawberry roan beside his silent companion's mount, a big, blaze-faced sorrel. "We're headed home to get hitched right and proper."

3

Seattle, Washington ~ October 31st, 2018

IT'D TAKEN LESS THAN AN HOUR TO DRIVE FROM THE HOSPITAL IN Everett to her loft apartment on the Seattle waterfront. Parking the late-model, black Lexus, Astra collected her briefcase and headed for the elevators, heels clicking on the cement floor. She glanced at her watch. Nearly nine p.m., much later than she normally arrived home, but she didn't have to worry about her three dogs since her neighbor, and apprentice witch, Rebekah Corbett, a young veterinary student would have looked after them.

Astra paused when she saw Latham Sellers lurking near the elevator, not that her ex ever admitted to skulking. He always came up with another excuse for his behavior. She stopped several feet away from him. Six foot tall, sun-bronzed and muscular in his three-piece, pinstriped suit, he must have come straight from the state capitol. Light reflected off his shaved skull. "You should have called. Why are you here?"

"I heard about Orion. I came to see if you're all right."

"I'm fine and he will be too." She kept her distance, her voice calm and detached, while she silently speculated about his motivation. She studied his handsome face and carefully manicured hands, wondering what she'd ever seen in him. "You don't like my family. What really brings you here?"

"I've never said anything against them." Impatience glittered in his reptile-green eyes. "Satir…"

"No." She held up her hand. "You don't call me by my witch-name. Not in this life, not ever again."

He took a step forward. "We've been together in four lives. While I haven't been one of them, I know you better than any of the other men who've shared your bed in this time."

"True, and you won't share it again. You ought to have shown respect and remembered my apprentice was off-limits. She serves me, not you. Trying to assault her last June was—."

"A mistake. One that won't be repeated."

"One of three mistakes." Astra kept her gaze on him, summoning the power she'd need to send him away. "All of them unforgiveable. You also broke into my home this month and stole my dogs to seek vengeance on someone who wronged you."

"You'd have done the same if he insulted you."

"I wouldn't have gone after his child's puppy in a dog park. When Freya refused to disobey my rules, you kicked her and broke her ribs. You tried to have Bamse and Ivor rip her apart. If I hadn't teleported her and her sons home, she'd have died."

"I didn't know *Healing* was one of your powers."

She inclined her head in acceptance. "It's not, but I can use my soul-matched mate's gifts and that is one of his talents. Now, it's time for you to go."

"I will, but you may want to walk carefully. Your mate escaped the death we arranged for him and he'll seek revenge."

"I never ordered you to harm him in this life. You make your own choices and act on your own, but you ought to remember he was a foot soldier in the beginning to earn the money necessary to train as a *Healer*. Since it was always part of his mage-craft, his talents won't have changed. You'll answer to him on the day and at the time he chooses."

"That's why I work out at a gym every day and take self-defense classes."

"You'll need them." She smiled. "*He'll* be stronger than Venus and she always defeats you. Walk carefully, Latham. If you had a part in arranging Orion's accident, she won't grant mercy regardless of how much you beg this time."

He stormed away and Astra pushed the button for the elevator. She had *magickal* work to do, but she took time to text Venus and let her younger sister know Latham might pose a threat. Her sister didn't respond in words, but with a line of laughing emojis mingling with crossed swords.

Three hours later, Astra finished the spells to protect her sisters and the children, including her half-brother. She hadn't needed the jewelry she kept in its velvet lined, wooden casket, locked away in a work-room cabinet for safe-keeping. No matter what her mother said about the *talipenlace* set as a *magickal* focus, Astra didn't wear the necklace with its pentacle in a triple spiral design, or the matching bracelets, or earrings. However, she chose her battles and allowed her youngest sister to believe what she wanted. Venus cherished her pendant but hadn't realized that its *magick* would be amplified when she wore the full collection created by her soul-matched wizard more than three hundred years before.

Leaving the work-room, she lingered to lock the heavy wooden door that kept her magick from leaching into the rest of the huge loft. She strolled into the kitchen and refilled the glass of wine. The three dogs slept near the fireplace in the large living-room and she headed for her favorite chair in the corner. A mix between English bull-mastiff, Bernese Mountain Dog and Rottweiler with a dash of black wolf-blood, Astra privately thought of the huge, ebony dogs as 'hell-hounds' although she never called them that where someone might overhear. She saved the endearment for private moments with her pets.

She heaved a sigh, leaning back in the recliner. She'd ordered the banishing spell so long ago. Was Meteor right? Had Venus cast an actual *'Undoing'* spell tonight? If so, problems would arise on the upcoming *Sabbat*. *Relax*, Astra silently ordered herself. *Breathe. Drink.* The black robe she'd worn to cast her spells felt as heavy as the responsibilities she bore. She reminded herself of the three steps to *magickal* accomplishment, *Prepare, Practice, Persist.*

Even if a wizard arrived and tried to claim her sister, it didn't mean Astra had to let him succeed. She sipped her wine, remembering last night's dream. She'd been one of seven judges in a stone-walled chamber where a dark-haired, dark-eyed mage stood trial for treason. He'd proclaimed innocence of all the charges she presented. His rage mounted when she displayed the evidence manufactured by her minions, although he controlled his anger better than most. Without apparent emotion, he'd accepted the punishment the justices decreed, death in the *Fires of Eternity* on the next *Triholath*.

Then, somehow, he'd been pardoned by the Queen-Regent and created the golden ornaments with dark blue gemstones that captured his mind, heart and soul. Astra saw the lethal promise in his eyes when he claimed her with the entire set of jewelry at their spirit-binding ceremony and knew he intended to kill her. No one else overheard his whispered threat, *'A worse punishment than the one you planned, Laspowima.'*

When they were left alone to consummate their union that night, she'd pleasured him with her mouth, part of a *Sex Magick* spell she'd used with great success to control men, mages, other witches, and even Latham before. It hadn't worked on her new *chapalmatand,* soul-bound mate. She opted for a different way to rid herself of him, poisoning a bottle of wine. She hadn't known that as a trained Healer-Mage from a foreign army, he had immunity to toxic food and drink. She'd fled to sanctuary in Latham's quarters, but her new mate found her. On the way back to their marital chamber, he'd protected her from the dreaded *dracklegons*, the enforcers of their laws refusing to let them burn her alive for breaking the promises her family made. Once they were alone, he demanded to know when she'd accept the fate her aunt decreed.

He'd told her she'd have to earn the privilege of being his eternal soul-match, his *laspowima*. Until she did, she'd be a secondary mate, a *vaslattel*, subordinate to his other wives and any servants in their new household. Even her *Sex Magick* spells and the long hours they spent in each other's arms while they fornicated hadn't changed his mind.

He'd dared to lock her in the room using a spell she couldn't break while they waited for the *Time-Gate* to open to a new realm, and that meant she wasn't allowed to see her sisters. It was the only time they'd been separated for more than a few hours and her hatred increased. Astra plotted vengeance. She couldn't negotiate with a wizard who ignored her unless they were having sex. Afterwards, he always demanded if she was ready to fulfill the vows in the eternal marriage arranged by her aunt.

When the portal finally opened to the new realm, he referred to her as his *'vaslattel,'* shaming her in front of the Army healers who'd accompanied them to the new world. He was lucky she'd only ordered him banished beyond *Time* and *Space*. She wanted him executed. He wasn't highborn so she didn't dare order it without even a mock trial. She couldn't offend the Goddess with his common blood.

Now, Venus had cast a spell that might bring him here. Astra remembered her younger brother's warning. Orion had said her long-time adversary was destined to return in this life and demand recompense for what she'd taken from him. Astra finished her wine. She wasn't weak-willed. Just because a wizard pledged himself to gain her 'love,' it didn't mean she was bound to him regardless of her family's arrangements or promises. She was an age-old judge, an attorney in this life-cycle and she knew how to use the law to talk her way out of anything and everything.

She put the empty glass on the table next to her chair. Leaning back, she closed her eyes for a moment. Soon, she'd go to bed, but for now she'd doze in the recliner, safe from the nightmares of the demon and his minions who tortured and sacrificed her. She heard the snap of the flames in the fireplace and glanced through her lashes toward the blaze. For a moment, she thought she glimpsed a lean, wiry man in *High Healer* blue robes, heard his gravelly voice.

'If you've shamed me, or yourself, *Vaslattel,* plan to face the consequences. No one uses my *magick* for ill purposes, especially not my mate, a dark sorceress.'

———

Music poured out the door when Jed Corbett entered the dimly lit cocktail lounge at the restaurant. Couples in assorted costumes filled the dance floor, gyrating to old-time rock. The catering company had gone all out for the party. Orange and black streamers criss-crossed the room, filmy cobwebs hung from the ceiling decorated with plastic bats and spiders. Stacks of wildly carved pumpkins filled the corners. He headed toward the bar where a small, shapely blonde in a sexy cat outfit filled pint jars with beer. He smiled at the headband with kitty ears holding back bright yellow, purple-streaked hair and the elaborate makeup.

"Give me a boiler-maker, honey."

"No mixed drinks tonight." She slapped a glass down in front of him. "Five bucks. Pay up or I'll give it to someone who does."

"Start a tab and I'll pay at the end of the night."

"Pay now or find a different place to drink." Hate and contempt mingled in her low tones. "You hurt the Jamison boy. If there was justice, you Corbetts would be in jail."

"Not when we own the law." Jed pulled out his wallet. Had he slept with her? The pale blue eyes surrounded by livid black and violet layers of liner reminded him of someone. He couldn't come up with a name. "Besides, it wasn't me. I didn't do anything to the kid." He removed a fifty. "Keep the change."

"Shove it." She wheeled to the cash register, rang up the sale and returned with his change, counting out the full amount, laying the bills on the counter between them, obviously refusing any gratuity. "I'm not for sale."

"I admire your spunk so I'll have you for free." Jed picked up the glass and watched her storm to the far end of the bar. He'd pass the word that she was his, for the other Corbett men to leave her alone. Otherwise, she'd be in a world of hurt.

His family liked to party in Eagleville and they wouldn't allow a smart-mouthed woman to remain here for long. She'd be the guest of honor at a gang-bang in Corbettstown. When her body was found, the pack enforcer, the police chief would claim she'd committed suicide. The state cops and feds wouldn't ask why her tongue had been cut out.

What happened to Orion Jamison? Was he dead? If so, the Corbetts would face three angry witches. Their mother never had been able to hold them back and they'd burn the town to ashes again, killing as many of the shapeshifters as possible. Battles didn't scare Jed. His uncle probably wouldn't be as complacent. So, why had Frank Corbett permitted whatever occurred? As head of the family and alpha of their pack, he gave permission for each and every act committed by the Corbetts and he'd definitely have to sanction whatever happened to Orion Jamison.

Four beers later, Jed waited at the bar. The party ended a half-hour earlier and he was one of the few remaining customers. He'd have been stinking drunk if the bartender served him with any kind of style or speed. He waved his empty glass at her. She ignored him. He laughed. What a spitfire. Maybe he'd take her back to his place, wash off the heavy makeup and see how long it took to make her explode in passion. She'd hate that as much as he enjoyed it. He might keep her until she fell in love with him. That would bore him and he'd give her enough money to leave Eagleville for good.

"Hey Jed, I've been looking for you." His cousin, Junior Corbett, plopped down on the stool next to Jed's. "Dad wants you to stop by his house tomorrow. That new contract came through for the school land. It's 'Clear-Cut City', boy."

"I'll swing by his office first thing." Jed waved his glass again. "I have plans."

Junior followed his gaze to the woman. "Fresh meat. When did she get here?"

"Watch your mouth." Jed signaled her again. This time, she sauntered forward, hips swaying. "Two beers, honey."

She smiled sweetly at Junior. "Only two?" She ran a finger across his meaty hand, nail dipped in blood-red polish. "I'm sure a big man like him needs more than that. Don't you, Handsome?"

"Sure." Junior beamed at her. "How's about a whisky as long as Jed's buying? What are you doing when you finish cleaning up after the party?"

"Anything you want." Her tone was a sexy purr as she sashayed off to get their drinks. "You'll want the best I have, don't you?"

"You got that right." Junior preened at the attention. He adjusted his position on the stool to hide the paunch of his belly. "You sure are a pretty thing."

"Careful." Jed tried to keep the edge out of his tone. "You're married, Junior."

"Oh, I'm sure only his wife is." The blonde smiled as she brought back their drinks. "A man like you shouldn't be kept on a short leash, Handsome." This time, she trailed a finger over Junior's beard-stubbled cheek.

"Enough." Jed leaned forward. "You made your point. Now, go get us some food to sop up the booze. I'm not fighting with my cousin over an Eagleville pass-around."

"You look a little heated." The woman's smile widened, danger glinting in her eyes. She picked up the glass of beer, threw the contents in Jed's face. "That should keep you cool."

He wiped his eyes with a shirt sleeve. He heard howls of laughter from Junior. She was gone. So were his plans for the evening. "Damn it."

"Hot-blooded little skank, isn't she?" Junior picked up his pint jar of beer. "So, you want first or will sloppy seconds, do you?"

Jed back-handed Junior and watched his cousin fall from the stool to the floor.

"Get up."

Junior scrabbled backwards on his elbows like an overweight crab. "I don't want to fight with you, Jed."

"Too bad. You should have thought of that before you opened your filthy mouth."

"Damn it. I'm sorry, Jed. I'm real sorry." Junior struggled to his feet and hastily hid behind an empty table. "Come on. I'll drive you home. I didn't know she meant anything. She's just a woman."

Jed clenched large fists. "I don't take sloppy seconds and nobody touches a woman I want."

"Hey, she touched me first." Junior hustled behind another table. "I'll leave her alone. I'll tell everyone else too."

"All right, Junior." Jed glanced over his shoulder and saw the blonde behind the bar again. "Just remember she's mine."

"Not in this life, Corbett." Her tone made the words even more of an insult. "You'd have to rape me and I'd press charges."

Suddenly, he felt as if they'd had this argument a hundred times before. "I've never forced a woman, sweetheart. I don't have to. You'll beg me to touch you. All women do."

4

Liminfovia, October 31ˢᵗ, 1888

HUGH ADDED A LOG TO THE FIRE, GLANCING AT ROWDY. HE'D healed the young woman who now slept while her affianced husband joined them around the campfire and sipped coffee. "Who attacked her?"

"Gary Smith. He's headed for jail again when the police arrest him." A wiry, brown-haired man in working garb, Kyle leaned back against his saddle. "Astra said she'd try to make sure he stayed there a while, but first she and her sisters arranged for us to head home."

"From where?" Rowdy asked. "Most folks don't find their way to *Liminfovia*."

"What's that?" Kyle asked, rubbing the scar on his cheek. "Or should I say, 'where's that'?"

"It's a *magick* place," Hugh explained. "Betwixt Time, Life and Death. Men end up here when they anger witches. It often takes days, weeks or even years to escape."

"I've never angered any witches," Kyle said. "The ones I know have always been plumb helpful. This must be the place that Astra calls the *'Time In Between.'* I ended up here before when Bethany opened the gateway for me to go to her world from mine, and today, the Jamison women arranged for us to go through the portal so I could take Nina home with me."

Hugh eyed Rowdy, then Kyle. "How many witches and where are they?"

"It's more like 'when', not where. They're still in Liberty Valley, but it's the future, more than a hundred years from this time."

"Reckon, we'll go look for that gate of yours and head through it in the morning," Hugh said. "We have some scores to settle with a pair of witches."

"It'll wait, Holt." Rowdy stirred up the fire and added another log. "They'll keep a day or so until Miss Nina is ready to ride."

"Astra said Nina would need to rest for a couple days once we reached the *'Time In Between'*. I can look after her."

"You'll help, but I'm a *High Healer*, born and bred. I've been one longer than you'd believe, and I've never forsaken my duty. I'll stay until she's fit as a fiddle."

Hugh knew better than to argue with his best friend when the man had a patient who needed him. "As you say, Rowdy. When she is restored to health, they'll go their way and we'll go ours and see if the *Time-Gate* will let us through."

He paused when he heard brush rustling near the horses. He didn't wait for an answer, but went to check the horses one last time. Six small black cattle had joined their mounts. "Rowdy, come look. You ever see stock like this in Washington Territory?"

"Can't say I have." Rowdy arrived with a makeshift torch, a branch from the fire. "They sort of look like those English short-horns we've heard talk of."

The light made it easy to inspect the cattle. The strange steers crowded around Hugh as if they were dogs. "We'll take them with us, Rowdy and find their owners. Odd they don't have brands."

"Another fellow might figure on keeping them."

"I don't steal."

"It's why I ride with you." Rowdy turned and started for his blankets. "Mornin' comes early. I'll get some shut-eye. Wake me for a turn at watch."

"What if Katiranika *Calls* again? You trust me to wait?"

"You won't desert me or the boy. She *banexorted* you in 1718 and sent us back three hundred years, Holt, so you need to think of what you'll do when she's angry and decides to rid herself of you once more."

Hugh nodded. "You have right on your side. Always have…ever since we ended up in the same pile of rocks fighting those renegades. I'm glad we ride the same trails."

"I don't plan on changing things."

———

With the Halloween party over, the caterers focused on cleaning and packing up in the lounge. Jed headed into the restaurant to get another drink and a steak dinner. Of course, his cousin accompanied him. Junior never could pass up a free meal. Two hours later, when they left the building, the lights were off in the bar. He'd have to track down the woman he wanted tomorrow. There'd be at least one or more celebrations around the area, although most people didn't recognize the pagan significance of *Samhain*.

Jed followed Junior toward his new truck. The empty streets glistened from soft rainfall. A stop light flashed two blocks away.

Junior unlocked the doors and walked around the front of the pickup. He clambered inside, started the engine, and turned on the lights. "Your place, right?"

"Yeah, you saw to that." Jed buckled his seat-belt. "You got anybody else to sleep with? That bartender was right about you. Only your wife is married. You've always been an oath-breaker who never keeps his promises."

"You're just mean because that gal in the fright wig left and you didn't get her number. You know full well that I'm all talk and no action with other women. I'd never betray Cherry's trust, or break her heart." Junior pulled an illegal U-turn, drove toward the intersection. Just before he reached the crosswalk, a large, dark shape hesitated on the sidewalk. Then, the animal streaked across the street.

Junior slammed his foot on the accelerator. "Kitty fricassee!"

Jed grabbed the steering wheel and yanked it hard to the right. The pickup veered, skidding as Junior slammed on the brakes. Then the truck crashed into the telephone pole on the opposite side of the street from the cat. The pole swayed but held.

"You stupid, son-of-a-wolf." Jed threw open his door.

He'd figured on saving the animal, but the cat must have received a glancing blow. The large feline lay half on the curb, half in the gutter where it'd been thrown. He scooped up the creature. It weighed more than he'd expected. It must be part wildcat or cougar. He carried it toward his house, several blocks away. "I'll take care of you, keep you safe from Junior and the others in the pack that enjoy killing cats. What bastards."

Jed glanced over his shoulder. His cousin cussed up a storm as he viewed the damage. Sirens wailed, and Jed smiled. "What goes around, comes around, kitten."

Drunk drivers in Eagleville at this time of the night went directly to the county jail. The pickup would be in the body shop for weeks. Junior would definitely pay, and his daddy wouldn't be happy. Frank Corbett hated it when any of the pack, especially his heir-apparent made trouble in the adjacent communities without his blessing. Blue and white lights whirled on the top rack as the first cop car arrived.

Jed laughed harder. He stumbled on the uneven pavement and clutched the cat more tightly. If the animal began clawing or biting, he'd be a bloody mess. He reached his house in the middle of the next block, shifting the cat so he could unlock the front door. He carried the huge feline to the couch in the living-room. He put it down, covered it with the afghan from the back of the sofa while he went for first-aid supplies.

He switched on the lights as he returned to the living-room and his injured four-legged guest. The cat was gone!

In its place lay a naked woman with a mane of blonde, purple-streaked hair, eyes closed, still unconscious. He immediately recognized her. The bartender!

———

Astra sat bolt upright in bed, blankets falling to her waist. Freya stood close by, a stiff black figure and growled her own warning. "You're right. Something's wrong with one of my sisters. But, what? And who?"

She threw the blankets aside, hurried to the closet and removed the green robe she used for teleporting. Another fierce rumble from the huge dog that paced beside her.

"Matiranika's in trouble," Astra said, using her sister's witch-name. "You're right. We'll go now."

It'd take extra energy to bring along the ferocious dog, but she might need the protection especially since the middle triplet insisted on hunting the Corbetts. Traveling on the astral plane, along with Healing weren't Astra's talents. She'd co-opted them from the mate chosen for her so long ago. Whatever cost came with the gifts, he paid. She felt no shame or guilt for that. She wasn't Venus, afflicted with so much survivor guilt that she lost track of her memories, unaware her sisters blocked them from resurfacing in this life.

Dressed, accompanied by Freya, Astra hurried to the *Circle* in her work-room. She lit the candles, spoke the *magick* words, and found herself standing outside a house in Eagleville. She recognized it as the one belonging to the mage who called himself, Jed Corbett in this life. Tonight, he stood on the front porch where he argued with a young deputy in the green uniform of the county sheriff's department.

"I'm not going with you. I haven't done anything wrong."

"Are you sure about that?" Resting her hand on Freya's massive head, Astra advanced on the two men. "Where is my sister? Have you hurt her again?"

"Oh, great." Jed ran a hand through thick, black hair. "Make this fool think I beat women. I haven't seen your bloody sisters, either of them."

"Then why did she call me from here for a ride?" Astra glared at Jed and Freya and rumbled her own threat. "You have her."

"I do not." Jed took a deep breath. "Look, my cousin tried to drive me home. I shouldn't have let him because he was drinking, but so was I. He hit that telephone pole." Jed stopped talking for a moment and pointed toward the center of town. "Oh, hell. Think what you like. You will anyway."

"Exactly." Astra gave him a mental push, went past the large man into the house, followed by the police officer. She heard the dog snarl at Jed and knew Freya blocked him from the entry. She spotted her sister sitting on the couch, wrapped in a hand-crocheted afghan.

Meteor raised a hand to her bruised forehead. "Astra, everything hurts."

"It always does." Astra flicked a quick glance at the young deputy behind her. "Honey, why don't you stay away from him? When he drinks and he always drinks..."

"It wasn't his fault this time." Pain filled Meteor's light blue eyes as she gently touched a swollen cheek. "At least, I don't think so."

"When it comes to him, you never do." Astra adjusted the blanket around her naked sister. "Honey, where are your clothes?"

"I don't know." Meteor leaned against Astra. "I want to go home. To my house, not yours. Help me get there. My ribs are killing me."

"Come on." Astra helped the other woman stand. "You'll be fine. I promise. I've told you before. You need to stay away from him."

"I'll call an ambulance." Pink, blue and white shone in the deputy's aura, revealing not only his sincerity but also his innate purity, goodness and decency. "Did he assault you, ma'am? Rape you?"

"I don't know." Meteor blinked at him, obviously bemused by

the innocence he wore. "Eagleville and Corbettstown aren't good places for you, Deputy Dawson. You should leave so you'll be safe. The Corbetts are going to kill you before Yule, aren't they, Astra?"

"I'm afraid so." Astra clearly saw the *Outcome* for the newly hired officer. "I don't know the exact date, but you shouldn't take any chances. Don't come back here until the Christmas holidays are over, regardless of the reason."

"I'm a law enforcement officer." Dawson straightened. "I take care of those who need it. I'm arresting Jed Corbett. He has outstanding warrants, and this looks like a case of domestic violence. One of them is going to jail and you can't, ma'am. I'll come to the hospital to do the rest of the paperwork. Where are you taking her?"

"Home to my house," Meteor repeated. "I don't want a doctor, especially not our aunt. Her lectures are worse than yours and I hurt too bad to listen to either of you, Astra."

"I know, baby." Astra carefully put her arm around her sister's waist. "Aunt Diana has beds at the hospital in Everett. I'll take you there if you need to go. The deputy will give me the papers and I'll complete them for you. It won't be a problem because I'm an officer of the court here as well as in Seattle."

Astra guided Meteor to the door, where they saw Jed handcuffed and put in the back of the squad car. Once she had the necessary forms, Astra took Meteor to the two-story duplex the catering company bought for their headquarters five years before. Freya escorted them, a silent, lethal, competent guard.

Upstairs in the bedroom, Astra healed her sister. "It seems as if you accomplished what you set out to do. The Corbetts will have serious problems what with Junior driving under the influence and Jed assaulting you. I'll see to the papers. When Dawson comes to interview you, stick to the story. You finished work and you don't know how you ended up at Jed's house."

"But it's not totally true. It's a full moon, and I had to shift. I was in my cat-form and Junior tried to hit me with his truck."

"Nobody will believe a story like that. Junior and Jed earn their *Outcomes* too."

"What about my clothes?" Meteor unpinned the lemon-yellow wig and removed it, revealing her natural cap of cinnamon, red-brown hair. "I left my things in a box in the catering truck before I *changed*. Dawson will wonder."

"He thinks Jed was about to rape you. Once he has a search warrant, the deputy will find your clothing crumpled in a corner of the living-room behind the couch. I'll see to that before I return home."

After she tucked Meteor into bed, Astra brought her a glass of warm milk, laced with Irish whisky. "Drink this. You need to watch for Edwin and bring him safely to us. Jed will have sufficient to worry him. He won't even think of your son."

"I'd do anything for my children. Thank you for coming, Astra. I feel better, but I didn't expect any of these events."

"Of course, you didn't. *Outcomes* are my province, not yours." Freya beside her, Astra made her farewells and left the house. She'd embellish the complaint against the Corbetts and forward the papers to the sheriff's department tomorrow.

She sighed, hating the idea of what would happen to Deputy Dawson. He faced a horrible future...tortured beyond human endurance, then while he bled from serious injuries, a pack of hungry, rogue shape-shifters would rip him to shreds and feast on his flesh, organs and bones. Of course, as her sire proclaimed, '*blood magick*' demanded the deaths of innocents. Did that mean she had to allow Dawson's sacrifice?

———

Booked into the county jail, Jed supposed his name was what granted him a cell of his own. He hadn't harmed the woman, but wondered again why he hadn't recognized her as one of the three Jamison witches. What passion drew them together? Why did he always want her? He knew her, but she'd looked so different tonight and he couldn't even think of her name. What was it? Melly? Mattie? What? When he tried to force the memories, a black curtain dropped into his mind and blocked everything.

He dropped down on the narrow cot. He slept and dreamed. He liked women. He always had, even when he simply looked at the female guards in the prison where he awaited his death in the *Fires of Eternity*. He'd expected to wed someday when he met the right woman, but unlike the prince he loved and served, he knew he'd choose his own bride. Of course, with a choice between being burned alive and an eternal soul-match to one of the *Trecesalty*, he'd opted for the arranged marriage.

The second queen had too much pride to suit him. He abhorred the display she'd made of herself at their mating ceremony. Six fully armored, lovely soldiers carried in a litter. One opened the silk curtains. She'd barely stirred from the pillows, forcing him to join her on the cushioned pallet to put his enchanted set of jewelry on her, the elaborate necklace with its golden sun around her neck, the matching bracelets on thin wrists, the earrings…

Once she wore the ornaments and he'd stepped away from the litter, the guards carried it and his new *laspowima* from the chamber. She hadn't remained for the vows. Instead, her aunt recited the promises for her the same as she'd done for her other two nieces. At least, his bride hadn't created a stormy scene like the war-queen who refused to join the prince at the bridal table. Even the eldest of the three royal witches couldn't convince her sisters to participate appropriately at the celebrations.

He grimaced. He'd stayed away from the room he and his mate were to share for several hours. He couldn't avoid her any longer. He had to speak to the woman. Perhaps they'd find common ground and become true friends, if nothing more. Otherwise, their lifetimes together would indeed seem like eternities. It wasn't as if he could leave her, not when the *talipenlace* set he created bound him, heart, body, and soul to her.

He opened the door to the shared chamber and stepped inside.

His new bride wasn't alone. A woman in the blue robes of a *High Healer* hovered over his mate.

"What's wrong? What's happened? Why are you ill?"

The question prompted a weak sound he recognized as a near giggle. "I die, *Warpath*—" A spasm of coughing broke off the words.

"Are you serious?" He reached the bed in three long strides and really looked at her. More coughing wracked the thin body wrapped in a scarlet robe and she spit blood into the cloth the healer held. "Why? Who harmed you? What has done this?"

"Her links to *Trilunon*." Putting aside the cloth, the *High Healer* held a cup of watered wine to the second queen's lips. "Drink. You need your tonic. The ceremony was too much for you and this journey to a new realm - - -."

"May cure me," the queen sipped the red liquid in the gold goblet, "or kill me."

For the first time, he saw dark bruises under the light blue eyes. He remembered the bright face-paint she'd worn at the ceremony. Royal pride must have dictated hiding her frailty. No wonder he hadn't realized she was so fragile. He sank to his knees beside the bed, covered one of her thin, finely bound hands with his. "How can I help you, *Chosen*?"

5

Liminfovia ~ Friday, November 2nd, 1888

TWO DAYS LATER, THEY BROKE CAMP AND WERE ON THE TRAIL shortly after sunrise, riding through rugged country filled with different kinds of evergreens, pines, cedars, hemlocks and spruce trees. Before the track wound down a steep hill, Hugh recognized thread-like *magick* hovering in the air, streaming downward. He and Rowdy exchanged glances. After they went through the portal, they stopped and turned their horses to face the psychic barrier. Waves of energy rolled, small ones followed by larger ones, creating a hazy view, a thin fog-shrouded screen blocking most of the path behind them.

Dropping the reins behind the saddle horn, Hugh lifted his hands and framed a wall of his own with his special symbol. He felt Rowdy adding *magickal* support beside him. '*Lord and Lady, hear my word. Cowboys ride through the pass and close this gate behind our herd. No outlaw will trespass here or otherwise flee, not during the rest of my lives, and while we live and breathe, we keep this sacred place under lock and key.*'

Hours later, he rode at the rear of their small group. He eyed the black cattle again. He'd never seen stock like this and he'd been a cowboy since he headed west twenty-three years before when his mother died. At thirteen, he was too old for the local orphanage.

"I bet a woman owns them." Edwin said, dark eyes bright and interested. "Mama always made a pet of ours because it makes it easy to milk and care for the cow, but when the pack killed her, that made Mama really mad. She told Pa she wanted to move away from Corbett's Town and be with decent folk, not the soul-less wolves in his family."

"These are steers, son, but you have a good point. Women aren't as strong as men."

"Reckon, you best not tell your witch that, Holt." Rowdy chuckled, a faint sound. "We'll call *Liminfovia* home for years."

"What's Lim—?" Edwin asked. "*Liminfovia*? Is that where we stayed the past two nights? Is it the place that kept us safe from the pack?"

"It's a *magick* place where wizards can rest," Hugh explained. "Sometimes, witches send us there, but we can go on our own too." He glanced at Rowdy. "What's the matter? You looked better after that last stampede when your horse died under you and rustlers shot you."

"Bad dreams." Rowdy reined his mount to a stop. "I didn't leave my blankets, did I?"

"Not that I saw." Hugh warded his old friend, saw new energies creep into the air around him. "Better?"

Rowdy nodded, pushed back his hat. "Makes me wonder where my witch lurks. She can use my *magick* for good or ill. With her, there's scant difference. She may serve the law, but she always views ethics as weaknesses."

"Then, you'll have to teach her otherwise." Hugh watched hope filter into Rowdy's dark gaze. If only it was that easy. They had to find both their witches soon, or he might lose his best friend to a dangerous spell or someone who continually drained the healer's life energies.

The cedars thinned as they rode further. Alders, maples, and scrub brush slowly replaced the evergreens. A wide road covered with rock lay before them. The cattle broke into a run.

"Let's catch them." Hugh pushed his horse to a gallop. As he went by, he glimpsed logged land piled high with slash – tree branches and unusable wood. Giant stumps dotted a few clearings where various plants began to grow, most of them inedible by livestock.

Rowdy rode up beside Hugh, gestured to the place where the cattle pressed against barbed wire. "There's a fence. Then again, maybe not."

"You're right. It's not much of one." Hugh took Mustard closer, through the cluster of cattle. He glanced over his shoulder, saw Edwin safe behind him. "These cows want into that grass. Can't blame them. You stay clear, son."

"Yes, sir. Want I should hold your horse?"

"No need. I'll ground hitch him and he'll stand pat." Hugh dismounted, stopped when he realized the boy had read his mind. "Reckon, you'll make a fair wizard one day."

"Pa says that too." Pleasure seeped into Edwin's face.

Hugh and Rowdy shared a look. Mayhap, there was more to Thojedescar than either of them knew. Hugh began to take down the rusty wire. After a moment, Rowdy swung down to help.

"We'll return these cows and then we'll track witches. They can't hide from us much longer."

"You've said that the last two nights in *Liminfovia*, Holt. It feels like my life-mate is near, but I've been wrong afore."

———

The telephone rang before the alarm went off on her radio. Astra rolled over to answer the extension on the nightstand beside her queen-size bed. "Yes? What is it? Who is it?"

"Your mother. I wanted to let you know that the doctor is

releasing Orion today. He's almost a hundred percent better except for a broken leg. He's even recovered from most of the effects of a concussion. The doctor thinks it's a miracle."

"Of course, it is. I'll look forward to seeing him later."

"This afternoon. I expect you at the ranch for the *Sabbat*. Bring whatever you need, your apprentice and your *talipenlace* set. Plan to stay for the weekend."

Astra sat up in bed, plumping the pillows before she leaned against two of them. "What if I have other plans?"

"We've discussed this too many times before and you know the rules." Impatience filled the older woman's voice. "When one of the leaders of the coven calls, you get on your broomstick and come where we want you. The *Lady* told me you were needed here and no, I don't know why yet. Besides, you've rescued enough horses and ponies for us to feed this winter. Have any others called Meteor so she has to send you to them? Does she or Venus have something else for you to do?"

"No." Astra pushed back the hair that fell in her face. "Why do you care?"

"Things haven't changed this month. As I've told you more than once, I'm your mother and I love you, Astra, even when you try to block me. I see the shadows under your eyes despite the makeup you wear. You're still not sleeping. Why not?"

"Because I'm busy. Do you want a list of everything I have to do?" Astra knew better than to share anything about the nightmares that left her shaking and shuddering in bed nearly every night. No one ever protected her from the demon who haunted her.

"It's what your brother told you, isn't it? What you do comes back three-fold even if it takes years or centuries."

"I've done nothing evil. I only defend the innocent. Everyone knows there aren't any guilty people in prison."

"Remember what Orion told you. In this life, you've tried to choose honor, but there were others when you opted for expediency. The *Guardian* opened the door when she passed through *Time's*

Portal, the *Seer* guides the dying, and the *Bard* records the past. He's coming soon and he'll make you pay the price you've avoided all this time."

"Wizard's *magick*." Astra struggled to sound unconcerned. "I ward myself and my sisters have 'white-lighted' me and mine."

"Well, remember that you answer to the *Rule of Three*. There's no need to play *Hecate* yet, my dear, or turn people over to your demon-father for him to use for blood sacrifices in one of his ceremonies. Your strengths are needed in other places."

"Is that your word, Aunt Diana's or the *Lady's*?"

"All of us. Why don't you try listening?"

"I would if you said something I wanted to hear. *Samhain* ended at midnight two days ago. Why didn't you insist everyone celebrate then instead of waiting for the weekend?"

"Because a wise witch doesn't waste energy, and the *Lady* doesn't mind if our observances last a few days beyond an arbitrary date. Grow up, Satiranika. You'll be twenty-nine years old before *Yule*. As I already said, you'll need your entire *talipenlace* set and your apprentice this weekend."

"Again, is that your order or *Hers*?"

"Mine, your Aunt Diana's and we always serve *Her*. Obey or you'll face the wrath of all of us and you won't like it, my dear."

"Very well, but I already don't like it." Astra knew she sounded childish, especially when her mother laughed. "I suppose you're going to call Meteor too."

"Yes, and I'm warning you both. Leave Venus alone to face what's coming. She deserves happiness after everything the two of you have done to her and I'm not talking about arranging for her to raise Meteor's children, so don't even go there. Your middle sister should accept the consequences of being with Jed Corbett, not foist off her responsibilities on others."

Venus signaled the young black Appaloosa she rode for a slow jog. The mare moved forward, picking up a steady shuffle step. Overhead, a bald eagle circled in the blue sky. Venus waved to her sister, wondering why Meteor used the bird form instead of simply visiting the ranch like a human. What worried her?

Their spells always worked, some faster than others, but this particular one needed more time because it affected more than the three of them, especially since Venus intended to trade herself for protection and help. Still, *magick* always happened. She focused on the job at hand, training Dancer. They went from the trot to the walk, then up to a collected lope on the left lead. A turn toward the center of the arena, a downward transition to the jog again, then up to a canter on the right lead.

She saw her adopted son, Quaid, climb up to sit on the fence and reined the horse to a walk, riding toward him. "What is it?"

"Grandma said she *saw* strangers with some of the Angus. They're tearing down the back fence and she says you need to go stop them."

"Oh, I will. Believe me." Venus unlatched and opened the gate with her mind, riding through it. "Thanks, honey. You stay with Grandma so I don't have to worry about you."

"Okay. Can I go with you to take care of the steers later?"

"Yes." Venus squeezed the mare with her legs and Dancer leaped forward into an eager gallop, slowing slightly when they headed up the ridge behind the house and barns. At the top of the hill, she increased her pace. The ten-foot track wound through pastures to the back fence.

As soon as she entered the meadow, Venus saw the two men. One was part Native American. Long black hair speckled with gray tied in a ponytail with a leather thong, he wore a suede shirt, brown pants and low-heeled boots. Wiry, lean and muscular with the lethal grace of a cougar, she thought, wondering why she enjoyed the sight of him.

She took a deep breath, glanced at his companion and jerked

Dancer to a halt. The filly trembled beneath her as if the two of them moved to the same rhythm of her thudding heart. The big blond topped six feet. Broad shoulders, a wide chest, long legs, narrow-hipped, he was the epitome of a clichéd, sexy cowboy in faded jeans and a flannel work shirt.

She rode forward. "Who the hell are you? What the hell do you think you're doing? Those are *my* Black Angus. That's *my* fence. This is *my* place and you're trespassing."

A dark hat shaded the stranger's face. High cheekbones added to the strong angles of his rugged features. He wasn't a pretty boy. He didn't speak as he stood and stared at her.

"Did you hear me?" She rode Dancer nearer. "You're stealing my cattle in front of me? Why put up the fence again? What are you? Born again, stupid?"

"It's not much of a fence, ma'am." He kept his attention focused on her as if he'd never seen a woman before. "You *need* a man to build you a better one."

"I don't *need* a man for anything." She tossed her head, red hair flying. "If I wanted one, I'd advertise on the Internet and find a real cowboy. You aren't him."

"It looks like a woman put up this fence the first time. It's all spit and vinegar. No wonder we found these cows wandering about in *Liminfovia*." He chuckled, pushed back his hat to reveal gold hair. "Now, afore you really pitch a fit, Missy, I suggest you move that cayuse. Otherwise, when these cows come home, you'll get dumped."

"Don't tell me what to do. I've sent for the police and I'll have you arrested as soon as they arrive. Now, return those steers."

The blond hunk didn't speak. He stepped over the bottom strands of barbed wire and strode toward her. He was even more attractive close up, but it was his eyes that snared her. She felt as if she'd drowned in the dark depths, the same emotion she had on summer nights when she couldn't sleep. She'd sit on her porch, stare up at the black velvet sky. She'd long for the stars and feel as if she could fly to them.

His eyes weren't dark brown, but a true black like obsidian and as unreadable. His gaze made her shiver and she couldn't meet it any longer. His mouth was wide and full, with little creases beside it as if he laughed more than he frowned. What would it be like if he kissed her? What a ridiculous idea. He was a thief. She'd have him jailed again. This time, no one would save him.

She glared at him when he caught hold of Dancer's bridle, close to the western curb bit. "What are you doing?"

"Saving you from a nasty fall, Missy." The stranger guided the mare to the far side of the field where small evergreens hemmed the grass. He stopped, but held the horse still while he continued to study her. "What's your name?"

"None of your business." She glowered down at him. "Release my horse. I'm not a child. I take care of myself."

"Not anymore. I'm here now."

She felt a blush scorch her cheeks when his gaze swept over her again. Why did he look at her as if she belonged to him? She didn't know. She struggled not to tremble.

"What's your name in this life?" He repeated the question, his muscled arm across Dancer's neck, close to the saddle. "Are you Kat—?"

"Go to hell!"

"Telling a man to go and making him do it are two different things, Missy. Reckon, it doesn't matter all that much. I'll change it."

"What?"

"Your name, Missy. I'm Hugh O'Connell. Most folks call me Holt because when I take a-holt of something, it moves."

She eyed his muscular build and broad shoulders. She didn't doubt it. Determined not to reveal that he'd impressed her, she adopted an arrogant tone. "I don't care what people call you. Unhand my horse, scum."

"Not in this life, Princess." His jaw tightened as he glanced past her. "Let in those cows, Rowdy. Edwin, stay clear until they've settled. Come in when Rowdy says, not before."

"Whatever you say, Holt." The dark-haired man obviously watched them for a moment longer. "Ain't we hunting witches? We've got miles to go today, don't we?"

"Nope. Not any longer. Where my *Chosen* is, yours can't be far off." Hugh arched a brow. "Isn't that right, Princess?"

6

Rocking J Ranch ~ Friday, November 2nd, 2018

VENUS CHOKED BACK THE QUESTIONS CROWDING HER MIND. WHO was he? How did he know she was a hereditary witch or suspect her *Craft* name? Had the Corbetts arranged this? Did they provide the cattle they'd stolen months ago for him to return? And Edwin? Had he brought her nephew with him?

She gathered up the reins as the steers shoved into the meadow. The Angus immediately began to graze on the fall grass. When she looked around, she didn't see a boy. Was Edwin the son Meteor expected? If so, where was he?

Venus took a deep breath. If she had to use her horse to escape, she would. "I've told you twice. Release my horse."

"Not until you answer my question. Names provide power. What is yours?"

"Not your concern. I do as I please."

"Here-on, you please me, Witch. Find that red dress. I'm going to marry you." He winked at her, amusement edging into the dark eyes. "Again. This time you speak for yourself."

"Never." She lifted her chin. "I wouldn't have a thief or oath-breaker like you in three hundred years. I don't sully myself with *garungap*. Be gone or I'll send you away and you won't like it."

The laughter vanished. He straightened, his face hardening with anger. "You need a lesson in manners, *Laspowima*."

"A peasant like you can't teach them."

He reached for her. She booted Dancer in the ribs. The filly leaped forward, striking him with her shoulder. He used the momentum from the blow to jump aside. He grabbed Venus' left arm and yanked her from the saddle.

"Damn you." She slapped him with all her strength. "Let me go!"

He pulled her against him. Breath whooshed from her lungs. "No!"

His head lowered. She fought, kicking and punching, cursing him. He ignored the blows, simply tightening his hold. He tangled one hand in her hair, pulling back her head. She stared up into his fierce, angry face. "Slimy son of a toad…"

His mouth stopped the words, the spell before she finished it. She moaned under the passionate pressure of his lips. She couldn't move. He kissed her as if he staked a claim. She struggled to deny it and him.

Sex Magick was too hard to control. She'd always avoided it. Her fingers gripped his shoulders and her lips parted, but he didn't deepen the kiss. It didn't matter. She wouldn't let it matter.

The kiss could have lasted for hours or all time when he finally lifted his mouth from hers. She felt as if the earth stood still, stopped by his touch, trapped. She shook in his hold. Her knees buckled. Grateful he hadn't released her because she didn't want to fall at his feet, she lifted her head and glared at him. "Filthy, lousy…"

He smiled down at her. "I ought to have done that a long time ago."

"We just met moments ago."

"Oh no, Witch. We knew each other long before today."

She gaped up into the black mystery of his gaze. She almost

believed him. She never could have forgotten this man. No, they'd never met. She shook her head, denied him. "No, I don't know you at all. You mean nothing to me."

"I will." He chuckled, his breath warm on her lips. He framed her face with calloused hands. "Count on it, Princess."

She shuddered when his mouth teased hers. This time, the kiss remained gentle, only a taste. Still, she felt possessed. It was as if he took all of her, body, mind, heart and soul. When the kiss ended, he slipped a finger under the chain of her medallion. He lifted it until the amulet met the fabric of her cotton shirt. She didn't resist, couldn't resist as he unfastened the top two buttons of her blouse.

He drew out the golden disk, holding it in his hand. The chain pulled against the back of her neck. She obeyed its pressure, stepping closer to him. He stroked the line of her throat. The feel of his fingers against her skin caused excitement to rocket through her. He tried to kiss her again, but she managed to turn her face and his lips brushed her cheek. Did the *Rule of Three* apply to *Sex Magick*?

She wasn't sure. No other man dared to touch her like he had. Most saw her as a friend, a pal, someone beyond physical needs. She took a deep breath. "No more."

"I'll wait a while." He glanced down at the amulet he held. "You keep all your promises to me and I'll keep mine to you, Katiranika."

"What promises? Are you insane? I already told you. We've never met before. I don't know you. I won't know you."

"Some vows were made for you, *Laspowima*. You've fought the ones offered at the soul-matching ceremony. I haven't wasted my time here. You won't *banexort* me again."

She recognized the words once she'd heard them. A *laspowima* was an eternal partner and she dimly remembered her oldest sister telling her that those women gave up their *magick* to their new mates at what would be considered their weddings in this realm. However, soul-matches couldn't be dissolved because those bound remained together forever.

As for the *banexort*, it was a spell that transported someone or something thousands of miles away. How could she have used the

Power to harm him? A *banexort* was a punishment cast against the will of the victim. Why didn't she remember doing such a heinous act?

"It's dishonorable. Astra said she passed judgement and I rendered it, but I never do evil or blood *magick*. No, I didn't send you anywhere." Venus shook her head, meeting his dark gaze. "I might have killed you in a fair fight, but a *banexort*? Never!"

"It'll come to you." Before she moved, he kissed her, a light, swift touch. "I can't tell you more."

She wrenched away. Anger and concern grew. Dread swept through her. Every witch knew three was the basic *magick* number. She'd learned that before she had her first wand. She held up her hand, tried to ward him off. She quivered when his mouth twisted into a wry smile. "I'm not ready. I mean it."

"I heard it too many times. Listening to you, keeping my distance, showing you respect...." He held out his hand. "All that got me was regular trips to *Liminfovia*. Come here."

She stared at him. She had to flee, but she couldn't move away. Her body had a will of its own, his will. She stumbled forward, drawn by the enchantment of his black gaze. "I'll be free of you. I swear it."

"You've had hundreds of years free of me, Witch. You're mine."

"In your dreams." She stood in front of him, a heartbeat distant. She wouldn't allow him to win. "You'll never have me."

"Yes, I will." His hands closed over her shoulders. "I won't wait this time. I promise you'll enjoy everything we do."

Held hostage by his dark eyes, she longed to run. Her boots felt glued to the grass. She pressed her hands against his chest, felt the heat of his skin through his shirt. She ought to push him away, but somehow she couldn't.

"No." She jerked her head, managed to tear her gaze from his. "I'm not yours. I won't be."

She backed a step, a second, a third, until she was out of reach. She risked a glance at him. Mockery filled his rugged features and she realized he'd allowed her escape. "You son-of-a—"

"No more cussing. I'll kiss you again. If I do, I won't wait to have you."

"I won't let you."

"Don't bet a lot on that card." He folded his arms and stood rock still. "I'll take you the way I should have when we waited to come to this realm."

"Try and you'll wish you were still *banexorted*."

"Not hardly, Witch. I led my army into wars before you left the school-room, but I appreciate the warning." He started toward Dancer. "I'll fetch your horse."

"Don't bother." Venus whistled and the black Appaloosa mare trotted to meet her. She picked up the reins. Before she swung into the saddle, she heard the distressed cry of a child. Leading the mare, she headed toward the dark-haired man and a young boy. Hugh was already there, attempting to comfort the youngster.

"What's the matter?" Venus asked.

"It's gone." The boy sobbed against Hugh's shoulder. "It was all I had left and it's gone!"

"What is?" Venus eyed the lean, dark-haired man warily. "What's he talking about?"

"His ma's necklace, *Trecesalty*." The stranger studied her with dark eyes. "She gave it to Edwin afore she passed."

"And Pa's dead too," Edwin wailed. "So's my baby brother. Everybody's left me and now it's gone too."

Hugh smoothed the boy's golden brown hair, patted his back and murmured low reassurances. "We'll find it, son. How do you know your pa's gone?"

"I felt it. I always *Heard* him no matter how far away he traveled and he stopped talking when we was in that *Limfovia* place where we camped last night."

Venus thought about it for a moment. If Meteor was around, then so was whoever sired this boy. "Well, turn on your ears and your brain, Edwin. You can *Hear* him just fine if you start really listening again. As for the necklace, one of these two barbarians should have explained how they really work."

"Watch it, Princess." Hugh's calm tone held a hint of menace. "Teach your nephew what he needs to know without the insults."

Edwin shifted slightly away and turned his attention to Venus. "What do you mean, ma'am?"

"Aunt Venus." She smiled at him. "No more crying or grieving. Your mother arranged for you to come here."

"But, she's dead. Me and Uncle Hugh and Rowdy were the only ones at her funeral. Rowdy said the words for her and my little brother. Honest, ma'am."

"Aunt Venus." She dropped to one knee and waited until his gaze met hers. "I don't doubt what you know, Edwin. Your mother asked me to bring you here for her. I saw her before I came up here. You might have too if you'd known where to look for her and what to see."

"She *Changed*," Edwin announced. "Didn't she, Aunt?" He pointed to Dancer. "Is that my ma?"

"No way. If I kicked your mother the way I did Dancer, she'd have given me flying lessons." Venus tousled the boy's hair. "Think again. What other animal did you see?"

Hugh frowned. "Rowdy, did you see Mary?"

"Yes." He gestured toward the sky. "Edwin, didn't you?"

"The eagle." Edwin wiped at his tear-stained cheeks. "But the necklace. She didn't take it away. Where did it go?"

"It returned to her or the mage who crafted it. That particular set of jewelry can't be with two people at the same time," Venus said. "She had it first and longest."

"I wanta see my ma." Edwin took a step closer to Venus. "Where is she?"

"Not here yet. If she shows up for the *Samhain* festivals in the shape of an animal, my mother, your grandmother, will be furious. Don't worry, Edwin. I'll let your mom know you're safe and you took good care of the necklace until you reached us."

"But, I want you to take me to her."

"Not yet." Hugh spoke before Venus could. "You stay with me and Rowdy, son. I promised your mother we'd watch over you.

Until she comes for you, we need to keep you safe. I'm not breaking my oath."

"I'm sorry." Edwin hastily apologized. "I'd never want you to be in trouble with the Goddess and God. Will you really bring Ma, Aunt Venus?"

"As soon as she arrives." Venus put the reins up on Dancer's neck, then swung into the saddle. She lifted her chin. "Once Meteor collects her son, the two of you can leave."

"I don't think so." Hugh stood, resting a hand on Edwin's shoulder. "We'll stick and stay, Princess. First thing, we'll rebuild that fence. It's a man's job and you're not one."

Venus turned her attention to Rowdy. "Well, you can talk for yourself, can't you? Since you're not welcome here, take your friend and go."

"Holt speaks for me." Rowdy took a step forward. "We stay. When you bring the boy's mother, fetch Satiranika too."

Venus gaped at him, stunned he knew her eldest sister's witch name. "Serve you right if I did. She doesn't need me to render judgements for her anymore. She'll send you beyond *Liminfovia*."

"I don't think so." Rowdy appeared unimpressed. "She will greet me as sweetly as you did your chosen mate."

———

Safe, at long last her son was safe. She swooped toward the balcony of the two-story duplex where she and her friends established their catering operation soon after they graduated from college. She'd guided Edwin and Rowdy Tall-Deer onto the trail that led to one of the *Time Portal*s and into *Liminfovia*. Then, she lost them in the gray mists. This afternoon, she'd seen them on the road and their arrival at the Rocking J. From now on, her boy would be protected not only by Hugh O'Connell and Rowdy, but by her family as well.

Just for fun, she swooped down and frightened two rabbits who froze before racing into the blackberry bushes. She started to smile, then remembered she lingered in bird form. Impossible to rejoice as a human when she was an eagle. She landed on the balcony, shape-shifted, opened the glass door, and stepped into the upstairs apartment. She glanced around the combined living and dining area. Everything looked as she'd left it, from the furniture to the antique spinet in the corner.

A cool breeze ruffled her hair, and she shivered. She crossed to the couch, scooped up the black silk robe she'd left earlier, and eased it over her naked body. She snugged the belt and enjoyed the way the material felt against her skin. Senses always seemed keener after she shifted to one of her animal forms and back again.

For now, she'd eat. Flying made her hungry. The rabbits hadn't looked that appealing and she hadn't taken time to hunt larger prey when all she wanted to do was watch her eldest son. She crossed to the kitchen, partitioned by cupboards and a breakfast bar from the dining room. When she remodeled the house, she'd contemplated tearing out the wall that divided the bedrooms from the great room. Instead, she'd opted to combine the three bedrooms into a giant one and expanded the bath so she could bathe regardless of her form.

She opened the refrigerator, removed a brick of sharp, aged cheddar, and the remains of a pot roast. Those with a loaf of home-made sourdough bread and a bottle of wine would make a feast. She pulled a butcher knife from the decorator block on the counter. She felt more than heard a footstep on the beige carpet.

She whirled, knife in hand. Blade up, the tip rested against the hollow of Jed Corbett's throat. "You!" She allowed contempt to fill her voice as she stared up, up, up to meet his black gaze. "Why are you here? How did you get inside? Why aren't you in jail?"

He ignored the blade. He reached into the pocket of his worn jeans, removed a key. "The Corbett family has an interest in most of the businesses here in Eagleville."

"Not me and not my company, not for long." She pressed a little too hard on the knife. A drop of red blood trickled from his throat. "Why are you really here? Revenge for the charges when you tried to kill me?"

"I've been out of the Gray-Bar Hotel since this morning, sweetheart, as soon as my uncle sent his lawyer." He replaced the key in his pocket and smiled down at her. "That's too long to wait, isn't it, Matiranika?"

How did he know her witch name? She and Astra blocked the memories five years ago on his thirtieth birthday. He shouldn't have any memories of her. He ought to view her as a stranger on the fringes of his mind. Instead, he still seemed to desire her and nothing kept him away for long.

She tipped back her head. Their gazes met, clashed. At six foot six, he towered above her by ten inches. Of course, he was also taller than most of the men in Eagleville. Thick coal black hair curled around his ruggedly handsome face. A nose broken in one of his many brawls saved him from looking insipid. He could have been a cover model or an actor if a director wanted a rugged, he-man type. Today, he wore faded chopped off jeans, a red plaid shirt that jarred with the bright orange suspenders and corked boots.

She kept the knife on him, not that he appeared to notice. "I've told you before that I don't want my hardwood floors scarred by those awful boots. You'll pay to refinish the wood."

"You always want money, Matiranika." He chuckled. "Trying to show me how mercenary you are won't drive me away. I know you."

"What did you call me?" She kept her tone matter-of-fact. "Another woman's name?" She shrugged but didn't move the weapon. "Handsome, if you have enough money, you can call me whatever you want."

7

Astra tested the temperature, then stepped under the shower spray. Warm water cascaded over her. She visualized all the negativity from the previous night washed away by the stream. She tipped her face to the spray, let the water soak her hair. These few moments were all she could have of blessed solitude before the weekend. She drew a deep breath, relaxed, and allowed her mind to drift. She craved peace, calm before she faced the drive to the ranch and the stress of *Samhain* with her family and fellow witches.

No, she wouldn't think of the ceremonies yet. For now, she'd be herself. When was the last time she'd felt centered? The answer came in a sudden flash. It'd been three hundred years and four life-times ago when she was trapped in that bedchamber with that healer-mage, Rowindache. She'd never shared how much she remembered of her own history with her sisters. Knowing their past would influence Venus and the choices she made, while Meteor was too bonded to her soul-match.

Astra had told herself more than once through her previous lives and this one how much she detested the mage selected for her. He'd no respect for her royal rank. Instead, he looked down on her. When he'd grown frustrated with her Sex Magick spells and refusal to do more than share his bed, he'd dared to threaten her with a return to her aunt's realm and a horrifying death in the *Fires of Eternity* where she'd be roasted alive, before being eaten by dracklegons. Then, he insulted her by claiming her as a secondary mate, a *vaslattel* and told her to read the laws of his country, *Warpathia* as if she hadn't already.

Yet, he challenged her. She had researched his background prior to his trial and knew he enlisted as a common soldier and saved his pay to attend the *Healer Academy* in his country. Before he had the necessary funds, the Army offered to train him. She wasn't sure why and he hardly spoke to her. A small part of her admired his determination. Still, when he completed his training, he returned to the *Warpathian* Army, a fool bound by his sacred honor. For some odd reason, her aunt felt they were a match.

During the first moon, they were together, he rarely spoke to her beyond asking how she liked what he did to her in bed. She'd had several lovers prior to him, and he never inquired about them. However, he was the only one to make sure she enjoyed herself as much as he did. Of course, he also annoyed her when he asked if she was willing to repeat the vows her aunt made on her behalf. When Astra refused, he either napped or read or watched a small view screen about their destination. If she distracted him too much, they'd have sex. Even so, he still refused to unlock the door to the chamber, and she couldn't since it was magically keyed to him.

The only way she'd be able to leave was by killing him. A spell usually ended with the death of the creator. She wasn't desperate enough to do that yet. Besides, the method would take some serious thought. He only ate and drank what she did after her first attempt, so that ruled out poison. Her dagger was for ceremonies, not use. She negotiated with her foes. She wasn't the war-queen who'd been trained to slay them.

That particular day, a knock on the door interrupted the mid-day meal which they'd shared in an almost comfortable silence. When Rowindache answered, Thojedescar waited outside. He claimed her sister was ill and he wanted Rowindache to come heal Matiranika.

"I'm going too." Astra had insisted. "I haven't seen her since our journey began."

"It was your choice," Rowindache pointed out in gravelly tones. "You never asked."

She held her head high, glared at him, then left the chamber. She'd led the way, annoyed when he caught up with her, taking her arm to guide her. Didn't the peasant understand his place? The *Trecesalty* led and others followed. She was the oldest of the royal Three and that made her the leader of her siblings, too. They never asked anyone for anything. Even the idea was an insult.

Remembering that humiliation as the servants and soldiers in the *Amalodian* army stared when she passed brought her back to the present. Arranging Rowindache's exile in the Middle Ages in this realm wasn't sufficient recompense for what he'd done to her. She should have killed him. Well, it wasn't too late. If he showed up in this life, she'd arrange a suitable death for him, one where he suffered agonies before his demise.

Her mother didn't allow the blood sacrifices that Astra remembered in her dreams and, to be honest, she preferred serving the Goddess and the Light although she wouldn't share that with her family. She took a deep breath. She needed to finish her preparations, call her assistant and make arrangements for them to leave for the ranch before it got much later. The last thing she wanted was another call from her mother.

For a moment, Astra wondered what evil her demon-father had in mind for tonight. He seemed to think the rites of manhood included his followers creating litters of babies for their mothers to support and raise, making more members of the were-pack unless the youngsters couldn't shapeshift. Granted, the leader of the shapeshifters, Frank Corbett, thought his orders made him the one in charge, but didn't realize who still held the real authority even after all this time, much less why the blood sacrifices pleased his ally.

When those children reached adulthood, they became servants to the pack or were sacrificed in Corbettstown ceremonies. During one of her visits, Astra saw the mark on Rebekah, the young woman who served as her maid. Astra demanded her as a minion before she could be killed. Amused, her father agreed, claiming that his dark sorcery held more influence on Astra than the light *magick* she thought she preferred, and one day she'd be a worthy successor to rule his realm.

Let the demon think what he liked. She knew better. She might not be able to save all his victims, but Rebekah proved a reliable ally, a willing channel for *magick*, and a suitable apprentice. Astra drew a deep breath, relaxed while she mentally reinforced the wards on her apartment, then her siblings, her nephew and niece, her minion and extended the reach outwards to 'white-light' the innocent among her clientele. It took a great deal of witch-power to maintain the protection, but she had what she needed—she took it not only from the node under her home—but also from Rowindache, the wizard who'd sacrificed himself so long ago.

———

Venus rode into the round pen directly in front of the twenty-stall barn. She dismounted, led Dancer into the stable, unsaddled, groomed and fed the young, black mare. Memories of Hugh O'Connell swamped her mind while she worked, making it difficult to focus on the ordinary chores of horse care. She'd met the man less than an hour ago. Why did she feel like she knew him? Worse, how did he know her?

She shivered, suddenly cold despite her flannel shirt, turtleneck and heavy jeans. It wasn't fair. She'd intended to trade her body to gain security for her family. Her heart, mind, and soul wouldn't be at risk with the spell she'd cast. Somehow, she knew he wouldn't accept anything less than *all* of her.

She reminded herself that they'd only met today, yet she suspected it wasn't true. She remembered seeing him at an elaborate ceremony. Was it the one he'd mentioned? She'd worn a red dress... she recalled it now, but she'd never seen a material, a color, or a design that matched it. Never on this planet, in this realm.

Ordered to select a set of jewelry from the three enchanted sets on an altar, she'd refused. Hugh picked the necklace he placed on her, along with matching bracelets and earrings. She usually wore just the amulet and left the rest of the collection for formal occasions, her *talipenlace*. They hadn't been a gift from her mother, Venus thought suddenly. *The tokens of Power always belonged to me. I just received them from her this time instead of the wizard who created them.*

There'd been promises made, but not by her. She felt as if her mother had been the one who spoke for the triplets, gave them away in some sort of ceremonious, magickal ritual. Love wasn't the problem. Venus knew she hadn't expected that, or romance, much less attraction in the bonds to a man. So, what started her war with Hugh O'Connell?

Why did she feel the need to fight him? She didn't know. She glanced at her watch. She'd told him she'd return with materials to repair the fence in a short time. What if he came to find her? No!

She had to hurry. She headed for the ranch pickup. She parked the truck in front of the tool-room, began to load it. Hammers, nails, staples, shovels, post-hole diggers, the wire stretcher and two rolls of hog-wire. She wedged the supplies in place with bales of hay she'd intended to spread in the fields for the horses. Instead, she'd take care of the cattle that he'd returned first.

He claimed he was here to stay. Would he after the Corbetts arrived to make trouble? Their logging company destroyed the boundary fences in the midst of clear-cutting trees on the parcels of land they'd bought from state agencies. The original fence hadn't been on the surveyed property line, so what Frank Corbett orchestrated was legal, if not ethical. Because the Jamisons had ties to the influential Dawson family, their relatives had rebuilt some of the pasture fences last summer, but there was so much work to do on the Rocking J that a one-day work party didn't make that much of a difference.

Astra fought the good fight in court, but so far nothing had been settled. Nobody seemed to care about the trouble caused when fences went down and Venus' herd of purebred Black Angus disappeared during the predicament. She'd found the butchered remains of what she thought were all of them, but somehow the last six head escaped. She knew the shapeshifters had killed her beef to gain more than one kind of *Power* because their deities demanded blood sacrifices, the more tortured the victims the better.

Venus shook her head. In an odd way, she wanted Hugh to be the man she'd sought. In another, she wanted him to leave. Why was she so ambivalent? He thrilled her as much as he frightened her. *No, I'm not afraid of him. I'm just not prepared to deal with him.*

It wasn't as if she hadn't dated during the last ten years, but she hadn't seen much point to it. Astra claimed she enjoyed sex as one of the greatest indoor and outdoor sports ever created. Meteor swore she hated all men, but couldn't stay away from Jed Corbett, admitting she was addicted to what he did in bed. Edwin, Quaid and Fallyn were proof of that.

Wasn't there a happy medium? Venus drew a deep breath. She had so many questions and so few answers. She still didn't have a clue about what she planned to do other than have the back fence rebuilt. She closed the tool-room door. She spotted her aunt's small red car in front of the three-story house. Diana waved, then resumed unloading pumpkins from the back seat.

Venus sighed and went to help. She really needed to return to work.

"Blessed be, Katiranika." Pleasure shone in Diana's face when she hugged Venus. "Haven't you had a wonderful *Samhain*? Someone really warmed up your aura. Who is he? Where is he? What does he look like? Is he super-yummy as Matiranika says?"

"I don't know what you're talking about." Heat flooded Venus' cheeks. She grabbed a large pumpkin and hurried toward the back door into the kitchen. "I'm the same as I've always been."

"Falsehoods don't do witches credit." Diana followed, a tall, stately woman in a brilliant orange caftan that should have clashed with the pumpkins she carried and her bright red hair, but somehow didn't. "Tell the child, Estelle."

"Tell her what?" Estelle glanced over her shoulder from where she spread newspapers on the table. "Has Venus done something I should know about, Diana?"

"Met a man." Diana put the three pumpkins on the table. "From what he did to her aura, I'd say he serves the *Horned God* for sure. What do you think?"

"How would she know?" Venus tossed her head. "She doesn't believe in anything my sisters and I do."

"Don't be rude, child." Diana winked at Estelle. "Do you still use the opposition technique with her?"

"Whatever works." Faint red crept into Estelle's face. "She's a stubborn witch who always tries to contradict me."

"Mothers and daughters." Diana shook her head ruefully. "When you two grow up, I'll be happy. Now, what about our young one's aura?"

"It's as you say." Estelle placed several spoons on the table, eyeing Venus. "What's his name? Where did you find him? Was he one of those who brought the cattle? Your energies were pure white after you put Fallyn down for her nap and left to work that horse. Now, your aura's a rainbow. What changed?"

"Nothing." Venus lifted her chin. She heard clumping footsteps in the hall and watched her younger brother struggle into the room on crutches. "What are you doing here, Orion? You should be resting. You just got home from the hospital this morning."

"I have duties today, Sister Mine." Orion hobbled forward. "I need to build the bonfire on the beach for tonight's festivities."

"Take a break, first." Diana guided him into a chair. "Help the children carve the pumpkins I brought and *Foresee* for us. Who put his lovely big marks on Venus' aura?"

"Along with the rest of her." Estelle brought over a glass of iced tea. "He must be powerful to leave gold, pink, and three shades of red in that white aura. She won't share. Talk, Chrisondear."

"I'll make you a sandwich, Chrisondear," Diana said. "And you can tell us everything Katiranika won't."

Her brother chuckled at the sound of his wizard name. "Are you two serious?"

"Don't you dare tell them anything." Venus glared at her brother, then her mischief-making aunt and mother, elder witches who led their coven. "Two men returned our missing livestock and volunteered to repair the back fence. I'm going to let them."

"That's not all." Estelle focused on her. "With those vibrant colors, one of the men is…" She paused to look at Orion when he stirred in the chair. "What is it?"

"They came in answer to the summons Venus sent two nights ago." Orion stared into the glass of tea, awe on the youthful, handsome face. "You'll receive what you most desire, Sister. Take care. He has as much *Power* as you do and it's trained."

"Anything else?" Estelle asked. "What's his name?"

"I don't know, but he has an old link to Venus." Orion frowned into the amber tea. "Why do I feel tied to him too?"

"We'll tell you later," Estelle said, glancing at Diana. "Now, take yourself up the hill and invite them to the party, Venus. I can't believe you haven't already."

"I won't. You can't make me."

"Either you go, or I do." Diana folded her arms, her tone stern. "If I do, I'll apologize for your poor manners, upbringing and ask his forgiveness for the disgraceful way you conduct yourself."

"You can't." Venus choked back a sob at the betrayal. "You're an Elder-Witch. To humble yourself to that arrogant…"

"Isn't a hardship for me." Diana pointed to the door. "You're the one who hasn't learned to rule her pride. Begone, Katiranika."

Venus wiped quickly at her tears and obeyed the command. It wasn't as if she had much of a choice when the request included her witch's name. She looked over her shoulder and saw her mother and aunt huddle over Orion and the glass of iced tea. The three of them laughed, then talked in low voices. Did they think they were Hollywood witches?

———

"Holt, come see this." Strain showed on Rowdy's features, his tone flat. "I never saw the like in these parts."

Hugh unwrapped the rope he'd dallied around the saddle horn. He dropped the lariat on the ground and left it with the cedar log he'd intended to drag to the clearing. He turned Mustard to follow Rowdy. The last time his friend sounded that concerned, they'd faced a band of armed men planning to cut the herd they were taking to the railroad.

In the middle of the field stood a red and white wagon, no team to pull it. Hugh reined his stallion to a halt. He stared. He hadn't seen a contraption like it since they arrived in this realm. "What is it?"

"Danged if I know. It looks somewhat like the land-cars we had back home in *Trilunon*, but those floated and this one has wheels. It made noise coming here. For a moment, I figured it ate her because she was stuck inside, and I didn't want to shoot for fear it might swallow."

"Sounds fair." Hugh swung off his horse and started in the direction of the new-fangled wagon. "Let's ask where she brought us."

"Think she'll tell us?" A smile slowly edged Rowdy's lips. "Want me to get my rifle in case it's still hungry?"

Hugh chuckled. "No need. We're both heeled and good shots with our pistols."

As they walked toward her, she tossed hay in the direction of the steers. Little wonder the critters couldn't look out for themselves since they depended on folks to tend them. Mustard snorted behind him, then trotted past to drive the steers from one of the piles of hay.

"Lucky for us, they didn't try to sleep in our blankets," Hugh drawled. "She pampers them a lot."

"Maybe, they need it."

When they neared the wagon, Venus called. "Are you two going to unload these tools or gossip all day? Hurry up. I have work to do and I don't have all day to waste on you."

Hugh pushed back his hat with a thumb and eyed her. He spoke softly, his voice calm. "Didn't your mama teach you manners, Missy? You're plumb out of hand."

"If you expect me to beg you to work, forget it." She tossed her head, red hair flying and glared at him, violet eyes narrowed. "I don't crawl to any man."

"I never reckoned being polite was the same as crawling, Princess. Will I have to teach you that too?"

"Go to—!"

Hugh raised his hand, blocked the curse. "I already told you not to try to *banexort* me again. Now, where did you bring us?"

She stared at him, then looked at Rowdy. "Do you think I brought you here?"

"Maybe-so. Maybe-no." Rowdy shrugged. "You finally *Called* for Holt. Me and the boy tagged along. I watch Holt's back. He does the same for me. You did your worst when you sent us to the Middle Ages in this realm. Between each life, we ended up alone in *Limin-fovia*. We finally found each other this time around, in our fifth incarnation."

"I didn't do that." She stared at them, then slowly sank down to sit on a roll of wire. "I couldn't do that. Why don't I remember? Astra said she passed judgement, and I rendered it, but why would I do something so heinous?"

8

Meteor stared up at him, pressing the knife into his skin. "Leave my place, *garungap*." She used *Trilunon* slang for the sludge found at the bottom of sewers.

He shook his head, feathered his thumb over her lips. "Put down the knife, Matiranika. You won't kill me here because you'll have to get rid of the body and you'll hate imprisonment, more than *Warpathian* justice. Besides, the blade tickles."

She pushed the tip further into his skin. "Like I care."

"Not again." He snagged her wrist. "I told you to stop."

"Agreed. There are better ways." She dropped the butcher knife, heard it clatter on the tile floor. She tried for a slow, sensual smile and watched the impact. His amusement faded and he tensed. "You want me. It's why you're really here."

"I'll always want you." Laughter filtered into his night-dark eyes. "How much will it take to have you forever?"

"More than you'd earn in a lifetime as a logger." She tiptoed up to nip his lower lip. "So, what do you have for me?"

"This." He patted the lump in his shirt pocket. "It's pure gold with diamonds, emeralds, and rubies. You'll love it. You can have it when you admit we belong together."

"I don't believe you have anything like that. It could just be a container of chewing tobacco." She held out her hand. "Let me see it."

"In a moment." He tipped up her chin between his thumb and first finger. "You're mine. Talk to me, my sweet. What will it take to get the truth from you?"

"A million dollars in the Caymans. I'm not cheap."

"That's for sure." He bent his head and his mouth found hers.

The long, slow tenderness of the kiss sapped her strength. She swayed toward him, unable to resist. She pressed her hands against his chest, longing to thread her fingers in his thick, black hair, and struggled to control herself.

Finally, he lifted his head. "I've missed you."

"Liar." She shivered when he dropped kisses on her brows. "I've seen you with those skanks at the parties this past week. They were all over you."

"So, you did see me there?" He grinned down at her, obviously pleased by the jealousy. "If you hadn't been sneering at me, I'd have sent them packing. Next time, you can."

"As if I'd give you that satisfaction."

"Oh, you'll satisfy me today, Matiranika. You want my heart, body, mind and soul, don't you?"

"Not anymore." She ran a scarlet fingernail to the top button of his flannel shirt. "I'll settle for cash, jewels, real estate, a new car. Whatever you feel like giving, Handsome, but it has to be worth major bucks. Expendable, I'd say."

"Like my son? You gave him away, didn't you?"

She hoped her expression hid the truth. She couldn't let him see how vulnerable she was when it came to her children. "I don't know what you're talking about."

"Edwin." Jed frowned down at her. "I remember my boy, too. You lied about me being his father and traded my son away to friends of yours."

She shook her head. "I'd say he was more mine than yours. I'd have done better by him if I hadn't been dying. Don't you recall that? You succeeded in killing me then."

"Some of your lies aren't funny." Pain flashed in his ruggedly handsome face. "I'd never hurt you. Why are you the woman for me?"

"Because you're a moron." She kept her voice as sweet as honey. To distract him, she threaded her fingers in his hair. "If you pay me, we can go to bed."

"I do like that sharp, nasty tongue of yours." He lowered his head and his lips brushed hers. "I won't pay any more than I already have for my woman."

"Charm won't work, Jed Corbett. I want money, but you can always leave."

"I'm staying." He reached into his pocket, pulled out a dirt encrusted gold medallion on a chain. "Yours, isn't it? I found it in the woods today, Matiranika. How did it get there?"

Lie, she told herself. She had to protect Edwin and their other children at all costs. She lifted one shoulder. "Who cares? I don't want it. I never did. If that's all you have, go find something better."

"I care." His tone grew impatient. "Answer me."

"I threw it there." She met his gaze and prayed he'd believe the falsehood. "Once a creek ran pristine for the salmon that spawned there and called it home. You Corbetts murdered the fish when you killed the land and the trees. Now, the stream's a sewer. It was a fit place for that *garungap*."

"I remember trading all of me to make this for you."

"Like I said, it's *garungap*." Her smile widened as she taunted him. "Just like you. *Garungap*. I want something better before I take you to my bed again."

"Just remember I'm the *garungap* you owe a son for the one you sold." Jed slid the muddy chain around her neck. "How do you remove this? It should remain where I place it and yet it never does."

She glanced down at the sun-shaped disk with its curling golden spokes. Tiny animals were carved into the center, their jeweled eyes dulled by dirt. The chain didn't have a clasp. The ends fused together when she wore it. Somehow the links changed so she wouldn't lose it when she shape-shifted.

He tracked the chain with a gentle stroke of one finger. "Are you going to answer me?"

"Why should I?" She trembled when he stepped closer. "Now, what?"

"I'm curious. It's the middle of the afternoon. Why are you only wearing a robe?"

"Maybe I knew you were coming." She struggled to breathe and not reveal the way he excited her. For a moment, she wanted to rearrange her hair, hide her breasts and the nipples that tightened, poking into the silk.

He lowered his gaze to the loose collar of the black robe. "Very difficult." He eased his hand into the opening. "Do you feel like giving me an answer yet?"

"I'll give you nothing. You'll pay." She bit back a moan when he cupped her breast. "Please."

"Oh, I fully intend to." He found her nipple and teased it with his thumb. "Tell me of the *talipenlace* jewels, Matiranika. I know they connect us. You wear the necklace if I force you, but why doesn't it remain on you?"

Relief almost made her laugh aloud. She controlled the impulse. He didn't know as much as he thought. *She'd* never worn the jewelry willingly, not from the start.

"Another secret, *Laspowima*? I'll learn it. As soon as I picked it up out of the mud, I knew more than I had in thirty-five years. I won't forget again."

"Yes, you will." She tilted her chin and met his gaze. "As soon as you sleep, Thojedescar, each and every memory will fade until it's less than dust. By dawn tomorrow, you'll know nothing."

"Thojedescar." He twisted a hand in her hair. "My own name. My real wizard's name." His low, flat tone made it a statement, not a question. "And if sleep is what makes me lose myself, then we won't sleep."

"We?" She shook her head, stepped away. The grit on the gold chain bothered her. She longed to remove the medallion, but knew he waited to see how she managed it. There was another way to resolve the problem.

The idea was the mother to the wish, a lesson she'd learned as a new witch when she first began studying *magick*. She visualized the amulet clean, shiny as it'd been when she gave it to Edwin and snapped her fingers. That was just for show. The gesture wasn't necessary, but she saw the quick wonder on Jed's face when the necklace gleamed as brightly as the day he'd cast it.

He followed, reached for her. "Like I said, you owe me a son." He swung her up in his arms. "I'll keep you with me while you carry him, through the birth and forever as long as we both live."

She turned her face into his shirt so he wouldn't see her tears. If only he meant those promises, but he didn't. He'd abandon her, return just to murder her for the last time. Not again, not in this life. She'd kill him first.

———

Venus sat still, watching the two strangers. The men had a bond stronger than mere friendship, and oddly enough, she felt as if she could trust both of them. *That bewilders me when I only met them an hour or so ago and yet they seem more reliable than my sisters. Why?*

"Where did you bring us, Princess?" Hugh climbed into the back of the pickup. He rested his hands on her shoulders. "Tell me."

"The Rocking J ranch, in Liberty Valley, Washington State, near Eagleville. It's Friday, November 2nd, 2018. Where did you come from?"

"You tell me." He released her, rocked back on his heels. "It'll come to you sooner or later."

"No, it won't." She reached for his hand, gripped it. "I only *See* a little, nothing compared to other witches in my family. Mostly I have to wait until my older sisters, or my younger brother, or my aunt, or my mother tell me what's going to happen."

"And you can't always rely on what they say." Rowdy lifted out the shovels, leaning them against the side of the truck. "Each witch's and wizard's truth is different. Doesn't mean it's wrong, ma'am, just that it's what your *relkinam* believe."

She nodded, grateful he understood. "I'm tired of them always keeping secrets from me. Will you tell me?"

"Not yet, *Trecesalty*," Rowdy said, respectfully. "Tomorrow is soon enough."

Holt squeezed her fingers. "You're very young and you don't have all your memories yet. We have time for you to remember, but if you don't, then Rowdy's right. I'll help you. Now, I've got posts to split and fence to build."

"All right. My mother told me to invite you to the *Samhain* celebration tonight. It starts at dusk."

"We'll be there."

Venus watched him jump down from the back of the truck. He pulled out the second roll of wire, hefted it onto a broad shoulder, and walked away. She heaved a sigh. Somehow, she felt like it wasn't the first time he'd left her to learn hard truths. Where was he when she *Called* him? Rowdy had said something about her sending them to the Middle Ages, but they weren't dressed in medieval armor. Where had they come from? Could she wait until tomorrow to discover the answer?

———

Brigid Dawson parked in front of the two-story building on the corner of what she thought of as *'Walk, don't walk.'* Most of the streets in Eagleville had names but lacked much signage beyond the main intersections. The same went for the businesses, which made it all the more surprising when her cousin, Meteor Jamison, painted a huge mural of fantastic creatures that included unicorns, centaurs, and winged horses frolicking on the structure as well as huge letters spelling out Captivating Catering.

Brigid appreciated the job here. She'd feared there wouldn't be many chances to bake the elaborate cakes she loved after the bakery where she worked for so many years had closed and she'd be stuck working on the family homestead or managing the Silver Lake Pony Ranch forever. She slipped out of the car and headed toward the two-story Victorian house. She had sandwiches to make from the baguettes she'd baked yesterday, two giant Halloween cakes to finish decorating, and sugar cookies to frost. What fun!

Happily humming her favorite song from *The Wizard of Oz*, she fished through her keys and unlocked the front door. "Meteor, I'm here. Are you?"

No answer, which meant she was the first to arrive. She paused at the main bank of light switches and flipped them, hearing the florescent lights thrumming as they came to life throughout the downstairs, and then entered the large kitchen. She crossed to the intercom, pressed the 'talk' button. "Meteor, it's me, Brigid. I'm here. The rest of the crew will be along soon. Anything special need to be done?"

Silence for a moment before her cousin answered. "Go ahead and start on the order for the party at the Rocking J. I'll be down in a few minutes. Remind Tolliver that we need non-alcoholic beverages for the kids, not just his fantastic wine punch."

"No worries. You've got it."

———

Astra glanced in the rear-view mirror as she pulled off the highway onto the gravel driveway at the Rocking J ranch. Her three large black dogs, lay in the rear of Rebekah's Ford Explorer eagerly anticipating the weekend. *Soon*, Astra promised silently. *You can hunt soon. Wait, my friends. Wait.*

Rebekah sat in the back seat, a twenty-four-year-old redhead, whose curves filled out tight blue jeans and a light blue sweater that not only matched her eyes but clung to full breasts and a narrow waist. "I don't know about this, Astra. I should have gone to see my family."

"Not a good idea." Astra focused on the drive toward the house, barely flicking a glance at the tall man in the passenger seat. Gard Devlin worked as a private detective for her law firm and thought he'd picked her up after one of their meetings. Nothing could be further from the truth she didn't share with him. She'd selected him, the way she did herbs for the poppets she used to wreak vengeance. "I've told you not to go to Corbettstown on holidays for the past five years ever since you moved into my apartment building."

"Why?" Brown-haired and eyed, Gard was brawny rather than lean. A green t-shirt stretched over muscled arms, wide shoulders and a broad chest. Faded jeans encased long legs. His battered boots looked more comfortable than fashionable. "Why don't you want her to go?"

"Because Rebekah isn't safe there and I won't have her harmed."

"You keep saying that, but you never explain why," Rebekah scowled. "Or why I had to apply to the University of Washington and live in Seattle with you. I grew up in Corbettstown. I can handle what happens there."

"No, you can't, and neither will I if something happens to you." Astra glanced quickly in the rearview mirror, then back to the road in front of her. "I've told you numerous times that my father has inappropriate plans for you and he's not the kind of man who takes 'no' for an answer."

"And that's why you want me to investigate your brother's accident," Gard said. "You think he had someone sabotage Orion's new sports car."

"Yes, and I'm trusting you to keep that to yourself. You can let my family think you're here as my date. They're constantly pushing me to take time for myself and enjoy life, although they weren't too happy when Beth Chambers and I partied at Billy Bob's on Friday and Saturday nights."

Rebekah heaved a dramatic sigh. "You know they're not going to approve of him. Your mother intends to choose your husband. It's the way our family has always done things. The elders want what they want when they want it and they plan for each next generation to be stronger than the ones before."

"I know." Astra smiled. "Having Gard here will definitely distract her from those plans."

"Oh, wow," Gard said. "That's what a guy enjoys most, upsetting an ambitious mom with plans. Thanks a lot."

"Oh, you'll enjoy meeting her and she's never rude."

"Good to know."

———

Hugh put down the roll of wire, stretched, and headed back to the wagon to finish unloading it. He stopped by Rowdy, who'd paused to take out the makings to roll a cigarette. "What do you think? Did we really travel more than a hundred years?"

"Wouldn't be surprised after what the marshal's brother said about coming back from here. Let's make a start on that fence or we'll be setting up camp after dark. I'll have to cook something special since it's a *Sabbat*."

"She said her mother wants us to join them for the festival. We don't want to offend the *Lady* and *Lord*. They'll send us somewhere a lot more inhospitable than *Liminfovia*. Besides, a body's better off not looking when you cook."

"I don't know what you're belly-aching about. I've told you plenty of times that you can take over the camp chores and you keep saying you want me to do them. I wasn't making soup that day. I was boilin' the winter dirt out of my socks." Despite the way their journey ended, Rowdy must be comfortable here if he mocked Hugh with the language they tended to use in the past.

He opted to continue the squabble as they sauntered toward the wagon. "I didn't reckon it was soup. Coffee, mayhap. I ought to have known better. It tasted too good." He glanced toward the horses. Edwin had taken over their care and happily unsaddled his own as well as Rowdy's. "Once the boy finishes up there, he can jump in to help us."

"He will. He's a hard worker." At the sound of hoof-beats, Rowdy looked toward the far side of the clearing. "And here comes his mother. He'll be thrilled to see her."

9

ASTRA DROVE ACROSS THE PRIVATE BRIDGE TO THE ROCKY BEACH
that bordered the Widow River where Orion directed several men
building the ceremonial bonfire. She slammed her foot on the brake
as she recognized the biggest, a dark-haired brute. Jed Corbett! Why
was he here? How dare he visit their home?

Freya yelped, then growled as she rose to push her cold nose
against the back of Astra's neck.

"Later, my pet. You can hunt later." Astra parked the rig. "Come
on, Gard. I'll introduce you to my brother. It looks like he needs
some good help. Rebekah, try to keep the dogs with you."

Gard sauntered beside her toward the group of men. She kissed
Orion's cheek. "Blessed be. I brought you help. You could use
some."

"Blessed be." Orion returned the kiss and hugged her. "Tell your
dogs to leave my small ones alone, or I will." He offered his hand to
Gard and they shook. "I'm Orion Jamison. You're welcome here
and well met."

"Gard Devlin." He gestured toward the cast on Orion's left leg
and the crutches. "You're hurting. I'll get you a seat." Gard headed
for the wooden chairs near the site of the bonfire before the teen
answered.

"He *Sees*. Does he know it?" Orion asked. "Or that he's a guard in nature as well as name? He has honor. Why do you have him?"

Astra stroked Freya's black fur when the dog pressed close. "Not for what you think, little brother. It's *Sex Magick* tonight and I've grown weary of the men in the coven who lack imagination and never ensure I enjoy myself. I wanted someone new who might be better in bed. Besides, Gard plays a game of his own, despite the integrity. He seeks justice for his dead."

"He doesn't know you're aware of his agenda." Orion ran a hand through his sandy-blond hair. "Do you aid him?"

"In my way. He'll pay with his body. It's a fair trade." She wondered whether to let the four-foot hemlock log that Jed carried remain on his shoulder and decided against it. She snapped her fingers into Freya's thick fur and watched the man stagger as the wood slipped.

"I told you already." Orion stopped the firewood from falling, long enough for Jed to steady it and take it toward the pit. "Leave my small ones alone."

"He's not small. Why is he here? Hasn't he done sufficient harm to our family? He had an affair with Meteor and left her pregnant twice, once while he pursued Venus. At least, he didn't try to seduce me."

"He probably didn't want to be castrated alive. Save that crap for a fool. You and Meteor worked *magick* on him. I *Foresee* trouble."

"Leave the *Outcomes* to me." She smiled at Gard when he arrived with a chair and helped her brother sit down. "I'll greet my mother for both of us. Don't let Orion do too much."

"It'll be an interesting afternoon." Gard chuckled. "I haven't seen a bonfire this big since I was in the Army and stationed in Europe."

"Have fun." Astra tiptoed up to kiss him, a quick touch of their lips. The dogs would stay with her since she might need them for protection. Once she'd visited the house, she'd return to the beach and see what mischief she could do to drive away Jed Corbett.

She nodded at him as she strolled toward the Explorer where

Rebekah waited with Bamse and Ivor. "Watch the boundaries today, Corbett. I will. You'll pay for any indiscretions."

"Good to see you too, Circe." He jerked his head toward Gard. "Should I warn him that you turn men into swine?"

"It's such an easy spell. It takes no time or effort. Maybe oinking comes naturally for you."

She didn't wait for a response. She ordered the dogs back into the SUV. Once Rebekah buckled up, Astra drove to the house. Despite what he'd said, Orion never invited Jed here. Who did? Not Meteor. It'd be too big of a risk that he might see his children.

At the three-story house, she allowed Rebekah to collect the bottles of wine. With the dogs to escort them, they headed for the back door. Her aunt met them on the porch and Astra smiled at her. "Hello. I'm glad you're here."

"Not for long. I saw what you did to Jed." Diana folded her arms across her middle and frowned. "You have so much *Talent*, Astra. Why play *Hecate*? You're far too young to act the *Crone*."

"With Venus the *Maiden* and Meteor the *Mother*, what other role is left for me?" Astra kissed the air above her aunt's cheek. "Blessed be. Don't worry for me. I prefer retribution."

"*Evil* done in the name of *Good*, remains *Evil*, Satiranika. I know your mother has told you that whatever you do comes back three times."

"Both of you have lectured me for years. I'm through listening." Ignoring the use of her witch's name, Astra headed for the kitchen, her aunt, Rebekah, and the dogs following. "Mother, I'm here. Why did you invite Jed Corbett to our festivities?"

"Why wouldn't I?" Estelle came to take the wine. Her dark blue eyes were calm, certain of the choices she made. "He was in Meteor's apartment when I phoned. Be kind to your sisters today, daughter. You shouldn't keep their mates from them."

Astra winced. She'd guessed correctly about the interference. Why did her mother have to meddle on today of all days? "A man answered Venus' summons?"

"He seems bound to her. She wants him too. Let them be in this life. If you fight me, you'll lose, Daughter."

"We stand together." Diana ranged herself beside Estelle. "If you try to ruin your sisters' happiness again, we'll stop you."

"We'll see about that." Astra whirled, starting toward the wing of the house that Venus claimed. "Are my sisters with the children?"

"Of course," Estelle said. "Where else would they be?"

"Fine. Come along, Rebekah." Astra didn't bother to explain what would happen when the three men arrived and were united. Chosen by Estelle long ago, they plotted with her to destroy the *Trecesalty*. Neither her mother nor her aunt realized her father, regardless of the fact that he was a demon and practiced his share of evil, warned Astra about their machinations. She had to protect her little sisters, keep them safe. No one else would.

At the door to the south wing, she turned around. "I'll take the dogs and look after my sisters. You need to stay with my mother and aunt, Rebekah. See what you can do to help them with the arrangements for the Witches Ball."

"And spy on them for you." Rebekah nodded, concern in her pretty face. "Astra, do you think these new 'mates' will harm your sisters? I know Jed Corbett's like the other guys in the pack. He just wants to screw around when he's not drinking and brawling. The summer before I left, he got in a fight with a motorcycle gang and hurled two of them through the local tavern's plate-glass windows. One nearly bled to death before the first-responders arrived."

"Then, you understand the importance of the task I've given you. It's up to us to keep my sisters and the children safe."

Rebekah nodded again, took a deep breath, and glanced back at the kitchen. "Magick always costs the witch or the wizard who uses it."

"I know and I'll be the one who pays it, not you. Do what I tell you."

Without waiting for the younger witch to answer, Astra turned the knob and entered the open-concept downstairs of her sister's home. The Great Room, a living area flowed into the dining room which in turn swept toward a large island with a granite counter that separated the kitchen. On the far side, the half-bath backed onto a pantry—laundry room and an entrance to the outside wrap-around porch.

In the small play corner that her niece, Fallyn claimed, Astra saw a small *magick* circle cast with stuffed animals in the quarters. She took a closer look, nodded with approval. The little girl might have started the pretend ritual, but her adopted mother, Venus finished it.

"Await me here," Astra told the dogs. Bamse grumbled a protest and Freya showed her teeth. Instead of romps in the woods, swims in the river, and hunting coyotes, there was work. "Exactly. Guarding can be fun. You get to bite the men who threaten us and ours."

The two younger dogs explored the common area while Freya jumped up on the couch, stretching her massive length on the cushions. Suppressing a laugh, Astra climbed the stairs to the second floor and the bedrooms. On the landing, a small body hurtled against her.

"Auntie Tra. Auntie Tra. Auntie Tra!"

"Blessed be, baby." Astra scooped up the naked child and kissed the top of the red-gold curls. She breathed in the scents of little girl, soap, and talc. "Where's your mama? Purifying herself and you for *Ritual*?"

"See my pretty?" Fallyn held up a sun-shaped disk she wore on a gold chain around her neck. "Auntie Mettie give. See!"

"I do, sweetness." Astra carried the two-and-a-half-year-old back to the large bath off Venus' room. "Did you lose someone?"

"Not really. She heard you and the dogs arrive." A white towel wrapped around her body, Venus dried her hair with a second one. A third lay on the floor where Fallyn had obviously dropped it. "Do you know what happened today? Hugh O'Connell came to my *Call* and *he's*…"

"I know who he is. Our aunt and mother shared with me." Astra picked up the discarded towel and proceeded to finish drying her wriggling niece. "Anything else I need to know?"

"He seems determined to stay."

"We'll see." Astra eyed her youngest sister. Energies shimmered around Venus. Someone had tampered with her aura. "We must cast a *Protection Spell* for Fallyn and Quaid since Jed attends *Samhain* here."

"Not just them." Venus drew a deep breath. "Edwin arrived today. He's with Meteor and Quaid in your wing of the house. She's thrilled to have her oldest son back with her."

"I'll bet." Astra gestured to the necklace Fallyn wore. "I see Meteor found her amulet again."

"I didn't know it was lost." Venus focused on rubbing her waist-length hair with the towel. "Edwin had it. That surprised me. I thought Meteor had it when we cast our last spell."

"She left it to protect him." Astra glanced at the hallway when she heard footsteps. She greeted their middle sister with a smile. "He's safe, isn't he?"

"At last," Meteor agreed. "He understands why I sent him away from the shape-shifter pack. I just didn't know how to stop Jed from coming here. I'd put him to sleep upstairs when Mother woke him with her phone call and invited him. When I went back to check on him, he was gone and I thought—"

Remembering the way they'd blocked his memories, Astra inclined her head in acceptance. She knew her sister thought that he'd awakened and found himself in a strange room and bed, so he'd discreetly left. "When did he arrive here?"

"I'm not sure," Meteor said. "I drove my SUV. He came with the catering crew, and it stunned me when he showed up in the truck. Orion took him away to help with the bonfire."

"It's okay. We'll deal with him appropriately." Astra kept her tone light so she wouldn't upset the child she held. "We're the royal *Three*, remember? Don't forget what he did in your past life when he endangered you and Edwin."

At the confusion on Venus' face, Meteor explained. "Edwin came early and weak because the Corbetts tried to poison me when I was pregnant. Jed attacked me after I learned he'd arranged for the town doctor to lace Edwin's asthma tonic with arsenic. Before I D.I.E.D.—"

"You asked Hugh O'Connell to look after him," Venus finished.

"Exactly. I'm sorry I brought deceit into our Circle when you led us in spell-casting last night. I didn't know how to tell you what I'd done with my amulet."

"It's all right," Venus said. "You're forgiven. If I'd been where you were, I'd have done the same thing." Speculation filled her face. "It means we did the *Calling Spell* with two, not three of the necklaces. They're stronger than I thought."

Astra didn't rebut the idea. She hadn't taken her set of antique jewelry out of the box in years, much less brought it with her to the hospital. She wouldn't share that with either of her sisters. They had enough trouble dealing with Jed Corbett and this new man, Hugh O'Connell. She cuddled her niece close, grateful for the distraction the child provided. "Everything will work out for the best."

Before she said more, she heard a tap on the window. Still holding Fallyn, Astra walked into the master or was it mistress suite and opened the French doors to the balcony. Three crows sat on the railing.

"My birdies." Fallyn announced, stretching, reaching for the nearest crow. "Pretty birdies. Mine."

"You're definitely your mother's child." Astra kissed the little girl's forehead. "What news?"

Cawing ensued, and she listened. She grimaced, thanked them and promised food later. She turned to face her sisters, who'd followed her into the bedroom. "I have much to do." She passed Fallyn to Venus. "I'll be right back. I sent Rebekah to help our mother and aunt with the preparations for the *Sabbat*, but I need to handle a more immediate problem."

"What did they tell you?" Venus asked.

"They fear the *Binding* on Jed loosens. Without it, his rages will break free and he'll K.I.L.L. Meteor and the children."

"Go then." Venus clutched Fallyn tightly. "Will you leave the dogs to guard the innocents?"

"My doggies. Mine." Fallyn tried to break free of Venus' hold. "Wanta see my doggies. Now!"

Astra heard Venus begin to discuss the importance of clothing and dressing for the party. How did her youngest sister manage to have so much patience?

If she ever had children, Astra knew she'd be likely to issue orders, not reason with her babies. She had a hard enough time training her apprentice, and Rebekah was an adult. Meteor trailed behind Astra into the hall. When they were out of earshot, she said, "Keep Venus occupied. She's our weakest link. I'll restore her purity. She can't be the *Maiden* without it and her aura has far too much color right now."

"Help me too." Meteor kept her voice low. "I don't want to be with Jed tonight. Three children are enough for me to shield."

"I will." Astra hugged her sister. "Go look after your boys. I'll handle everything else. I promise."

———

With their experience, it didn't take long for two of them to set up a campsite. Their ritual clothes in the saddlebags, they rode toward the track Venus had taken with her strange wagon. Meadows divided by rows of giant evergreens covered rolling hills. Hugh supposed another man might miss the neglected fences and the ramshackle barns.

"How much stock do you reckon she runs?" Rowdy asked. "I haven't seen many cows, other than those we brought."

"There's horses." Hugh pointed to the herd that galloped along one fence and whinnied at their stallions. "Maybe, she's more for training them than having a cash crop of cattle."

"Could be." Rowdy gestured toward the sky and the plume of smoke that wavered. "Let's find the bonfire first and help with that. Don't want any man thinking I'm lazy."

Hugh nodded agreement. As they reached the bottom of the ridge, he saw corrals and pens. More barns and sheds caught his attention. The dirt road parted, with one branch leading to the left, shaded by maples, cottonwoods and more cedars. To the right, he saw a large house. It was even bigger than the one where Mary died, and that had been the fanciest in Corbettstown. This one had towers, wrap-around porches, a squared-off wing, and balconies. Sun glittered on the glass windows.

Hugh reined Mustard to the left. If the folks who lived here had such an elaborate home, why didn't they put money into the ranch? What was wrong? If he asked, would Venus tell him? He didn't know, but it'd be worth a try. He heard water rushing over rock and saw the river before they arrived at the end of the track. Several men tried to start a bonfire on the rocky beach, but the flames continually died before they took hold on the piled-up wood.

Beside him, Rowdy whistled softly. "Holt, look. There's Thojedescar. Why does he help these fellers when he's never been one for ceremonies?"

"Ask him before I question him about Mary."

"No, you can't expect straight answers from him." Rowdy swung his bay horse in front of Mustard. "Don't you see it? He's ensorcelled. He reeks of women's *magick* and not only that of his soul-matched mate. He's bound, banished, and beguiled. It's not a new casting, but one wrapped up in his past four lives."

"You see all that from here? You haven't even spoken to him. Can you *Heal* him?"

"I'll do my best." Rowdy scowled when a shadowy figure moved near the fringes of the roadway. "She plays with the fire and stops it from being lit."

Hugh frowned, seeing the woman for the first time. She was oddly familiar, not a total stranger. She wore a purple, black and silver striped shirt over tight black pants. A crow perched on each shoulder. Red-gold hair tumbled down her back.

"She's a *laspowima* to Thojedescar—" Hugh stopped when he saw a rare anger rise in Rowdy's dark eyes. "Yours."

The woman turned to face them. She lifted her hand, made signs that Hugh didn't recognize.

"Ward yourself." Rowdy forced his stallion to take a step. The bay reared and exploded into a bucking frenzy.

"By the *Lord and Lady*." Hugh booted Mustard away from the frightened, enraged stud. He hastily guarded his own buckskin and advanced on the witch. "Cease your mischief. If my saddle partner suffers the smallest scratch, you'll have three."

"And you will die." She laughed, cobalt blue eyes dark with hate. "As will he."

"Not before you receive my justice, *Vaslattel*." Horse under control and safely protected, Rowdy rode forward. "To mind-bend a helpless creature breaks the first rule of *magick*, to do no harm."

"And you'll do what, peasant?" She made another peculiar sign. "Return to your wallow and root with your *relkinam* in the mud, swine. Learn courtesy."

"You dare much, *Vaslattel*." Rowdy vaulted from the saddle, flung the reins toward Hugh, and advanced on her. "You think to change me and my prince to farm animals? Haven't you learned anything while we've been apart?"

10

HOLDING THE REINS OF HIS FRIEND'S BAY STUD, HUGH WATCHED Rowdy stalk toward the woman. She had courage, Hugh granted her that much respect. Few men dared to taunt Rowdy with his origins unless they were prepared to die. He'd earned his station in each and every life. It wasn't granted by birth.

The woman stood perfectly still. She stared at Rowdy as if the anger meant less than nothing and so did, he. She laughed at him again, then vanished—no dust or mist remained behind. She was simply gone in less than a heartbeat. The crows circled for a moment before flying away.

Rowdy studied the ground and the lack of prints from her boots. He wheeled, paced back to his horse. "You'll leave her to me, Holt."

"Unless she succeeds in killing you. If so, she goes alive in your coffin and the two of you travel to the stars together."

"I wouldn't have it otherwise." Without using the stirrups, Rowdy vaulted into the saddle as gracefully as a boy half his age. He stroked the blood bay's neck. "Take care when you approach her. She walks the astral planes as I do by day or night and has her witch's *magick* as well. If I'm not there to defend you, she will kill you."

"I *See* it." Hugh kept his buckskin from moving. "Rowdy, we accepted them as the highest of the high, as *laspowimas*. We vowed to treat them the *Warpathian* way. We would *Know All, Accept All and Love All*. To take a queen as a *vaslattel* breaks your oath and diminishes your honor."

"Our way is based on respect for both." Rowdy narrowed his gaze on the men building the fire once again. "As I told you before, she attempted to poison me on our soul-match night. She abandoned me for one of her lovers. When they realized what she'd done, the dracklegons offered to release me from our bond and to kill her since she was a *Vow-Shredder*. I protected her from the law-givers and refused to let them break our tie to each other. I won't have her burned alive in the Fires of Eternity. Instead, I took her as a *vaslattel*. Even now, she seeks to destroy your bonds to your mate as she did those of Thojedescar to his."

"But, why a *vaslattel*? She's one of the *Trecesalty*, the three royal queens of *Amalodia*, the ancient rulers of our ancestral home in *Trilunon*. Even with the lawgivers granting permission, you can't mean to shame her in front of her royal *relkinam* in this life."

"When she earns the privileges of a *laspowima*, I will grant them," Rowdy said, his tone even. "Be grateful I haven't taken the evidence of my deaths by rogue shapeshifters in my last four incarnations to the *dracklegons*. They'd insist on roasting her for one of their feasts regardless of her fitness to be my *vaslattel*."

"It will take at least another two hundred years to show she's worthy of being your *laspowima*." Hugh shook his head ruefully. "Rowdy, you're thirty-eight years old and you've had time to remember everything that happened in those four previous lives before we found each other as well as when we lived in *Trilunon*. Forgive some of her mischief. Like Venus, she hasn't turned thirty yet. She's too young to have the memories you do. Consider granting her the opportunity to be your *laspowima* in this realm."

"Not yet. Not after being disemboweled, ripped to shreds, and eaten alive four times while I heard shapeshifters quarrel over my bones. If you hadn't kept the fight fair when we were in Corbett's Town, it would have been a foul, fifth death." Rowdy shook his head. "You think of the evil she does and see if you understand my feelings."

They rode through the gates, onto the sparse grass and gravel-covered river beach. Smoke rose from the bonfire.

"Welcome." A youth with a heavily bandaged leg struggled to rise from a chair. "Did you arrange for us to start the ritual fire? Accept my thanks. I'm Orion Jamison. My sister, Venus, told me about your arrival."

"Hugh O'Connell and Rowdy Tall-Deer." The boy looked famil-iar. Hugh stiffened in the saddle. No wonder. He saw the same features in the mirror each morning when he shaved. "Your father?"

"The same as yours." Orion leaned on wooden crutches. "My mother told me today when we learned you'd come to the Rocking J."

"And who is she?" Somehow, Hugh knew it wasn't the same as his own. Was his father here in this time? Would he find his own *relkinam* close by? Or even his army?

Before Orion answered, Rowdy interrupted. "Thojedescar!"

Hugh looked at the group clustered around a man lying insen-sible on the ground. He dismounted, dropped Mustard's reins in the dirt, and followed Rowdy. "What do you need?"

"Water. My bags." Rowdy knelt beside their one-time friend, covered Thojedescar's soul-eye with a hand. "Find my *Chosen* and distract her so I can remove part of this *hex-death* created by one of her spells."

"As you say." Hugh brought the saddlebags from Rowdy's horse, while a tall, brown-haired fellow fetched water. "I'll deal with her, all right."

"I'll aid you." Anger filtered into Orion's face. "I warned Astra to leave us alone to prepare for the festival."

"Does she have the Power to call the crows of death?" Rowdy glanced up from his patient. "And the hounds from Hell?"

"As long as you don't touch them without permission, they're fine dogs," the brown-haired stranger said. "Many animals prefer women to men. I'm Gard Devlin."

"You've served me well in lives past, Gardarsolter, but Thojedescar was always your commander. Here-on, you'll guard him from those who mean to harm him. There are many and he won't be able to tell you of the most dangerous. It will take a moon or more to restore him."

"You mean Jed?" Sarcasm entered Gard's deep tones. "How do you plan to arrange that? He claims he's tough."

"Gard's right." Orion eyed Rowdy. "Jed won't like help. He's whipped every male shifter in the pack between the ages of eighteen and forty. How do you even know Gard? Astra only brought him here for the first time today."

"Too many questions, *Hisprinling*." Rowdy used the title for a second royal son who might ascend the throne of *Warpathia*. "If you watch and listen, you'll learn more than you do with demands."

Glimpsing the younger man's impatience, Hugh hid a smile. Rowdy's teachings could be irritating at times. "Anything else, Rowindache?"

"Yes. Astra will serve as High Priestess today. Arrange for me to be her High Priest. Find a place for us to live. We require fighting wages because we'll certainly earn them."

"Especially when you deal with my sisters. They are a challenge when the three of them stand together."

"You will leave them to us," Rowdy said. "We are their soul-matched mates. As it was decreed in the beginning, let it be so now. Do you hire men, *Hisprinling*? If so, we start to circumvent their whims."

"As you will then, Brother." Orion gazed at Rowdy before glancing at Hugh. "I'll show you the bunk-house. It's been repaired, but it needs cleaning since Kyle Morgan moved out nearly a month ago."

"Astra will do it." Rowdy's attention returned to Thojedescar when he stirred. "Tomorrow. There's no need to spoil *Samhain*. It will give her time to think of the changes she wants to make in the New Year."

"I want to see that," Orion muttered. "She always leaves the dirty work for Venus and Meteor."

"Not anymore." Hugh winked at the boy. "Rowdy does his own kind of *magick*."

Would the *Healing* his friend practiced on Thojedescar be enough for the man to regain his soul? Before they'd traveled through the *Time Gate* to this realm in 1718, the three of them had grown up together on *Trilunon* and once they'd been closer than most brothers. Could they be that close again?

———

Brigid Dawson fastened one end of the orange crepe streamer in the corner of the ceiling, then passed the roll to Daphne Hollister, one of the owners of the catering company. A tall, pale ash-blonde with gray eyes, the woman utilized her complexion to emphasize her Snow Queen costume. If Daphne stood against a white wall, she'd be invisible in the ivory dress she wore. She'd hung her sparkling cape in the cloakroom and intended to put it on when the ball started. While the two of them decorated the huge barn loft for the party, the other two partners in the catering company set up tables for the food and beverages.

The door opened and Brigid saw her aunt enter with another woman, a statuesque redhead, in a vibrant orange caftan. Each of them carried a cardboard box. The two crossed the room to confer with Tolliver, a stocky, short man who surprisingly exuded a strong sex appeal in the satyr costume he'd worn all month. It amazed Brigid when none of his partners complained about his bushy beard, or the surgically altered, pointed ears that looked like an elf's, and the two tiny horns that poked through his thick long, carmine hair with the consistency of a horse's mane. Granted, it was Halloween, but he'd been wearing variations of the same outfit for the past two weeks, down to the boots that covered his legs in fur and made his feet look as if he had cloven hooves. It always reminded Brigid of what her uncle had said about 'selling the sizzle, not the steak.'

Lizzie Blake, the other cook who created fabulous meals, opted for tattoos that covered nearly every inch of her small body, most of which had something to do with dragons. She'd dyed her hair in varying shades of green, but it didn't clash with the purple, pink and electric blue makeup she used as a fantastic fairy mask over her eyes, forehead, and the top of her cheeks.

Next to them, Brigid felt dowdy in her cowgirl outfit, although she'd thought she looked pretty sexy in a white tank top under a black and white cow-print vest and tight blue jeans under the matching chaps, with a bandana around her neck. She'd polished up the Ropers she wore for Saturday nights at Billy Bob's because she certainly couldn't wear her barn boots to a party. Her fringed gloves and hat were in the cloakroom with Daphne's cape. Next year, she'd do better, Brigid told herself.

She watched Tolliver carry a small table over by the door and set it up in the front corner. The two older women began to decorate the table, covering it first with a black cloth, then with another one that looked like silver spider webs.

"What are they doing?" Brigid asked Daphne. "I thought we were in charge of the decorations."

"We are. To show respect, the Elder-Witches have to set up the *Samhain* altar. It stays in place for the next three days and they'll put out objects that signify the importance of what we're celebrating."

"Like what? Isn't Halloween just for fun?"

"Not for us." Daphne shook her head, smiling. "This is the end of harvest time and the start of winter. It's why it's nicknamed, *'The Witches New Year,'* but it's also when the dead are the closest to us, so we remember them and send them off to the *Summerland* with our good wishes."

Not knowing what to say, Brigid returned her attention to the task at hand and taped up the black streamer beside the orange one. She heard the door open and glanced over her shoulder to see a young woman carrying a basket with pumpkins, squash and other root veggies join Estelle. "Where are the triplets?"

"They'll be along. They're probably helping the children get ready for the nature walk. It's why Astra sent her assistant in her place."

Brigid nodded again, remembering what her older sister had said when she heard about the new job. 'Keep an open mind and see what you learn. The world's a bigger place than most people think.' Obviously, Audra knew more about the mystical nature of the Jamisons than she admitted.

———

After taking the boys to join Venus and the rest of the children whose parents belonged to the coven, she'd returned to the apartment she shared with her eldest sister. It wasn't as big as the south wing of the house where Venus lived, but then again, it didn't need to be since Meteor and Astra had homes elsewhere.

Meteor adjusted the lemon-yellow wig and pinned it into place. She'd opted for the same black cat-suit she'd worn to nearly every party during the past two weeks. It clung to her curves, and she didn't look like the mother of three children, although only Edwin called her, 'Mama'. The other two thought she was their aunt and for now, that provided them protection. She longed for the day when she could claim all three, even if it'd break her younger sister's heart.

Venus deserved to have a family of her own, but Meteor wasn't sure the man who'd ridden in today was the answer to the spell they'd cast. What if he'd been sent by the Corbetts to wreak havoc? They hadn't hesitated to turn Jed against her in their past lives until he actually murdered her. Granted, he was responsible for his actions, but his *relkinam* weren't innocent by any stretch of the imagination.

She glanced over her shoulder when her bedroom door opened and Astra entered, followed by the largest of the three black dogs. "What took you so long?"

"I told you that I had to check on Jed and reinforce the bindings.

Then I saw Venus and cleansed her aura. She's pure as winter snow now."

"That means you erased the memories made today. She won't know her match if he comes to visit."

"And when she treats him as a stranger, he'll undoubtedly leave, just like all the other men who've shown interest in her."

Meteor nodded. "Don't you worry that someday she'll realize you've played mudpies with her mind and emotions?"

"Careful." Astra's dark blue eyes narrowed in warning. "You're beginning to sound like our mother and aunt. Remember, they're the ones who set this plan in motion and arranged for your death again and again at Jed Corbett's hands."

"I could never forget or forgive that." Meteor started toward the adjoining bathroom to apply her makeup. "Where's your costume?"

"Aunt Diana told me I serve as the High Priestess for the next three nights and she will be the Crone Goddess. She's sending me a black dress and a matching robe. Haven't they arrived yet?"

"No, but Rebekah will bring them soon. She's helping with the two altars, so you have time to shower before she gets here."

Astra heaved a sigh. "I know they're up to something, but it's almost impossible to read an Elder Witch's mind."

"You're not joking about that." Meteor turned in the doorway. "Our mother wants all of us to wear our jewelry sets tonight. I'm leaving my necklace with Fallyn."

"Venus will wear hers like always, but I'm not taking mine out of the box." Astra ran a hand over her hair. "I haven't worn it in eons, and I don't plan to break that tradition, especially since the man who made it arrived with Katiranika's match."

"Why does he worry you? I remember him as an honorable mage and *healer*."

"Isn't that reason enough?" Astra shuddered. "I'm not virginal like Venus or faithful to my soul-matched mate like you. I've participated in the *Great Rite* since our fourteenth birthday, when our father demanded one of us serve him."

"In every life?"

"Yes, and when he and his minions didn't use me first, he gave me to Latham for a sacrifice, which was even worse. He always laughed as he raped me and then slit my throat. Jarvesel and Latham killed me in three of my past lives, but I managed to defeat Latham in my last incarnation and seriously wound our demon father."

"And our mother and aunt didn't protect you from them?"

"Never. I've always been the one they sacrificed to satisfy our demon father's whims. There are worse things than dying, Matiranika and I've learned all of them."

Meteor hurried to draw her sister into a warm embrace, holding her tightly. "I'm so sorry. What can I do?"

"Stay with me during the ceremonies. Don't let them win by giving me to a mage who will slay me for my actions before he came here. I couldn't bear being his blood sacrifice too."

11

SEVERAL SLEEPING BAGS SPREAD ON THE GREAT ROOM FLOOR TOOK up most of the area. Venus swept a gaze over the children who ranged in age from two-and-a-half-year-old Fallyn to the four teenage girls clustered around the remains of the pizza. Quaid and some of the other boys tutored Edwin in the finer points of their latest video game.

Venus wondered again why Edwin's grown uncle chose to stay with them. He sat in her favorite rocking chair, half his attention on her and half on the kids. She focused on Fallyn when the little girl wandered to her, picking up the child. "What is it, baby? Are you ready to go to bed?"

"No, Mama." Fallyn snuggled a jam-sticky face against Venus' neck. "Want –tory."

"What kind of a tale?"

"Our –tory."

Venus wished for her chair. It surprised her when the man stood and offered the seat. All brawny cowboy, he must be more sensitive than he looked. She thanked him with a quick smile and strolled to the upholstered rocker. She sat, cuddled her exhausted daughter close and set the chair to moving slowly. Then, keeping her voice soft to soothe Fallyn into slumber, she began reciting the *Wheel of the Year'* story. "At *Yule*, which is what we call Christmas, we cele-brate the coming of the sun, for the *Goddess* brings forth the *God* and thus warmth and fertility enters our dark world—"

Fallyn sighed, stretched her legs, and then yawned. "*Wish tree*, presents, cookies, and candy. *Holly King* comes."

"Yes, the whole family did come for dinner and the *Holly King* arrived with his sleigh full of gifts. Then, in February, we celebrate the *Goddess* and her recovery because—"

"*Imbolgc*. Pretty fires."

"That's right." Venus kissed her daughter's strawberry curls. "We light lots and lots of candles and rejoice for the birth of the land as it renews."

Cassandra, a blonde fourteen-year-old, offered a warm, damp washcloth to Venus, then sat on the floor by her feet. The other girls joined her and the rest of the group slowly came to listen to the ritu-alistic tale. Venus smiled at them as she washed away the remnants of Fallyn's last snack.

"At *Imbolgc*," Cassandra took up the story, "spring begins. The *God* grows. The snow—"

"All gone." Fallyn yawned. "Flowers come."

"Yes." Venus felt a steady gaze on her and looked up to meet the stranger's dark eyes. Why couldn't she remember his name? She felt as if there'd been some connection between the two of them, but it seemed to have melted as easily as the snows in the first spring sunshine.

"*Ostara's* next," Quaid said. "We have rabbits and colored eggs and chocolate and a really great party."

"You're being majorly shallow," Cassandra decreed. "It's not only a good time. It's when the *Light of the Earth* appears. It's the middle of the spring festivals. Right, Venus?"

"Absolutely." Venus winked at her son. "And it's a fun party-time too."

With help from the children, she continued describing the rest of the Sabbats until she reached *Samhain*, the 'Witch's New Year.' She was careful not to frighten them when she explained this was a time to celebrate the lives of those who'd gone to *Summerland.* It was when they paid respect to ancestors, family members, elders and all other loved ones who'd died, including pets. To help guide them to their rest, she'd put a white candle in the window and the children had chanted a prayer with her earlier in the evening, so now she reminded them of that.

"And we each wrote down a bad habit we wanted to change and threw the papers in the bonfire," Edwin added. "That was fun, wasn't it, Uncle Hugh?"

"Definitely." He stirred, but continued to lean one broad shoulder against the far wall near the fireplace. "And it's almost one in the morning. It's time for young-uns to hit the hay if they want to be awake for the *Closing of the Circle* and the dawn feast."

To Venus' astonishment, his tone prompted obedience from all her guests, even the teens. They headed for their sleeping bags. She stood, carried Fallyn to her spot, and tucked the little girl into the pallet.

Fallyn opened big blue eyes. "Want doggie, Mama."

"Okay. I'll get one for you." Venus rose to her feet, started toward the corner and the toys. She stopped at the cry of bewilderment. "What, baby?"

"Outside doggie." Fallyn sat up, pointed to the front door. "Her come now."

"If you let in one, you'll have to let in the others on the porch," the stranger commented. "It's a warm night and they'll be fine outside if all of them stay together. Go to sleep, little 'un."

"No." Fallyn began to crawl out of the bag. "Me want doggie."

"All right, Guinevere." Edwin propped up on an elbow. "Go back to bed and Aunt will fetch her. Do it quick, or you'll be in big trouble."

Venus frowned at the name he called her daughter, then slowly turned to eye the boy. "Her name is Fallyn."

"Mama said when she had a girl, she meant to call her Guinevere," Edwin said. "Fallyn can choose to change her *Craft* name when she's older."

"Now, you should let in the dog, Mama," Quaid said. "She's plenty scared. She's been running for ages."

Venus stiffened as the truth seeped into her mind. The three children weren't talking about a 'dog'. They referred to Meteor, who'd shape-changed. For her to do it on a *Sabbat* meant she faced some sort of trouble, and as usual, it undoubtedly had to do with Jed Corbett.

Venus went to the door, opened it as a large black shape hurtled inside leaving behind Astra's three dogs. "Peace be on you and with you." She closed the door and locked it. "You're safe here. There's food and shelter for you and yours as long as you want it, now and always."

The big, black dog panted, shuddered and pressed close. Venus dropped to her knees, drew her sister near and crooned a low Protection spell into the false canine's ear. "—*I call you at this hour to help us, I pray. Bless us with your protection and love each and every night and day. Keep all harm from us, all evil at bay. Let us walk in the circle of your light—so mote it be, as I say.*"

She repeated the charm three times and felt Meteor relax. Because of the children, she wouldn't revert back to human form. Instead, she broke free and went to lie between Fallyn and the boys.

Fallyn beamed, kissed the dog and moved closer. "Night, Mama. Night, Quaid. Night, Wynn. Night, man."

Venus smiled and fixed the covers on all three of her kids, including Edwin. She rose, warded the youngsters in the coven, and went toward the kitchen. She switched off the lights, aware Edwin's uncle seemed fascinated by each motion. What was his name? Why couldn't she remember it?

She hadn't lost her mind. They must have talked at some point because Orion mentioned agreeing with her at the bonfire. When she questioned her brother, he told her that she'd hired this man and his friend to help on the ranch. She frowned at the holes in her memories. "Where's your buddy?"

"Claiming his *vaslattel*."

"His what?" Venus blinked, curious. She felt as if she knew the meaning of the word, but somehow it stayed just out of reach. "Who are you talking about? Did he meet someone at the bonfire or the *Great Rite*? If he did, how would you know? You're here, not there on the beach with them."

"Because it's what I'd do if we'd known each other longer, Katiranika." He paced toward her, a golden-haired giant, all lethal grace in a black shirt and pants under a dark robe. "You forgot me, didn't you? Who be-spelled you?"

"No one." She shook her head, began to clear dishes from the table. "You can leave. It's late and I want to sleep before the morning ceremonies too."

He stopped in front of her, catching her chin in calloused fingers and lowered his head. "What's my name? You oughta recollect it, considering the way you kissed me."

"What? Are you crazy?" Her voice shook, and she stared up at him. "No way. I'd never kiss someone I don't know."

"Good. I don't cotton much to sharing. I'm not Rowdy." He bent his head, his breath warm on her lips. "I'm Hugh O'Connell, Hughondear. Remember me, Katiranika."

His deep tone almost broke through the fog in her mind. With her hands full of plates, she couldn't push him away. His mouth brushed hers softly. She swayed. When he stepped back, she hurried to the sink, nearly dropping the dishes.

Her brain felt fuzzy. In her mind, she saw his face. It'd grown harsh when she cursed him. Then, she stood locked in his arms while he kissed her senseless. She'd fought him, but finally surrendered to those kisses which drugged her soul.

"It must be a dream," she muttered. "I couldn't do that and forget."

"Not by yourself." He strode to her, twined a hand in her hair and turned her face up to his. "Who ensorcelled my war-queen?"

"I'm not. I belong to no man."

"Except me." His mouth claimed hers, a sweet, gentle yet insistent pressure.

Tears slipped down her cheeks as she capitulated. She wouldn't tell him that her sister betrayed her. How did Astra do it? Take away the events of a day so nothing remained. Why had her older sister done such a thing? Worse, had it happened before?

"Now, you know me." The flat certainty in his tone roused her. "Don't you, Katiranika?"

"Yes, but it doesn't matter much." She pushed at his broad chest. "Get you gone."

He chuckled. "In a kiss, *Laspowima*. Make me regret leaving if you can."

The challenge taunted her. She rose on tiptoe, threaded her fingers into his golden hair. She nibbled at his lower lip, sucked on it for an instant. Slowly, she allowed her mouth to rove over his, kept control of the kiss, although she didn't deepen it. Innocence was so much fun. He followed her lead, responded as she directed and yet she knew the embrace entranced both of them.

He trailed a finger down her throat to the gold amulet nestled against her breasts. "I keep and protect you, Witch. I don't want you to forget me again. Now, I'll go."

"Why?" She rested her hands on his shoulders. "You could stay. I'd like that."

"I will another time when it's just us." He kissed her forehead. "For now, I'd best track down Thojedescar before he drowns himself in a vat of wine. If he shape-shifts before he learns his true *magick*, he may dishonor himself and me."

"I didn't know Jed Corbett could change—"

"It's why he and your sister matched." Hugh took a step toward the back door. "Rowdy took Astra, but our marriage was arranged while you were still in the nursery before you received your first wand. Dream of me and our wedding."

"I'm not marrying you. I barely know you."

"Too late, *Laspowima*. You already did." He walked out the door into the night.

———

The early portion of the ceremonies had ended. The young witches and wizards were off and away with Venus, who would guard them. Behind him, Rowdy heard laughter on the beach near the bonfire. Now, the adults tried to decide the right game to start the *Great Rite*. There were always babies nine months after a *Sabbat*.

He saw a woman walk toward him and he paused on the path so he wouldn't frighten her. It wasn't his *vaslattel* who eyed him with hate while she allowed any of the other men close and permitted them to kiss her while she avoided his touch during the ceremonies. She'd even flirted outrageously with Gard and laughed at his witticisms.

Rowdy stiffened as the unknown woman advanced on him. Small, plump with gray in her red hair, she matched the description Hugh had given of Estelle Jamison, the matriarch of the family. He knew her as someone else, someone much more powerful than a mere Elder Witch. He dropped to his knees, lowered his head. "Your will, High Queen?"

"Cease this nonsense, Rowindache. In this realm, I haven't a title." She tossed him a black cloak. "I have work for you."

He rose, robe in hand. "What is your wish, *Majeenler*?"

"My daughter." The older woman shrugged. "Niece. Whatever you wish to call her, but she is yours. You will bond with her tonight and bind her to you for eternity."

"If it's her will, she chooses the time and place." Rowdy felt a rare anger rise but continued to use the title for the regent of their home realm. "I will not be played, not by her and not by you, *Majeenler*. I'm not a token for your games."

"You've been a pawn far too long, but I'm not the one who sent you hurtling through *Time*. I tried to find you and Hughondear for nigh on six hundred years, but Astra is a powerful witch despite her youth. Her spell hid you from rescue."

"She didn't cast it. She ordered the war-queen to *banexort* us."

"Yes, but Venus merely read the spell her sister provided. My youngest daughter never would have dishonored your *healers* by giving them to the shape-shifters to be blood sacrifices before they're grown in each and every life."

Rowdy shuddered, recalling his own gruesome deaths. "Is that why I never found them in my past lives?"

"Yes, and it's why Hughondear always found himself leading his army into one battle after another until they all died. We, my other Elder Witch and I, managed to cast a protection spell over you in your fifth lives so you could find each other and be free to come here. Now, you must guide your *Chosen* to a better path, one that leads to the *Light*, rather than the *Dark*, or she will continue her journey to evil and become her demon-father's true successor."

"How do I manage it?"

"By invoking the entire *talipenlace* set tonight. You'll find the box you created in the bunk-house. It contains the necklace, the earrings and bracelets. Once Astra willingly dons the jewels you designed, it will guide her soul. When she repeats her vows to you, then and only then, do you have her mind. She must give you her body three times before dawn. It will take longer for you to win her heart. She has scorned love longer than you know."

"What do you mean, '*invoke the talipenlace*'? It's been hers since our soul-matching ceremony when I gave it to her and helped her wear it the first time."

"She keeps it in the box you created and uses your *magick* for *Power* to control lives and create *Outcome*s which aren't hers to offer." The older woman shook her head ruefully. "I thought I knew how to unite our countries by arranging marriages between *Warpathia's* strongest mages and *Amalodia's* best witches when Jarvesel poisoned *Trilunon's* air, water and food sources. I didn't realize he'd already turned Astra against her own people, and I don't think she knows the depths of his maneuverings."

"Does he force her to use my *Powers* to do harm?"

"I'm not sure if he still influences her or if she does it on her own, but the results are the same. When she exercises retribution, she prevents people from their true destinies."

"And mocks justice as she did at my trial when she arranged for false evidence to be given to ensure my conviction."

"Whether she believes it or not, I love the child. I will do anything to save her." A tear trickled down Estelle's cheek. "I can't believe she's bad when she has such wisdom and protects her sisters and the young witches and wizards in our coven. She means to save the helpless, but her vision is blinded at times."

"You don't have to convince me." Rowdy held up the dark cloak. "Why this disguise? I could simply take her from the festivities."

"Yes, but it might spoil the ceremonies and the *Great Rite*. Orion will host the candle game and you will agree to participate. When the rest of the men do, there will be cloaks to hide them as well. Astra will blow out the candle while you hold it and you take her away from the bonfire for the *Trilunon Nine-Time Kiss*."

"It seems you've planned everything."

"I've had far too long to do so while I searched for you and the prince. I intended to undo the harm my girls caused. I should have realized they didn't enter the soul-matching with clean hearts. Astra convinced her sisters I meant evil. Now, they'll never believe I wanted to save them, to unite the witches who remained with the wizards who survived the plague." More tears fell. The woman turned and hurried away, obviously upset by emotions that threatened royal bearing.

Pity swelled as Rowdy watched her return to the large house. Behind it, he saw the dim shadow of the bunk-house where he, Hugh and Edwin would live for a while. But not tonight. Edwin slept with the rest of the children. Hugh remained with his *laspowima*, even if they didn't fulfill their destiny.

Rowdy swung the cloak around his shoulders and pulled up the hood before strolling back to the bonfire. The High Queen was right. It was beyond time that he claimed his *vaslattel,* and taught her the manners she'd never learned.

12

Rowdy arrived at the bonfire in time to hear Orion explain the rules of the game, along with the *Trilunon* embrace of where each kiss landed, from foot to ankle to knee and onward. His suggestion met with quick approval. Amid laughter and teasing, the adults took their places, men to the inner circle, women to the outer. Each time the lit candle made it all the way around the male circle, the women owed their mates the *Kiss*. If a woman managed to blow out the taper when her partner held it, he owed her the carnal debt.

Rowdy felt a hand touch his arm and heard Astra's low, amused voice. "Are you sure about this, Gard? We don't have to stay. The guest-room is made up for you in my mother's house. Do you want to play?"

Rowdy nodded, wondering how the High Queen managed to steal the other man's cloak. Had she convinced the former soldier to give it to a friend of his one-time general? Either Astra wasn't as good at reading auras as she thought, or the robe had been disguised.

Orion lit the taper and passed the candle onto the man next to him. Rowdy waited his turn, focusing on the orange candle, not the love promises his *vaslattel* whispered in his ear to distract him. She might not mean them for him, but he intended for her to keep each one. He wondered how many men she'd been with and decided it didn't matter. He wouldn't be her first, but he'd be the last. She was his, just as he was hers and this life was for them.

———

Astra smiled at her young half-brother. How did he devise such antics? She'd have to ask him when the *Sabbat* ended. Tonight, she'd have Gard Devlin, see how well he performed in bed. It'd show Rowindache he meant nothing to her, he never had. It'd delighted her to mock him with the men who flirted with her as the High Priestess, not that she admitted it to her mother or aunt. They'd have chastised her for disrespecting their rituals.

She watched the candle come closer, leaned over his shoulder so her breast rubbed against his back. He tensed, totally aware of her. She nipped his ear in quick teasing. "I'll make you happy."

He held the candle. She blew, suddenly aware he kept it a moment too long. The flame flickered, went out. So much for his proclaimed honor. He wasn't as decent or moral as he claimed.

With a chuckle, he passed on the taper to the next man. "So, I'm the first to win."

"No." Breath lodged in her throat, she fell back a step. "It can't be."

"It is." He laughed again, then stood. He'd have three inches on her if she hadn't worn her favorite black dress boots with four and a half inch stiletto heels so she could look down on him. He snapped his fingers, and the candle burned once more. He offered the traditional farewell to the group clustered around the fire. "Merry meet until we meet again at dawn."

She stared into his dark eyes, shook her head, her voice a bare whisper. "I won't."

He caught her fingers, guided her away from the fire on the beach in the direction of the house. "I prefer my kisses without an audience, *Vaslattel.*"

"You won't have mine." She stumbled on the dark trail, wishing she'd brought at least one of the dogs with her instead of leaving all three of them to guard Venus and the children.

He shrugged. His shoulders weren't as broad as Gard's, but they weren't narrow either. His grip tightened. "You can fight me, *Vaslattel*, but sooner or later, you'll want to please me."

The taunt infuriated her. "You'll leave this place and plane. I'll see to it that you return to the hell from whence you came. I swear it."

"Not again. It's not happening, Princess. Your sister vowed not to *banexort* me or my prince, so you'll have to do your own dirty work. Reckon, I'll stay and make my second-wife howl for me like one of her she-bitches from that hell."

The insults added to her rage. She froze, swung at him. He caught her wrist before the slap connected with his face. "I'll never want you."

He pulled her a step forward, against his lean body. "You don't know what you want, Satiranika. The evil you do poisons you as much as it does those you fight."

"I'm not yours." She strained to see his face in the night, amazed he remembered her witch's name. "I'll be rid of you."

"You'll change your mind by dawn." He lifted her into his arms, carried her toward the bunk-house. "You'll wear what I made for you and be happy to please me. None will interrupt us while we sort out our concerns. We'll have the place to ourselves."

"Are you crazed?" She tried to wriggle out of his hold, amazed at his strength. Wiry, light on his feet, he moved as if he were part panther. "I saw that hovel. It hasn't been cleaned in weeks."

"Then it will suit you fine." No humor shone in the dark eyes. "You can clean it tomorrow. How many men have had you?"

"You dare to ask me that? You, the lowest of criminals!"

"That many?" His mouth came nearer.

She tried to turn away, but he held her tighter. His lips captured hers. The pressure forced her head back into the hollow of his shoulder. His tongue made its way inside her mouth and he proceeded to conquer that area as well. He didn't seek her participation. He kissed her as if he owned her, whether she permitted it or not, whether she liked it or not.

She reminded herself that she should fight him, or at least be as cold as ice in his hold, but somehow the idea didn't make a lot of sense. Not when she longed to respond to him, to this mage who treated her like a woman instead of the men she met who tried to get her to pay their way, as well as her own.

She kissed him back, her tongue engaging with his in a duel she was determined to win, but he didn't allow her to explore his mouth. He continued to maintain control of the fierce kiss until she surrendered. When he finally lifted his head, she could barely breathe, much less talk. She struggled for air, almost panting. She let him carry her into the dark cabin.

How did he see when she couldn't? He opened his arms, let her fall, and she landed on her back on a small, narrow bed. He turned away, left her to go light a lamp on the table in the center of the room. Then, he closed the door. He lingered there for a moment before removing the black cloak, hanging it on a nearby peg. He still wore dark pants, a loose shirt, and boots. He sat down on a simple wooden chair and began to remove his boots.

She watched him warily for a moment. She rolled off the bed, rose to her feet. "As far as I'm concerned, I owe you nothing." He wasn't the only one who knew special names and she opted to use his. "You can tell people whatever you like, Rowindache. I'm finding Gard and going with him."

"I don't think so. You won't get out the door, but you can try." Rowindache toed off the second boot, gesturing to the carved box on the table. "Put on the *talipenlace* set, *Vaslattel*, or I will."

She shivered at the sound of his gravelly voice. "How did that get here? I left it in my room in the house."

"Ask your mother tomorrow."

Astra moistened suddenly dry lips. She looked around the cabin, one long room with three bunks on the inside and three more on the outside walls. He sat in the combined kitchen and living area. At the far end, she saw three large steamer trunks lined up beneath a curtained window since the bunkhouse didn't have dressers or closets to store extra clothing or personal belongings.

She eyed him again. She wanted to untie the leather thong that held his long black hair speckled with gray in a ponytail and run her fingers through it. His wiry, muscular build stirred her. "If I put it on, will you agree to let me leave?"

He shrugged. "That's a risk you'll have to take."

"And that isn't an answer, Rowindache."

"It's the only one you're getting."

Taking a deep breath, she sauntered to the table, deliberately letting her hips sway, knowing he watched her every move. He must remember the Sex Magick spells she used on him as much as she did. She opened the box and eyed the golden ornaments. Like her sisters' necklaces, hers had a gold chain, but the center disk was a pentacle, a five-pointed star inside a circle. The dangling earrings matched, and the two bracelets had healing runes carved into the gold accentuated with dark sapphires.

He waited, silent, like the cat he reminded her of, while she began with the earrings, taking off the ones her aunt had sent for the ritual and replacing them, then the bracelets and finally the pendant.

When she finished, she turned to face him, feeling the *magick* in the air. "Now, what?"

He leaned back in the chair, wearing only his pants. Neatly folded, his shirt lay on the table. "Have they always been yours?"

"Of course. Who else would have them?"

"Your father wanted them."

"That demon?" Astra shook her head, stroking the pentacle on its chain. "No, Rowindache. You sacrificed your heart, mind, body, and soul to me of your own free will. Nobody else can have those, least of all, my father. I'll keep these toys along with your powers and use your *magick* as I do mine."

As it had in the past, the disk warmed beneath her touch. Somehow, the heat felt different tonight. She dismissed the notion. On *Samhain*, the veil between the living and the dead, the old and the new was much thinner when *magick* ruled. Of course, the tokens held extra energies.

"You wear them of your own free will?"

"Certainly. Nobody makes me do anything."

What was he, stupid? She froze, choked on words, suddenly feeling trapped. What had she done? She ran past him for the door, grabbed the knob. No matter how she twisted it, pulled on it, the door didn't budge. Meanwhile, the jewelry felt as if it branded her, hot against her skin.

"It's sealed." His hands closed over her upper arms and he drew her back against him. "Look at it."

She stopped, stared at the pair of parallel lines on the wooden panel, visible only to witches. "What have you done?"

"This glyph blocks entry to the outside. You've willingly admitted you wear my devices, *Vaslattel*. That makes you mine."

"I already told you. I'm not yours. I won't be."

He chuckled, turned her to face him.

She gaped at him. He stood naked in front of her. When had he finished undressing? Black hair fell halfway to his muscled chest, mixed with the scant hairs between brown nipples. Before she stopped herself, she looked down to his narrow hips and lower. He was larger than she'd remembered, and he wanted her. She wasn't ready for him.

Quickly, she met his gaze. The dark eyes revealed nothing of what he felt. She shook. His hands went to the collar of her black robe and he unfastened the clasp. The cloth parted, and he pushed it off her shoulders until it pooled on the floor.

He focused on the knee-length, ebony dress with its form-fitting low-cut bodice that clung to every inch of her breasts and narrow waist before flaring out into a full skirt at her hips. "Remove this."

"If I don't?" She raised her chin, their lips a breath apart. "What are you going to do?"

"Have you in it." He pulled the skirt up toward her waist. "Do you want to hold this?"

She shook her head. Suddenly, she had a plan, one meant to

embarrass him. She wouldn't respond when he kissed her this time. She'd ignore his touch when he caressed her. No man wanted a woman who dismissed him as if he were less than dirt. "You can't be serious. We haven't talked. We need to discuss what we're going to do—"

He raised a brow. "Discuss? I'm having my *vaslattel* now. I've waited long enough."

"You haven't even been here a full day."

"And if you'd had your way, I wouldn't be here now." He gathered up the skirt in one hand, holding it between them. "So, I'll make up for the time I wasted waiting for you to be a true mate."

She gasped when he cupped her, sliding a finger inside her, then pulling it out and slipping it in again, in a slow, deliberate motion. Why hadn't she worn panties? Since the dress her aunt brought had a built-in bra, Astra opted for lacy thigh-high stockings and her spike-heeled boots.

She'd figured on having Gard tonight and hadn't wanted anything in the way of wild sex. She arched her head back against the door when Rowindache's thumb found the perfect spot to rub. How could she remember that she meant to be ice when he touched her like this? When she was wet and throbbing and he'd stopped moving his fingers?

He paused, and she stared at him. He smiled, shifting his hands to hold the bottom half of the dress. He gripped her waist, lifted her, pinned her body against the door.

"What are you doing?"

"I already told you." He moved forward, parting her legs even further. "Having my *vaslattel.*"

She clutched his shoulders, determined not to fall at his feet. "You can't. You haven't even kissed me. You need to—"

"Take what's mine." He drove into her. "It's been too long since I had you, Satiranika."

She gasped, cried out at the sudden possession. His thrusts rocked her into the door, his mouth claiming hers in a series of fiery kisses. She wrapped her legs around his narrow hips and held on, matching his movements. He went deep inside as if he intended to breach her soul. She sank her teeth into his shoulder and rode the storm. Tossed on the winds, she rose and fell, snared in the onset of a sexual hurricane while they traveled together on a journey toward the stars. He was hotter, harder than she'd remembered. A raging fire burned within her, the flames rising ever higher until she reached the sun, climaxing moments before him. His fierce strokes continued until he groaned with satisfaction as he reached the heights.

They collapsed onto the floor, her dress still twisted around her hips. He'd treated her as if she were a woman he'd hired for the night. He hadn't even tried to give her pleasure. So, why did she have an orgasm with him when those were so rare for her? She glared up at him, where he sat less than a foot away.

He held out a hand. "Come to me."

"Return to the swamp where you were conceived, *Garungap!*" She knocked away his fingers before he touched her. "You're worse than sewer slime!"

"Even lower than that, *Vaslattel.*" He laughed at her, a short, sharp sound. "You belong to a man whose parents met profession-ally. She was a space marine and he was a licensed sex provider."

Her lips curled in disgust. Venus' mate was the heir to the throne of *Warpathia*. Meteor's came from the wealthiest family on *Trilunon*. Did her sisters know of this shame? Her aunt did. Why else arrange such humiliation?

"And I got you." She shoved away his hand when he tried to smooth her hair. Contempt laced her tone. "You've had me. Now, open the door. I want to take a bath, to wash away your stink."

"Not yet, *Vaslattel.*" A wry smile twisted his lips. He stood, offered his hand a third time. "Let's try the bed."

"Go by yourself." She sneered at him. "Your father must have taught you that much back in the day."

"Tell me why no one washed out your royal mouth with soap, Princess." His smile didn't reach his eyes. "Or spanked your regal backside."

"Try anything like that and you'll spend eternity as the pig you are." She stifled a scream when he bent, caught her ankle, and pulled her to him. She trembled when he joined her on the floor. "I told you before—"

"I'm not listening." He drew her close, lowering his head. "Kiss me."

"No." She pushed against him when he covered her with his body, easing her legs apart, resting some of his weight on his elbows. "You can't be ready this soon."

"You inspire me, *Vaslattel*." He slid into her.

Her hips arched to meet the first thrust. She reminded herself that she meant to freeze, but the idea was moot. She met each stroke, some fast and shallow, others long and deep. Somehow, she managed to hold back a little, make this only a physical union. She writhed, twisted under him, catching his mouth with hers in kisses that didn't seem to last long enough. She clawed at his back, trying to hurry the pace he set. Nothing altered the steady thrusts. They seemed to go on forever until he exploded inside her and they climaxed together among the stars. This time he lay next to her. His fingers stroked her hair.

"Some lover," she scoffed, trying to shift away from him. She stopped when his arms tightened around her. "You can't take your time with a woman so she really enjoys sex, can you?"

He laughed, pressing a kiss to her forehead. "Take off the dress, Vaslattel, and I might try a little harder, but you certainly enjoyed the last two times. I don't believe your lies, my own."

"Rot in hell."

"If it gets torn, you'll have to explain to the Elder Witches why it's unfit to wear at dawn."

She pushed him away and sat up. "I hate you."

"I know." Lying on his side, he leaned back on an elbow. "After being tortured and killed so many times at your instigation, is it a surprise I enjoy that too?"

PART II

"Let the magick take you where you want to go."

— METEOR JAMISON, SHAPE-SHIFTER,
ENTREPRENEUR, AND HEREDITARY WITCH

13

DESPITE THE CALMNESS HE'D SHOWN WITH VENUS, HE FELT A NEW anger with her sisters. On his way back to the bonfire, he glanced toward the bunk-house. Light flickered in the windows and he knew his partner wasn't alone. Tomorrow would be soon enough to warn Rowdy of his *vaslattel's* latest manipulations.

At the beach, he saw Thojedescar, and another man seated at the bonfire, the one Rowdy had assigned as a guard. It'd dwindled down to a small blaze, almost a campfire. Hugh joined the other two. "No *Great Rite* for either of you?"

"I'm not much for sex with a stranger," Gard Devlin said. "It's too dangerous. Astra disappeared before I arrived so I'd say she agreed with me."

"Is that right?" Hugh sat down on a convenient log, took the bottle of wine from Thojedescar. "Or did she go with Rowdy?"

"Not willingly. I think it surprised her when she learned who wore the cloak given to our new friend for the festivities. For a *Healer*, Rowindache knows much of the mischief between a wizard and a witch."

"Still, she agreed? He didn't force her?" The question was more for the benefit of the other man. At this point, Hugh personally wouldn't have cared if Rowdy dragged his *vaslattel* kicking and screaming from the fires. Still, if he had, their laws required Hugh to intervene. "She wanted him?"

"I'd say so." Thojedescar gestured to the wine bottle. "If you don't intend to drink with me, give it back. It's not beer, but it'll do. Whisky would be better."

"You've had enough." Hugh hefted the bottle. Less than half the wine remained. Before his one-time friend left in search of more liquor, Hugh continued. "You need your full mind. Your woman fears and hides from you."

"Not her cloak or ritual clothes." Thojedescar waved to the pile of cloth at his feet. "She's out there naked in the dark with another man. I hope the mosquitoes get both of them."

"That's some threat." Hugh took a swallow of the sweet wine. It didn't sound like much peril awaited Mary from the man she named her killer. It was time to learn the truth. "Anyway, she's with Venus and the children. She arrived as I left. My *Chosen* guards her now so I'll take her raiment to Mary before dawn."

"Meteor," Thojedescar corrected. "She was Mary in our last life. Didn't it shock the kids when she showed up nude? Of course, I didn't see hardly any youngsters. So, maybe not."

"Are you half blind?" Gard asked. "There must have been fifteen or twenty of them at the dance. How long have you been drinking?"

"Not long enough to miss that many kids. What did Circe do to me?"

"Who's Circe?" Gard asked. "I met most of the people here and they've been really nice. I don't recall a woman with that name."

"It's what I call Astra." Red crept into Thojedescar's face. "She always makes a pig of me." He frowned thoughtfully. "Why would she prevent me from seeing children?"

For the moment, Hugh avoided that question and reverted to the original subject. "Meteor shape-changed. Why didn't you do the same, Thojedescar?"

"You two are insane." Gard took a swallow from his own bottle of wine. "I've heard and seen a lot of foolish things since I arrived, but that's impossible. It's loony enough to believe in *magick*, but impossible creatures like werewolves and vampires. No way! Next, you'll be telling me there's angels all around us."

"We don't care for the name 'werewolves'. We're shifters," Thojedescar said, "and we don't hunt humans. That's an old mortal tale."

"You've drank too much," Gard told him. "She could have gone to her sister's if she wanted. She'd didn't have to make a show of leaving her clothes behind."

"She ran away from me. She owed me three *Trilunon Nine-Time Kisses,* and I'd have collected mine when I gave her one. She already knew I wanted a son to make up for Edwin. She'd have been pregnant by dawn."

"No, no more babies," Hugh said. "You'll have Edwin back when the two of you are ready to protect him. For now, I'll guard the boy. Mayhap, you can convince Venus to return the daughter and son she raises for you, but it will take much effort."

"What daughter and son?" Thojedescar propped his chin on a fist and thought. "I dated Venus for a while three years ago to irritate Meteor. I remember that, but what have I forgotten? She gave Edwin away more than a hundred years ago. Shouldn't he be grown and dead by now?"

"Too much booze. You're drunk, man. First, it's shape-shifting. Now, it's traveling through *Time*. Soon, you'll tell me about reincarnation and we've all had a hundred lives before. It's crap."

"Then, why'd you visit and stay with us, Gard?" Thojedescar rested his hands on his knees, eyeing Hugh. "He's right about one thing. How did you get here if Mary gave you our son a hundred-plus years ago?"

"Venus did a *Calling and Love-Bringing* spell. It opened a portal for us." Hugh saw disbelief on Gard's face and acceptance on Thojedescar's. "So, Rowdy and I rode here. We brought Edwin with us."

"And the portal?" Thojedescar asked. "Will others follow you?"

"No, a cowboy always closes gates behind him. We did." Hugh held his one-time general's gaze. "Do you still serve me?"

"Sure. Always have. Always will."

"Wait a second," Gard said. "I don't serve anyone but myself. I don't know how that long-haired, freaky guy made me promise to watch over this logger, but I said I would. And I will, but that doesn't make me a slave."

"Except to your honor," Hugh said. "How old are you?"

"I'm thirty-eight, but what does that have to do with anything?"

"At thirty, your memories should start to return unless they've been blocked like Thojedescar's." Hugh turned his attention on the big, dark-haired man. "When I left Corbett's Town, Mary was dead, but she'd told me that you threw her down the stairs and broken her back along with several other bones. She couldn't shift and heal because she was pregnant, close to birth. She died in agony and your second son did too."

Anguish swept across Thojedescar's face, landing in his dark eyes. "I'd never hurt her. I don't know why she'd say something like that."

"Because she thought you murdered her," Gard said. "If you did it, I'm turning you into the cops. Beating up guys in tavern brawls happens. Hitting a pregnant woman? No way! It's disgusting."

"I didn't do it." Thojedescar paled, but he met Hugh's gaze evenly. "I swear I never lifted a hand to Mary in any of our lives. She's one of the *Trecesalty*, a royal queen. She doesn't bear false witness. She calls her father a demon and hates what he's done. She tries to live honorably like her mother. To perjure herself—"

"Would be as if I'd done it." Hugh grimaced at the idea. He didn't doubt other royalty in his line and that of the *Ranika relkinam* had oath-breakers. *Vow-Shredders* dishonored all families, but most rejected those outlaws. "So, she told the truth as she knew it. Why would she think *you* slew her?"

"Because whoever did it stole his shape." Gard drank more wine. "It's obvious."

"No, it's as bad as oath-breaking," Hugh said. "It can't be done. No decent shifter would—"

"Oh, get off it." Gard snorted. "Honorable? Decent? You're talking about a guy who beats a woman. Where's the dignity in that? And the low-life bastard throws her down a set of stairs and leaves her to die when she's pregnant. Why wouldn't he steal somebody else's likeness? It makes for a perfect alibi, especially if he arranged for someone other than the victim to see him."

"Like who?" Hugh knotted his fists. "Edwin. He saw it. Why didn't he tell me?"

"Is he the kid?" Gard asked. "Think about it from his point of view. No matter how bad he knows his old man is, he won't admit it to himself. Not for a while, anyhow. He'll make excuses, try to protect his dad."

"It can't be done," Hugh insisted. "I'd have heard tales."

"We hush it up," Thojedescar intervened. "It's a shame to us. It's done on rare occasions, usually to save or protect a virtuous one. Meteor did it almost three years ago. She took on her sister's shape and seduced me so Venus wouldn't fall in love with me."

"Told you so." Gard finished his wine, leaned over to take the bottle Hugh held. "As long as we're talking bull-crap, anything's possible."

"And what happened to Meteor?" Hugh asked. "She appeared as fine as frog's hair tonight."

"She is. She accepted the *Rule of Three* and the consequences of borrowing a shape to use it for harm." Thojedescar slowly shook his head. "That's the only time I've seen it done. I could ask my uncle. He'd know if anyone else in Corbettstown had done it."

"I don't remember being introduced to him," Gard said.

"He's not here," Thojedescar said. "He abhors witches, especially powerful ones like Estelle and Diana. He wants to buy this place, or at least log off the old-growth cedar and they won't sell, so he plagues the life out of them."

"And you allow this disgrace?" Hugh eyed his friend sternly. "Here-on, no more liquor. Shifters have a weakness for it and so must you. That ends now. You will make amends for the dishonor your *relkinam* does in each and every way."

"How am I supposed to do that alone?" Thojedescar narrowed his eyes, snarling. "I've fought. It does no good. Mary dies and leaves me without a soul. I'm empty. Nothing refills me except alcohol."

"You're no longer alone. I'm here," Hugh said. "So is Rowdy. This man with the big mouth will go along to watch over you, to guard your shape. Whoever the killer is, he will try to take it again and arrange for you to suffer the results. It must not happen *again* or you and Meteor will never be together. Your children will never know how much their parents love them."

"Why are you helping him?" Gard asked. "What's in it for you?"

"I owe him loyalty as he does me." Hugh leaned forward to add another log to the fire. "Besides, I want time alone with Venus. As long as we raise their children, it will take much time and arranging. And I'm a lazy man."

The wry comment brought laughter from both men. Gard shook the bottle of wine, drained it. "Sounds like bull-hockey to me. You're setting us up to track a woman-beater and murderer. I'll bet if the fight comes here, you'll kick some real tails and take a few names."

"Oh, I'll even read them from the *Book of Shadows*," Hugh agreed. "Rowdy will unleash the *HellHounds* on them. He's a *Healer*, but he was a swordsman first and no slouch in a fight."

"How does he plan to take Circe's dogs?"

"Astra," Hugh corrected. "No name-calling. That ends too. She's your sister by marriage. You owe her respect."

"I nearly wish you back a hundred years on the other side of that portal. Will you make her be nice to me?"

"Of course not." Hugh waited a moment too long before he grinned. "It's Rowdy's task. I never attempt the impossible. He'll have his work cut out for him. I lose patience with her when she blocks my *Chosen's* memories of me."

"Not for long, if I know you. I'll bet it's why Meteor abandoned me tonight. Astra did some charm to prevent us from joining. I will be the one to deliver my *laspowima's* clothing to her. Next time, she shape-shifts, I will too. For now, it'll be enough to confuse her."

———

A muffled sob woke him. Rowdy lay still, listened. A second one came to his ears. Where was she? He was alone on the pallet they'd made of her robe. He turned his head, saw her. She huddled against the door, a dark shade in her black dress. Dimly, he saw the red of his glyph burn into the oak, brighter than earlier. He stood, went to her.

Faint pity stirred when he saw the tear-stained cheeks. Virulent loathing shone in the blue eyes, along with something more. He brushed a strand of sunset hair from her face, admiring the high cheekbones and rounded chin. "What troubles you, my—?"

"You've had me twice, but I'm not yours." She cradled one hand in the other. Fury, pain and abhorrence mingled in her tone. "I hate you."

"Of course, you do." He took her fingers, pried them open. He winced when he saw the burned skin on her palm. His sign shone as brilliant on her skin as it did the oak door. "How did you come by this?"

"You fell asleep while you waited for me to remove my clothes." She lifted a shoulder. "I decided to leave."

"Foolish to tamper with another's *magick*." He released his hold, turned and walked to the spare bunk where he'd left his saddlebags. "You should have expected my spell to rebound. One of yours would have."

"Mine would kill you." She glared at him, cobalt blue eyes darkening. "I'd dance on your grave, spit on the marker and plant nightshade there."

"When I take the *Journey to Rebirth*, you will love me." He winked at her. "Or I won't go."

She muttered curses while he studied the room. Several bunks lined the walls. Trunks took up the far end of the room. Chairs clustered around the woodstove that heated the place. Two of his symbols glowed on two other windows. "You tried thrice. No wonder you were hurt. Why didn't you heed the first warning, *Vaslattel*?"

"I needed to leave here." She tossed her head, her tone venomous. "I craved to wash off your stink in my own place, *Garungap*."

He laughed softly while he hunted in his bags for the container of salve. He pulled it out, removed the lid. "If you ever say sweet words to me, I'll know you're ill or I am."

She tried to step away. "What is that? Poison?"

"I'd never harm what belongs to me." He snared her hand, smoothed balm over the burn. He chanted a low charm to ease pain, heal the injury. He could totally remove the wound, but she had lessons to learn in respect, reverence, and refinement. Then, she'd be a better queen to those she ruled.

He'd considered treating her with gentleness, tenderness, and compassion. However, he'd trained enough wild horses to know some couldn't be tamed with sugar and sweet words. She viewed kindness as weakness, so he chose harshness. When she admitted she belonged to him, he'd soften toward her.

"Is it better?" He wiped his hands on a cloth. He found a bandage in his bag. "Almost done."

"Fine. It takes you forever." Scant heat filled the scornful words. She bent her head and watched him wind strips of white cloth over the burn. "You've done this before. When?"

"You know I'm a *High Healer*." He finished bandaging her hand, leaned forward to brush her lips with his. "Take more care with yourself, my own."

He'd intended the endearment to mock her and himself but heard a note of sincerity in the words. He trailed a line of kisses from her ear to the gold chain around her neck. "What is it, Satiranika? What worries you?"

"Nobody ever looks after me." Her voice was soft, barely a

whisper. "I thought you'd snipe or sneer at me. I didn't expect you to tend me."

"You're mine." He kissed her forehead. "I've told you before. I always take care of what belongs to me. Ask me nicely and I will give you the moon, the stars and throw in the sun."

She smiled, lifted her face so their lips touched. "Do you still want me to remove my dress?"

"Yes." He rested his hands on her hips, turned her so he saw the row of buttons marching down her back under the red-gold curtain of hair. "And I will help you."

"You want to have me again, don't you?"

He gathered up her hair, shifted it out of the way and unfastened the first set of buttons, revealing the pale skin of her shoulders, her arms. "I'm going to have you, *Vaslattel*."

She gasped when he kissed her neck, following the path down her spine that the falling dress revealed. "The bed is—"

"Too far away." He pushed the gown to the floor, leaving her in stockings and boots. He stroked the flaring hips, the soft, plump cheeks of her behind, and slid two fingers into her. She was hot, wet and ready so he urged her forward a little. "Steady yourself."

She moaned when he moved his hand, rocking his thumb against the bud of flesh. He nipped her ear. "Soon, you'll beg to please me, my own."

"Never. I do as I wish."

He caressed her once more, relishing the way she moved with his hand. Then, he removed his fingers, probed again, this time with himself, and pushed deep inside her, gripping her hips and holding her still for a moment. "Now, you'll move as I wish, *Vaslattel*."

14

THEY LAY TOGETHER ON THE FLOOR OF THE BUNK-HOUSE. ASTRA turned her face against his chest, breathing in the scent of sweat, the faint odor of wood smoke from the bonfire mingling with a smell of herbs that was peculiarly his own. He wasn't her first man, but she didn't remember one tenderly holding her between bouts of sex. She felt his mouth move against her cheek and shifted enough so their lips met for a moment. "This is temporary, Rowindache. After these three days are over, we'll return to our 'real' lives."

"Is that what you think?" He adjusted the chain and the pendant she wore until the pentacle was between her breasts. "A witch of your skill and talent should know better."

"Know what?" She bit back a low groan when he bent his head and blew softly on her nipple before he drew it into his mouth and sucked. He fondled her other breast, rolling the nipple between his thumb and fingers. "You didn't answer my question."

He lifted his head. "I'm enjoying my *vaslattel*. You'll have to wait to interrogate me." He lowered his head, found her other nipple, and claimed it with the warmth of his mouth.

His hand sought out the curls between her legs, curving over the mound. She shuddered at the touch, anticipating what came next. "I'm serious. This means nothing."

He chuckled against her skin. "You're wrong. It means everything. Remember what I told you on our very first soul-matching night. After being with me, no other will satisfy you for all of eternity."

She clutched at his shoulders when his fingers began the entrancing dance they'd started before, one finger sliding in and out of her, joined by a second while his thumb rocked against the small bud of flesh. Her hips rose and fell, unable to resist the need to move with the pattern he'd begun. She clung to him, kissing his neck, nipping at his ear.

He adjusted their position and his body claimed hers. She responded to the rhythm he set, meeting the strong, urgent strokes as they whirled through the storm together. Dimly, she heard his harsh voice grate in her ear, chanting some invocation. Between the words, he kissed her, each kiss seeming longer than the last.

He paused after one kiss, holding still and waiting. "Say the words. Tell me who you are."

"I, Satiranika, first daughter—"

Her reward was a long kiss, one where his tongue explored her mouth and the motion of his hips started again, short strokes alternating with longer ones. And the spell continued, his gravelly voice asking questions, demanding answers that she had to give.

"—eldest of the *Trecesalty*, born to Dianaranika and Jarvesel, thirteenth witch in the *Ranika relkinam* give myself, soul, mind and body to—"

She struggled, managed to stop the assurances for one moment, then a second, a third. The powerful thrusts continued. A whirlpool of emotions overwhelmed her. Through it, she heard him encourage, insist on the promises.

"I, Satiranika take Rowindache as my *capostrol*, his *vaslattel* now and always, through all my lives—" She froze, horrified by what she'd vowed. How could she agree to that? She was from a long line of queens who ruled not only a continent but also an entire realm. She wasn't destined to serve a peasant.

"Finish it with me. Say all the words."

She met the movement of his hips with hers and the oaths continued between kisses. "I follow my *capostrol's* ways for three eternities—"

"As I keep my *vaslattel* for three eternities." He began the shared pledges. "*Lady and Lord*, be joyous within us—"

"View with our eyes." Her voice joined his. "Listen with our ears. Breathe with our nostrils. Touch with our fingers—"

They completed the last of the covenants in the final movements of their mating. One fiercer stroke propelled him to the pinnacle. He achieved ecstasy while she didn't. She felt him pour himself into her and shook with new terror. What if he impregnated her? What would she do?

She'd bound herself to him in an eternal soul-match, although she hadn't intended it. How did his demand for a commitment differ from that of other men? The longest she ever remained with a lover was three weeks when she wanted more than the pleasure derived from a mechanical sex-toy. At least now she knew why she never received it. How dare Rowindache cast a sex *geas* on her that lasted for so many lifetimes?

She lay beneath him, her borrowed robe between them and the floor. She reared up, scarlet fingernails like claws. She went for the thrice-damned black eyes. He'd enchanted her with his night-dark gaze, dared to compel her to take part his *Sex Magick* spell. He'd never do so again.

Hate and rage combined within her, and she dug her nails into one lean cheek, managed to tear his skin before he snagged her wrists, held them over the wide, gold bracelets. "If I have a child of yours, I swear I'll drown it in the nearest sewer."

"Your promises preclude that, *Vaslattel*." Blood dripped from his cheek onto her skin. He shook his head, faint admiration in his tone. "You swore not to dishonor me. Harming my child disgraces my second-wife and me."

"You disgust me." Tears burned behind her eyes at the threatened humiliation of him choosing a different woman that he'd place on a higher level and insist she, the daughter of royalty serve. "You'll pay three-fold."

"I already have. When you tried to poison me that first night, I forgave you because it didn't work. Then, rogue shape-shifters tore me to pieces four times at your behest. Didn't you realize I'd want recompense when I didn't choose vengeance?" He held her wrists beside her head, bent to kiss the line of her jaw. "Wait until I finally make you mine. You'll lose control, shatter in my arms and scream your love for me. When you do, I'll expect a knife in the heart."

She trembled when he kissed the dimple in her chin, the corners of her mouth. "If I fail to kill you the first time, what do I expect? Death?"

"Oh no, my own. That's too easy for a queen who thinks she's better than everyone else. I've never intended to let you die. If I did, I'd have turned you over to the *dracklegons* the first time you killed me and had them burn you in the *Fires of Eternity* so you couldn't return to another life."

"You're soul-bonded to me. You'd have died too."

"Not when they severed our bonds before your death as they promised, Satiranika." He retained his grip on her wrists. "No, if you try to kill me in this life as you've done in all my past incarnations, you'll feel my justice, along with a sore royal backside. You'll eat your meals standing up for a week and we still haven't discussed what you did to my *Healers*, but we will."

She gaped at him, shaking her head. "I did nothing to them. I don't know what you're talking about."

"Denial of her actions doesn't suit my *vaslattel*." He tightened his hold on the bracelets and her wrists. "Because you haven't turned thirty yet, you may not have all your memories, but you turned my *healers* over to the shape-shifters who devoured them. What did you do to Robinaranika and her cadre from the *Amalodian* army?"

"Who?" Astra twisted beneath him, unable to break away. "I don't know what or who you're talking about."

"Your older half-sister from *Trilunon*. She came through the portal with us three hundred years ago and protested mightily when you arranged for Venus to *banexort* Holt and me. Remember her!"

His tone made it an order, one Astra couldn't refuse to obey. She caught flashes of a tall redhead in light blue *Healer* robes who cared devotedly for Meteor, when her health failed because of the strong connection to their land and its inhabitants. Since she was their mother's child from a previous love-match unsanctioned by the royal family, Robinaranika wasn't in line for the throne. She offered regular advice to the triplets. Meteor and Venus usually listened and followed her suggestions, but Astra only did when it suited her convenience.

She winced, recalling the confrontation she'd had with her half-sister after the first *banexorting*. Her sire overheard and offered to take all the *healers* with him and the shape-shifters he led since Thojedescar had committed suicide. Astra agreed, once Jarvesel promised to treat them as they deserved. She hadn't realized he meant to murder them again and again. "He was supposed to honor and respect them."

"Who was?"

"Jarvesel, the enforcer for the shape-shifter pack."

"And you trusted him to do it when he'd done his best to wreak havoc, destroying our home in one of his rages after he learned he'd be your mother's consort, but never a king even if he sired you and your sisters?"

"Why wouldn't I trust him? He's my father. He may have become a demon rather than honoring his heritage as a mage-priest, but he's never lied to me."

"When you recall the past, you'll realize he never told you the entire truth, shifting it to suit his desires. But you're my *vaslattel* now and you won't lie to me. I'll give you a loose rein unless you try to balk, or buck my plans, or buffalo me."

"Any other rules you think I'll follow?"

"Oh, like it or not, you'll do as I wish. You'll treat others with the respect due them. You'll let your sisters and their *Chosen* decide their paths alone." Rowindache lowered his head. "And finally, you won't stray off any trail I set for you."

She twisted her head to avoid his kiss, but his mouth claimed hers anyway. She found herself surrendering to the pressure and responding when his tongue enticed hers into a duel. When he lifted his head, she demanded, "Do you plan to punish me for everything that happened three hundred years ago? Will you try to beat me?"

"If you try to kill me again, I will not be happy." His tone became even more matter-of-fact. "If I still breathe, you'll face my justice. If you succeed, Thojedescar and Hughondear have promised me *Warpathian* equity. You'll travel alive with me in my coffin on the *Journey to Rebirth*. I won't let the *dracklegons* have you for meat in one of their fires. You're mine."

"Barbarians. All of you are barbarians." She struggled beneath him, but it frustrated her when he didn't relax his hold. "Let go of me."

"No." He bent closer, brushing her mouth with his. "You're mine. If you carry my first son, I'll be gentle when you attack me."

"What if it's my first daughter?" She couldn't believe the words escaped her lips. "Will you deny her as my father did me and my sisters when he realized we were witches like our mother?"

"Never. I'm not such a fool. My daughter will need me to teach her to be tolerant, kind, and how to use a sword as well as her *magick*."

"My sisters and I can raise her." Astra glared at him when he laughed and grinned down at her. He'd hardened inside her, and she knew he planned to have her once more. How many times did he intend to take her before dawn? "My daughter won't be weak."

"Not with you as a mother." He still held her wrists. His hips rocked back and forth, a gentle thrusting, slow and easy, not like before. "Admit you're mine."

"If I do?" She groaned when he kissed her breasts. Why did she want this man so much? Usually, she simply enjoyed the exercise of sex although she rarely had an orgasm. "What happens if I speak nonsense?"

"This." He sampled her nipple in one kiss, a second, a third. He sucked gently, rolled the aching nipple on his tongue. His dark gaze met hers. "When will you admit you like having me —"

"Never. When will you let me go?"

"I won't." He maintained the steady motion. "As my *vaslattel*, you must admit you prefer *Sex Magick* with me, whenever I have you. Now, I know I'm your first mage."

"How can you be so stupid?" She caught her breath, writhed beneath him, their hips meeting, but nothing she did incited him to increase the rhythm of his thrusts. "I've had many partners since my fourteenth birthday when I attended my first *Great Rite* and served as the altar for my father and his minions. At least they didn't slay me as one of their blood sacrifices in this life."

He stopped, stared down at her. She thought she saw pity in his face and lifted her chin in defiance. How dare he feel sorry for her? "You're not my 'first' anything."

"Then, I'll be the last." A tender smile warmed his dark eyes as he continued his slow movements, rocking against her. "I'll watch our daughters closer than your mother watched you and keep them safe from any who'd dare to harm them. You haven't learned real passion in this life yet. I'll teach you, *Vaslattel*."

———

Frank Corbett scanned the group of partiers in the large living-room. Various tables held a variety of meats layered on platters. He knew how, what, and who to feed his pack of shifters. Most of the people here worked for him or were related in some way. Music filled the air and couples danced. A few had slipped away to mate in different rooms of his house, and he didn't mind. He stood alone, a glass of whisky in his hand, and counted the absent members of the pack. They'd pay for refusing his summons on *Samhain*. Chief among the truants was his nephew. Where was that boy?

He glimpsed Police Chief Gunnolf Marvin in the doorway and Frank signaled the large man to join him. Despite being in his early fifties, the law-enforcement officer was more muscled than some of his younger deputies. "Well? What did you learn?"

"No sign of him anywhere in town." In his tan uniform, with a shaved head, he exuded a raw sexual power that still attracted attention from many of the pack females, but tonight he was all business. "I've got my deputies searching here and in Eagleville. His truck is parked in the driveway of his house in Eagleville, but he's nowhere around."

"That's no surprise," Frank mocked. "He dropped off the company pickup and left here yesterday. He only brought me a half-cord of firewood. I barely had enough for the prey I roasted."

"Yes, I know. We had to scramble all over town to make up the difference. I still don't have a clue where to look for Jed. Let me speak to Junior again. Maybe, he'll have remembered something else."

"All right." Frank looked at his oldest son, crooked a finger and Junior hurried over. "Tell Marvin what you told him already."

"Like I already said three times, we were cutting firewood. Jed got a hair cross-wise and stopped. Said he was leaving. He jumped in the truck. Damn near left me to walk home."

"It wouldn't have hurt you." Frank cast a sour look at his grown son's beer gut. "If you'd gotten tired, you could have always shifted and come across country as a wolf. It'd do you good to get more exercise. Jed doesn't disobey orders, and he knows I need a truck-full of green wood for the barbeque. Why did he stop cutting?"

"How should I know?" Junior complained. "He found something. Looked like jewelry, a necklace of some sort."

"What?" Frank stiffened, eyeing the younger man. "You didn't say anything about that before."

"Describe it," Gunnolf Marvin ordered. "Color? Size? Design?"

"I think it was gold, but I barely saw it. Jed shoved it in his shirt pocket, slammed his chainsaw in the back of the rig, and peeled out. If he hadn't needed to turn around, I'd still be walking."

"Because you're too damned lazy to shift without a full moon."

Frank didn't bother to hide his contempt. "Where'd he head once he switched vehicles? Did he stop anywhere in town?"

"Not that I noticed. It looked like he went straight toward Eagleville." Junior's dark gray eyes filled with hate. "If I hadn't shown up tonight, you wouldn't be worried or sending your tame cop hunting for me."

"Oh, I would." Frank bared his teeth, "but I wouldn't stop him from dragging you in here by the scruff of your neck, pup, like he's wanted to do forever. Your cousin is an honest man, the same as his father, and those are rare. Of course, I worry he'll be harmed. Even when he enlisted in the Marines, Jed came and asked my blessing first. But you've never served—not your pack, your town or your country."

"All of us aren't cut out to be warriors." Junior ran a hand through dark brown hair. "I'll bet at least half the pack hasn't seen action."

"The Corbetts have always been fighters," Gunnolf said. "Your father and me had some good times when we were stationed overseas in the Army, a few real dandy pig-hunts. Those little ones are feisty and smarter than hell."

"We've had some good hunts here too and there will be more." Frank chuckled. "Don't fret, Marvin, I told Trina to save you a plate of barbeque."

"Appreciate that, Frank. I'll eat after I find Jed. I've checked out everywhere in the county, but I'm going to start contacting other sheriff's departments in the state. If he raised a ruckus somewhere, he could be sitting in a local Gray-Bar hotel."

"Sounds good. Thanks, Marvin."

"Before you do that, you might want to track down the bartender from the catering company. Jed really liked her."

Frank knotted his hands into fists. "Do you mean the witch who had him arrested a couple days ago? I told him to forget her. I'd take care of her."

"He told me to leave her be, that he wasn't sharing her with any of the Corbetts." Junior sneered. "How much do you want to bet that includes you?"

Frank waited until Junior walked off, belly leading the way. Meteor Jamison owned the only catering company in Eagleville. She'd be at the old Widow Ridge ranch for *Samhain*, oh yes, they called it the Rocking J now, but he remembered the past all too well. "You may as well stop looking, Gunnolf. You won't find him, not if that witch warded him."

"I have an informant at the Rocking J. I'll reach out to her."

"Not yet. Tomorrow is soon enough. If we don't hear from her, you made her suffer before and we'll make her pay again."

"I'll want more than that if I have to go up against Diana and Estelle. They've warded themselves and the *Trecesalty* far too well this time around."

Frank nodded. "I know. If they hadn't, we would have had them years ago at our feasts. Let's take Junior on the hunt at *Yule*. He can help us load up the barbeque. We'll need twice as much meat in December as we have tonight, and he'll learn he's not irreplaceable. It will do him good to watch you force the change on our prey and see what we really eat at our festivities."

"I don't know if that's enough payment since I'll enjoy taking care of that disrespectful whelp more than you do."

Frank chuckled, slapped his best friend on the back. "Come on, old wolf. Let's find Trina and some supper. Afterwards, you can take her upstairs."

"She thinks she's your mate now."

"I know. She's overstepped too many times. You're the pack enforcer and you'll teach her better manners without killing her and I don't have the patience to train her in this life, much less contend with her snobbery."

15

Rocking J Ranch ~ Saturday, November 3rd, 2018

SHORTLY BEFORE DAWN, METEOR WOKE. SHE SLOWLY EASED OUT from between her sons and small daughter. Remaining in her dog form, she padded to the door that led to her apartment. She nudged it open and climbed the stairs to the apartment she shared with Astra. Meteor found her sister's assistant sleeping in the double-bed in the guestroom, but it wasn't a restful slumber. Rebekah cried out, twisting in the blankets, sounding more like a frightened child than a woman grown.

Meteor crossed to the bed and nudged the other woman's hand, growling softly while she sent her thoughts into the younger witch's mind. *'Ward yourself from those who haunt you. Send their evil back on them thrice-fold and 'white-light' yourself as a servant of the Goddess.'* It wasn't enough to offer advice, so Meteor leaped grace-fully onto the bed and curled up beside the apprentice, mentally guarding her from the monsters that tormented her.

Why hadn't Astra dealt with the nightmares that plagued the girl? It was a mentoring witch's job to teach more than new enchantments or spells. Meteor took a deep breath and slipped into the dream. The woman in the torn remnants of a blue *High Healer* robe being dragged toward a fiery barbeque pit by three shape-shifters wasn't a stranger, but her half-sister from a long-ago life. Blood ran down the inside of her thighs, red and purple bruises covered her face, arms, and ribs. Bite marks lined her throat and breasts.

The men who intended to roast and eat the *Healer* had already raped and tortured her. That was obvious. Death would prove a release, but it didn't appear to be a merciful end. Meteor nosed the girl's shoulder. *'Listen to me, Robinaranika. Stop your pulses, heart, and mind. Choose when and where you die since there isn't an escape. Make your body anathema to these outlaws.'*

'I'm the last to die. They killed my healers in front of me and purloined all our powers. I don't have much strength left.'

'You have enough. You haven't forgotten the first lesson a healer learns. To put a body together, you must know how to take one apart. Do it now! Discorporate!'

Silence while the *healer* in the dream took a deep breath, used the last vestiges of her *magick* and dissolved into a heap on the ground, poisonous fumes rising from her corpse. A howl of rage erupted from the silver-haired mage by the fire, but it was too late. Meteor recognized him as her father, shuddering at the sight of the demon-mage prince. Despite his efforts, he couldn't force the spirit of the departed woman to return or stop the noxious odors from killing her last three attackers. He still howled vengeance would be his at some later date.

Rebekah's breathing slowed, calmed and she opened her eyes. She rolled over on the bed and clutched Meteor's dog-shaped neck tightly. "Thank you. How did you know I needed you?"

'I've comforted the children enough to recognize their night-terrors. You'll have this dream again as your age-old memories reoccur. Just repeat the same escape. You may eventually want to try taking more of them with you.'

"I don't know how far I'll be able to go."

'What do you remember now?'

"That demon warlock." Rebekah shuddered and clung more closely to Meteor. "Jarvesel used his dark powers to tear away my healers' talents once he murdered the soldiers who tried to protect them. He arranged for some of the shifters to assault my personal guard and after I *'Healed'* him, I was chained to a wall. Jarvesel stripped away most of my *magick*, which enraged my protector because it was the first time I was tortured and seeing it was worse for him."

'A Healer's magick is part of her mind, body and soul. You must have felt ripped to shreds. But it wasn't the most dreadful. What happened next?'

"Jarvesel gutted and disemboweled my guard and there wasn't anything I could do to save him. It took more than a day for him to die in agony and Jarvesel raped me in front of him."

'You were untouched before that.'

"By my choice, not by the dictates of the *Goddess* or the priest-esses who trained me to be a *Healer*. As an *Empath*, I needed to find a life-mate first since my *magick* runs on emotions." Rebekah closed her eyes for a moment. "My mate feels closer now, but why didn't I recognize him yesterday?"

Meteor licked the younger witch's cheek, a swipe of the dog tongue. *'Because you had to face what happened in the past in order to have a future. Where is he?'*

"He came with Astra and me to the celebration. I thought she wanted him, so I didn't go to the *Great Rite*."

'He's not for her, not now, not ever. Her soul-matched wizard arrived yesterday, and he'll never share her with another man, mage or not.'

"But she made Venus send him away along with her *Chosen* three hundred years ago."

'And Venus called them back two nights ago, much to Astra's dismay. She told me our father ordered her to attend a Great Rite at one of his celebrations when she was fourteen and worried how that might affect her Chosen.'

"I've served her since I was a child whenever she visited

Corbettstown, but your father swears he adores her. He tells everyone he'll give her whatever she wants. She claims he'd arrange for the shifters to abuse and kill me in one of the ceremonies, but I can't believe that's the case. When she wanted me to attend her in Seattle five years ago, Jarvesel immediately agreed and ordered Frank Corbett to release me."

Meteor considered the idea, then asked. *"Do either of them ever contact you or ask about her?"*

Silence as Rebekah thought before she slowly nodded. "Yes, but it's only Jarvesel, known as Gunnolf Marvin and he doesn't have much in the way of *Power* anymore. He's the police chief in Corbettstown and he either phones or sends one of his deputies to check on her if she's too busy at the law firm to call him every week."

Shaking her dog form, Meteor rose to her paws, not sure what or who to believe. Astra claimed she'd been sent by their mother to their father and now, Rebekah had a different tale. *'I need to shower and dress for the Closing of the Circle. What about you? What are your duties?'*

"I'm to help your mother and aunt, so I'll find out what they want me to do and get started."

————

It was a soldier's trick to doze, sitting up with his eyes open and Hugh always opted to rest when the opportunity presented itself. He'd never been one to seek the easiest path and his war-queen, Katiranika, undoubtedly pose a challenge even in this time. He allowed the memory of their first 'soul-matched' night to seep into his mind.

A brilliant red dress swirled around her ankles as she stalked the chamber in the palace where they stayed until the *dracklegons* opened the *Time Portal* to a new realm. It might be days or months away. No one knew but the highest priests and they weren't talking, at least not yet. Gold flashed from the *talipenlace* set she wore.

She'd allowed him to put the jewelry on her but refused to speak any of the shared vows. Anger and hatred mingled in her violet eyes when she mutely glowered up at him while her aunt, the High Queen repeated the sacred, eternal oaths.

He sat on the edge of the wide bed, watching her pace, fury in each step. "So, Princess? Do you intend to be silent for the next thousand years?"

"And you?" She whirled to glare at him. "Do you plan to rape me this night? It's your way, isn't it, *Hisprinarch*?"

He winced at the title, aware of the insult. He wasn't his father's heir and wouldn't be allowed to ascend to the throne any longer. "I will never harm you, *Trecesalty*. We have several long lives to share together. You'll come to me eventually and I can wait."

"You'll die before I come to you, *Warpathian*." She cast a scathing look at him and a knife appeared in her hand, so swift the motion that he didn't see her draw the blade. She was a skilled warrior, but he was better. "Now, I'll join my sisters."

"Not tonight, *Laspowima*." He admired her tactics, *'attack, always attack.'* "I've sealed the door. The morning's soon enough for you to visit them."

"If I kill you, your spell ends, and the door opens." She juggled the dagger in her hand as if she meant to throw it. "I won't be in your reach either, *Hisprinarch*."

"Call me, *Huspowner*." He chuckled at his own mockery. "It's how a woman refers to her *Chosen* in my country."

"I'll consider it." She tossed the knife in the air, caught the jeweled hilt with her other hand. "If and when I choose a mate. But you? I'll butcher you in your sleep if I wait that long."

"Then, you'll pay, Princess." He returned the dangerous smile with a narrowed look. If she actually threw the blade in an attempt to strike him, he'd roll off the bed to the floor. "You won't care to lose your pretty toy. It's very distinctive. Everyone will recognize it when I wear it and proclaim it a gift from my loving mate, one she offered in surrender."

"*Garungap!*" She tensed in rage. "You dare much."

"Try to slit my throat and I'll dare more, *Trecesalty*. We've been pledged since you were an infant. When you reached soul-matching age, you should have had enough honor to come to me without an invasion and a war." He didn't move but kept a careful watch on her. "Start a fight with me tonight and I'll finish it. If you succeed in killing me, you'll face *Warpathian* justice."

"Your country has no justice. My eldest sister warned me of your laws." She tightened her grip on the knife. "Try to rape or enslave me and your *Journey to Rebirth* begins this night."

"What? No civilized people do such evil, not even the *dracklegons* who roast their meat alive."

"My sister is a High Judge. Do you claim she mis-spoke? She serves the *Goddess* and *Her Truth*."

"Very well." He inclined his head in apparent acceptance. His new bride would never believe him over her sister, at least not yet. He'd warn Rowindache not to allow his mate to rule over the law-courts here in this castle or when they arrived in their new realm. "Did your sister tell you of the punishment for *Warpathian* murderers? Killers go with their victims on the *Journeys to Rebirth*. The victims have the peace of death—their killers go alive until they suffocate in the shared coffins."

"You sicken me." She lifted the blade. "If I kill you and your friends, then my sisters rule with me. In *Amalodia*, any woman may defend herself from rape."

"As in any civilized place." He took a deep breath and tried again to reason with her. "I will not touch you without your permission. Think, Katiranika. You will not manage to slaughter my army. For now, they try to court your women. It has been a long time since they believed in such dreams." He gestured to the time-piece on the stone wall. "Wait until dawn, *Chosen*. I'll take you to your sisters then."

She hesitated, swung toward the door. She tried a few passes with the dagger, murmured some unlocking spells. When they didn't work, she spun around and subsided onto a chest of her belongings. Her voice was low and deadly. "Stay away from me."

"For now."

"Forever." She trailed a finger across the sharp blade. "Break your word and I'll kill you and your men. If they harm my sisters, your friends die. I swear it."

"The High Queen ordered your powers bound."

"Stealing our thrones didn't endear her to our people and the *Healer-Mages* led by my half-sister refused to commit such folly." Katiranika tossed her head, shaking back flame-red hair. "Afraid now?"

"Actually, I'm relieved, *Laspowima*." He ignored the insult to his courage. He was old enough, smart enough to choose his battles. "To have such a powerful witch bonded with me assures me of a bright future in our new home."

"You think you have all the answers." She laid the dagger across her lap. "I will never accept you as my mate."

"When you know me better, you will." He studied her slender form. She was the perfect size. Her head just touched his heart when they'd stood beside each other at the soul-matching ceremony. The red dress fit tightly over full breasts, hugged a narrow waist, and smoothed over long legs. Finally, she was his.

High cheekbones made the violet eyes appear larger. Her mouth was too wide for pure beauty, yet the pointed chin and fierce line of her angled brows made her more than lovely in his view. Every emotion she felt flitted across her face and shone in those eyes. He could watch her for eternity and never grow weary or bored, although he wanted more.

He smiled at her. "You'll love me someday and our younglings too."

"I will never give you children. Never!"

"A long time." He removed his boots and swung his feet up on the bed. "I'll remind you of your words next year when our first baby comes."

16

QUESTIONS CROWDED JED'S MIND. HE'D EXPECTED TO FIND A BED somewhere and sleep after they *Closed the Circle* and enjoyed the *Dawn Feast*. It probably wouldn't have been with Meteor, at least not yet, but even if he'd had to nap in the catering truck, it'd be worth it to stay at the Rocking J for the festival instead of dealing with the drama in Corbettstown at his uncle's. Jed knew there'd be repercussions for his absence and he'd deal with the fall-out later. For now, he simply enjoyed being with those who honored the true meaning of the *Sabbat*.

However, instead of the nap he'd planned to take, he found himself in the barns tending to the livestock with Hugh. Next, he, Gard, Rowdy and Hugh headed for the back fence with most of the other men. Surprisingly, Gard was one of the best cat-skinners Jed had ever seen, seeming to have a wizard's touch with the forty-year-old, 450B John Deere crawler. He'd have this part of the property line cleared in hours, not days. Jed fired up the borrowed chainsaw and cut another cedar log into posts.

Hugh gestured to the hodge-podge of alder, maple and cotton-wood trees dropped into a tangled, criss-crossed pile. "It appears to me that someone wished to destroy the boundary fence and make trouble for these women and a boy still learning his powers. Did you take part in such evil-doing, Thojedescar?"

"By omission," Jed admitted, letting the engine idle before turning off the saw. "I didn't stop those who did it, although I didn't participate."

"Could you have prevented it alone? Or would you have died, or been hurt beyond mending? I am the first *Healer-Mage* to arrive here and without someone like me, you'd have gone to *Summerland.*" Rowdy joined them. "Only a foolish soldier fights overwhelming odds unless he plays *'Coyote'* and plans to lure his enemies into an ambush."

"Evil must always be fought." Hugh picked up a post. "It's what a man does."

"Nobility is your weakness, Holt." Rowdy pointed to the hole he'd just dug, the appropriate place for the post. "You should remember that he who fights and runs away lives to fight another day."

Jed didn't recognize the quote, although it made sense. They'd have to watch out for Hugh's sense of honor and duty. New admiration for the older man struck Jed. He had questions for Rowdy, but didn't know if he'd choose to answer.

"How did you change Astra's robe from black to silver?" Jed tightened the chain on the saw. "Or get her to sit beside you this morning at the feast after the *Closing of the Circle*? Or be so polite to me? I've never seen her that respectful to her mother or aunt. What kind of spell did you cast?"

"I said last night that Rowdy has his own *magick*." Hugh returned to the cedar log split into several posts. "I can find more work for a man who has enough time to think of rude questions about another's *Chosen*."

"Let me deal with Thojedescar's manners." Rowdy paced off the distance to the spot for the next post and started to dig the hole, waiting until Jed joined him. "First, her mother sent a new robe for my *vaslattel*. As for your other concerns, the answer remains the same—the invocation of the *talipenlace* and renewal of our soul-matching vows. For the next three days, she loses her fears and allows her heart to show."

"Why do you think she's scared of anything?" Jed shook his head. "No way. She argues with everyone and picks more fights than I do when I'm drunk. Many of the local police are her friends and she uses them to arrest her enemies and have them thrown in jail."

"She lacks your size to protect her family. She resorts to words, curses and hexes." Rowdy stopped digging for a moment. "She'll help me guard you on the astral plane after I remove the blocks she put on you. When you return to Corbettstown, nobody must realize you regain yourself, especially not your *relkinam*. Your kinfolk will continue to hunt and try to kill you and your mate as they've done before."

"I can see that." Jed started back toward the pile of logs waiting to be cut, then swung back around. "I want a life with Matiranika and our children this time, not to die again. What do you mean '*invoke the talipenlace*'? I've returned the necklace to her numerous times and even put it on her, but it never remains on her, and I don't know what she did with the rest of the set of jewels I created. They don't make her treat me the way Astra did you this morning."

"Nor will they. Your *laspowima* is a different woman than her eldest sister. You'll be the next of us to invoke the *talipenlace*. You wait until *Yule* in December when your mate wears the entire set of jewelry you made for her."

"What good will that do? She has before and nothing changes."

"You're not listening. She must wear it of her own free will. Then, you ask her if she wears it as her desire, not that of her mother and aunt. If your soul-match does, she'll admit it in thought and words."

"Like that's going to happen." Jed glared at the fallen timber. "It'd be easier to stand up those trees or add two more moons to the one in this realm's sky. Now, I'm in the miracle business. Then, what?"

"You repeat your vows together."

"It's been three hundred years and I've died four times since then. How am I supposed to remember the soul-binding spell? I can barely recall what happened on *Samhain* eve when I found the necklace I made in the woods."

"You have almost two moons to regain your memories." Rowdy leaned on the post-hole digger. "Do you want to know what comes next?"

"Hopefully, something easier. If I have to part the oceans or stop a volcano, don't tell me." Jed scowled as Hugh neared. "What about him? Why doesn't he have to *'invoke the talipenlace'*? Is it because he's a prince?"

"Like us, he does, but we do it in birth order of the *Trecesalty*, the three destined queens of *Trilunon*. If you fail at *Yule*, you try again at *Imbolgc*, the first of the spring celebrations in February. After you succeed, then Holt tries his luck."

"I make my own luck." Hugh dropped a post into the hole. "What do you two have to talk about? There's fence to build before we take the livestock through the balefires and move them to safer pastures for the winter."

"Rowindache tells me how to *'invoke the talipenlace.'*" Jed stopped when Rowdy raised a hand. "What?"

"You can't teach him what he needs to know until you've done it." Hefting the post-hole digger, Rowdy started to walk down the new fence line. "Come with me."

Jed followed. When they were out of Hugh's earshot, Jed asked, "What's the last thing I have to do?"

"It's not all you. After the two of you share your vows, you and your *laspowima* must unite your bodies three times before dawn."

"That's it? We make love three times." Jed grinned. "Wonderful. It's easier than the rest of it." He eyed Rowdy with new respect. "You did all of it last night with Astra and she didn't turn you into a pig and banish you to the sty with the other hogs?"

Faint humor twinkled in Rowdy's eyes. "We're not done yet. Claiming her as a *vaslattel* will take three days. Besides, I want my first child. With the *banexort* spell she ordered cast on me, I've been in this realm far too many years and never a son."

Jed whistled softly, watching Rowdy turn back to the task of digging the next hole. He intended to spend three nights of *sex-magick* with a powerful witch and still remain human. What a wizard!

With renewed energy, Jed fired up the saw and started to cut the fallen evergreen trees into posts. He'd sweat out the alcohol in his system first and then he'd recall those missing memories. When he did, perhaps he'd recall the differences between a *laspowima* and a *vaslattel*. It definitely didn't sound like the same thing, but he was certain Meteor wouldn't tell him and neither would Rowdy or Hugh.

––––––

Carrying his bedroll as well as that of Hugh's and Edwin's, Rowdy entered the bunkhouse. He stopped when he saw a petite redhead putting clean dishes into a cupboard. He dropped the blankets inside the door, took a step forward. "Robin?"

"I'm Rebekah in this life." She turned to face him. Tight blue jeans emphasized curving hips and long legs. A light blue sweater clung to full breasts. "Rowindache?"

"Rowdy. Remember, we vowed to be as brother and sister *healers* long ago? You were the first to sincerely welcome me to your *relkinam*, even though when you learned I'd soul-matched with Satiranika, you said—"

"You may not have made the wisest choices, *siblerbro*. We are an annoying batch of hatchlings." She ran across the room, flung herself against him and hugged him before bursting into wrenching tears torn from the heart.

He held her tight, stroking the flame-red hair and rocking her as if she were a child, not an ancient *High Healer* whose powers had rivaled his own although she'd been several years younger. He'd wondered what she'd accomplish as she matured, but that was never discovered since she died so soon after their arrival in this realm. "I'm glad to find you safe."

"She had you killed horribly again and again."

"And you punished for daring to speak up, for trying to thwart her plans." Rowdy didn't need to read Robin's, or rather Rebekah's memories to recognize the trauma she still suffered. "What are you doing here?"

"Cleaning the cabin as you requested." She took a step back, tilting her head. "Didn't you want it done?"

"I did, but not by you." He glanced around. Recently washed, the wood-paneled walls gleamed. Late afternoon sun shone through the sparkling windows, but he still saw his protective glyphs on the glass. A cast-iron teakettle sat on the recently blacked woodstove. Bright patchwork quilts covered three of the bunks. Someone had spent hours cleaning the bunkhouse.

He smiled down at her. "You're a *High Healer*. You need to go to the balefires and keep all safe, down to the smallest kitten."

"But I was ordered—"

"Not by me." He covered her soul-eye with one hand, sent pure healing energies into her mind and aura. "Remember who and what you are. Serve the *Goddess* as you're meant to serve. You've too many responsibilities as a *High Healer* destined to be a *Guardian* in this time to be less than you are."

He heard footsteps and glanced over his shoulder as Gard came up behind him, carrying two saddles. "Leave those there and escort Robinaranika to get what she needs from the house. Then go with her to the balefires to attend the animals and people at the ceremonies."

Gard nodded, eying her. "Why do I suddenly remember Jed ordering me to watch over you and protect you from anyone who wanted to hurt you?"

"A new memory restored by our arrival," Rowdy said. "More will come, but Robin was once assigned to serve as *High Healer* to Thojedescar's *Chosen*."

"He feared for my safety because the diseases plaguing *Trilunon* poisoned Matiranika as well since she was tightly linked to the realm and all its inhabitants, not just the people." Faint amusement lit Rebekah's blue-green eyes when she glanced at Gard. "I remember you daring to flaunt my requests while we waited for the *dracklegons* to open the portal to this realm."

"Only those that countermanded the orders I'd already been given." Gard looked appalled as the words escaped. "Why do I know that, Rowdy?"

"Your age-old memories were undoubtedly blocked since they should have started returning when you turned thirty in this life and were old enough to handle them. You're my age and I've had mine for eight years," Rowdy said. "Some will feel like nightmares, Gard, but Robin can help you through those dark mazes."

She lingered in Rowdy's embrace a moment longer. "How do you two know each other well enough to shorten your *Trilunon* names?"

"Gard may not recall it yet, but we shared the same table at meals, the same desk at school and slept in the same room as boys in the orphan housing. We grew up as brothers and joined the *Warpathian* Army at the same time."

She took a deep breath and eased away. "You became a *Healer*."

"Yes and Gardersolter went on to be one of Thojedescar's most favored officers." Rowdy picked up the bedrolls and carried them over to the trunks below the windows. "Where do I find my *Chosen*?"

"With her mother and aunt," Rebekah said. "They wanted her to help plan the rest of the weekend festivities, which is why she sent me to finish the cleaning here. She'd already done almost everything, but she wanted the dishes washed again."

"I'll see it completed." Rowdy watched the two leave, carefully not touching, at least not yet. His *vaslattel* had a great deal to answer for, even if she'd brought those two to the ranch to observe *Samhain*. They'd never been allowed to share the destiny the

Goddess intended, dying instead at Jarvesel's hands as blood sacrifices.

When Gard remembered who engineered the horrific demise of the healer he'd sworn to protect, he'd seek vengeance and with most of her powers bound to Rowdy's, Astra wouldn't be able to defend herself. He carried the saddles to the stands in the far corner of the room. He heard the padding of paws on the porch and glanced toward the door.

Astra entered, accompanied by a large black dog. "What are you doing here?"

"Not the most respectful, or appropriate greeting, *Vaslattel.*" He enjoyed the flash of rage that darkened her deep blue eyes. "I'd prefer one of your kisses instead."

She folded her arms, unmoving from her stance on the threshold, fury in an embroidered silver robe. "And I'd prefer you rot in this realm's Hell. Conjuring while you fucked me last night was out of bounds, *Garungap.*"

"I've heard worse so stop trying to shock me with your choice of language. It doesn't befit a dark sorceress with your powers. Exchanging vows during a *Sex-Magick* mating has always been the way the promises are offered between a *vaslattel*, a captive witch and the wizard who claims her."

"I'm not your captive." Her fingers slipped into the huge dog's black fur. "No one owns me."

"Don't do it, Satiranika. He doesn't deserve to die because of your spite and anger."

Her breath hissed between tightened lips and her eyes narrowed. He barely saw her hand move before the dog leaped forward, eager for his blood.

Rowdy flung his hands up, creating an invisible, brick wall between him and the hunting animal. The giant, black canine slammed into the barrier, head first. He slid down, landing in an unconscious heap on the floor, blood seeping from his nose and mouth.

"No!" She started forward. "What did you do? You hurt Bamse."

"I told you what I'd do if you tried again to kill me, *Vaslattel*." Sparing a glance at her shocked, pale face, Rowdy slowly lowered his defenses. "Mind-bending a helpless animal is beneath you. While I heal him, finish the work you foisted on someone else."

17

VENUS ROLLED HER SHOULDERS AND STRETCHED AS SHE ENTERED her mother's kitchen, grateful Meteor insisted on taking all the children, even two-and-a-half-year-old Fallyn down to the river beach and the balefires where the animals would be blessed by Aunt Diana. It'd allowed Venus the opportunity for a much-needed nap. Yawning, she headed for the coffee machine, inserted a pod and waited for a fresh cup to brew. She watched her mother fill a box with groceries. "What are you doing? I dropped off a large donation to the food bank before our *Samhain* celebrations."

"This is for the men you hired. It's part of their wages. I agreed to pay extra, so they'd prepare their own meals instead of expecting one of us to cook for them."

"What? Who do they think they are? It's well into the new millennium. Household chores aren't decided by gender anymore."

Estelle dropped a bag of dry beans into the box. "Frankly, having two grown men work for a hundred dollars a month each strikes me as more of a bargain for us than it is for them. Will Dawson insisted we pay Kyle Morgan minimum wage when he was here and that was tough to manage since he worked sixty-plus hours a week. I don't know why these two are different, but I'm grateful to the *Goddess* for one of her miracles."

"They're certainly not from around here." Venus picked up the steaming cup of coffee, wondering exactly where the two men came from. Her spell had drawn them to the ranch, but she hadn't demanded to know their current whereabouts when she cast it. She sipped the strong, black beverage, enjoying the way the brew warmed her. "Why isn't Astra helping?"

"She needs to finish cleaning the bunkhouse and then she'll go to the balefires." Estelle added a bag of cornmeal to the box and finished with a pound of ground coffee. "Take this out and put away the food for me. Bring back the carton. I'll want to use it tomorrow when I send lunch up to the fencing crew."

"Be right back. Don't wash my cup while I'm gone. Leave my coffee alone so I can drink it in a few minutes." After another quick swallow, Venus put the mug on the counter, picked up the box and headed out the kitchen door. A large black dog rose from his position, lying by the back door, and escorted her across the wraparound porch to the long, low cabin nearby.

Glass windows sparkled in the November sunshine. The rockers on the covered porch sported clean cushions and the wooden deck had been swept clean of dust and autumn leaves. The bunk-house door stood open and Venus entered, the big wolf-dog at her heel. Ivor whimpered; a strange sound she'd never heard him make before. She watched him charge across the room to where Rowdy knelt beside his injured littermate. Long black hair speckled with gray tied in a ponytail with a leather thong, he wore the same kind of work clothes she'd seen him in yesterday, a suede shirt, brown pants and low-heeled boots.

Venus put the box of food on the counter and joined the others, dropping to her knees to put a comforting hand on the youngest dog's side. "What happened?"

"Your sister ordered him to attack me." Rowdy didn't lift his gaze from the black dog. "A foolish mistake she'll come to regret."

"I'm sure she already does. She delivered these two when Freya had her first litter last year and raised them from puppy-hood." Venus looked around the room but didn't see Astra. "Where is she?"

"Finishing the cleaning she tried to make Robin do." Rowdy's attention remained on the dog. "Now, grant me silence so I can complete healing this overly loyal creature."

Venus nodded and rose to her feet. There wasn't any work left to do in the cabin. Even the white linoleum floors gleamed, but she saw the bathroom door ajar and went across the room. Her sister crouched near the toilet, retching. Her silver-white robe had blood on the hem, undoubtedly from the dog. She turned slightly and Venus saw tears pouring down Astra's face.

"What were you thinking?" Venus hurried to her side. "He's not helpless. Orion warned you and so did our mother and aunt."

"Nobody else ever stood against my dogs." Sobs wracked Astra's body. "How was I to know? And he won't let me help undo the harm I did."

"You're not stupid." Venus flushed the toilet. Turning to the sink, she filled a glass with warm water, then helped her sister rise. "Rinse and spit. You came into your powers long before I did. You should know a wizard when you see one."

Astra clutched the glass tightly, more tears raining down her face. "I was so angry, and I killed my puppy."

"Not yet. He sleeps." Rowdy stood in the doorway. "When he wakes, he remains with me to finish healing."

"You can't keep him away from me. He's always been mine since I helped him take his first breaths."

"Grow up, Astra." Venus sighed, impatient with the drama. "Clean yourself and listen to what he told you. Until he's a hundred-percent healthy, the pup needs to be with Rowdy." She headed for the door and shoved the man's arm. "Now, fix her. Yes, she did wrong, but she suffers and it's your job to make her whole too. Step up, *High Healer*. I'm putting away the food and taking the box back to my mother. You two settle this without me and no more drama to spoil the weekend and the *Sabbat*. Neither of you will be happy if I have to be involved any further."

Embarrassment flooded through Astra, burning a path into her cheeks. What was wrong with her? She was a wreck, and she never allowed her emotions to rule her. She glanced quickly at him before going to the sink. "I'm fine. You can go now."

"And face the wrath of the war queen alone?" He shook his head. "No, *Vaslattel*. That would be the act of a braver wizard than me. I'll wait for you."

She felt a tremulous smile quiver into life and shook her head, dismissing it. She rinsed her mouth, spit into the sink, wishing she had a toothbrush. She glanced in the mirror, grateful her expensive mascara hadn't run and given her the look of an overwrought raccoon. "Then, tell me what is happening to me, *Healer*. Why am I so out of sorts, so weak, so emotional?"

"You'll never be weak, but this remains from our spell last night. You're no longer afraid to show your heart."

"What?" She spun to face him. "You did this and didn't warn me of the ramifications."

"I had other concerns." He shrugged, faint amusement flickering in the dark eyes. Taking a witch like you isn't an easy ride for any wizard. I remember that when I had you at the beginning of our soul binding."

Instant fury replaced the shame she'd felt. Grabbing the glass, she hurled the remaining water at him. He ducked and was across the room faster than she expected. He caught her upper arms and pulled her against him.

"No!" she shouted.

"Not what I want to hear." He lowered his head. "I never did get my kiss when you arrived."

"I thought you threatened to beat me if I tried killing you again." She lifted her chin defiantly, their lips a whisper apart. "What about that, Wizard?"

"You've punished yourself worse than I ever would, and you'll suffer more while the pup heals."

That was true and for a moment, she admired him for recognizing it. She enjoyed the feel of his lean body against hers, although she didn't plan to admit it. "This vulnerability? I don't like it. When am I myself again?"

"Tomorrow night. For now, we put each other first."

She brushed her lips across his, a teasing invitation. "Do you plan to fuck me here, *Capostrol*?"

He chuckled, his breath warm on her mouth. "I thought to make you wait, *Vaslattel,* but why should I? From now on, you won't use that word for our mating."

Before she could tell him that she wouldn't allow him to control her language, or her actions, he kissed her. It wasn't light or provocative as hers had been. Instead, the fierceness sparked a fire within her, and she surrendered to the claim he staked. She wound her arms around his neck, pressing closer, lips parting beneath the pressure of his.

Moments later, he lifted his head. She gasped when he caught her waist, boosted her onto the vanity. He pushed her legs apart and stepped between them. "What are you doing?"

"Having my witch."

She shuddered when he unfastened the clasp at her neck and opened the robe. She shrugged out of it, let it fall onto the counter. His gaze narrowed on the skimpy red shift she wore. He lowered his head, kissed the hollow of her throat, and slowly began to undo the top two buttons of the dress she'd chosen since she thought nobody would see it or the fact that she'd skipped underwear. She moaned when he cupped her breasts, his thumbs rubbing the cloth against her nipples. "Now, Rowindache. Have me now."

"Soon." He smiled. "I don't think you're ready yet."

She squirmed on the counter, trying to move closer to him. "I am."

"Let's see." He kissed the rise of her breast, his lips moving downward until he drew her nipple into his mouth and sucked.

She threaded her hands into his hair and arched against him, gasping as the damp cloth of her dress rubbed against her nipple. Then, she felt his calloused palms slide up her thighs before one large finger slipped inside her. A second followed and he started a steady rhythm, his thumb rocking against the small bud of flesh. She rose and fell with the motion of his fingers. At the same time, his mouth teased her nipples through the thin material of her dress, roving from one to the other and he continued to suck.

It wasn't like the previous night. This time he didn't stop, his fingers moving in and out of her while she matched the pattern he set, pleading, begging for more and calling his name. She exploded in what seemed like a hundred pieces, convulsing to the point of collapse. When she returned to sanity, she saw him opening his pants. "Are you serious?"

"You're about to find out, *Vaslattel*."

"You haven't even taken those off or your boots."

"I don't need to."

She caught her breath when he eased his hands under her hips, brought her closer to the edge of the vanity and then drove deep inside her. "It's just *Sex Magick*. I don't love you. I won't."

"Not yet." Buried inside her, he started to move, and she met him, motion for motion. "You don't have to as long as you please me like this, Satiranika."

———

After the evening meal, he chose to return to the bunkhouse to check on his newest patient. His *Chosen* hadn't joined the rest of them for supper and her aunt had told him that she'd see both of them in the morning for the greeting of the dawn and the New Year ceremonies. Hugh and Venus were together in one of the barns, tending the horses while Meteor minded the younger set and her mate remained with Gard and Robin.

When Rowdy opened the door, he saw his mate offering broth to the injured dog. She'd changed clothes, leaving behind her robes for a striped tunic and black pants. The pup licked her hand before trying the golden liquid in the bowl. Her face sober, red-gold hair confined in a long braid that fell to her hips, she glanced at Rowdy before returning to her task. "I want to take him home with me tomorrow."

"We'll see how he feels." Rowdy closed the door behind him, glimpsing the platter of meats, cheeses and different types of sliced bread on the table. "Is that for us or for him?"

"For him." She didn't take her attention from the large black dog. "I brought wine and cakes for us. Normally, he doesn't get 'people' food, but I didn't think his dry food would tempt him to eat."

"And the broth?"

"Chicken soup. Meteor makes it when any of the children are sick and she gave it to me for him."

Eyeing the bottle of wine warily, Rowdy pulled out a chair and sat down at the table. He picked up a piece of cheese, pausing when she frowned at him. "What concerns you?"

"I didn't bring that for you."

"I know, but the last time you served me any food, it killed me."

"That was three hundred years ago, and the poison was in the wine." She rose, stalked to the table, took the slice of cheddar from him and bit into it. After she chewed, swallowed, she held out the other half to him. "Do you trust me now?"

"Not yet, *Vaslattel*." He chuckled, snagged her wrist over the bracelet and drew her down on his lap, nipping the last of the cheese from her fingers. "If we drink from the same glass and share the same food, it's a beginning."

She sighed, turned her face into his neck. "What if I promise not to kill you until tomorrow afternoon when you've finished healing Bamse?"

"A strange bargain." He touched his lips to hers in a whisper of a kiss. "What if you tell me how to please you in bed instead? What do you want most from me tonight?"

"To be kissed three hundred times while you spend hours worshiping me." The truth escaped and bewilderment flickered across her face. "How did you know to ask a question no one else ever has?" She lifted her chin. "Never mind. I didn't mean it and I want to look after my puppy."

"He seems to be finishing that broth just fine on his own." Rowdy found her mouth again. "One. Who chooses where I kiss?" He brushed her ear with his lips. "Two. You or me?"

"You choose. No, I do." She met his mouth with hers for an instant. "Even if you make me beg in bed, I won't love you."

"You don't have to say those words." He kissed the hollow of her throat under the gold chain of the necklace, continuing the count. "You grant me body, mind and soul, Satiranika. Your heart comes later when you're ready."

"Never. That will never happen. I learned a long time ago not to love any man."

He framed her face with his hands, staring into the dark blue eyes. He was healer enough to know an injured woman when he saw one. She'd obviously survived more than one trauma and he didn't doubt he knew the man. He wouldn't tell her again that a father should protect, not harm his child.

She doesn't need to hear it and I'm not adding to her burdens. It would take a long time to gain her trust, but they were together, and he could wait. Rowdy kissed her gently. "Thirteen."

Fifty kisses later, he paused to take the dog outside. When they returned from a short walk, the pup opted to remain on the porch with his mother and brother. Back inside, he found her opening the bottle of wine. "If you ride slowly, he may be able to keep up with you on the journey."

"Where did Venus find you and Hughondear? You came in answer to her summons. From what year?"

"You tell me." He leaned against the door, watching her fill one glass. "Did you ever share the truth with your sisters? Did you tell them why you wanted to be rid of me?"

"They didn't ask." She stared into the red wine for a moment, then turned to face him. "I meant to protect the sister I had left after Meteor was murdered."

"I know, but you chose the wrong wizards to punish. We'd have helped you find the murderer and see he faced real justice. Your middle sister wouldn't have suffered the consequences in so many lives. She and Thojedescar could have lived happily, raising their youngsters."

"Venus *banexorted* you through Time, three hundred years from when we arrived in 1718. You didn't come from there or then." Astra frowned, obviously calculating the answer. "You brought Meteor's oldest son with you and she said she gave him to you before she died in her last life a hundred years ago. You came through the *Time Portal* we opened."

"Yes, and we closed it behind us." He shook his head, locked the door, and crossed to her. "Sloppy *magick* always costs the witch or wizard a higher price. Next time, finish what you start, Satiranika. Speaking of that, I still have kisses to count."

"We have to return you and Hughondear to your *Time* to live out your lives. We'll keep Meteor's boy."

Rowdy lifted the glass to Astra's lips. "This is our *Time* now and we'll stay with our soul-matches."

"You're not listening. You're leaving."

"Not this time." He put the glass on the table next to the bottle. He drew her close and kissed her forehead. "Fifty-one."

Seventy kisses later, they lay naked on his bunk. He focused his attention on her breasts. She arched against him, demanded he take her. He refused, drawing one nipple into his mouth, sucking gently. At a hundred and fifty, he'd started on her right leg, paying close attention to her knee.

She wriggled, squirmed under the kiss. "Do it, Rowindache. Do it now."

"I haven't reached three hundred yet. Isn't that what you asked? I want you happy."

"If you take me, I will be." She caught his arms, tried to pull him to her. "I promise."

He remained where he was, beginning a new line of kisses up the inside of her thigh. He smelled her readiness before he found it with his mouth. His tongue flicked at her in a series of darting kisses. His lips moved against the nest of red-gold curls as he counted.

She threaded her fingers in his hair, holding his lips on her as she twisted and arched against him. Low moans escalated to cries as she commanded him to do more. He granted the wish, taking her from peak to peak. He rode the storm with her, sending her onward beyond the stars. She clutched his shoulders, rose to meet his lips, and finally screamed in rapture.

He wanted to slide deep inside her, but decided to wait. Instead, he started on her left foot, nibbling at her toes.

She stirred. "What are you doing?"

"I've only kissed you two hundred and twelve times." He brushed her big toe with his lips. "I have further to go."

"And I won't survive if you do." She propped up on her elbows. "I absolve you. No more kisses. Please."

He stopped, met her dark blue gaze. "It's the first time you've asked me for anything. Even in bed, you issue orders, my queen."

"Your point?" She smiled at him. "You have one, don't you?"

"Certainly." He snagged her ankle, bent her leg so he could kiss her calf. "I like you asking, the way you said, 'Please.' It makes me feel more your man, so I'll complete the task you set. You'll speak to me with respect, *Vaslattel*."

"I'll do it without kisses. I swear it, *Capostrol*."

Ignoring the promise, his lips trailed along her left leg while she moaned and wriggled beneath the kisses. Spasms of joy seized her before his mouth touched the small bud in the curls between her thighs a second time and licked it. At three hundred kisses, he eased into her. Within a few strokes, she reached the heights. After several hard, fast thrusts, he followed, and she came again as he finished.

She pressed next to him, her arm across his chest. Her lips moved in the hollow of his throat. "I'm not a patient, kind or particularly sweet witch even in this life, Rowindache. Why do you want me?"

"I leave pure sweetness to those who like honey which cloys

over time." He pulled her closer, their bodies fitting together on the narrow bunk. "I prefer your sharpness, your strength."

She rolled on top of him, admiration filling her voice. "The way you took me the first time against the door. I liked it. You're not afraid of me. You don't make allowances or crawl to me. You renounced me as a *laspowima,* and you meant it."

"Truth-speaking honors both of us." He smoothed his hands over her back to the curve of her hips. "Your point, *Vaslattel.* You have one."

She grinned down at him, danger in her gaze. "I like vengeance even when I'm not angry. So, I'll give you three hundred kisses and make you beg for mercy."

"You can try." He chuckled. "When you fail, I'll have you bent over that trunk by the window."

18

Rocking J Ranch ~ Sunday, November 4ᵗʰ, 2018

THE LAST MEMBERS OF THE COVEN DEPARTED WHEN THE *SAMHAIN* celebrations ended, shortly after lunch. As an Elder Witch, she could have sent for anyone on the ranch she wanted to see and had that person come to her, but it was time for truth speaking, so Diana Yarbro climbed the stairs to the apartment Meteor and Astra shared during their visits to the ranch and knocked lightly on the door.

Meteor greeted her with a smile. "Are we late for Sunday dinner, Aunt Diana?"

"No." Diana hugged the younger woman and kissed her cheek. "I need to talk to Satiranika alone so would you mind giving us privacy?"

"Not in the least. She's packing and threatening to leave early. She's in a total snit about something." Meteor jerked her head in the direction of one of the bedrooms. "You're welcome to her."

"Thank you, child." Diana hugged the younger woman again and waited until she left the apartment, closing the door behind her.

In the bedroom, Astra stood over a suitcase on one of the beds.

The robes and gowns she'd worn on the weekend hung neatly in the closet; the door still open to the room. She obviously didn't intend to wear one of them to the late afternoon meal since she'd dressed for travel in black slacks and a black top with a Southwestern design. She glanced over her shoulder, anger rising in her face and landing in the dark blue eyes. "What do you want, Aunt? Or should I say, Mother?"

Diana winced. "This wasn't the way I planned to tell you or your sisters about the way Estelle and I saved the three of you from your demon-father, but you left me little choice."

"Saved?" Astra carefully placed a pair of folded pants in the suitcase, then spun around, advancing two steps. "What did you save us from? The two of you have always tried to control us, including the wizards you chose for our mates. I don't call soul-matching us to men who plan to steal our *magick* anything but evil. I have to protect the three of us from everything."

"Those three wizards are honorable mages and uniting with one of them doesn't take away from your strengths, Daughter, but adds power to what you do. If they couldn't be trusted, your aunt never would have commuted their death sentences or offered them the opportunity to sacrifice themselves and serve you and your sisters." Diana drew a deep breath. "This is an old argument and one we're not having now. You need to prepare for your sire's attacks when he learns of their arrival. He did his best to destroy our home in one of his insane rages and this realm is already in jeopardy."

"You keep saying that, but you never explain anything in detail." Astra folded her arms, gold bracelets gleaming on her wrists, and waited. "The Corbetts run a logging empire, but they adhere to the letter of the laws and re-plant saplings where they cut trees."

"Have you visited those sites? Most of the young evergreens don't grow to maturity and don't hold the dirt in place. Deforestation causes mudslides, erosion, pollution and that doesn't even touch on the impact to the animals that live in the forests, global warming or climate change."

"They call it progress here and you can't blame everything that happens in this country on my father, especially since he isn't in charge of the logging operation."

"No, but he is responsible for unleashing the plague that wrecked our land and killed so many. It spread from the animals to the humans and in our country, most of the men died, down to the smallest male infants. It mutated in *Warpathia*, affecting their girls and women."

"That's what Aunt Estelle says, but how do you know it's true? None of us have even visited *Trilunon* in hundreds of years."

"We can't because the *dracklegons*, the high priests sealed all the portals to our home to keep the toxicity from spreading throughout the connecting realms, not just this one. They've been trying to find a new domain for us, but so far, they haven't had much luck. Macartundear hasn't returned from his visit to the latest discovery, but before he left, he told us that the *dracklegons* said *magick* runs weak there and they don't know if we or they can restore what's been lost."

"I thought my stepfather, or should I say, my uncle was dead."

"The three of us felt it best to hide his trip from those who would stop his travels and anyone who might report his activities to our enemies."

"If you mean my father and his minions, say so. Will you stop hiding things from me?" Astra plucked at the gold chain of the necklace she wore. "Which one of you took the jewelry to the cabin and told Rowindache how to use it to try to control me?"

"We love you, child, and we're not your enemies. Neither is he. You've used, or should I say, 'mis-used' his power from the time of the soul-matching. He's shown you more mercy than many mages would, since he remembers the way you had him killed in his four previous lives."

"I'm not responsible for what Latham or the Corbett pack did. It's no secret they serve my father, your one-time lover. I don't have the power to cause harm to others if I controlled the *Time-Streams* like a *dracklegon* even when I walk the eternal star paths. I never said I wanted rogue shapeshifters to murder Rowindache. I don't care if any of you believe me or not."

Relief swept through Diana. She hadn't lost the girl, at least not yet. Crossing the room, she drew her eldest daughter into a tight embrace. "Of course, I believe you, child. As much as we battle with each other, you've always told me and your aunt the truth, even when you flaunt the *Rule of Three* and imperil your own soul."

Astra took a ragged breath. "He made me his *vaslattel* and threatens to force me to wait on a first-wife."

"Words have power." Diana stroked the fiery red hair and felt sobs shake the younger witch's body. "However, before he can bring in a new mate, he needs your permission. If you don't accept the new match, he won't have harmony in his home and that will affect any spell-casting he does, including his power to heal."

"Really?" Astra drew back, tears shimmering in her eyes. "I don't recall that from reading the *Warpathian* laws in those scrolls."

"Of course, you didn't." Diana saw past the defiance and knew the younger witch craved the love and acceptance she denied wanting. "You read them three hundred years ago and even though you've had most of your memories, more will come now."

Astra touched one of her earrings. "No matter how much I try, I can't remove the *talipenlace* set. I could before. What changed?"

"Admitting it's yours and you wear it willingly. The jewelry links you and Rowindache for the rest of your lives here."

"I despised him before, and I hate him even more now. Will I be able to break the bond when I kill him?"

Diana laughed, smoothing the bright red hair again. "That threat would be more believable if the two of you hadn't enjoyed so much *Sex Magick* during these past few days, my dear. You can't kill your children's father any more than I can. Jarvesel has given me much more cause, especially when he tried to sacrifice you and your sisters in one of his blood rites."

"I've been sexually active almost half my life and have always taken precautions. Even with him, I won't get pregnant."

"What works with mortal men doesn't always with mages."

Diana kissed Astra's forehead. "Blessed be, child. Finish your packing and come to dinner."

———

Venus helped with the clean-up after the early evening meal. It was only fair since Meteor had taken her three children to watch a movie in the family room and Astra disappeared outside, supposedly to check on the dogs.

Her aunt glanced at the doorway when Rebekah arrived with more used serving dishes and put them on the counter. "We'll finish here. Will you please go clean the work-room and prepare it for Rowindache? He wants to cast a *Protection Spell* on Thojedescar and Gardersolter before they go to Corbettstown."

"He can't go there. Jarvesel will recognize—" Rebekah's voice trembled, her hands shaking, her face pale with fear. "He'll torture and kill Gard like he did before."

"Not when Thojedescar claims him as a friend, at least not until whoever has been murdering him tries again and Gardersolter has agreed to take the risk of keeping Thojedescar safe."

"I don't understand," Venus said. "Meteor says she's been killed repeatedly in her past lives and that her soul-match did it."

"That's impossible." Diana put the leftover roast beef into a plastic container. "A *chapalmatand* can't harm his *laspowima*, his forever mate, without inflicting permanent damage on himself and dying horribly. That's why we arranged for the three wizards to sacrifice their hearts, minds and souls in an ancient rite before we bonded them to you and your sisters. Jed's aura lacks the marks it'd have if he'd been the one who harmed your sister or threatened their children."

"But Meteor said she died at his hands several times and she's absolutely certain about who injured her. That's why she arranged for Hugh and Rowdy to bring us Edwin."

"She's as confused as he is, but together we'll discover the truth." Diana shooed Rebekah from the room. "Venus, go find Astra and send her to the workroom to help her mate. After that, mind the younglings and have Meteor join Astra, Rowdy and Jed for the spell-casting."

Venus nodded agreement, wondering why her mother opted to allow her best friend to manage the *magickal* elements this time. It wasn't Estelle Jamison's style to take a back seat to anyone, not even the woman who'd shared so much with her over the years. Of course, she and her sisters were closer to Aunt Diana, Venus thought, and they tried harder to please her, because none of them doubted that Orion was their mother's favorite. Amazingly, their brother didn't take advantage of the fact.

When she entered the bunkhouse, she found Astra sitting at the small kitchen table, busily writing on a yellow legal pad. She glanced at Venus. "I'm leaving instructions on how to work the electric stove, the refrigerator and the freezer. You'll have to teach them how to do laundry. We can't afford to put in a new floor if they flood the place."

"What are you talking about? I'm not their maid. They're grown men. They can look out for themselves."

"In a lot of ways, they will, and they won't hesitate to protect you, the children, Estelle, Orion, or the ranch. I have several large trials coming up and I can't be at the law firm, or the courthouse and here at the same time." Astra wrote a few more words. "Well, I could be, but I won't return until Rowindache leaves."

Venus saw her sister's hand quiver at the mention of the wizard's name. "Astra, what happened this weekend? Did he hurt you?"

"Not like you think." Astra shoved back from the table. "I need some air."

Venus hesitated, then followed her sister outside. "Talk to me. What's wrong?" She put her arms around Astra. "Come on, Satiranika."

"Don't call me that." Astra shook like one of her dogs after a swim in the river. She turned into Venus' hold, clutched the younger woman. "You've got to warn Meteor."

"About what?"

"These thrice-damned things." Astra pulled back enough to tug on the center disk of her necklace, a five-pointed star inside a circle. "I can't take off any of the jewelry, Venus. I tried several times today. No matter what, Meteor has to refuse to wear it willingly. She must deny it's hers and you've got to do the same. Neither of you can repeat the soul-matching vows, or we're all lost."

"Did you bind yourself to him?"

A flush brightened Astra's cheeks. "Not knowingly. It was sex, great sex, but just sex. At least, that's what I thought. Then, I found out otherwise."

"All right. I'll tell Meteor." Horrified, Venus stared at her older sister. "Astra, what are we going to do? Should I try sending them away?"

"I don't know if you can." Astra took a deep breath. "Don't try, at least not yet. I'll study my *grimoires* at home. I have several different *Books of Shadows,* and one may hold the answers we seek. Play along. Distance aids a little, but so does any distraction. He's busy with something else, or I'd never be able to warn you about the *talipenlace* jewelry. He doesn't know how strong I am."

"I won't tell him or Hugh." Venus promised, meeting the dark blue gaze. "Is that why you've been so odd this weekend? You've taken a step back from the ceremonies and allowed Mom and Aunt Diana to lead them. You've been super sweet to everyone, even when some of the younger witches and wizards made 'stupid' resolutions for the next year. That isn't your style after you've had sex, although it was 'great sex'."

"Because it was what he wanted." Astra buried her face against Venus' shoulder. "Do you have any idea how it feels to be locked inside, silently screaming while your body does the opposite of what your mind says? If he comes near, I'll follow his orders regardless of what I think, or what you and Meteor need."

"Listen to yourself. It was *Sex Magick*. He doesn't have the power to take you from your sisters."

"All he has to do is touch me and I will go anywhere he wishes, do whatever he asks. As I am now, I'd follow him through a *Time*

Gate. It wouldn't even take an actual spell casting." Astra eased away to turn back to the cabin. "I need to finish writing out the directions for the appliances. Why were you looking for me?"

"Aunt Diana sent me to fetch you to help Rowdy cast a *Protection Spell* on Jed Corbett and Gard Devlin before they go to Corbettstown. You're supposed to go to the workroom up in the attic."

"All right. I'm almost done here. I'll go in five minutes."

Alone, Venus studied her necklace with its embossed disc of an engraved warrior on a horse. She'd worn it almost seven years in this incarnation. Would hers do the same thing, turn her into some sort of 'Stepford' witch who surrendered all her individuality to some wizard?

No! Not if she could help it!

She reached up, wrenched at the chain, and threw the pendant as far as she could. Somehow, she'd save both of her sisters.

Three hours later, she pushed the wheelbarrow loaded with hay up the barn aisle, feeding alfalfa to the horses. She continued the chore even when Hugh joined her, quietly helping with the task. Once all the animals had been fed, she followed him to the hay room off the stalls. "I need a bale for morning."

"I'll load it in a moment." He parked the wheelbarrow near the large stack of bales. Then, he reached into his shirt pocket, pulled out a necklace. "Why did this return to me?"

"I have no idea." Venus frowned at the jeweled disk on the gold chain. She'd thrown it away near the bunkhouse and she didn't remember seeing him there. "It doesn't matter. You can have it. I won't waste time tossing it in the garbage."

"You dare much." He took a step toward her, caught her shoulder. "Replace it, witch." A muscle twitched in his jaw. "You won't turn me into a husk of a man."

"I won't wear it again." She lifted her chin, met him glare for glare. "Nobody makes me into a brainless doll."

19

THE LAST THREE DAYS HAD BEEN BUSIER THAN HE'D EXPECTED, OR even dreamed they could be when he thought of having his full powers returned. Leaning back in a chair near the woodstove, sipping a cup of coffee, Rowdy studied the cabin. It felt like the home he hadn't realized he missed. He'd enjoyed the time he spent with his mate here.

He'd had women before. He hadn't waited for his *Chosen* during the last six hundred years. A *chapalmatand* had to remain unwaveringly faithful to his soul-matched mate, his *laspowima*, but Satiranika was his *vaslattel*, and fidelity wasn't required since he could have more than one woman in his house until she proved herself a worthy match. Still, *Sex Magick* with her had been surprisingly blissful at moments, especially when she slept in his arms, allowing him to hold her close. Undoubtedly, it was due to the fact that both of them worshipped the *Lady and Lord*. No shame attached to physical lovemaking. Yet, it was more peaceful since Astra departed with the three dogs earlier this evening.

She'd threatened not to return while he remained at the ranch, but he'd ignored the words when he kissed her goodbye. She could run as far as she wanted, although a city less than fifteen leagues away wasn't beyond his *magick's* reach. He'd rein her in when he chose and both of them knew it. For now, let her keep her pride. He glanced at the sleeping boy in one of the bunks. Playing with other children, including his two new-found siblings, had worn out Edwin. The bunkhouse door opened and Holt stalked inside, closing the door behind him with carefully controlled force.

"Someone singed your tail feathers." Rowdy rose and went for another cup. He filled it with strong coffee from their old, blue enamel pot and passed it to his friend. "What happened with your witch?"

"She removed my necklace." Hugh patted his shirt pocket, then pulled up a chair. "She said some nonsense about me wanting her for a toy. Who'd fill my *laspowima's* head with such silliness?"

"Her sister, my *vaslattel*." Rowdy sat back down and chuckled, raising the mug to his lips. "I should have expected her to fight my orders and try to outwit me. She's been a lawyer for a long time. I told her to allow her sisters and their *Chosen* to decide their paths and leave the four of you alone. She helped ward Thojedescar and Gardersolter, but I'll strengthen their protections. I'll also ask the High Queen to take us to Matiranika so we can ward her against the one who steals her *Chosen's* shape."

"And what about this game your mate plays with Katiranika and me?"

"You're smarter than most men and you know how to defeat one wily witch."

Hugh took a swallow of strong coffee as he considered the matter. "Sometime in the next week or so, your *vaslattel* will block my war-queen's memories of me again. When she does, I'll return the necklace and my *laspowima* will be grateful to have it."

"Exactly. Once she has her memories, she'll defend herself from any mischief my *vaslattel* creates, but since I've bound her powers to a certain extent, it won't be a fair battle between sisters. You'll have to keep the war queen from wreaking havoc."

"Not a problem." Hugh raised his mug in salute. "Still glad to be here despite the storms we face?"

"Definitely." Rowdy winked at his old friend. "My *vaslattel* not only provided the pleasure of her company these past few days, but we will be blessed with our first child shortly after the *Summer Sabbat* in June."

"What?" Hugh almost choked on his coffee. "Does she know?"

"She will before *Yule*." Rowdy grinned appreciatively. "And I don't doubt she'll give the war queen a lesson in rages and tantrums."

———

The weekend party had started to wind down and the only one of the pack who hadn't checked in was his nephew. Frank Corbett frowned as his current bedmate, the town doctor's daughter, Trina Corbett, a tall, slender blonde, approached, a wary look on her pretty face, blue eyes concerned. "What worries you, my sweet?"

"We're down to the last of the barbequed meat. What do you want me to serve for dinner?"

She flinched when he put an arm around her waist and Frank hid a smile. Marvin had evidently schooled her well during the last few days, although it would be impossible to see any bruises because of the long-sleeved, clinging, vintage black hostess gown she wore. She always bored him with days about the details of every shopping trip. He still had to admit the pride she took in her appearance and the exquisite care she used with her cosmetics provided him with a lovely woman to run his house and made others envy him.

"Look in the big freezer and warm up the leftovers from the *Mabon* feast in September."

"I will." She eased out of his hold and hurried toward the kitchen, black heels tapping on the hardwood floor. She paused long enough to greet two late-comers at the door, then vanished into the hallway.

Carrying two bottles of beer, Marvin joined Frank. "Well, there's your nephew at long last. Who's with him?"

"I don't know." Frank took one of the bottles and waited while the two younger men approached. "We'll find out."

Marvin nodded as Jed neared. "Good to see you, son. We've been worrying up a storm that you got yourself arrested and missed the party."

"And you'd have had to pull more strings to save my sorry butt." Jed shook hands with the police chief. "No, I pretty much behaved myself this year."

"Where were you?" Frank couldn't help smiling when his nephew stepped in to greet him with a manly hug. Jed was one of the few shifters who always showed affection as well as respect. He embraced the dark-haired giant, patting the big man's shoulder. "Marvin's right. We've been missing you this weekend."

"That's my fault." When Jed stepped back, the brown-haired stranger, who was nearly as rugged, came forward and held out his hand to Frank. "I'm Gard Devlin. Jed and I served together a few years ago. When I got to town, I called, and we went drinking. Time got away from us. He invited me to tag along when he came here. If it's a problem, I'll go."

"No problem at all." Frank shared a glance with Marvin, and the police chief gave a faint nod. He'd run a background check on Jed's buddy. "Any friend of Jed's is welcome in my house. Trina is loading up the buffet tables again and there's still some beer at the bar, but Jed knows where I keep the good stuff. The two of you can help yourselves not only to the booze but also the food."

"We ate in Seattle before we headed up here," Jed said, "but a cold beer sounds good."

"I'll grab a couple." Gard sauntered toward the bar, obviously eying the women who returned the interest.

Frank noticed the first to come forward and greet the stranger was Junior's wife, Cherry, a curvy, little brunette that surprisingly remained faithful to her idiot husband.

"Gard wanted to catch up with a guy we knew who worked on the docks in Seattle, but he wasn't around." Jed ran a hand through his dark hair. "Pissed off Gard, because he was promised a job and with a dishonorable discharge, his prospects are in the toilet. You got something for him, Uncle Frank?"

"Depends on what he can do." Frank didn't say he'd hire the man to watch Jed and report back. "I don't need a troublemaker on the payroll."

"Nope, you've got me for that." Amusement flickered in Jed's jet-black eyes. "Gard's a hell of a cat-skinner who can make a dozer dance. He can fix it when it breaks down too. He's got a bit of a temper, but he'd never hit a woman or a kid unless they really ask for it. Mostly, he brawls with other guys, but he's always has my six."

"Then he could run a dozer up where you'll be cutting timber with the new crew next week," Frank said. "So, where did you go the other day? Junior told us you found some token and ran off with Meteor Jamison."

"The witch who had me tossed in the Gray-Bar? You told me to stay away from her, Uncle Frank, and you know I respect what you say." Jed scowled. "Pretty sure Junior didn't tell you that he kept dragging his ass on Wednesday when he knew I had to meet up with Devlin, but I didn't wax my cousin. Yet. He keeps lying about me and that can change. I took out better guys in the *sandbox*."

"Easy, Jed." Marvin took a slug of his beer. "Let me handle your cousin. Making trouble with his dad, the pack leader is one thing. Lying to a cop so we're all chasing our tails for days is another."

"Go have a drink with your buddy before he offends someone by messing with a mated female." Frank patted his nephew's shoulder again. "Leave Junior to us. We've got your back this time."

"All right." Jed started away. "I'll give you time to handle it, but if you don't, I will."

"I think he just threatened us." Frank struggled to hide a grin, clinking his bottle against Marvin's before lifting the beer to his mouth. "You scared, old friend?"

Marvin chuckled. "Nope, but I'm not the alpha of the pack with a young wolf nipping his tail."

"Yup and when I'm gone, he'll be the one running things." Frank's grin broadened. "So, we're right about taking Junior hunting with us. He doesn't have the guts, the attitude or the libido of a real

Corbett. If his mother wasn't dead, I'd take that witch on a hunt. She swore he was mine when she was dying."

"She wasn't a real witch, either. If she was, her son would use his *Power*, not hide from it."

"That friend of Jed's has *Talent*," Frank said. "If he didn't, he'd avoid my nephew, not be drawn to him."

"I'll check him out, but I don't *See* anything to be concerned about." Marvin glanced at the bar. "Shall I tell Trina to bring them food?"

"Not necessary since you heard Jed say they ate elsewhere. He rarely joins us for meals and when he does, he won't eat the meat I serve." Frank drank more beer. "If you're still enjoying Trina, she's yours for as long as you want."

"She claims she's yours and hasn't done anything that requires punishment. She fights me every time. It's been too many years since a woman did that. I'd forgotten how enjoyable bed battles could be, even when they leave bruises and bite marks on a man." Marvin finished his beer.

"You've had your share of the pack women."

"They're not like her. They only surrender because they know better than to refuse your enforcer." A slow smile crept across Marvin's face. "It's a treat for a man my age to realize he hasn't lost the ability to make a young thing howl for him while she comes again and again, especially when he knows how much she hates it."

Faint jealousy stirred in Frank. He'd chosen Trina at *Beltane* six months ago and while she never refused to do anything he wanted, she didn't show a great deal of excitement about being in his bed. The platinum credit card he gave her caused more pleasure and so did long shopping excursions in Seattle.

"The fact that she ends up begging for more when I'm ready to sleep is music to these old ears. But, she's yours and taking her was just a reward for the weekend."

"Not if you still want her." Frank smiled at his lifelong friend, deciding to be amused by the revelations.

Marvin never let anything interfere with his duties and at times, his sense of responsibility could wear on the nerves of those who weren't as devoted to serving the pack. Normally, he'd have visited the festivities between rounds in Corbettstown, not changed to civvies, faded jeans, a plaid shirt and boots to fit in with the others for the weekend. He hadn't prevented Trina from fulfilling her duties as a hostess, but he'd often disappeared with the woman, a matter other shifters hadn't hesitated to report, especially when Marvin locked the doors to the wine cellar, Frank's office, the pantry and an upstairs guestroom behind the pair.

"Keep her and have sons of your own. We need to know if Cherry can bear young. She's never been pregnant, not in the five years she's been mated to Junior. Perhaps we should take her on the hunt with us. I'll groom her to be my new companion."

"Then we both have plans for the *Witch's New Year*." Marvin inclined his head. "Thank you, Frank. If you don't require me any longer, I'd like to take my new toy to my house and have privacy to appreciate her antics in my own bed."

"Go and have fun." Frank watched his long-time friend head for the hallway that led to the kitchen. He doubted anyone else heard the outraged screams a few minutes later, but crossed the room to stand inside the archway and enjoy the scene of Marvin carrying Trina over one broad shoulder toward the front door.

Her black dress was bunched around her thighs and she pounded his wide back with fists. He kept walking, but smacked her rounded rump when she stopped yelling long enough to try and bite him. Seeing him, Marvin paused mid-stride. "Are you sure, Frank?"

"Yes. She never had that much energy with me. If she'd shown any fire, then she wouldn't be such a bore." Frank waved a hand for the shape-shifter standing guard to open the door. "I'll send her things to your house."

"You know I love you, Frank." Trina writhed in Marvin's hold, struggling for freedom. "I wouldn't have hurt you by telling you that your friend assaulted me more than once this weekend. You're a bastard. You'll pay for setting me up. Both of you will pay."

Marvin chuckled, stroking one of her shapely legs through a

black stocking. "I don't think so, but you will. Would you arrange for my assistant to run the office for the next few days, Frank, so I don't have to respond to any calls?"

"I'd be delighted." Laughing, Frank returned to the party. His house belonged to him again, and he had a new conquest to pursue. He sauntered toward Cherry. Marvin was right. The New Year would prove satisfying for the two of them.

———

Back at her company headquarters, Meteor helped carry in the equipment from the catering truck. She put away the clean stainless-steel pans in the pantry while Tolliver locked away the remaining bottles of wine in their cellar. Lizzie had left the remainder of the cooked food at the Rocking J, but stored different ingredients in the cupboards and walk-in cooler.

It'd been one of the best *Sabbats* in a long time, Meteor thought. All three of her children were safe with Venus, who'd guard them beyond death, but for once the war-queen wasn't alone. She'd have the help of the two skilled wizards who remained at the Rocking J. Once again, Meteor found herself wondering what the results would be of the spell cast by Rowindache. He insisted that her soul-matched mate wouldn't harm her, much less commit murder numerous times.

Meteor wasn't as certain and knew her elder sister had concerns, too. This wasn't the first time that Astra had tried to protect the *Trecesalty*, but she'd resorted to blocking Jed Corbett's memories instead of warding him from anyone who attempted to harm him.

Her cousin, Brigid, came out of the office. "I've confirmed the upcoming events for the next week. The answering service didn't have any emergencies, but we had three calls for parties in Corbettstown."

"We don't serve the shifters," Daphne said, before Meteor could. "I'll call and refer them elsewhere."

"I'm the newest employee and scheduling is one of my responsibilities."

"Not when it comes to Frank and his pack." Meteor smiled at her cousin, a tall, curvaceous redhead, a typical ornery Dawson, down to her laced-up riding boots. "Daph is right about them. Corbettstown is too dangerous for witches who serve the *Goddess* and the *Light*."

Brigid frowned thoughtfully. "I'm not a witch and I don't mind baking a cake for someone to pick up here for their child's birthday, even if the family lives in Corbettstown."

Meteor shared a glance with Daphne, then said gently. "You're not in touch with your powers yet, my dear Brighty. The *Law of Contagion* applies to all of us, from the newest in the *Craft* to the eldest. We avoid fights until we can win them."

"I don't understand everything you're saying." Brigid shrugged. "But, you're the boss and I do know there's a murder investigation ongoing near Corbettstown. Our cousin, Donald is up there, helping with the interviews."

"I hadn't heard anything about that." Curiosity sparked in Daphne's pale face. "Who died?"

"Nina Armstrong and her fiancé, Kyle Morgan disappeared under mysterious circumstances at a cabin outside of town last week," Brigid said. "We've been waiting to hear what the police, state law enforcement officers, and federal agents discover, but so far there's nothing."

20

WHILE SHE DROVE TOWARD SEATTLE, ASTRA FLICKED A SIDEWAYS glance at Rebekah who sat in the passenger seat of the SUV answering messages on her phone. "Did we miss anything important this weekend?"

"I'm not sure. My sister, Trina, texted me several times during the past few days, but now she's not responding."

Astra frowned, focusing on the freeway traffic. "She lives with Frank Corbett up in Corbettstown, doesn't she?"

"It's not like she had a lot of choice at *Beltane* last May. When the alpha decides he wants an unmated female shifter, she goes, or she dies."

"Good point. Did she prefer someone else?"

"No, she was real careful about dating since she didn't want a mate yet. She was saving money to move to California and join a more progressive pack with an alpha that would let her finish graduate school rather than whelping pups for Frank. That's all a woman can do in Corbettstown. She says he's been hassling her a lot because she's been with him almost six months and hasn't conceived."

"You did something to help her prevent pregnancy, didn't you?"

"Of course. Doctor Gideon Corbett may be our biological father, but he's not much of a parent and Trina knew better than to ask him for help. He won't do anything to upset Frank and preventing more babies definitely would. Trina and I made sure that none of the higher-ups or the older females know most of the younger women are practicing birth control and plotting their own escapes from the pack."

"We'll have to ward them, so my demon father doesn't find out. We'll do it as soon as we get home."

"Are you serious? You've never offered to help us before. Is this because of Rowdy?"

Shaking her head, Astra narrowed her gaze on the other vehicles on the freeway. "He doesn't control me. Rescuing you from being barbequed alive and eaten by the pack was the most I could do. You've never told me about the subversive element in Corbettstown, or I'd have aided them before."

"Trust isn't an easy lesson when we learn deception early. Frank intended to have Diana killed once her memories returned, and she realized she was a true witch. My father may be a doctor, but he's not a real healer since he abides by the laws of the pack rather than adhering to the Hippocratic Oath sworn to by most physicians in this realm. He agreed to turn Diana over for the sacrifice when I was a toddler. She told me that she intended to take Trina and me with her when she fled, but she was betrayed by some of the other women in the pack. Luckily, she'd already arranged to have the three of you smuggled away by Estelle."

"That makes it even more incredible that I could save you when our mother couldn't."

"I know that now." Rebekah glanced over her shoulder at the three large dogs sleeping in the back of the Explorer. "The Elder Witches shared a great deal this weekend. So did Rowdy."

"I'm sure my mate would agree to help you and your friends because he's a true *High Healer-Mage*, but he's busy at the ranch right now and I don't think we need him."

"But if things change—?"

"Then, I'll contact him," Astra lied, keeping her tone even. She wouldn't, but her apprentice didn't need to know that. "Have you shared everything you learned from the three of them?"

Silence and when she flicked a quick sideways glance at Rebekah, the younger woman's attention remained on the phone in her hand as she texted an answer to someone. Her half-sister never managed to keep secrets for long. She'd spill whatever was on her mind in the next few days.

Grimacing, Astra focused on the highway traffic again. "When you finish with your messages, get my phone out of my purse and check mine."

———

It'd been a busy weekend, and she tucked the children into bed early. For once, Quaid didn't complain about going at the same time as his younger sister. Pouring herself a glass of wine, Venus sat in the living-room watching and not watching a lame sitcom on the large-screen television at the same time. Normally, she'd have spent the evening cleaning her house after a celebration, but Rebekah had organized the teenagers in the coven and arranged for the younger witches and wizards to sweep, vacuum, and do the dishes after lunch. The counters gleamed and so did the floors. They'd even done the laundry, changed the sheets in all the bedrooms, and washed the windows.

Once this wing of the house was physically clean, Rebekah led the younger set through a psychic cleansing, saying they needed to be sure their teacher and her children could *'live without fear and nothing evil would enter here.'* Finishing her red wine, Venus wondered about her older sister's assistant. She'd said Astra was busy with other tasks and the training of younglings to the Craft was everyone's responsibility.

Why do I feel as if I knew Rebekah before? In another life? Or was it in another place? By another name? Venus set the empty glass on the end table and leaned back on the couch, closing her eyes to allow the answers to come as she remembered the first night with hersoul-matched mate, Hughondear. They'd been alone in a bedchamber in a castle waiting for the *dracklegons,* the *Mage-Priests* who would open a portal into a distant realm.

She'd meant to remain awake, to guard herself with her favorite dagger so he couldn't come near, but eventually she fell into an exhausted slumber. She felt the warmth of his skin, heard his heart-beat, and realized he carried her. Where?

She still held the knife. She opened her eyes, pressed the tip of the blade against his neck. "Release me."

"In a moment." He took a step, a second, a third. "You don't need to sleep on the floor, *Chosen.* You can have the bed."

"I won't share it with you." She kept the knife on him. "Trust that truth if nothing else."

"I believe you." He lowered her to the wide bed, walked away. "Sleep well and dream of me."

"You can wish, but it won't happen." She caught her breath when he turned back, but it was only to toss a light blanket over her. "I'm my own witch, not yours."

"Someday, we'll share our powers as well as our hearts and bodies and I can wait, Katiranika." He strode to the door. "For now, I'll rid you of my presence so you can rest. I'll have a meal sent in six hours."

She gazed after him, amazed when he left the room. Didn't he want her? He hadn't even tried to kiss her. Granted, she'd have fought him. What kind of warrior-prince was he? A gutless coward? She'd inform him of that the next time she saw him. With the idea to comfort her, she tucked the blade under the pillow and drifted off to slumber.

Hours later, when she woke, she was still alone in the room. Where was he? Why did it matter? He was her mate, she told herself sternly. They were committed to each other, and she was of the *Trecesalty.* Royalty of her rank and in her extended family had their marriages arranged. She'd honor the bonds, even if they weren't of her choosing. She was her mother's daughter, not her sire's.

Her mother had fallen in love once and Robinaranika was the

result. However, when their mother married, it was ordained by her mother, Katiranika's grandmother following the spiritual guidance of the *dracklegons* of *Ethlestial*. Nobody ever expected that husband, a mage-priest linked to them to murder Dianaranika after she gave birth to the triplets. The babies were viewed as a blessing from the *Goddess* throughout the entire realm of *Trilunon*. Even the priests who foretold the future hadn't *Seen* it, which meant Jarvesel cloaked his evil from them.

Katiranika rose to her feet, pulling the dagger out from under the pillow. For now, she'd bathe and dress. She'd visit her sisters and see how they fared with their soul-matched wizards. She heaved a sigh as she entered the cleansing chamber. She missed the three soaking tubs back in her palace where bathing was a luxury and a ritual. This castle had been designed and built by the *Ethlestials* who preferred dry heat over wet and that meant she wouldn't feel clean again until she returned to *Trilunon* or arrived at their new home.

She grimaced. She ought to feel some bond to the huge creatures that were half human and half reptile. She didn't. The giant, winged lizards always frightened her, reminding her of the pictures Matiranika found on the view screen of the Terran crock-diles. Katiranika hoped she'd never showed her fear. The *Ethlestials* didn't have such large jaws or teeth and the *dracklegons* walked upright.

The sight of Lavarutesel, the mage-priest who'd been her father's apprentice at the soul-matching ceremonies made her stomach lurch. She couldn't touch the food at the meal afterwards. If she'd had to watch him charming her oldest sister for another moment, Katiranika knew she'd have stolen her new mate's sword and attacked the envoy. Instead, she started an argument with her aunt who'd invited the monster to the rites.

The quarrel continued when she and Satiranika were alone. Her eldest sister actually wanted to bond with the creature and share his nest, rather than her new mate's. She claimed she didn't care if her children hatched with tails and scales. She'd adore them the way she did their sire.

Katiranika shuddered at the idea. At least, her new *Chosen* was human. The streams of warm air ended all too quickly, and she stepped from the tube, regretting she couldn't towel dry her hair and body the way she'd do in her own chambers. Once again, she missed her home. She even felt lonely for the young soldiers who waited on her, although their giggles and chatter could be annoying. She didn't want to recall the argument with her sister any longer and hoped her angry words would be forgiven.

Shaking back her long hair, she returned to the bedchamber and found clean clothing in her trunk. She didn't intend to be unnoticed in the castle, although most folk would stare at the jeweled necklace, earrings and bracelets binding her and the former prince of *Warpathia*. Still, today was the first chance she had to see her troops in a month. She chose purple leggings, a silver under-blouse, and a silver tunic with purple stripes. She braided silver and purple ribbons into her waist-length red hair. Here, she could carry her usual weapons and she would. After all, she was the war-queen.

She belted on her sword, tucked matching knives into the sheaths in her boots. The dagger she used for *magick* went into the scabbard she wore inside the full sleeve of her tunic. A tap on the door interrupted her preparations and she tensed. "Who is it?"

"Me, Kat. Robin. I brought you a meal."

"Wait." Katiranika unsealed the door and waved it open, eying her half-sister, who stood in the corridor. "Welcome and blessed be. Did he send you?"

"Who? Your mate?" Robinaranika arched a coppery brow. "No. I haven't seen him." She turned and took a tray from the soldier behind her. "I suppose you won't leave, so guard the door."

"As you say." The tall man in the *Warpathian* uniform bowed to Katiranika respectfully. "I am Gardarsolter. I watch over your sister as my commander ordered."

"I'll gamble she likes that." Katiranika hastily suppressed a smile when Robinaranika narrowed sky-blue eyes and glowered. "Then again, maybe not."

Amusement flickered in the warrior's dark gaze. "Exactly."

"I've taken my share of orders over the years so we won't leave without you," Katiranika promised. "I wish to see the rest of the *Trecesalty*. Send them word when possible."

"Only to Matiranika, not to the oldest of the *Trecesalty*, and I will explain what occurred last eve while the war-queen breaks her fast." Robinaranika poured three goblets of wine, blessing them with the charm to prevent poison. "Sister, come join me. We must talk."

"Very well, Robin." Katiranika took one of the glasses of wine to the soldier in the hallway before sealing the door. "Now, share your ill tidings. What harm has befallen Sati?"

"I haven't seen her this day." Robinaranika drew a deep breath. "She tried to kill her *Chosen* and fled to Lavarutesel's chamber. He accepted her, at least until her mate arrived and reclaimed her."

"Who died in the battle?"

"No one. As a *Warpathian healer*, Rowindache was immune to the *Vensonxic* syrup she poured in the wine and Lavarutesel claimed his privilege as a diplomat to avoid swordplay. Because of his shameful conduct, the priests renounced him and refused to face Rowindache on his behalf."

"And our sister?" Katiranika trembled, gripping the back of a chair and prayed only her concern showed, not her fear. "Her new mate didn't turn her over to the *dracklegons*. He hasn't harmed her either. I'd feel her pain and death."

"What else do you feel? She's blocked me from her thoughts. When I went to their chamber, her mate refused me entrance. He says nobody may see her."

Katiranika considered the tactic. Solitude was often used to break a captive's will, but it wouldn't work on their sister. "It will punish him more than it does her. He'll change his mind when he grows less angry and more frustrated."

"He seems a merciful man." Tension seeped from Robinaranika's body. "He spoke up for my *healers* when she interfered with their duties so I would not turn them over to the *dracklegons* for meat."

"You didn't?" Katiranika gaped at her half-sister. "What were you thinking?"

"They abandoned their patients, which enraged me. They swore the same oaths I did. Even royalty may not order *healers* to do less than their honor bids."

Katiranika nodded, sitting down and reaching for the glass of wine. "Join me and share the meal you brought. After we eat, we'll visit Mati and tell her of Sati's disgrace. If someone arranged for me to fight with several half-human, half-*dracklegon* soldiers, I'd be furious too. If all her new mate does is refuse visitors, then Sati has more luck than she knows, or deserves even if she won't admit it."

Relief filled Robinaranika's face. She had six years on the *Trecesalty* and always worried about them, although she didn't share their royal standing. Katiranika struggled to smile and hide the despair she actually felt. How could Satiranika forsake her sacred name and honor? The three of them participated in the soul-matching ceremony, however reluctantly, and oaths were everything to the citizens of *Trilunon*, not just the *dracklegons* who guarded and enforced their laws.

Breaking one's word meant death and not the kind that was an early departure on a *Journey to Rebirth*. *Vow-Shredders* died in the *Fires of Eternity* so they would never return and continue to dishonor their *relkinam*. Knowing the customs every child was taught in the nursery made the feat Satiranika's *Chosen* accomplished even more extraordinary. The eldest of the Trecesalty should have been roasted alive and eaten, not rescued by a *healer-mage*.

Katiranika forced herself to eat the bread and cheese on her plate, washing it down with the sweet, breakfast wine. She wouldn't touch the meat. She never did, not unless she tracked, hunted and butchered it herself. She wasn't about to eat a shape-shifter or someone turned over to the *dracklegons* for justice.

When they finished eating, she rose. "Where are my younglings? This chamber needs cleaning, as do my uniforms. I want my extra weapons sharpened too."

"Do you wish the bedding changed?"

"Why? I didn't share it with my mate. We don't know each other well enough for that, although I offered to slay him there."

"How good of you, Kat." Robinaranika shook her head ruefully. "We cannot let others know you and your *Chosen* have yet to seal your bonds. This match has been arranged since you were in the nursery."

"I've heard those words so many times I could scream." Katiranika lifted her chin. "I won't share his bed until I am ready. I mean it, Robin."

"It is always your choice, Kat."

"Then, always remember that, Sister."

21

After Astra returned from a long, hard run on the waterfront with the dogs, she showered and changed into purple, lace-trimmed pajamas. Shrugging into a matching fleece robe, she snugged the belt around her waist. "I need a drink."

The sound of her own voice surprised her. She shivered, slid narrow feet into fluffy slippers, headed for the kitchen and the small cupboard she used to store bottles of wine. It wasn't the first time she'd had sex during a witch's weekend. Still, normally she didn't limit herself to one partner. She screwed any single guy in the coven she wanted, avoiding not only the married ones but also the ones other women claimed. She rarely had more than one encounter with the same man, claiming she needed space.

She missed the nights she and Beth Chambers had squabbled over who was picking up which man at their favorite local watering-hole, Billy-Bob's Cowboy Bar. Beth was one of the few friends who understood Astra's philosophy that some women talked too much about their sex lives, enumerating previous lovers to new ones. Most guys couldn't handle it. The two of them decided when they found Mr. Right rather than Mr. Make-Do, neither would share what they knew about each other's former bed partners.

Astra heaved a sigh. When she was done, she was done since

she abhorred emotional entanglements. For all the nonsense about 'women having to be in the mood and men having to be in the room', she hadn't found that to be the case. Even when she 'hooked up' with a shifter or one of her father's disciples for a quick romp, they sniveled about wanting more than a one night stand. She usually told them to stop acting stereotypically 'girly'. She didn't want to hear it, which made her sire laugh and say she was destined to rule his kin and kingdom.

His favorite, Latham Sellers, continually pursued her although she'd repeatedly rejected him in this life. More than once, he'd called her a slut when she picked up a shifter in Corbettstown during a visit. He said she wasn't a 'cock-tease' because she always delivered, and she definitely wasn't a 'whore' since she didn't demand payment in one form or another, but only wanted her own pleasure, which rarely happened. It didn't take a rocket scientist to know he intended to hurt her feelings because he didn't think she was telling the truth about wanting someone better than him. He no longer had the power to break her heart or mind and he'd never had a claim on her soul, even in the bygone days in their old realm.

Carrying a glass of Chardonnay in one hand, the bottle in the other, she headed for the living room and her recliner. She sank into the chair, eyeing the remote on the table beside her. She decided to wait before turning on the wall-mounted flat screen. Why had she succumbed to the spell Rowindache cast? It didn't make sense. She still heard his gravelly voice insisting on promises she'd no intention of making, much less keeping.

"I, Satiranika, eldest of the Trecesalty, born to Dianaranika and Jarvesel, thirteenth witch in the Ranika relkinam give myself, soul, mind and body to Rowindache, Healer—"

Astra took a hasty swallow of the golden wine, wishing she had a confidante. Her sisters depended on her to keep them safe. She didn't dare show any vulnerability and somehow she had to live down the humiliation of Venus finding her in tears yesterday morning, another score to be settled with her so-called life-mate.

Wincing, Astra sipped more Chardonnay. Light glinted off the etched bracelet she wore and she trembled. He'd kissed her before she left and she'd told him she wouldn't return while he remained at the ranch. He'd laughed, wrapped her braid around his hand, kissed her again as if he owned her and said he'd find her when he 'wanted' her. The inflection when he drawled the word, 'wanted,' made her knees weaken and dampened her panties. *Garungap*!

She refilled the glass and picked up the remote. She'd watch a mindless TV sitcom and be grateful she'd arranged to go to the office after lunch tomorrow. She had several cases and an upcoming trial, which meant motions to prepare for the defense. Undoubtedly, the prosecuting team had sent more paperwork for her to read, study, and respond to in a timely manner. She didn't have any more hours to waste on a lower than sewer sludge wizard who didn't know his place and despite what she'd claimed, she knew she'd return to the ranch for Thanksgiving in a little more than three weeks. By then, she'd have found a way to deal with Rowindache.

She spent the next two days in a whirlwind of activity working at the law firm, eating lunch with different partners in the executive dining room, taking her dogs for long runs on the waterfront, shopping at the famed Farmer's Market below First Avenue with Rebekah. Tuesday night, Astra collapsed into her recliner, a glass of her favorite golden wine beside her on the end table. She dozed off and woke later at the sound of a low, rough male voice.

"Don't just drink your supper. Eat something, *Vaslattel* and sleep soundly in your bed even if I'm not there to share it."

She opened her eyes and saw him standing nearby, an insubstantial form in jeans, a plaid work shirt and boots. He wasn't really in the living-room of her penthouse. She'd traveled the astral planes enough to recognize it when someone else did. "I didn't invite you here, Rowindache. Leave."

"We're soul-linked, my own." He shook his head, chuckling. "I don't need a formal invitation to come to you when you're troubled or hurting."

"I'm not 'troubled or hurting'. The likes of you couldn't do either."

"Lies don't become a witch of your power. If you haven't realized it yet, I'm one of your strongest allies. I'll never harm you. Take care of yourself so you can care for others."

She felt a sudden surge of warmth before he vanished and realized he'd provided a quick dose of *Healer magick* to soothe hidden pain. She rose to her feet and headed for the kitchen to warm up the leftover Chinese food in the fridge. She'd do it to please herself, because she was hungry, not to follow any suggestions from a wizard who didn't know his place.

After eating, she took the last of her wine and strolled into the workroom. She'd study the grimoires and find a way to rid herself of this new man determined to stay in her life. She wouldn't count on anyone else, not after the fiasco that resulted when she tried to use the poisonous syrup Latham provided so many eons ago.

Over the next two days, she found herself repeating the same pattern, working to exhaustion first at the law office, then going for extra runs with the dogs and spending her evenings in the workroom, researching a new toxic spell. In bed late Thursday night, she drifted toward sleep. She felt a hand smooth her hair. "Go away, Rowindache."

"You're a stubborn witch, Satiranika. My stubborn witch." He stroked her hair again. "I've warned you not to try to kill me. Did you think I wouldn't be aware you contemplated brewing a different type of poison?"

"I haven't given it to you yet."

A low chuckle from the wraith sitting on the edge of her bed. "True enough. Come walk with me on the star-paths, my own. Let the threats wait for another day or night."

"If I go with you, it doesn't mean anything." This time she knew he kissed her forehead as if she were a child. "I'm serious."

"I know." Amusement filled his gravelly voice. "The night is ours. Let's wander it together. We'll return soon, early enough for us to sleep a few hours before dawn."

While she read responses to interrogatories in her office Friday afternoon, she remembered the astral journey the night before with

Rowindache. They'd visited the ranch so she could see the sleeping children. Edwin had moved into Quaid's room and slept in the bottom bunk while his younger brother claimed the top one.

With the children asleep upstairs, Venus practiced an elaborate sword dance in the living-room, adapting her movements to classic rock and roll pouring from the stereo as she spun from one turn to another. Astra lingered to watch the lethal moves. A favorite broadsword in her right hand, her younger sister combined karate blocks, kicks, and strikes with parries and thrusts of the steel blade, altering her pace from slow to fast, matching the music. No wonder Venus faced few challenges. Nobody wanted to lose body parts or sustain cuts and bruises in mock battles and luckily the youngest of the *Trecesalty* wasn't at war yet.

"Holt should watch this," Rowdy commented. "It takes a great deal of strength to carry a sword and move that deliberately."

"Where is he?"

"Guarding my body as the dogs guard yours." He rested a hand on her shoulder. "We want to be able to return to our forms without facing a foe."

She nodded agreement, sliding away from him. "Let's go. I want to see Meteor."

"What about the rest of your family on the ranch?"

"Estelle and her son aren't really related to me."

"Perhaps not by blood, but in their hearts they stand as mother and brother to you and your sisters. It doesn't become a queen to dismiss the devotion of her allies."

Shaking her head, Astra dismissed the memory if not the advice. She frowned at the papers on the desk. She still didn't understand why Diana Yarbro abandoned her children in this life, giving them to a friend to raise, or why Estelle Jamison agreed to pretend the triplets were hers. The two were powerful witches and the coven they led one of the most important in Washington State.

Did they truly fear Diana's demon mate? Why hadn't they severed the bonds that tied the two? Even if Diana hadn't admitted it, Astra knew her parents weren't soul-bonded. Her father shared that much during one of her visits to Corbettstown. He'd said their maternal grandmother sought aid from the Council of Elders and they arranged the match to unite powerful *magick* clans and save their realm from civil wars. According to him, rebels led by Diana's sister killed her and stole the triplets before they could walk, taking them to their aunt's castle.

So much of the past remained shrouded, affecting the present and the future. Astra couldn't yet see the truth behind the stories that her mother, foster mother, and father shared. Adding Rowindache to the maze didn't help resolve any of the puzzles. Was he trustworthy? He must have his own agenda. Did he truly intend to be an ally?

Too many questions and not enough answers. Her personal life had to wait, Astra told herself. She'd be in court next week and she had preparations to make. She narrowed her gaze on the stack of legal documents. An hour later, the intercom buzzed on her phone. She picked up the receiver. "Yes, Vonnie. What is it?"

"Tasha Endicott from the FBI is here to see you."

Her young Dawson cousin sounded way too impressed, and Astra muffled a sigh. "I have work to do and she doesn't have an appointment, or a warrant, does she?"

"No, but she's from the F.B.I."

"She still has to adhere to the law. Failing that, let's consider common courtesy. She can't just barge into my office."

"But, she's from the F.B.I."

"And you watch way too many crime dramas on television." Heaving another sigh, Astra replaced the receiver, stood, and walked across her professional sanctuary to open the door. She glanced at the dark-haired, mixed-race woman standing by the receptionist's desk. Tasha Endicott wore a navy-blue blouse with the dark-gray belted pantsuit, and Astra glimpsed a shoulder holster under her jacket.

"Good afternoon, Agent Endicott." Astra eyed the curvaceous redhead, almost quivering in the seat behind her counter desk, obviously thrilled by the visitor. "Vonnie, would you bring us coffee? Be sure to include a cup for yourself since I'll need you to take notes in case I miss any details. Tell your sister to take over the phones while you're assisting me."

The college student nearly jumped to her feet, then obviously remembered her professionalism. "I'll be right back."

"Thank you." Astra met Tasha's amused, dark gaze. "My cousin, Audra Dawson, arranged for her younger sisters to work in the office because the twins told her they want to be lawyers. They didn't believe me when I shared how boring my job is most of the time."

"Rather like being a F.B.I. agent," Tasha said. "I spend a great deal of time shuffling papers and reading reports."

"Exactly." Astra ushered the other woman into her office. "Well, pull up a chair and tell me how I can help you. Have you found Nina Armstrong or her fiancé, Kyle Morgan?"

"Not yet. We may have to use information from their interviews to locate other living witnesses. Without their bodies—"

"Gary Smith won't stand trial for their murders, much less witness tampering." Astra held the door for Vonnie as the younger woman entered, carrying a small tray with three coffee cups and a plate of shortbread cookies. "You need more evidence. I don't have much to offer. Without breaking confidentiality, I can tell you that my client feared him and thought he continued to stalk her."

"I heard that much from Detective Watkins at the Eagleville Police Department. He told me there was a fire at the rescue where Nina kept her horses. She was gone when the first responders arrived, and so were the horses. What happened to them?"

Before Astra answered, Vonnie did while she passed around the coffee cups. "My sister arranged for five of them to move to Snohomish and Elinor Killian's new pony farm before the fire. Besides that was on the trails, nowhere near Nina's barn."

Astra allowed the silence to build, wanting the federal agent to believe any admission to sound reluctant. "When he called to tell me that Kyle had been arrested for carrying a gun without the proper paperwork, I had my brother take the four remaining horses to the

Rocking J. Once I had Kyle released, he went to find Nina and I haven't seen either of them since."

Tasha nodded, waiting to hear more details, but Astra chose not to finish the story. Early on Halloween morning, she and her sisters went with Kyle to Smith's cabin between Eagleville and Corbettstown, where they found a seriously injured Nina. Astra healed Nina before the three witches used their powers to open a gateway to the past. Then, Kyle and Nina rode their two geldings and led the two mares equipped with pack saddles and their extra gear through the *Time Portal* to Liberty Valley in 1888. The federal agent would never believe *magick* existed.

"Kyle knew we'd look after their four-legged critters until he and Nina came to get them."

"I see." Tasha leaned forward to take a cookie. "If I asked to see the horses, would you show them to me?"

"Certainly, if you had a warrant," Astra said, super sweetly. "Let me know when the paperwork is in order and I'll have my sister bring the stock up from the pastures so you don't have to hike all over the ranch. I have to protect my client's interests."

"Even if nobody's seen her or her fiancé in a week and a half?"

"Even then."

The careful fencing continued as they finished their coffee, ate the cookies until Astra ushered her guest to the elevator. When she returned to her office, Astra studied her younger cousin with what she hoped was a casual gaze. "So, what did you observe?"

"She's suspicious. She thinks you know more about Nina Armstrong and Kyle Morgan than what you're saying."

Astra nodded, approving. "The sign of intelligent people is how much they agree with you. Why do you think she came here without her partner?"

"To disarm you."

"It didn't work. I've been a lawyer too many years and as the saying goes, this isn't my first rodeo."

That night, the three dogs slept in the living room. Apple wood crackled in a blaze in the fireplace. In her star-splashed robe and matching pajamas, under a multi-colored afghan that Meteor crocheted, Astra curled up on the couch ready for an evening of mindless television entertainment. She'd opted for a platter of fresh vegetables, ranch dip, a variety of crackers and cheeses for dinner, along with a bottle of wine.

She'd called Venus this afternoon, giving her youngest sister a heads-up about the F.B.I. agents who might visit the ranch to try and find Nina and Kyle's horses. Venus had pointed out it wasn't like the 'good ole days' when folks could tell equines apart. She had enough stock in the ranch remuda of fifty head to confuse the issue. One large, blaze-faced sorrel gelding, a gray mare, bay filly and battle-scarred strawberry roan looked enough like the missing horses to bamboozle any number of law enforcement officers.

Freya lifted her head, emitting a soft growl of welcome. Bamse yawned, stretched to his full height and crossed to the archway that opened into the kitchen, followed by his bigger brother. Astra tossed the blanket aside and rose, ready to defend herself. She stopped when she saw the lean, dark-haired mage petting the younger dogs. "You're still uninvited, Rowindache, so why are you here?"

He straightened, smiling at her. "Courting you is never an easy task, my own, and I've been without you too many nights."

Amused, she suppressed the urge to smile back at him. He'd traveled the way she often did, teleporting from one place to another. This time, he was real flesh and blood. She glanced past him to the mixed bouquet of gold roses and red tulips on the break-fast bar, then gestured to the living room. "You may as well join me. I'll fetch another glass."

"As I've said before, to remain alive and well, I'll share yours."

"Do I honestly frighten you?"

"Oh yes, *Vaslattel*, but what I feel for you scares me more."

22

Eagleville, Washington ~ Sunday, November 18th, 2018

TWO WEEKS LATER, SILENCE FILLED THE CAB OF THE TRUCK AS Gard and Jed headed toward Eagleville after Sunday dinner in Corbettstown. Occasionally, the cold, November rain stopped long enough for the crescent-shaped moon to peek through the clouds. The wet pavement of the winding, tree-shrouded, narrow road gleamed under the pickup's headlights and street lights at rare inter-sections.

Gard waited long enough for Jed to speak, and finally asked, "What's bothering you? We haven't seen anything or anyone acting strangely while we've worked at that new logging site. Your uncle seemed fine tonight when the whole family was at his place."

"Something's off and I'm not sure what."

"Trust your gut. What bugs you?"

"My uncle's never been without a woman as long as I've known him. He was happy to have his daughter-in-law, Junior's wife, Cherry, in charge of the pack meal tonight. Uncle Frank hasn't done that before. He's always had a woman of his own to act as a hostess. The last one was Trina Gideon, the town doctor's daughter but I haven't seen her anywhere in almost three weeks. Plus, some of the men were missing, and he wasn't concerned."

"Is it a big deal?"

"Yes. He'd have tried to kick the crap out of me if he hadn't accepted our story when we missed his *Samhain* celebration." Jed stiffened, hitting the brakes, and stopping the truck on the side of the highway. "Come on."

"What's wrong?" Gard opened the passenger door and followed the other man through the ditch and into the evergreens. He reached under his jacket, pulled out his Glock from its shoulder holster, and lowered his voice. "Are we hunting or being hunted?"

"That won't kill anyone in the pack unless you have pure silver bullets." Jed barely looked over his shoulder. "It will wound shifters, so keep it."

Gard listened and heard the howls. "Wolves?"

"Shifters. We aren't high enough in the hills for real wolves." Jed stopped, glanced at the ground and dropped to one knee, touching a dark, damp spot. "Damn it. She's losing too much blood. They'll find her before dawn."

"Who?"

"The pack. If she's not dead, she'll be punished for fleeing."

Gard glimpsed a flicker of white and touched Jed's shoulder, then pointed. "There."

Jed nodded and eased further into the dark grove. Gard followed, spotting a pale shape huddled low to the ground, trying to edge into some sort of a den under a large, fallen log. Wolves didn't usually have snow-white fur so it must be a cross-breed.

Jed removed his shirt as he approached. "We have to hide the blood and the smell or they'll track you to me."

The animal whined, a low sound, and pushed forward a duffel bag with one paw.

"Smart. You took your clothes with you." Jed wrapped his shirt around her. "We'll hope they don't use your other belongings to find you."

"It's a dog," Gard said. "It doesn't understand what you're saying and obviously it's someone's pet. We'll get it to a vet, but we can't stay here. I can hear those wolves getting closer. If you're worried about someone finding us, we need to go."

Jed chuckled, wrapping his shirt around the injured creature's leg before he lifted it into his arms. "He's learning, but he's been with the humans too long. A vet won't help her. We need a *healer* and luckily I know a good one."

At the truck, Gard opened the back door to the super-cab. Jed carefully placed the wolf-hybrid on the narrow seat, covering her with a blanket. Then he picked up the gas can.

"You're not setting the woods on fire, are you?"

"No, of course not. I'm a shifter and a logger. I love the forest more than most. I need to hide the smell and a little of this will do the job." He gazed at the white wolf. "Remain as you are and that will start the healing. Gard, call my mate and tell her to ward my truck and us so nobody realizes we stopped between Corbettstown and Eagleville."

Gard found himself reaching for his cell phone as the other man disappeared in the direction of the trees. "This place gets weirder and weirder. His mate? Why doesn't he just call Meteor Jamison, his girlfriend? What does he think she can do?"

Lying on the bench, the wolf tilted its head, eying him with oddly light blue eyes. A soft, feminine voice echoed inside Gard's head. *'The witch will do as Jed bids and cloak us.'*

Gard gaped at the animal. "I didn't hear that. What's going on?"

'There are none so deaf as those who refuse to hear, or as blind as those who won't see.' The wolf turned its head, licked the blood from the wound on its shoulder. *'Call the witch.'*

Gard stared at the wolf, barely hearing footsteps crunch on the gravel. He glanced over his shoulder and saw Jed. "She talks."

"Of course, she does. She's a woman." Jed put the can in the truck bed behind the cab. "The only one I've ever known who doesn't is mine. Did you call her?"

"Not yet. I will now."

———

Humming along with the Christmas music filling the air from the classic country radio station, Brigid Dawson slid three more pumpkin pies into one of the ovens in the big kitchen. Once she'd closed the pony farm and taken care of all the livestock that afternoon, she'd driven up to Eagleville to do the kind of work she'd preferred. The catering company only hosted a few Thanksgiving celebrations, but Meteor and her partners made up the difference by providing prepared holiday dinners. That meant Brigid switched over from creating cakes to baking different kinds of pies.

She glanced at her older sister, Audra, who'd arrived to celebrate the holiday with their family and offered to help so they could gossip at the same time. The two of them emailed, texted and talked regularly on the phone, but it wasn't the same since Audra came out of her writing closet, proudly proclaiming her identity as bestselling, erotic romance author, Destynee LaFleur.

Because she'd moved to Eastern Washington a few months before, she didn't have to deal with their mother's disdain for her creative endeavors, or their younger sisters' daily dramas which often included criticizing Audra's appearance and actions since the petite brunette looked more like their gambling addicted father than the rest of the red-haired, statuesque Dawson clan. Tonight, she still wore the faded blue jeans and a bright red Washington State University sweatshirt, she said were her 'dressing for success' writing uniform.

Her new husband, Joe Watkins, a professor who taught veterinary medicine, the dean of his department at the Pullman campus, was handling emergency calls for his father's clinic today and met them in Eagleville. He'd been put to work with Tolliver. Joe didn't act as if schlepping cases of wine from the cellar was anything but a lark. He'd said that he hoped he'd learn the recipe for the punch that Tolliver made for parties, but Meteor only laughed and told Joe not to get his hopes up because her partner kept the ingredients of his brews a secret.

Wrinkling her nose, brown eyes amused, Audra gazed at the jars of mincemeat mixture she'd carried out of the large cooler and put on the counter. "I can't believe anyone actually likes this kind of pie. I never understood why you insist on serving it at our dinners at the Lazy B."

"Uncle Will always asks for it." Brigid carefully lined the next pie pan with the last piece of homemade crust. "It helped me get my job here. It thrilled Meteor when I explained that our family recipe combines different kinds of meat and fruit. I age it for at least two weeks before preparing the pies and Cherry Corbett ordered ten of them."

"What's the big deal?"

"Your sister does *magick* in the kitchen," Meteor said, as she entered, "and I'll always be grateful you sent her to me for training in witchly arts. Gard Devlin called, and he's on the way here with Jed. Where are the cleansing herbs? They need them to wash Jed's pickup."

"In the special pantry." Brigid turned away from the island counter where she'd set up the ingredients to make pie crust. "Let me wash up and I'll get them. Audra, will you cut the next pound of chilled butter into cubes?"

"Sure, if you tell me what herbs are used for cleaning."

"It depends on the type of wards you intend to set." Meteor opened a cupboard, removing several bottles of distilled water. "This is to keep anyone from discovering that Jed rescued an injured shifter who escaped the pack enforcer's justice, or as Astra says, injustice."

"Wait a minute." Audra lowered the knife she'd just picked up, placing it on the counter. "Are you trying to tell me there really are werewolves in Eagleville?"

"No, there's a pack in Corbettstown and they prefer their wolf shapes when they shift. We talked about this before when you wanted to use my sisters and me in one of your books, Destynee. There's a reason why my mother calls you the *Bard*."

"You told me you wanted total freedom of shape." Audra frowned, folding her arms. She tilted her head to one side as she obviously took the time to recall a conversation from months before. "You could be anything from a wolf to a cat to a bear to an eagle. Was that for real?"

"Of course. As my mother and aunt taught me when I was a child, lies don't become a witch and they always rebound three-fold."

"Astra told me she wanted 'wild, raunchy sex' with a bunch of hot guys. Did she get that in real life, or was it just in my book?"

"Her romps with shifters, the pack enforcer's crew, and those she picked up at Billy Bob's on Friday nights ended at *Samhain*. Her soul-matched wizard doesn't share."

"Wait a second." Audra ran a hand through her short, brown hair. "Are there really wizards?"

Brigid laughed. "I don't believe you, Audra. You should know if you have sexy witches, you need their male counterparts. Now, wash your hands and cut up the butter for me. We have work to do, and you can interview Meteor later."

"All right. All right." Audra took a deep breath. "What about Venus? Has she 'clouted' her hero with a broadsword yet? Does she even have one?"

"Well, she has several, but the one she uses most often is known as an 'arming' sword. It has a heavy, double-edged blade about thirty inches long and she likes the grip because she can use it either on horseback or on the ground. As far as I know, she hasn't chal-lenged her 'hero' yet. She never takes any guy to her 'salon' and only people in the *Craft* or who ride in renaissance reenactments willing to spend big bucks realize she trains horses for combat."

"Excuse you," Brigid started for the pantry. "The butter is getting warm, Audra, and I don't want to chill it again. My crust doesn't wait for anyone and I have several pies to finish tonight."

"Okay, okay. I'm stepping up here. We're not finished, Meteor. I have a lot to learn that needs to be incorporated into my stories."

"Undoubtedly. You are the *Bard*, after all, and you want to know the truth before you tell it." Meteor glanced over her shoulder when the doorbell rang. "That's probably my aunt. She was stopping at the ranch to pick up Rowdy. You'll be polite and wait until they finish *Healing* the shifter before you question them."

"Definitely, but can I watch?"

"Only if you prepare the butter first. I don't want to deal with a kitchen witch's ire."

"Because you know you'll lose." Smiling, Brigid went into the pantry, crossing to the adjacent room where they kept herbs, spices along with the various syrups, elixirs and powders derived from plants, grasses and flowers. She didn't know all the uses for the remedies yet, but allowed what Meteor referred to as her 'third', or 'soul' eye and what Brigid thought of as intuition to guide her to the appropriate shelves and the jars she needed.

"There's more to do tonight than *Healing*." Rowdy glanced at the older woman who'd come to fetch him in one of the newfangled wagons that moved without horses or oxen. A tall, stately woman, she dressed appropriately in a sunset blue gown. Bright red hair coiled in braids around her head didn't show a hint of gray. "At some point, you and I will have to come to terms about your eldest daughter. She's still torn between what she hears from her father, her aunt and you."

"He's a demon who lies when the truth would serve. Now, that you, Holt, and Jed are together with my daughters and can serve as the *chapalmatands* Estelle and I chose to protect them, I'll ask the *Dracklegon* Council for my freedom. Be warned. It will enrage Jarvesel."

"And you rightly fear him, but as your new son, it is my duty and pleasure to guard you. I know Holt and Jed will aid me."

Rowdy saw tears fill her eyes and one streak down her cheek before she blinked hard, then focused on the road ahead of them, driving toward a cluster of lights on the horizon. "Didn't you expect this when you arranged the match with your eldest child, Mother?"

"No, I didn't, Rowindache. I just wanted my baby girl to be safe. Her father has killed me more than once, and this is the longest I've lived in any incarnation, perhaps because my friends and I have struggled to guard my daughters from him. He wants to slay them in his blood magick rites the way he did before so he can steal their *Powers*."

"It's beyond time for his evil reign to end. My children will need their grandmother to give them their first wands and teach them *magick*."

"I look forward to doing so." A smile slowly formed on Diana's lips. "You'll have to get Astra's permission. I've made mistakes, and she has much to forgive."

"We all err in different ways. Only the *Goddess* and her consorts are perfect." Rowdy gazed out the window as the town spread before them. Houses, shops, and well-lit businesses lined the streets. "This place is larger than some of the cities I visited."

"And Eagleville is considered small by our standards." Diana parked in front of a two-story house, the headlights picking up a bright mural of various animals frolicking on the structure as well as huge letters spelling out 'Captivating Catering'. "Have you been to Meteor's place before?"

"Not yet. She promised to set wards on the doors to keep whoever stalked her in previous lives away." Rowdy opened his door. "I created wind-chimes as well as amulets to protect her and Thojedescar from the one who steals his shape. We'll do the *Protection Rites* after the healing."

Diana inclined her head in agreement. "I'll gather our things."

Rowdy waited while another vehicle parked next to the one Diana drove. He nodded a greeting when Gard slid out of the passenger side. "And the injured creature?"

"In the back." Gard lowered his voice. "She talked to me. In my head. Nobody has ever done that before."

Rowdy smiled, gripped his friend's shoulder for a moment. "I removed the blocks on your memories, but you'll also find new talents emerge."

Gard glanced around the parking area warily before opening the rear door to the blue pickup. "What are they?"

"Warrior arts. Ask Thojedescar because my *magick* is that of a *Healer-Mage* and differs from yours." Rowdy eyed the injured white wolf lying on the seat, seeing the bloody gash on her shoulder and torn paws. "What happened to you?"

'His minions brought my captor a new guest. I was sent to prepare food because my new owner enjoys torturing for hours and likes certain appetizers and wines while he performs evil acts. When the fools in charge of me left me alone, I escaped.'

"After she undressed, packed her clothes in a gym bag, broke a window and shifted, running through broken glass, using her blood to lay several false trails." Admiration filled Jed's tone. "Once she's healed, I want her as one of the officers in my new pack. She brought the bag with her."

"Was it his? If so, he'll use it to track her."

'Not my first rodeo, cowboy. I smuggled the bag into the kitchen days ago when I first began cooking. I scrubbed all the floors, walls, furnishings, the bathrooms, and everything I touched with cleaners, including the linens and rugs. I poured bleach down the drains too.'

Rowdy gathered the wolf into his arms, preparing to carry her inside. "Why did he allow such behavior when it'd prevent him from keeping you?"

'I did most of it when his duties distracted him from using me in his bed. I told the idiots guarding me that the stench of puke, crap, and urine from former victims in the house offended me because I'm a female shifter. Their blood, meat and bones made me hungry enough to hunt my captor's slaves even if I was punished and suffered for it after killing and eating them, since my new owner thought I should 'lose weight' and kept me on a strict diet. So, they

believed the fairytales I conjured for them and allowed this 'lowly female' to clean.'

Rowdy started toward the house. "And they never doubted you?"

'Why would they? Pack women are only allowed to cook, clean, breed and bring forth more male children. The idea a mere female would lie to suit her own ends and plot to escape was beyond their comprehension.'

23

METEOR HELD OPEN THE FRONT DOOR AS AUNT DIANA AND ROWDY came toward her, the man carrying a white wolf in his arms. Jed Corbett and Gard Devlin followed, flanking them. "Daphne and Brigid have what you need to cleanse the truck so nobody discovers what you've done tonight."

"Afterwards, I want to return to see how she does." Jed paused on the doorstep. "Will you allow that?"

"It'd be helpful if you did," Rowdy said, his tone even, his gaze meeting Meteor's. "Diana and I wish to set up wards so we're fore-warned when someone steals his shape to commit evil and tries to harm you."

Meteor nodded, trying to hide the inner excitement that always coiled inside her when Jed approached. "All right, but first take care of the pickup."

"Does it require both of us, or can I do it on my own?" Gard stood beside Jed. "He'll be safe enough here with all of you."

"But that leaves nobody to watch your back, Gardersolter," Rowdy said. "Go with him, Thojedescar. The shifters will hesitate to attack him if you're there and his death again at their hands would devastate Robin."

'What does my little sister have to do with him?

Meteor rested her hand on the wolf's head, blocking the men from overhearing the answer. *'She blames herself because he died trying to save her back in the day and the last thing he saw was the beginning of her torture.'*

'Someone should tell her that wasn't her fault, but my would-be owner's.'

"No one truly owns a shifter and I've told her more than once, but it will take time for her to believe it. You can help with that.'

'And I will.'

"It sounds like we need to heal more than your body, Trina, or the pack alpha and the enforcer will find you." Diana shifted the box in her arms. "I haven't been here since you remodeled. Where is your work-room, Meteor?"

"I tried moving it, but discovered I still preferred the 'she-shed' in the back yard." Meteor saw Brigid and Daphne and gestured for them to take over with Jed and Gard. Once they did, it was time to proceed to the hallway that bypassed the kitchen.

Joe Watkins came up the stairs from the basement, carrying a case of wine. He stopped when he saw them, his gaze sweeping over them, then locking on the injured wolf. "What happened? I'll get my bag from my truck."

"Not needful," Meteor told him, signaling for Tolliver to step up and distract the veterinarian. "My aunt and brother by marriage will handle putting Trina back together."

"I don't think so." Joe narrowed summer-blue eyes. "Your pet obviously has a broken leg and without X-rays, I can't tell if she's cracked the shoulder blade, or if it's just swollen from abuse." He passed the box to Tolliver and approached Rowdy. "Don't let her bite me."

'I won't unless you hurt me. Then, all bets are off.'

"Be nice." Meteor stroked the top of Trina's head. "He's mated to the *Bard* and you don't want her telling your story."

"I never get used to your family calling her that." Joe gently probed the gash on the shoulder, removing a fragment of glass and turning it over in his hand. "Your wolf-dog must have jumped out a window, but I didn't see any broken ones here. Was it a car?"

"No, someone tried to steal her," Meteor said. "She broke out of his house and came home."

"Lucky, she didn't bleed out. There's more glass and at least one of the pieces is close to an artery."

'I'd rather be dead than his play-thing and I don't want to bear his spawn.'

'I'll make sure that doesn't happen. Rowindache, let's have the animal healer help us. Trina will be able to remain in this shape longer, which aids in her mending. After he leaves, we'll go to the work-room and we'll be able to help her shift back.'

'Agreed, Mother. Find a place for us to look after your 'pet,' Sister, one away from where you do magick.'

Meteor nodded, then turned slightly to open the door to the distillery where Tolliver created beverages for their enterprise. She flicked a quick glance at her partner, a stocky, short man in jeans and a sweatshirt, appreciating the way he nodded agreement and didn't say what he'd heard during the silent conversation. Half satyr, he'd enjoyed October when he didn't have to disguise his pointed ears, or horns, or furry legs and hooves. Now, he had to suppress his true nature when strangers were around.

Rowdy carried Trina over to the stainless steel table and lowered her onto its gleaming surface. "Let's begin with cleaning her."

"Give me your keys, Doctor Joe, and I'll fetch your bag," Tolliver said.

"I'll go with you," Joe said. "I need sedatives as well as antibiotics, and those are locked in the back. I'm glad I brought the rig from the clinic instead of going back for my Jeep."

Trina looked after the two when they left. *'You're not letting him give me any drugs, are you?'*

"Of course not." Diana passed a glass bowl to Meteor. "Warm water and I'll add witch hazel to it. He's accustomed to animals, my dear Trina, and you can play the part. Rowindache is right. Better to avoid questions and if you shift now, it will be too big a shock for your system as well as startling the guests who don't need to know all our secrets."

———

The Wednesday before Thanksgiving meant a long day in court. It'd exhausted her, but she'd made several good points and enraged the last witness, an experienced law enforcement detective, leaving that impression with the jury before the extended break. She didn't blame the man for his momentary loss of control on the stand. He'd viewed the bloody crime scene and had to go to the hospital to interview her client's badly injured former boyfriend. Astra counted on the jurors holding the police officer to a higher standard than she did. She always remembered the cops were human beings too and cleaning up the messes others made took its own toll.

Her client was home for the holiday weekend. She'd reminded him to behave appropriately for the next four days since being arrested in a brawl with his family would create a bad impression when the trial continued on Monday and the jury would certainly hear about it from the prosecutor. She parked her car, collected her briefcase and started toward the elevator, coming to a halt when she saw Latham.

As usual, he wore a dark three-piece suit, but dirt and mud marred the pants. Someone tore one of the jacket sleeves and she spotted dried blood on his shirt and his arm. By the way he cradled the other arm against his side, she suspected his assailant cracked the bone and broke his ribs. Dark bruises covered his face. "What happened? Who hurt you?"

"Your father."

"You're one of his favorites. You have been since our days in *Trilunon* when he chose you as his novice. You're still more important to him than I am. How did you offend him?"

Impatience glittered in the reptile-green eyes. "Why is that important?"

She shrugged. "It's not my prime concern, but it should be

yours. If he remains angry, you won't get off with a beating the next time he sees you. He'll skin you and make your *dracklegon* hide into new boots. It won't do any good for me to try to intercede for you." She kept her tone calm. "Or do you plan to use me to make amends the way you've done in more than one of my lives?"

"It won't work unless you know where the female shifter is that the alpha gave him at *Samhain*. Your father wants her back and blames me and his deputies for her escape."

"You were stupid to try and steal his reward from Frank Corbett. My demon-father serves the pack well and rarely receives any recognition. I don't blame him for being upset. I have no idea who she is or where she is, or what you've done with her."

"If I'd taken her, she'd be with me, but she isn't. When he turned me loose a few hours ago, he gave me until tomorrow noon. If she isn't in his home to attend the pack dinner with him, he'll imprison me along with his other minions, and change us into prey. We'll be hunted and the alpha will roast us at *Yule*."

"And what happens to her?"

"I don't know and I don't care." Latham took an angry step forward. "He claims he'll collar and leash her so she learns to respect and obey him. He can drag her to Thanksgiving dinner in her wolf shape. I didn't die for you and I'm not dying for some female I don't know."

Astra shuddered at the idea, feeling a wave of sympathy for the unknown woman, and tightened her grip on the briefcase. "I can't help you."

"You must."

"No. I don't owe you or my demon-father anything." She lifted her chin. "I've rejected you several times in this life. Perhaps, you'll listen tonight. I'm done being one of your blood sacrifices. Be gone and don't return."

He advanced on her. "I'll make you listen."

"I've heard all I want to hear. Go!" Growls erupted from the staircase and out of the corner of her eye, she glimpsed the three dogs loping toward her. How had they gotten out of her apartment?

Had Rebekah seen the confrontation when she brought them back from their evening walk and turned them loose? The dogs surrounded her, Freya standing sentinel between Astra and Latham while the two males took up positions flanking their mother.

Latham fell back one step, then another, continuing to glare at her. "Jealous over a mere shifter? You know she means nothing to me."

"And I never did either." She glanced over her shoulder at the sound of a man's booted footsteps. An odd relief swept through her when she saw Rowdy coming towards them, a lethal figure in dark clothes, before she focused on Latham again. "How long did you think it'd take me to realize I was merely a convenient tool the pair of you used at my demon-father's whims?"

Latham gaped at Rowdy. "You're here?"

"As you see." Rowdy rested a hand on Astra's shoulder. "We stand together and if someone hadn't already beaten you, I would demand justice tonight. However, I'll give you time to heal before we meet. I'll send the challenge to the Council and your *relkinam*. As the injured party, I choose swords. I hope you still have yours."

"He does." Astra stepped closer to him, feeling the solid warmth of his body. Obviously, he was really present, not merely walking astral paths as he had over the last three weeks during many of his visits. "I've renounced him more than once in this life, but he still pursues me for his own dreaded purposes. He's practiced for this day because he always feared you."

"As anyone should who comes between soul-matched mates."

"I only did what she wanted." Latham narrowed his eyes. "She told me to kill you. She was the one who said to give you to the shifters for fresh meat time after time."

"Lies. All lies." She stiffened in fury. "You gave me poison to put in the wine for him. If I murdered him instead of accepting him as my mate, you promised we'd be together and have the soul-matching ceremony of my dreams. Another falsehood."

Latham stared at her, obviously shocked. "How do you know this?"

"Do you think I'm stupid?" She lifted her chin and glared at him. "You and my demon-father plotted to slay me before we ever left *Trilunon*. None of us expected Rowindache to survive, follow and save me not only from the *dracklegons*, but also from the two of you in my first life. He wasn't there to rescue me from your blood sacrifices in my second and third lives. I killed you before you killed me in my fourth life. Luckily my mother and aunt saved me in this life, or you'd have slain me when I was a child.

"You're prevaricating and you fully know witches may not bear false witness without offending their *Goddess*." Latham took an angry step toward her. "He'd have been dead if you'd actually used what I provided."

"She told you to go." Rowdy gestured toward the exit and the street traffic beyond the garage. "Do you require an escort?"

More growls from the dogs and Freya bared gleaming teeth. A muffled curse came before Latham wheeled and stalked away. Astra watched, then met Rowdy's gaze. "Despite what he claims, I never ordered him to harm you."

"I know that now." He kissed her forehead. "I told you not to lie to me, *Vaslattel*, when we repeated our vows and you haven't."

"When I kill you, I'll do it myself and I'll brew my own poisons, too. I won't serve anyone else's purposes ever again."

"As befits a queen." He guided her toward the stairs, the three dogs leading the way. "Tomorrow morning is soon enough for your mischief. Let me have tonight with my mate."

"Not if I have to climb to the penthouse." She laughed and swung back to the elevator, signaling for Freya and her sons to join them. "I won't have enough energy to enjoy you, Rowindache. We'll arrive my way."

24

Seattle, Washington ~ Wednesday, November 22ⁿᵈ, 2018

WHILE SHE BATHED AND CHANGED, HE POURED WINE AND CHECKED the meal Rebekah prepared. She'd called it a Yankee Pot Roast. Although he wasn't familiar with the name, he recognized the vegetables she peeled, carrots, onions, and potatoes. When she chopped celery into small pieces, he seared the beef roast, then created gravy with its drippings along with a few other ingredients, amusing her when he included two cups of freshly brewed, strong coffee.

He'd explained that on the range, they'd eaten everything they hunted and most of the meat was tougher than boot leather. When he was a boy, he'd been hired on as a 'hoodlum' or cook's helper on one of his first cattle drives. The old *cocinero*, chuck-wagon cook taught him that coffee broke down the fibers and made any cut of venison, or elk, or beef tender. Even after he learned to rope and work stock, he still enjoyed helping with camp chores.

He'd spent most of the afternoon with Rebekah once Diana dropped him at the building. His mother by marriage said he didn't need to use *magick* to travel here. Other means were available and at some point, she'd teach him to drive one of the newfangled machines she called a car. After seeing the large numbers of them on the highway and the streets in this huge city, he still preferred his horse.

During the afternoon, Rebekah reminded him to call her the name she had in this life instead of her *Trilunon* one. She taught him how to use the fancy five-burner stove, the ovens, the lights, the view-screen she'd called a TV. She'd set the table with lovely china, white candles in silver holders, the flowers he'd brought from the ranch and showed him where Astra kept her wine. He'd explored the entire loft but hadn't tried opening the door to the work-room where his mate practiced her *magick*. He'd wait to be invited.

He filled two glasses with red wine. He turned, held one out to her when she approached, pure beauty in a black and silver gown with alternating blocks of shimmering color, silver in an inverted 'V' that emphasized her curves and hugged a slender waist. Red-gold hair hung in a shining curtain to her hips. His jewelry provided the only ornamentation she needed. "You're ravishing."

"And your arrival surprised me." She smiled, taking the glass. "Why did you come?"

"To see Robinaranika." He sipped his own wine. "Her shifter sister, Trina, asked me to ward her."

"How do you know Trina?"

He picked up the bottle, led the way to the sitting area and the small table where he'd placed a tray of meats, cheeses and slices of the homemade bread sent by Brigid. "That's a long tale best shared here and now before we eat supper."

"I'm listening." She sank into a chair, curling bare feet under her skirt. "Tell your story, *Capostrol*."

Hours later, they lay in her wide bed while she brushed kisses over his forehead, eyebrows, and cheeks, bypassing his mouth, reciting her own count. At a hundred and fifty, she'd explored his chest, nipples, arms and even sucked on his fingers. They'd already had sex twice, so he didn't lose control when her lips trailed downward. She avoided the area he expected her to claim and kissed his leg. He clenched his fists to keep himself from dragging her mouth where he wanted it. He felt sweat beads pop on his forehead.

The kisses continued. She sat up between his legs and looked at him. "Two hundred and thirty. You're a stubborn mage, Rowindache."

So hard he ached for her, he met the smile with his. "You can stop at any time, Satiranika. I will only tease you a little."

She tilted her head to one side as she considered the idea, then shook her head. "No. I'm having fun tonight and tomorrow we'll be at the ranch for Thanksgiving. I don't know if or where we'll find a place to make love. You, Edwin, and Hugh will share the bunkhouse while Meteor and I stay at the house. I mean, I'm not sure where we can have sex while I'm there."

"I heard you the first time." He grinned at her. "Before *Yule*, you'll admit how much you care for me."

"And then I'll cut out your heart." Her tone remained amused. "For the moment, you entertain me. I'll keep you until I'm bored."

"I'll stick and stay regardless." He eased the tight rein he kept on himself. "It's part of my vows to you, *Vaslattel*. I protect my witch, my queen, and do what she desires, but she serves my needs as I demand."

"My *capostrol*, but I'm not his slave. Nor is he mine." She ran her fingers up his right leg. "You don't own me anymore than I own you. We're together because we choose to be and I repeated the oaths of my volition."

"You say that now, although you wouldn't admit it at *Samhain*." He measured the sincerity on her face. "We'll still battle as part of our mating dance, but we can remember this courtship as a special time."

"Definitely and now I'll finish my kisses." She smiled, lowered her head and tormented him with quick, butterfly touches of her lips.

Her tongue stroked him and he shuddered. He couldn't wait. In a moment, he'd embarrass himself, spill his seed like a boy. "Enough.

You win." He leaned forward, caught her waist, pulled her toward him. "Your turn to ride, Witch. Take me."

"I only reached two hundred and forty," she protested. "I have more kisses to count. We settled on three hundred, remember?"

"Not right now."

She smiled and lifted herself above his hips. She descended slowly, impaling herself, inch by inch, as if intending to continue the torture.

"I can't wait." He lost patience. "Take your victory." He grasped her hips, brought her down on him. Buried in her heat, he urged her to move, directing the motion.

She paused, rested a moment. "If I win, then I set the pace."

"Do it. Please."

"Just remember, you asked for it."

This time she began the movements, sliding up and down. He struggled to allow her to keep control, to determine how fast she'd go. She moved quicker, leaned down to kiss him, her nipples brushing his chest. He felt her tighten around him, knew she was close, but couldn't wait any longer. He rolled on top of her, took both of them flying to the stars as he increased the pace of his thrusts.

Afterwards, she lay half on top of him, her breaths ragged. "You cheated. It was my turn to be in charge."

"Perhaps, next time will be different, but I'm not sure." He stroked her hair, straightening the tumbled, hip-length mane. "You're too enticing."

"Enticing. Ravishing." Her lips teased his for a moment. "Tell me more. I like your words. You make me feel beautiful."

"Hasn't anyone ever told you that you are?"

When she shook her head, he drew her down for a long, slow kiss. "Then you've been surrounded by fools. I won't make that mistake, *Vaslattel*."

"Will you make others?"

"Undoubtedly." He framed her face with his hands. "And I trust you'll point them out to me."

She laughed. Delight shone in her dark blue eyes when she mocked him. "Undoubtedly."

———

He'd taken the dogs for their morning jaunt along the waterfront, leaving her to create breakfast. Since she'd be gone for a long week-end, she opted to clean the perishables out of the refrigerator and use them in a frittata. She'd just started chopping up the leftover pota-toes from the roast when someone knocked on her door. It wouldn't be her *Chosen* because she'd provided him with a key. She wiped her hands and went to answer.

Rebekah stood outside. "Good morning."

"You have a key so you can look after my dogs," Astra said, eying her apprentice. The younger woman had already dressed for the holiday in dark blue slacks and a blue-green tunic sweater. She'd opted for low-heeled boots, a concession to the ranch visit where the ground could be uneven. "Why didn't you use it?"

"I didn't want to intrude on you and your mate."

"No intrusion. Come in. How is your sister?" Astra turned and led the way back to the kitchen. "Have you spoken to her?"

"On the phone last night before she shifted again. She's staying with Meteor and they'll meet us at the Rocking J today."

Astra pointed to the fresh fruit waiting on the counter. "Make a salad while you tell me why she's shifting when there isn't a full moon."

"Because she feels powerless as a woman since Frank gave her to the enforcer."

"And what did my demon father do to her? Did he rape her?"

"She says, no. He kissed her at *Samhain* and she pushed him away, biting his tongue the first time. He continued to corner her in the dining room, the study and kitchen, and kept kissing her. She said he didn't act like an old man and couldn't believe he was able to pack her upstairs, thrown over his shoulder like some kind of battle prize."

"She's a shifter. She could have broken loose at any moment." Astra added onion to the baking dish. "She must have gone willingly, right?"

"Yes. She said she knew she shouldn't be with him because Frank had chosen her last Beltane, but the alpha just used her and was really lousy in the sack."

"Please tell me she was smart enough to keep that to herself."

"Well, she told me and Cherry and some of her other friends to count their blessings that he didn't pick them. All she wanted for her birthday was a new vibrator unless he kicked her out before March since she didn't have a single orgasm with him in the past five months."

"Wow, I hope that doesn't get back to him. No man wants to hear he's a total bungler in bed and botches it, especially the leader of a shifter pack." Astra added the last of the roast beef to the pan, then chopped cooked bacon and pieces of ham. "So, what did she say about my demon-father?"

"He was different. She gave me way too many details about what he did. Your father told her he was having her for dessert when she brought him a late supper and went down on her. She struggled then, mostly because she was afraid of what Frank would do, but nobody heard her yelling or saw her fighting Marvin although the house was full of shifters. I said he'd cast a spell to maintain silence around them, but she doesn't believe he's a mage."

"I've told you before that he's a warlock, not a wizard, because he prefers evil," Astra said. "There are several reasons why my mother, my aunt, and I call him a demon. When he had her, he ensured your sister enjoyed it too, didn't he?"

"Yes, every time. Afterwards, she went with him all weekend, although she always struggled if any of the shifters might see them. She was happy when he arranged for her to be with him and got her out of Frank's house, but she didn't tell either of them that."

"Good choice. If going with my demon-father was consensual, what's the problem?"

"She realized something was wrong when she didn't fight him.

He didn't want tenderness, and was appalled when she told him she might fall in love with him, mocking her feelings. He prefers sex to be violent so he can conquer his bed-mate."

"He draws more *Power* that way and essentially drains his partner of all her life energies through sex." Astra began grating cheese. "She outwitted his minions and fled. That will pique his interest. If he thought he'd broken her will, he'd start planning how to get rid of her body when he finished her off, because he hates emotions. Now, he'll decide everything she did and said was to aid her escape from him and the pack. She intended to trick him and since she succeeded, he'll be furious."

Standing at the counter, Rebekah shuddered. "Fooling a demon isn't something I'd want to do."

"Because you know the repercussions will be hellish." Astra poured the beaten egg mixture over her concoction, then topped the dish with the cheese. "By now, he believes she truly loathes him. He won't realize she may be heartsick and feel she made a fool of herself. The hatred will intrigue him more. It's why he beat Latham into the ground and threatened him. My father normally considers the outcomes of all his actions long before he strikes, but this time he lost it."

Rebekah relaxed slightly and picked up the paring knife to peel the cantaloupe. "So, what are you going to do?"

"Well, Rowindache and our mother already healed her body. Meteor will help heal her spirit. I'll ask Venus to teach her to use weapons, especially a sword. The exercise will be good and heal her mind. Trina needs to be ready to protect herself from him and the wards on the ranch will disguise her."

"She's very proud. She won't agree to hide from him even if we think it is the best action for her to take."

"What if we ask her to help Venus guard the children?" Astra slid the baking dish into the oven. "According to Rowindache, someone has been killing their parents in every life and we still don't know who."

"That's a good idea, and she'd do it in a heartbeat. She rages whenever the alpha begins sorting the younglings in the pack. It's why she and Cherry decided to stop the birthing of new babies until the killing ends." Rebekah sliced chunks of melon into the bowl. "Fallyn is especially at risk from the Corbetts and your father, since she's a budding *Animal-Healer*."

"What?" Astra froze, dread sweeping through her body. "How do you know?"

"I saw her at *Samhain* talking to all the animals at the balefires. Some might think she is destined to follow in her mother's paw-prints, but that's not quite true. Fallyn will probably be able to shift like her brothers, but her strongest gift will be closer to mine or Rowdy's. She'll be a *healer-mage* like us."

25

IN THE PAST FEW WEEKS, JED DREAMED MORE THAN HE HAD IN years, but the majority of those memories were of his last life with Meteor. He'd met her while doing business with shapeshifters in Texas. It'd taken almost a year to win her heart, and she'd finally married him. She hadn't wanted to go to Washington Territory, but he couldn't refuse to obey the summons sent by the alpha of his own pack, so they'd reluctantly moved to Corbett's Town where Edwin was born a few months later.

This time was different. Somehow, he was remembering where he'd first met her so many lives ago. Jed recognized the chamber where she lay sleeping, her features waxen and breathing shallow. She lived, but only by sheer will. Her lashes fluttered and her eyes opened. She reached for the glass of watered wine on the table next to the large bed. Her hand shook. "Where is Robinaranika? I need her."

"I sent her to rest. Let me help you instead." He sat on the edge of the bed and held the jeweled gold goblet to her lips. "If you still desire the *High Healer*, I'll have a messenger go to her chamber and wake her."

"No." Matiranika leaned back against the pillows. "Let her

sleep. She comes often enough. It will be hard on her when I die. She'll blame herself although she's done her best."

He nodded, placing the cup back on the table. "You fell asleep before your *healer* and I finished talking. I am your *chapalmatand*. What affects you, affects me." He brushed his mouth over hers in a whisper of a kiss. "And mayhap, the other way around, *Laspowima*."

"Do that again." She lifted her hands, rested them against his chest. "Please."

"Do what? Kiss you?" He touched her lips with his. "Why?"

"This *Sex Magick* makes me feel stronger." She slid her arms around his neck, pressed closer. "Kiss me again."

"Let's see what a real one can do." His mouth claimed hers with a long, slow tenderness, promising all she could ever want from him. When he finally lifted his head, he saw a new brightness in her light blue eyes. "I think you'll have more energy after we truly unite."

She frowned in sudden concern, but didn't appear frightened. "I won't be raped. I choose what I give and I'm not giving myself to a *Warpathian*."

He smiled, kissed her brows, the long eyelashes and then the tip of her nose. "You'll choose me, my love. I enjoy a woman who wants me."

"I don't care what you enjoy." She sighed as he kissed the hollow of her throat. "I've sworn by the *Goddess* that you won't have me unless you take me by force."

"I've never forced a woman and I never will." He smiled and nipped her ear. "I'll wait until you beg me to take you. After you ask seven times, then I'll have my queen."

"Never." She threaded her fingers in his hair. "Your kisses are enough to heal me, *Warpathian*. With those, you can't make me beg you for anything."

He chuckled, trailed a line of kisses along her neck. "Wait and see, my own. It all depends on where I kiss you."

"It won't matter. I still won't beg. I'm one of the *Trecesalty*."

"You are also my *Chosen*." He eased his hand into the loose collar of her robe and parted it so he could kiss the rise of her small breast. "With the *Trilunon Nine-Time Kiss*, I can teach you to want me."

"First, you would have to explain what such a kiss entails." She nipped his ear. "My match with an *Amalodian* wizard ended when he died in the first wave of the plague before the *dracklegon* priest performed the sacred rites. My aunt arranged that marriage as well, and I was never alone with my promised mate, or any other male."

He stopped, measured the honesty on her face. "You are untouched? I don't deserve such a treasure, especially when I cannot offer the same."

"I may not be your first woman, but I am your last." She flicked her tongue into his ear. "If my aunt didn't tell you when she ordered the sacrifice of your heart, mind, body, and soul, I'm telling you now, a true *chapalmatand* never strays from his mate's nest."

"An interesting choice of words." He bent his head, captured her mouth in a quick, fierce kiss. "Nest, not bed? The Ranika *relkinam* has *Ethlestial* ties?"

"My sire was a priest-mage of the *dracklegons*." She bit his ear again. "Another secret of my aunt's?"

"Probably not, but I never expected to have a queen for my mate. What happens if I stray from your nest?"

"The same that would happen to any other female *dracklegon's* soul-match. I will roast you alive and feed you to my daughters."

"I suppose that should worry me." He stroked the bright red hair that reminded him of the bonfires on the *Triholaths*. Her lethal promise wasn't to be taken lightly. However, there also wasn't a family on *Trilunon*, his included that didn't have ties to the *dracklegons*.

She tilted her head so she could nibble on the other side of his neck. "Have I frightened you?"

"No, we have *dracklegon* blood in my *relkinam* and in *Warpathia* too. A shapeshifter like me often takes the risk of being roasted alive."

"Is that really your *magick*?" Her eyes widened as she gaped up at him. "Once it was my *Gift* too."

"It will be again." He kissed her. "While I will never harm you, much less roast you alive, no other man will share your nest. Agreed?"

"Of course! I am mostly human and I try to be like my mother, not my sire." She met his gaze. "I'll swear it on her tomb if you wish."

"Your word is enough, *Trecesalty*." He smiled, lowered his head. "Now, I'll describe the *Nine-Time Kiss* and show it to you. Then, you will beg me to have you."

————

Hitting the big sales with her sisters and Astra's assistant on Black Friday was their tradition, but one that drained Venus, especially since Fallyn threw a fit about staying home with Trina, the babysitter Meteor hired. Ten hours of traveling from mall to mall, store to store and shopping with so many other bargain hunters was an endurance contest, especially with a toddler in tow, although her daughter didn't seem as emotionally wiped out as Venus felt.

Next *Black Friday* will be different, she told herself, parking the dark blue 2015 Ford Escape in front of the house, close to her door. By then, Fallyn would be accustomed to the new nanny, or alternative arrangements could be made with Aunt Diana. Climbing out of the SUV, Venus opened the back door and freed her daughter from the prison of her car seat, ducking the large chocolate chip cookie the two-and-a-half-year-old held.

The little girl charged toward the porch, still waving the cookie and chanting a series of names. "See Wynn, Qway, Gamma—" Her voice trailed off, then she squealed with obvious delight. "Unka Hol, Unka Hol, Unka Hol. Where Owie?"

Venus collected three large bags and hurried after her daughter. The child obviously found someone she recognized from his previous visits to the ranch. The tall, solid, blond man in jeans and a denim jacket came down the steps to meet her, Fallyn trotting beside him, still demanding to know about 'Owie'.

"Let me take those for you." A smile warmed dark eyes. "Looks like you need the help."

"Thanks." Venus surrendered the department store sacks, then turned her gaze on her daughter. "What 'owie', honey? Are you hurt?"

"She doesn't appear to be." The stranger paused, glancing down at Fallyn. "Rowdy's putting up the last roll of wire on the back fence. Edwin and Quaid are helping Trina and your grandmother fix supper."

Venus walked beside him toward her wing of the house, admiring the way he spoke to Fallyn as if she'd understand every word. But who was he? If he worked on the ranch, why didn't she know him? What was the matter with her short-term memory? No answers came by the time they unloaded her rig, packing the presents into the kitchen. Still baffled, Venus picked up her daughter and put her into the high-chair at the table to finish the cookie.

"I appreciate the help." Venus glanced at the man who stood just inside the back door. "I didn't get your name."

"I didn't offer it this time." He opened his coat enough to reach inside to a shirt pocket, pulling out a gold chain and medallion. "This is yours, isn't it?"

"Pretty." Fallyn beamed at him, a sunshine smile. "Mommy's pretty."

"That's right." Venus crossed to him. "Where did you find it? I've been going out of my mind looking for it during the last two and a half weeks."

"Let me help you." He repeated his previous words, shaking out the chain, then holding the necklace in a calloused palm. "It is yours, isn't it?"

"It always has been." He was too slow, and she snatched away the vintage necklace.

It felt warm in her hand, and she wondered how long he'd carried it around. She slid the chain around her neck, felt the ends link as they closed, nestled the gold disk with the engraved warrior between her breasts. Warmth flooded into her cheeks as she realized he still watched, faint amusement mingling with appreciation in his dark eyes.

She backed a step, opened her purse. "What reward do I owe you for finding my necklace?"

"None for now, Katiranika. I'll claim it when you wear the entire set I made for you." He folded his arms, waiting in the doorway. "Do you remember me yet?"

She started to shake her head, then paused to study his face. High cheekbones added to the strong angles of his rugged features. His mouth was wide and full, with little creases beside it as if he laughed more than he frowned. "How do you know my witch name?"

"The same way you know my wizard name. Remember me, witch."

Suddenly, she knew he'd told her that before. Leaving her purse, she returned to him, rose on tiptoe and brushed her mouth over his. "Hughondear."

"That's right."

"You kissed me before. Why did I forget again?"

He twined a hand in her hair and turned her face up to his. "You tell me. Who dares to ensorcel my war-queen?"

"I'm not yours. I belong to no man."

"Except me." His mouth claimed hers, a fierce pressure that enticed and charmed.

She swayed against him, hands resting against his wide chest. How did Astra do it? Take away the memories of him so nothing remained. Why had her older sister done such a thing? Worse, how often had it happened?

"Now, you know me." The flat certainty in his tone roused her. "Don't you, Katiranika?"

"Yes." She turned her face so he couldn't see the tears dampening his jacket. "I don't want to lose myself again, but I'm not sure how to prevent it."

"Tell your sisters you're a grown witch. You can protect your-self. They don't need to guard you from me." His arms tightened around her. "You're the war-queen. If need be, you can slay me on your own."

She tipped her head back so their gazes met. "I have other desires, Hughondear. Shedding your lifeblood isn't one of them." She paused. "Well, unless you anger me beyond all reason and then, you'd better be afraid."

He chuckled, lowering his head. "In that case, I'll conquer you with kisses."

"You can try." His breath was spicy and warm on her lips. "You may fail."

"I don't think so. Let's see."

————

Astra yawned and stretched, rolling her shoulders. She'd secured the gifts she'd bought in the closet of the bedroom she shared with Meteor. There wasn't much point in taking most of them back to Seattle, since she'd spend *Yule*, known as Christmas with her family at the ranch. She'd left the presents for the other lawyers and her office staff in the Explorer. She normally rose early on working days in order to jog three miles along the waterfront with the dogs, return to her apartment to shower, dress, make breakfast and still be at the law firm by eight.

She shrugged. The nightmares that plagued her had faded in the past month and she slept better in Rowindache's arms than she had in eons. The reason for her sudden fatigue didn't matter, not when her bed beckoned, and supper was at least an hour away. After removing her boots, she curled up on top of the covers, closing her eyes. Before sleep claimed her, she heard the door open and the soft sound of padding feet as Meteor entered the room.

"Are you okay?" Meteor came over to stand next to the queen-size bed. "Do you need something?"

"Some privacy." Astra rolled onto her side away from her sister, turning her back. For once, she didn't rise to her feet or open her eyes. "Is that possible? Or do I have to step and fetch something for you, or Venus, or one of the kids, or the Elder Witches? Just leave me alone."

"You got it, Ms. Grumpy Witch." Meteor pulled up the afghan from the foot of the bed. "Take a nap and see if you feel ready for lasagna in two hours."

"I might if you'd shut up and go away."

"I will after I cover you up."

———

Smiling, Meteor closed the bedroom door, turning to walk down the hall. Her older sister's snotty attitude amused her more than it baffled her.

"Where's Astra?" Venus came toward her, Fallyn trotting at her heels. "I want to talk to her."

"She's napping. I'd guess she's been overdoing it again." Meteor scooped up the toddler, nuzzling her neck. "Let's go join the family and I'll wake Astra in time for supper. She rarely gets into a snit with either of us, but when she does, she needs space."

"Sounds good." Venus took a deep breath, deliberately keeping her tone sweet. "You two need to stop protecting me. I can't prepare for a battle when I'm less than myself."

Meteor stopped and stared up at the younger woman. "What battle?"

"Don't you feel the coming storm?" Venus narrowed violet eyes, frowning. "Maybe not. It's warrior *magick* to know when an enemy approaches."

"The strongest shifters train the pack to prepare for strife." Meteor held her daughter tight. "Some of the most powerful women protect the pups."

Venus nodded. "Rowdy and Aunt Diana severed Trina's tie to the pack a few days ago replacing it with the connection to you."

"I know. I was there. She promised to keep my younglings safe."

"Hopefully, the alpha and his enforcer will think she's gone."

Meteor appreciated the fact that her sister didn't say, 'dead', in front of Fallyn. Carrying the child, she started toward the door at the far end of the hallway. "Jed talks about having his own pack."

"Has he told his uncle yet? Frank will see splitting the Corbettstown pack as a challenge."

"It's not a split. Jed won't accept most of those shifters, not when they constantly fight with him. He'll mark Eagleville and the western portion of Liberty Valley as his territory and leave the eastern region to Frank."

"It'd be a peaceful solution, but not an acceptable one to Frank Corbett who prefers to rule everything and everyone." Venus held open the door to the staircase that led to her mother's wing of the house. "No wonder I feel the need to train the young witches and wizards for war."

PART III

_____

"Thoughts and images guide a warrior's magick and actions."
Venus Jamison, crusader, entrepreneur, and hereditary witch

26

Eagleville, Washington ~ Friday, November 23rd, 2018

JED FROWNED WHEN HE SAW THE LATE MODEL PICKUP PARKED IN THE driveway of his house. The rest of the employees at Corbett Logging had a four-day weekend, but his crew was behind on their quotas and he didn't want to discuss the issue at Sunday dinner with his uncle, not when there were more important subjects to address. So, Jed insisted his loggers drop trees and ship logs to the local mill on Black Friday, not that his guys would want to hit the malls anyway. They'd prefer hanging out in the local taverns and leave shopping until the last evening before *Yule,* when they'd need holiday presents for their mates and pups.

He glanced quickly at Gard in the passenger seat of his pickup. "Looks like my cousin wants something. We'll finish with him first. Afterwards, we'll clean up and head to the Rocking J for dinner. Stick around."

"That's my job."

"For now. Eventually, I'll have to choose an enforcer for my new pack." Jed carefully pulled up beside the other truck, so he didn't block it, and Junior would be able to drive away when they concluded their business. "Let's do this."

In jeans and a flannel plaid shirt, Junior hurried to meet them. "I have to talk to you."

"I figured that's why you were here." Jed shut the driver's door of the pickup. "What's going on?"

"Cherry told me to come see you and ask if you'd help us move to Eagleville."

"What? Why does your wife want to live here? Isn't she the new hostess for the pack?"

"Not willingly, but none of the women refuse Dad when he wants something. For that matter, nobody else does either. No one wants to be turned over to Marvin for discipline." Fear flickered across Junior's face. "Cherry said Dad tried to jump her last night, and it's not the first time. She doesn't want me to confront him."

"He'd kill you and then she wouldn't have anyone to protect her." Jed scowled, ran a hand through his hair. "You two are mated, aren't you?"

Junior nodded. "Since high school. I know I mess around with other females, Jed, but I've never actually cheated on Cherry. If I lose her, it will destroy me, and she says she'll be a dead woman walking. It'll be the same as when he sent me on a suicide mission in our last incarnation. Cherry says it wouldn't have happened if you'd still been alive, but he'd already murdered you and your mate."

Jed studied his cousin. They resembled each other. Both had Corbett black hair, muscled bodies, but Junior barely topped six feet. He tended to gain weight because he preferred a sedentary lifestyle to logging and he liked greasy food with his beer.

Somehow, Jed didn't doubt Cherry's words. No wonder the Elder Witches at the Rocking J wanted to protect Meteor and him. Did others in the pack suspect that Frank had more names of adult shifters on a proverbial hit list? "Have you told your dad you intend to leave Corbettstown?"

"Not yet. I will once you agree to help us move here."

"Living here means preparing for a battle, since Uncle Frank has control issues. Even if he agrees it's time for me to start my own pack, he'll try to take it away, Junior."

"I'll fight to keep my mate. She told me last night that she's been taking precautions because she doesn't want any of our children murdered if they can't shift and we know you won't do that."

"No, I won't." Jed rested a hand on the hood of his truck. He'd kill to protect his children, hell, he'd die for them. He had an odd sense that he already had more than once, not only for them, but also for Meteor. He certainly wouldn't stop loving them, much less annihilate his family if they couldn't shift. "All right. I'll talk to your dad about the new pack after Sunday dinner. What kind of house do you two want?"

———

She woke as suddenly as she'd fallen asleep. Yawning, she pushed off the blanket and headed for the bathroom. Her sisters had worn jeans and sweatshirts when they went shopping, but she'd opted for a light blue, long-sleeved, western shirt with darker blue, ivory, blush and burgundy floral embroidery, and a mid-calf length denim skirt. She sat down on the edge of the bed, drew on spike-heeled, blue cowgirl boots.

Her sisters and Rebekah wanted to hit the midnight sales, but Astra didn't know if she was up for that or not. Sighing, she stretched and arched her back, twisting at the hips. Coffee, she thought. She'd have coffee with dinner and then she'd be re-energized. Downstairs, she caught the scent of tomato, garlic and onion. Her stomach lurched, and she stiffened, trying not to gag. Was it food poisoning from the lunch they'd grabbed at one of the Chinese restaurants in the mall? No, it couldn't be. Rebekah, Venus, little Fallyn, and Meteor hadn't complained, and they'd all eaten at the same place.

Astra took a step forward into the living room, choked as another wave of marinara sauce hit her nose. Estelle always made lasagna on Black Friday, a family favorite, but just the idea of a huge cheesy slab was enough to send Astra reeling. She leaned against the wall, an unwelcome suspicion teasing her mind. Things had changed since *Samhain*, but not as much as she'd dreaded when she learned the soul-matched wizards arrived.

Still, she didn't feel the same as she had a month ago. Fatigue, nausea, moodiness—new symptoms, but why did she have them? She didn't have the flu or a cold. What else could it be? She took a deep breath, her mind returning to the first idea. She'd counted on her own precautions preventing pregnancy. The birth control pills she'd taken since she was a teenager meant she didn't have regular periods, so she couldn't use that as a barometer.

She glanced across the large room. A fire blazed in the river-rock fireplace on the far wall. Orion napped in a recliner in front of it, his crutches nearby. The comfortable old couches were empty, and someone had turned off the flat screen TV, not that her aunt watched it very often although she had a few favorite dramas and sitcoms. Heavy white drapes covered the picture windows. She saw Rowdy and Hugh standing by the sideboard where Estelle kept liquor.

Although they'd undoubtedly worked all day on the ranch, they'd cleaned up to come to supper. Rowdy wore black pants and a white shirt, his black hair braided back with a leather tie. He must have felt her gaze because he turned to face her, raising the glass of red wine he held in a salute and greeting. She stalked toward him, fury rising. "You son of a—"

"Wait, *Vaslattel*." He glanced at the tall, blond man beside him. "You don't need to hear this, Holt. Grant us space and privacy."

His friend nodded, amusement in his dark eyes, and walked away, carrying a glass of wine in each hand, leaving them alone.

"Start again." Putting down his glass, Rowdy strode behind the bar. "What concerns you, my own?"

Astra paced toward him, resting her hands on the edge of the wooden counter. "You didn't take any precautions to prevent pregnancy when we had sex, did you?"

"Why would I?" He dropped ice cubes into a tumbler, studied the bottles, chose one and poured clear liquid, filling the glass. "I've waited too long to have a family and children with you, *Vaslattel,* hundreds of years in this realm."

"I might be pregnant now."

"It's definitely possible. I knew after *Samhain,* but I still wasn't totally sure." He smiled, enjoyment deepening the lines around his dark eyes. "If not, we'll keep trying."

"Not funny and I'm not laughing." Fists clenched, she struggled to take a deep breath. "It's my choice too."

"You should have expected consequences when you had me unfairly banished, much less when you learned your father and former lover elicited rogue shapeshifters to murder me time and again." Rowdy picked up a second bottle. "The *Goddess* has *Her* own sense of justice which doesn't mirror yours and *She* didn't believe I deserved to be tortured, disemboweled and eaten alive over and over in four different lives."

Rage swamped sense and Astra grabbed the glass of wine, prepared to throw it in his mocking face.

"Consider the result before you act, Satiranika." His hand closed over hers. "If I wear that wine, you will be embarrassed by your first spanking in front of your *relkinam.*"

"You wouldn't dare."

"Try me and see, my queen."

Her gaze clashed with his. Dimly, she heard voices in the adjoining dining room and knew her family gathered around the table. "I hate you."

"I know." He leaned close. "I've told you before. I enjoy your hatred too."

His lips brushed hers and she trembled. She didn't know if she wanted to scratch out his dark eyes, surrender to the kiss and drag him upstairs, or scream in outrage. Why did he muddle her thoughts? What *magick* made her crave his touch?

He released his hold on her hand, came back around the bar and held out a glass. "Take this. It will settle your stomach as will supper."

"I don't think I can eat." She accepted the tumbler he offered, smelling ginger. "I want to puke and that's your entire fault too."

"Drink first, my own." He chuckled, feathering his thumb over her lips. "And if you can't eat what your aunt prepared, I have a pot of bean soup on the stove in the bunkhouse."

———

Venus adjusted the tray on Fallyn's highchair. She glanced up at Hugh when he came to join her. "I thought you and Rowdy intended to discuss tomorrow's projects on the ranch."

"His mate put a stop to that when she arrived, enraged by something my saddle partner has done."

"I'm going to talk to her tonight about using her powers on my memories. It needs to stop, but I'll wait until after supper when we're alone."

"I'd save that lecture for another time, *Laspowima*." Hugh handed her a glass of red wine. "If you upset her, she'll undoubtedly cry and that's something you'll hate."

"Cry? Why would she?" Venus eyed Meteor as she arrived with a plate of food. She'd chosen peas and a breadstick along with a small serving of lasagna cut into bite-size pieces for the toddler. "Is there some reason Astra is freaking out? Hughondear says she's close to tears. The only time I've seen her cry was at *Samhain* when she ordered one of the dogs to attack Rowdy and he defended himself."

"She's off on a tangent and I'm not sure why." Meteor put the plate on the tray and drew up a chair. "Give her time and space to center herself, Venus. If you don't tell her you have your memories and want to keep them, she won't feel the need to protect you from everyone. You've always been special to her, and she doesn't trust Estelle to keep you safe."

Venus blinked, glancing past her sister to their mother where she stood chatting to their aunt. "I don't understand. Why are you and Astra calling Mom by her first name?"

"It's one of those memories you'll regain soon." Meteor sat down beside Fallyn, who immediately tried to grab a handful of peas. "No, sweetheart. Use your spoon."

"Good luck with that," Venus said. "When she's hungry, she goes for fingers first."

"Go away, Venus." Amusement lit Meteor's soft blue eyes. "She needs to learn to feed herself appropriately, so let me teach her since she bullies you."

Hiding her smile, Venus nodded and stepped away. She saw Quaid and Edwin holding out chairs for her mother and Aunt Diana. Quaid's manners always were a credit to her, Venus thought, but they'd improved even more with his older brother's arrival. She allowed Hugh to pull out a chair for her and sat next to him. She noticed that Jed Corbett had chosen a seat next to Meteor's. He'd brought along Gard Devlin, who came into the dining room accompanied by her younger brother.

After Rowdy gave the blessing and Diana dished up the lasagna, everyone focused on eating. Conversation swirled around the table. Topics ranged from the shopping trip, logging in the foothills and the next pastures to be fenced on the ranch. When Fallyn finished most of her meal, she waved a breadstick like a conductor while Meteor ate.

Once they'd enjoyed dessert, Rebekah organized the boys to help with the dishes while the adults lingered over their coffee and apple crisp. Jed glanced around the table. "My cousin and his wife are looking for a place to live in Eagleville."

"I have a small two-bedroom cottage available for rent," Diana said. "Will that suffice, or do they need something larger?"

Trina held up her hand. "Hold on. Why would Junior and Cherry decide to leave Corbettstown? Do they have the alpha's permission to live away from the pack?"

"That's part of their issues." Jed eased further back in his chair, putting an arm along the back of Meteor's. "I'm going to see my uncle on Sunday and tell him it's time for me to start my own pack."

"He'll view that as a challenge." Fear flickered across Meteor's face, and she closed her eyes for a moment. "He'll kill you."

"I can take him in a shifter battle and we both know it so there won't be one." Jed glanced at Trina. "I'll need an enforcer to keep the peace."

She nodded. "I'll watch your tail, but there are conditions. No younglings are sacrificed."

"Agreed and the three of us will discuss your other demands later." Jed touched Meteor's shoulder. "You need to stay here when I confront him. Gard will be with me and Trina will protect you and the children."

"I'll go with you, Thojedescar," Rowdy said, his tone even. "You'll want someone to ward you from evil *magick* and keep anyone from stealing your shape."

"No." Astra stirred in her chair. She put down the fork she'd used to toy with her barely touched dinner. She still seemed washed out, her face pale, but her cobalt eyes were resolute. "You're not going to Corbettstown to die again, *Chosen*. If there's a price for this new pack, *I'll* pay it. It's my doing that my demon-father and his minions had the opportunity to torment and destroy innocents in our past four lives. I need to make amends. You'll remain here to guard Matiranika and the children."

"They'll have enough protection without me." Rowdy covered Astra's hand with his, gripping the gold bracelet on her wrist. "We'll stand together, the way we should have before."

Venus saw tears shimmer in her older sister's eyes, but Astra still shook her head. "No. I've made mistakes, but I take responsibility for the consequences, all of them."

"A witch who expects different results from the same spell she cast several times before is a fool," Diana said, her tone gentle. "Change the ingredients and elements and you affect the outcomes, my dear."

"What do you know of outcomes? Foretelling the dark future is my province, not yours." Astra pushed back her chair and stood, abandoning any pretense of eating. "He stays here and you and Estelle guard him with all the strength you never used to protect me. I face my demons alone, just like always."

When she left the room, Rowdy rose to follow, his black gaze sweeping over the older women. "Before we travel to Corbettstown and face the alpha and his enforcer, you need to *Heal* the divide between you three witches, or it will be used against us. I know an injured child when I *See* one, even if she's grown now and matched to me. A witch who carries the burden of the past with her is always a hazard to those who fight beside her."

27

A STRAINED SILENCE FILLED THE ROOM AFTER ROWDY'S DEPARTURE. Venus shifted in her chair, eying the concern on her mother's face and her aunt's tense figure before glancing at her sister. "I don't remember our father at all, much less visiting him when we were kids. Do you know what they're talking about?"

Meteor stood and removed Fallyn from her highchair, balancing the little girl on a hip. "They've sent Astra to serve him and his minions as a virgin sacrifice in each and every one of her lives when she reached puberty, as a punishment for writing the *banexort* spell when we arrived in this realm."

"But I was the one who cast it after she gave it to me." Venus stared at her sister, then at her mother and aunt. "Did you really do such a horrible thing to your own child, your own niece?"

Diana paled, shock filling her face. Beside her, Estelle stiffened. Her hands tightened into fists on the table.

Before either of the older women spoke, Meteor continued, "Like Astra says, they view her as expendable. She struggles not to show the scars of being his altar fourteen years ago and she still remembers the times she was one of his or Latham's blood sacrifices. She reasonably dreaded her *Chosen's* scorn when he arrived last month. Even in these so-called modern times, many still blame the victims of rape, not the abusers and you brought Rowindache and Hughondear from long-ago times. Because Astra fears our father and didn't want him using us the way he used her, she kept him away from us and blocked your memories of him."

Knotting her hands together under the table, Venus focused on the two Elder Witches after Meteor left the dining room with her daughter. "How much of that is true?"

"None of it. Meteor doesn't know what she's talking about." Estelle lifted her chin, narrowing dark blue eyes. "Your sister ran wild from the time she turned fourteen, regardless of my rules. She insisted on visiting your father even when I forbid it. She drank, smoked everything, not just tobacco, did drugs and of course, had sex with a variety of partners. I made sure she had birth control pills and condoms in her backpack so there wouldn't be unwanted complications."

"All obvious symptoms of deeper problems or traumas." Venus turned her attention on her aunt. "What did you know?"

"In this life, she disappeared after a football game the three of you attended when you were freshmen in high school." Diana's tone was measured, but she winced in pain. "Now, I realize she didn't go to a party with a bunch of older teens like she told me and Estelle. Your father must have abducted her for his own purposes and then released her afterwards, keeping her from remembering his ceremonies for some time."

"And neither of you tried to intervene or keep her safe?" Venus shuddered, shaking her head. "It's amazing she even comes to the Rocking J anymore, much less has a relationship with either of you. No wonder she's willing to sacrifice herself to protect me, Meteor and the children. She doesn't want us to suffer what she did."

"We aren't responsible for his actions," Estelle said, narrowing her eyes.

"You're both responsible for not protecting my sister from being gang-raped by her own father and his disciples and from allowing those bastards to kill her in their demonic rites." Rising to her feet, Venus planted her hands on the table and swept the older women with a scathing glance. "I'm going to need time to consider all of this, but the first priority is guarding the younglings. I wish my sisters had told me earlier that neither of you are trustworthy, but better to know before the battle than during it or afterwards."

"Being so judgmental isn't like you, Katiranika." Anxiety seeped into Diana's face. "What changed?"

"She knows who she is, the war queen." Hugh stood. "Where we come from, real warriors have their own codes of justice and we protect the innocent from those who'd harm them. Demons are punished, not repeatedly rewarded with a novice, untouched witchling."

"What he said." Venus turned and stalked from the room, aware he was behind her, obviously guarding her back. In the kitchen, she gestured to the boys and Rebekah. "Where is Astra? Did she go upstairs to her apartment?"

"No, she was really upset. She told me she wanted to be alone. She went outside to be with her dogs, but Rowdy went to join her."

"He'll know best how to take care of her." Venus gestured to the door that led to her wing of the house. "Come with me."

"We haven't finished cleaning up." Rebekah slipped the last pan in the dishwasher. She turned, tilted her head, curious. "What's going on?"

"My rooms. Now, Robinaranika." Waiting until Edwin parked the broom in the corner, Venus ushered the three of them to the hallway door. "Where is Meteor?"

"She took Fallyn up for a bath before bed."

"Good. While I talk to her, you can help the boys find a movie to watch before their bedtime."

"It'd be better if Quaid practiced his reading and Edwin finished his homework for school." Hugh closed the door behind them, leaving it unlocked. "They've already had two hours of 'picture time' today."

"It won't take long to do that stuff, Mama," Quaid said. "Afterwards, can we go downstairs to the 'salon' and fight with swords?"

Venus nodded. "Exercise is a good idea and then you'll both

sleep well. I'll take you to the basement when Hugh says you're ready."

"I'll need to fetch my sword." He grinned down at her. "We've never crossed blades before. I'll look forward to the bout."

"To losing?" Quaid cocked his head. "That's strange. Mama defeats everyone."

Heat rose in her cheeks and Venus struggled to control her breathing when amusement filled Hugh's dark gaze. She lifted her chin. "He's right, but I could use a new challenge."

"Oh, I'll definitely provide one, *Laspowima*."

———

Hugh walked out the kitchen door, across the back porch, heading toward the bunkhouse. He'd never thought he'd pity the woman that Rowdy chose, much less feel the need to protect her. Yet now he understood why she'd tried so hard to defend her younger sisters in this life with any weapon at hand.

Being reborn five times to the same parents who couldn't be trusted to look after her and abused her in every way possible would take its toll on any witch, turning her bitter and angry. He wondered how well he'd have done in the same situation. Would he be like Rowdy, determined to heal the past and survive into the future or like his mate willing to sacrifice herself one more time to save those she loved?

Two huge black male dogs rested on the porch and watched him approach. They growled, baring large white teeth, but neither stirred, allowing him passage to the door. When he opened it, Hugh saw Astra sitting at the table, a bowl of bean soup in front of her while she ate a slice of homemade bread. The matriarch of the canine trio lay by the chair. Rowdy stood at the counter, sorting through different jars of herbs.

"What are you creating?" Hugh closed the door and leaned against it. "Protection spells to take with you to Corbettstown?"

"That's the plan."

"I still don't like it." Astra scowled at him. "It's not safe for you to go there."

"I'll consider your feelings when you start taking better care of yourself and stop blaming yourself for what others do." Rowdy glanced over his shoulder at her. "That's a weakness we can't afford."

"Spare me another of your '*healer*' lectures. You've been nagging me since you arrived here, and it gets old in a hurry." Astra picked up the spoon. "I own what's mine to own and take responsibility for my actions."

Hugh opted not to participate in the ensuing discussion of warding spells, since he didn't know enough of what each specific weed or flower did, or how they'd affect the outlaw shifters in Corbettstown. He left that sort of *magick* to Rowdy now augmented by the skills of his soul-matched witch-mate.

Instead of herbal lore, Hugh relied on the mage-crafted, silver war-blade given to him when he graduated from the *Warpathian* military academy back in the glory days of *Trilunon*. The sword followed him, appearing in each of his lives where he'd find it on his thirtieth birthday. He wouldn't hesitate to use it on lawbreakers who attacked him. It took a long time for a shifter to heal from a non-lethal blow and silver generally left scars.

He opened the trunk holding his belongings and removed the sword, turning when he heard what sounded like the buzz of a bee. He saw Astra staring into the small screen of what Venus called a phone. "What is it?"

"My demon-father wants to meet."

"Why?" Rowdy asked. "Does he know Trina lived after her escape from the pack? Is he demanding her return?"

"He doesn't say that. He has a client he wants me to defend."

"An innocent?" Hugh asked.

"No, my father's followers are always guilty of something." Astra sent back a response. "I told him to meet me at the outlet mall and we'd talk. I've never invited him here to the Rocking J and never will, not tonight, not ever."

"I'll finish these spells so I can go with you."

"I don't need you. I've faced him by myself forever."

"You may not want my protection, but the mother of my child does." Rowdy left the containers on the counter and crossed the room to place a hand on her shoulder. "You'll never confront danger alone again."

Tears filled the dark blue eyes and one slipped down her cheek before she wiped it away. "I hate you."

"Repetition weakens that claim, my own." He smoothed a lock of bright red hair from her face. "How much wolfsbane did you say to add to the mix?"

Smiling, Hugh left the pair and the cabin. He had matters of his own to settle and looked forward to the next few hours with his *Chosen*, but he'd also tell her about the upcoming meeting between Astra and their father so none of the women ventured forth undefended.

———

Jed leaned back in the chair, allowing his gaze to sweep over the Elder Witches to his guards before glancing at Orion. The teen frowned in concern and Jed nodded in unspoken agreement. Dealing with his half-sisters' dramas undoubtedly consumed some of the young wizard's energies but learning they had so many reasons for their actions would have startled the boy too.

"So, what's your plan?" Jed asked. "How do you intend to ensure everyone's on the same side when I confront my uncle?"

"I don't know," Diana said. "I'm open to suggestions. What do I say to Astra and Meteor?"

"Try the truth." Trina neatly placed the spoon by her empty dessert dish. "I lived with the enforcer for almost a month. He always has an agenda and using up people, especially those with *Power* in each and every possible way ranks high on his list. Hurting Astra undoubtedly provided more pleasure than any of you can imagine."

"Clarify that." Orion ran a hand through sandy blond hair. "I don't understand."

"He had her pain and that of those who love her, which gave him incredible power to use in his schemes." Gard stood and drew out Trina's chair so the tall blonde could stand next to him. "Excuse us. We need to plan how I'll defend Jed when we visit Corbettstown and face his uncle. We'll leave you to debate how to establish an effective alliance with the *Trecesalty*. As Rowdy said, if the three of them aren't united with us, they'll be used to defeat us."

"I'll join you later," Jed said, "and you can bring me up to speed." He turned his attention to the Elder Witches and the young wizard. "Like Trina, I'm familiar with the key players in the pack. My uncle and his enforcer relish division even when they're not the ones creating it, so let's discuss strategies to unite us against them."

"Fair enough." Diana took a deep breath, then reached for the coffee cup in front of her. "At *Samhain*, I told Astra that her father constantly lied to her, but until he admits it, she probably won't believe me. He's managed to convince her that Estelle is not only my ally, but the enemy my daughters should fear."

"Why start with her?" Orion asked. "Make peace with Venus and Meteor first. If they trust you, they'll pass it on to Astra."

"He has a point but be sure you tell them the unvarnished truth about everything," Jed said. "Don't leave the slightest opening for my uncle or Gunnolf Marvin to exploit."

Diana shared a long glance with Estelle before nodding agreement. "It's time for me to tell them what we did when they were little witches playing with their first wands and why I sent them away with you. I didn't want Frank or Jarvesel sacrificing them in one of their blood rites."

———

Cuddling the sleepy toddler in fleecy, pink unicorn sleepers, Meteor sat in the rocking chair near her daughter's crib. Thumb in the corner of her mouth, Fallyn sighed. "Want –tory, Auntie Mettie. 'Bout my prettie."

Meteor dropped a kiss on the child's forehead under the strawberry-blonde curls, eying the sun-shaped disc the little girl insisted on wearing. "Once upon a time, a queen gave gold and gemstones to a brave shifter captured in battle and ordered him to make a *talipenlace* set of jewels."

"Fadda," Fallyn announced around her thumb. "My fadda, the wolf."

"Yes, your father," Meteor agreed, surprised by the young witchling's knowledge. There wasn't much point in asking for details the child might not be able to share. "For many days, nights and weeks, he worked very hard. He chose the sun's shape because he'd loved running through the woods on days when the three-ringed sun shone bright. He engraved all sorts of animals into the gold, animals he remembered shifting into when he was home."

"My birdies too and my fishies."

Meteor rocked in the chair, snuggling the child closer. "Yes, he included those because nothing compared to soaring through the sky with wind below his wings unless it was swimming in icy rivers."

"I do it someday."

"I'll teach you when you're older."

"Fadda too." Fallyn blinked big blue eyes sleepily. "Him show me too."

"That's right." Meteor glanced toward the door when she heard footsteps and saw Jed. As usual, just the sight of the tall, muscled, dark-haired man made her shiver. She rose and carried Fallyn to the crib. "Time for sleep, my sweetie."

"Want my blankie and my pony and—"

Meteor lowered the child into the bed, tucking a handmade patchwork quilt over the small body. The stuffed toy horse came next, along with its companion, a shaggy wolf. She raised the side of the crib, making a mental note to talk to Venus about bringing down an actual bed from the attic. It was time for Fallyn to make the transition to a larger child-size bed.

After switching on the unicorn-shaped nightlight, Meteor crossed to the doorway, clicking off the overhead light. She waited for Jed to step aside so she could close the door, leaving it slightly ajar. "What do you want?"

"My mate and pups in my house where we'll have a real home, but that's going to have to wait, isn't it?"

She glanced up at him, measuring the sincerity in his face and dark eyes. "You say all the right things at night, but come dawn, you leave. When you return, you kill me and try to slay my babies. Never again, Thojedescar."

"I may not have all my memories yet, but I'll swear any oath you like that I'd never harm you or them. When I go to Corbettstown on Sunday, Trina will be here to protect my family."

"Not me, only our little ones." Meteor lifted her chin, met his dark gaze. "As much as I fear the pack, I'll go with you, stand with you. Rowdy and my mother are right. When I hide from him, it gives your uncle more *Power* than he deserves. We need to change what we've done in the past in order to have a different future."

"One where we're together."

"No, that's impossible. Our time has passed. We'll order Trina to help Venus and Holt guard our young because they'll be the next to lead the pack."

"I'm their father."

"Yes and while I won't prevent you from seeing them, helping to raise the three of them, we're not together on anything else."

He took a step forward, framed her face with his hands. "I understand it will take time for you to trust me."

It'd be so easy to lean against him, to allow him to kiss her, but that way led to madness, to fiery sex and more children held hostage to an uncertain future. She allowed herself to relish the touch of his work-calloused fingers for another moment before easing backwards, shaking her head. "We're done."

"Not yet. Not while I draw breath." He traced her lips with his thumb. "Meantime, I'll have to create another necklace to trade for the one you're letting our baby girl wear, or it will break her heart when you take it away."

"I won't take it from her since I'll never wear it again."

"I traded all of me, my heart, mind and soul to make the *talipen-lace* set for you, my shape-shifting queen, not one of our wolflings."

"You did it to suit my aunt's desires, not mine. Give it to her the way I did the rest of the jewels when she tried to foist those on me. I've never worn the set willingly in this life and I never will."

28

Astra glanced around the food court, seeing several shoppers who had the same idea of taking a break from the stores, but didn't spot her father waiting at any of the spindly-legged tables. She strolled toward a large one in a corner surrounded by greenery. Before she pulled out a chair, Rowdy did, waiting until she seated herself and then taking a chair beside hers, facing the courtyard. She eyed him warily. "I can't believe you're adjusting so quickly to this time."

"What choice do I have when it's where you are?" Faint amusement filled his voice and lines crinkled around his dark eyes. "I never did see much use in complaining. It doesn't cure anything and generally only makes matters worse."

Astra looked at a laughing group of people passing by on their way to another sale. Some wore blue jeans and casual tops. One of the girls in a short, tight black dress sported several tattoos on her arms and legs. "What do you find most unusual?"

He followed her gaze. "How fast things happen. Depending on the weather and the horses, it took days for Holt and I to travel to places unless we created a portal and that used too much *Power*. If we hadn't been in Washington Territory when Mary sent for us, we wouldn't have arrived in Corbett's Town before she died."

Astra nodded. "I can see that as a major difference, but I haven't heard you say anything about the clothing styles, or the way women wear pants now."

"A lot of gals wore pants or divided skirts back in the day. Did it ever occur to you that if they didn't have a problem, town councils wouldn't have made laws dictating what women could wear?"

"No." She tilted her head, fascinated. "What else?"

He shrugged. "Folks used to say that if a feller was perturbed because a woman could rope the wind, ride a cyclone, brand what needed branding, shoot what needed to die, *he* was out-classed, because *he* wasn't much of a man."

"And the fact that I'm a criminal attorney isn't a problem for you? It took until well into the nineteenth century for women to be able to practice law in America, and even more time to run for polit-ical office."

"I'm a *high healer*. We've always had trouble finding enough folks with talent and keeping those who have different shapes from fulfilling their destinies makes no sense. I'd like it better if you protected only the innocents, not those who hunt them. It diminishes your soul when you send the wicked to die at the hands of your father or his minions."

She stiffened, trying to read his intent, but his face suddenly seemed impassive and calm, too calm. "Are you ordering me to do that?"

"No, it has to be your decision." He leaned forward, his fingers touching the bracelet she wore. "As I told you before, you'll treat witches, wizards, and healers with the respect due them. You'll allow your sisters and their *Chosen* to decide their paths without your interference. And finally, you won't stray off any trail I set for you, which also means not manufacturing evidence. Let others have the outcomes they deserve."

"I always have." She started to pull free, but his hold tightened on her wrist, and she stopped. "You may not like it but my guilty clients either end up in jail or I send them to Corbettstown to serve my father and the pack as prey to be slain and eaten. That in turn protects many of 'your innocents' from becoming sacrifices, which is what Trina faced when my father tired of her."

"Not just 'tired', he'd have taken all of her shifter *magick* as well before killing her."

Astra glimpsed the distinctive light brown of her father's cop uniform and watched him approach, a powerful, muscular man in his mid-fifties. When he'd started balding years ago, he shaved his head. A thin, gray-haired man in a tired, black suit accompanied the police chief. The two might be close to the same age, but not a wisp of his dead victims trailed her sire, unlike his companion. She didn't see the actual victims, but enough of their residue remained to let her know that once again, she faced evil in a human form.

She forced herself to remain still and not reveal she recognized Gary Smith. Someone placed a white cardboard cup in front of her and she smelled peppermint in the rising steam. She flicked a quick look over her shoulder and saw her sisters, Meteor, holding another cup while Venus stood sentinel beside her.

For once, Meteor had abandoned her favorite lemon-yellow wig. In faded, tight blue jeans and a purple University of Washington sweatshirt, red hair braided back from her face, she bore an even stronger resemblance to Venus. Their younger sister opted for black pants tucked into black boots and a dark navy-blue blazer over an ebony tank top. She'd coiled her hair into a bun on the back of her head, difficult for a foe to grab.

Astra wasn't fooled by her sister's innocent appearance. Venus wouldn't enter any battle unarmed. She hid matching daggers under the full sleeves of her coat and undoubtedly had another pair sheathed in her low-heeled boots. Her favorite sword would be in a scabbard on her back, and a pink Glock in the shoulder harness barely disguised by the cut of the jacket.

Astra eyed the pair. "What are you two doing here?"

"We're the *Trecesalty*, the three queens destined to rule our realm and all our people," Venus said. "The *Three* stand together. As it was once, as it will be now and forever, you pronounce judgement and I'll render it."

"It's not safe for you to be here."

"I'm not a child you need to protect any longer, Satiranika. I'm the war queen and I choose my battles."

"And I'm the matriarch who protects the land, the sea and the air, along with their inhabitants," Meteor said. "One of those is my elder sister."

"But your children?"

"Are safe with their father and his guards along with my *Chosen*," Venus said, her violet-blue gaze holding a lethal purpose. "Now, let's get this done so we can shop for *Yule*. Rebekah's holding our place in line at the toy store. We promised to bring lattes and mochas for the people near her."

Astra took a deep breath and met her father's dark brown eyes when he joined them. "As you asked, I'm here. What made you decide one of your followers needs a defense attorney?"

"You're not introducing me to your companions?" He raised an eyebrow, obviously amused. "Afraid I might go after them?"

"You?" She mirrored the look, letting just enough contempt fill her tone. "You don't recognize my sisters? Your other two daughters?"

"I haven't seen them in years. You and your mother kept them away from me." Marvin drew out a chair and sat down, gesturing for his companion to do the same. "I didn't expect a family reunion tonight."

"Good, because this isn't one. What do you want?" Astra barely flicked a glance at Gary Smith. "Why haven't you arrested him?"

"My jurisdiction stops at the town limits, and he hasn't committed any crimes in Corbettstown. You will turn him in at the county courthouse and represent him in the legal brouhaha."

"No. He's a killer."

"Alleged." Gary Smith spoke for the first time. "Never convicted."

"Not yet," Astra said, "but I *See* your doom coming. You defied the restraining order and attacked my client, Nina Armstrong and her fiancé, Kyle Morgan last month."

"I'm only one of several suspects." His tone smug, Gary Smith smirked at her. "Law enforcement doesn't have any proof, or any bodies after the fire at my cabin on All Hallows Eve."

"Evil surrounds you, an odorous miasma and the wraiths of those you've tortured, maimed and murdered follow you. As one of *Hecate's* handmaidens, I *See* what remains of their spirits, even if others can't." She returned her attention to her father. "Why haven't you or Frank Corbett taken him as prey? If anyone deserves to be butchered and fed to your rogue shifters, he does."

"Again, he hasn't done anything in my town, or harmed the pack."

She narrowed her gaze on him, recognizing a truth he hadn't yet shared. "He serves you and harms those you want injured. So, you allow him to hunt as he pleases and take out his rage on any females who fight you, plus women and girls who can't defend themselves, even the ones I serve as a lawyer. He doesn't observe my boundaries or yours."

Gary Smith stirred in the chair. "Speak to him with respect."

"Watch your words and attitude." Rowdy spoke for the first time. "If you wish anything from my mate, you owe her civility."

Marvin froze, his dark gaze narrowing. "I thought he was just your latest toy. You've taken him?"

"He's mine to do with as I please." Astra met her father's eyes, glare for glare. "I choose what happens to him, how long I keep him until I finish with him. You don't have a say. If you send your disciples, or any of your favored minions to attack him in this life before I'm done playing with him, I will end them."

"And you say you're not mine." A slow smile creased Marvin's face. "You'll always be more mine than your mother's with her silly, weak, white *magick*. I took your heart years ago." He leaned back in his chair. "So, you won't speak for my servant. Open the portal and I'll send him to safety."

"I didn't shut it, so I can't open it." Astra rested her arms on the table, closing a hand around the cup of tea, letting it warm her fingers. "It won't do you any good to perform a blood ceremony."

"If Smith hadn't already tried that, we wouldn't be here." Marvin stood. "However, you don't control all the doorways to the past, my dark enchantress. He's served me well, so I'll take him to a different gate, the one near the Canadian border."

"I'm training a new Dawson witchling," Meteor said, her tone icy and calm. "Don't use her blood for your rites, or your home in Corbettstown will be smoke and ashes when you return."

"Another threat." Marvin's smile widened. "Does your mother know two of you are more mine than hers?"

"You truly are an idiot." Venus took a step forward, closer to the table. "Fair warnings and refusals to do your bidding don't darken my sisters' hearts or souls, *Jarvesel, Soul-Eating, Demon-Prince of Transgressions and Untruths*. Ward yourself. Light conquers darkness, as it was and ever will be—"

"You destroyed *Trilunon*, but we protect our home here," Rowdy said.

"You can try." Marvin gestured to Gary Smith, who rose, ready to follow. "You're not the only ones who issue warnings, my darling daughters. Thwart me and you die after I take your loved ones and skin them alive for my pleasure. As it was before, I'll enjoy eating their hearts again."

Watching the two men leave, Venus said, "Well, that's over for now. It went smoother than I expected."

"It was a declaration of war. He means to destroy all of us." Astra shuddered, tears burning behind her eyes. "Everything I've done to protect you, Meteor and the younglings was for nothing."

"That's not true." Meteor placed a hand on her shoulder. "You kept us alive and safe until we could defend ourselves from him and his ilk. Don't degrade yourself or the risks you've taken for all of us."

"Listen to your sisters." Rowdy leaned close, his breath a whisper against her forehead. "Trust them as you trust me to guard you, my own. I'll protect you as you try to defend me."

Astra pulled away, rising to her feet. "Why should I trust you, *Capostrol*, when you only serve yourself and your ends?"

"Because I always look after what's mine, *Vaslattel*." He chuckled, standing up and coming around the table. "Now, let's buy that coffee and go join Robinaranika before she leaves the line at the toy store to come find us."

Astra waited until her sisters were out of earshot, standing at the mocha booth. She stopped in front of Rowdy, toe to toe with him. "I was honest with my demon-father. I will be the one to destroy you, not him."

"I appreciate that, my own, even when I know we have a future together, one where we happily raise our children in our home." Rowdy tipped up her chin. "While a witch like you isn't an easy ride for a wizard like me, I don't expect you to say you love me until the words come from the heart, but I welcome these new attempts to guard me."

She caught her breath. "That's not what this is about. I'll never love—"

His kiss kept the rest of the words from escaping and she trembled, then melted against him. She longed to be safe in his embrace, but she knew better. She'd never find the sanctuary she'd sought, yet for this moment she'd allow herself to pretend this time was real, not just some sort of strange game. He was one more hostage she'd have to save since she wasn't allowing him to be sacrificed by the pack again.

———

Amused by the debate Meteor and Venus had over the various stuffed animals, trying to find the perfect dog-shaped one for Fallyn, Rowdy leaned on the half-full cart two hours later. Further down the aisle, his mate and Rebekah viewed different dolls. Shopping seemed to have all the women's attention, but he wasn't easily fooled. Even if the faint scent of brimstone departed with Jarvesel, his threats remained, and Astra's concern for her family would increase as time passed.

Two men in dark suits accompanied by a middle-aged store

guard approached and Rowdy shifted to face them. From the corner of his eye, he saw Venus stalk forward to stand at his shoulder, watching his back, but leaving him room to fight. "What do you seek?"

"I'm Special Agent Wardrow Roberts." The older one, a tall, stocky man, stepped forward, opening a black billfold, and revealing a badge. He gestured to his companion, a young mixed-race fellow. "This is Agent Fletcher Gaines." He glanced at Venus. "Are you Astra Jamison?"

"No, but you already know that. She's my sister." No humor shone in the narrowed violet eyes. "Why do you want her? Do you have news about Nina Armstrong or Kyle Morgan? Did you find them?"

"That's not our case," Fletcher Gaines said, as the store security man departed. "It's part of Newsome and Endicott's since they were the first ones in Liberty Valley investigating what happened to Detective Chambers."

"Who?" Rowdy asked.

"Beth Chambers, one of the Dawson cousins," Venus said. "She was an Eagleville homicide detective who disappeared in Mount Baker National Forest when she went after Gary Smith."

Rowdy frowned thoughtfully. "Wasn't he the fellow we saw with your father tonight?"

"Yes." Venus shrugged. "Beth was the first to link him to a series of murders. She was pretty much the only one who cared about the prostitutes that ended up dead. The feds showed up a month ago when they discovered she'd vanished in the national forest last spring."

29

"That's a fair summary, although Fletcher was working with Detective Chambers. Very few people realize that since the sheriff's department hadn't officially asked for our help." This time Wardrow Roberts spoke. "Who is your father?"

"Your records show that too, and I'm sure you read them before you tracked us down," Venus said.

"Even so, there's no harm in saying he's Gunnolf Marvin, the police chief in Corbettstown." Astra obviously heard the last question as she joined them. "He wanted me to defend his friend, Gary Smith, but of course I couldn't since Nina Armstrong is one of my clients and her needs come first. Did you find her and Kyle?"

"Again, that's not our case." Fletcher repeated. "We're looking for our agents. A local officer found Tasha Endicott injured in a wrecked bureau car. He called for back-up and the paramedics quickly arrived. They stabilized her and transported her to the hospital in Everett. No signs have been found of her partner."

"Will she be all right?" Astra asked. "I've talked with her a few times about Nina and Beth Chambers. What does Agent Endicott say?"

"She was unconscious when Officer Dawson found her. She's in a medically induced coma now so she can't provide any assistance in locating her partner."

"Couldn't he have gone for help?" Astra asked. "That'd be perfectly natural."

"Yes, but the local officers say that nothing turned up when they canvassed the area," Fletcher said. "They've been extremely cooperative."

"Is that normal?" Venus inquired, a little too sweetly. "From what I've seen on TV and read in the papers, aren't you guys supposed to be adversarial?"

"Territorial would be more accurate." Wardrow Roberts eyed her. "You think we shouldn't trust them, don't you?"

"When a lawman asks his daughter to defend a killer and gets addlepated because she refuses, it's downright stupid to rely on his deputies." Rowdy eased closer to Astra. "Figure Venus will say you already know that."

She grinned appreciatively. "I don't have to now."

"Will you two stop picking at them?" Astra sighed, shaking her head. "They're just testing us. They probably already called out their agents to rip Corbettstown apart, and this is a case of keep—"

"Your friends close and your enemies even closer," Rowdy finished. "If that's true and they need nothing from us, reckon we should finish your shopping here so we can make those other stores you wanted to visit."

"Good points." Astra glanced at the agents. "We're done here, aren't we?"

"For the moment," Wardrow Roberts agreed.

"You can contact me at my office on Monday if you need anything else." Astra handed each of them a business card, then deliberately turned her back. "Let's go."

"And if we visit your home tomorrow?" Fletcher asked. "What happens then?"

"You'll be alone because we're not there," Rowdy told him. "Don't make a mess."

Astra glanced swiftly over her shoulder. "And leave the search warrant on the kitchen island counter."

———

As he drove through the night, north toward the Canadian border, Gunnolf Marvin thought about his daughters. He hadn't seen the three of them together in years. Some fathers would be proud of their obvious beauty so like their mother's. He preferred their undoubted intelligence, the danger and lethal threat they emanated. *My princesses* and he smiled. Of course, he'd threatened to destroy what they loved before killing them, but they wouldn't make the upcoming battle an easy one. And it'd been years, no, several lifetimes since he had adversaries worth fighting.

Gary shifted in the right bucket seat of the Crown Victoria. "Wish I was going to be around a while longer. I hate missing a bloodbath."

"You should have thought of the consequences before you took that woman to your cabin," Marvin said. "I told you there'd be time to deal with her, but you've always been too impulsive. You ought to have counted on her man following, since he already knew what you intended to do to her. They may not have been a mated pair like the shifters in the pack, but it didn't mean there wasn't a bond between them."

"I didn't expect them to escape while I established an alibi elsewhere, or to burn down my place."

"Good story, but nobody's going to believe you didn't kill them and dispose of the bodies before setting that fire. Even I don't." Gunnolf signaled for a lane change. He'd take the next exit and drive as close as possible to the *Time Portal*. "My girl, Astra, couldn't get a jury to buy it and she's pulled off some damned fine work in the courtroom, freed a lot of real scum for us to feed the pack."

"I'm telling the truth. I didn't finish them."

"Then why hasn't anyone seen them? The Armstrongs are

raising all sorts of hell and their political cronies are keeping the search alive for their missing chick and her fiancé. Do you think they'd hide the two of them and throw fits to distract everyone?"

"Wouldn't be the first time somebody's done that."

The road narrowed, winding up into the forest and Marvin concentrated on the highway, pleased there weren't many oncoming vehicles, which meant he wouldn't have to be concerned about witnesses. He'd close the portal once he sent Smith through, but there wasn't any point in telling the man no escape route existed. Let him live and die in nineteenth century Liberty Valley while the Corbetts cleaned up the messes he'd made. "Will anyone find the one you sacrificed?"

"If they do, they'll think he fell off the cliff in a drunken stupor, but the wildlife should take care of what's left of him."

Huge cedars crowded close to the two-lane highway. "Who was it? Someone you picked up in a bar or a prostitute from a street corner in Seattle?"

"No, I got tired of the feds snooping around and following me everywhere, so I eliminated them."

Marvin's hands tightened on the steering wheel, his knuckles whitening. "You killed a FBI agent? Did you even consider what happens to the rest of us?"

"He wasn't quite dead when I left after the portal didn't open. The bears and the other predators will take care of him."

"You're lucky this is one of the few mistakes you've made." Marvin pulled into a darkened parking lot at the trail head. "We walk from here. Let's go."

"Won't we need a blood sacrifice?"

"You may, but I don't." It wasn't quite true, but he wouldn't say he'd collected sufficient *Power* punishing his crew when they allowed his new toy to escape. Oddly enough, he missed Trina more than he'd thought possible. She didn't bore him, unlike other women in the pack. He had to watch for poison in his food and beverages, physical attacks when he entered the same room and the battles didn't end even after sex. Once when the two of them were in bed after a particularly wild bout, she'd said she loved him. He'd laughed at her and she'd damn near smothered him with a pillow.

When she fled, he'd been tempted to skin his deputies and cook them in his barbeque pit, but he decided to let them try to make amends first and find her while they healed from broken bones, gashes and concussions. He'd told them the dying started at *Yule*. Only Latham Sellers had the guts to point out that the woman would have been meat when Marvin tired of her. That was true, but it could have taken years especially if she gave him children. He'd looked forward to the challenge of raising sons with her fire and golden hair since she'd undoubtedly have taught them to hate him from infancy.

———

Studying the latest video games in the display case, Astra felt someone watching her, and she glanced over her shoulder, wondering if she blocked another shopper. An older man wearing a dark suit stood nearby, right arm holding his middle while blood flowed from several knife wounds, drenching his sleeve. More blood from a gashed forehead trickled down the side of his face, through graying beard stubble, landing on his shoulder. Oddly enough, none of the blood splattered on the tile floor.

"Help Endi—" He choked and sputtered through broken teeth. "Help her."

Astra glanced at the busy salesclerk talking to Rowdy, making sure she wouldn't be heard, before she murmured, "It's already done. Where are you?"

"Doesn't matter."

"It does to me." Astra approached him, sending more energy to the wraith. She saw drying mud on his knees, pine needles in his short, silver hair and the silhouettes of ramshackle cedar shake buildings behind him. She heard water rushing over rocks and smelled something like rotten eggs. It must be sulfur from old mine tailings. "We're coming. Stay alive until we arrive."

"Who are you talking to?" Rebekah froze beside her, gaze pinned on the dying man. "Is he—?"

"The missing FBI agent." Astra drew a deep breath. "Take your S.U.V. and go to the ranch and get Freya. She can track him. Leave her sons to protect the children. Meet me and Rowindache where the road ends near Monte Cristo."

"The old ghost town?"

Astra nodded. "Tell Meteor to call Brigid and have her contact Deputy Dawson. Tell him to join us there. He'll be able to call in law enforcement and the paramedics."

"What will you tell them when they have questions?"

"I'll claim attorney–client privilege as much as possible and throw my demon-father under the proverbial bus when it's not."

"That will work," Rebekah said. "I'll see you there."

———

At three in the morning, they returned to the Rocking J. Venus stopped her rig in front of the dark house. She'd thought everyone would be asleep, but that didn't appear to be the case. She flicked a sideways glance at Meteor when Hugh and Jed came off the porch, striding toward them. "What do you suppose this is about?"

"They undoubtedly want to know what Astra and Rowdy are doing."

"Do we tell them?"

"Of course. We're not following the same paths that our mother and aunt have taken. Concealing truth only aids our father and his minions in their dark arts." Meteor opened the passenger door, glancing up at Jed. "Make yourself useful and help carry these pack-ages into the house. We need to put them away before the younglings see them."

"All three pups are sound asleep in their beds."

"Do you really think your children will remain there and not start snooping before the holiday?"

Venus suppressed the urge to laugh. Her older sister might have said 'no secrets' but that didn't mean she wouldn't make the men work for the information they sought. Jed picked up the largest of the boxes and Meteor led the way toward the east wing of the house.

Hugh collected several bags, pausing to give Venus a steady look.

"Problem?" She arched an eyebrow. "Are they too heavy?"

"No. What are your sister and her apprentice doing with my partner? Is he in jeopardy?"

She shook her head. "Not from them, and the shifters are busy dealing with the FBI scouring Corbettstown. Astra went after an injured federal agent. He'll need healing before the paramedics and law enforcement arrive. That's Rowindache and Robinaranika's task."

"What about protection from whoever attacked him?"

"My demon-father and Smith are miles away."

"Will they remain there? What if your sire sends his disciples to clean up a perceived mess? Should we arrange a distraction?"

"Wouldn't that be fun?" She tilted her head, reminding herself that true warriors didn't giggle regardless of the urge. "What are you thinking?"

He glanced at the night sky. "It's the annual time of the year for meteor showers."

"Those were ten days ago, but most mundane folk wouldn't be surprised if they saw a few more streaks before dawn. Shall we go to the workroom?"

"Definitely. What do you have to create fireballs?"

"We've collected quite a few igneous rocks when I take the children on nature hikes in the Cascade foothills, and I store them in a cupboard upstairs. We can choose from the granite, basalt, shale and conglomerates."

"Did you tell the young-uns that anything can be a weapon?"

"Of course. I'm the war queen, and it's my duty to train young witches to protect themselves with a variety of armaments. Even the youngest can learn to hurl a fireball, although two and three of them need to link up for distant targets."

"Allying with other warriors is a much-needed skill."

"Exactly." She led the way up the stairs to the warded room. "My sisters couldn't block all my knowledge even when they suppressed my memories. I always knew I had to be able to fight and nothing is worse than being defenseless when strong adversaries approach."

———

Shrouded by night, large evergreens surrounded the gravel parking lot at the trailhead. Astra heaved a sigh as she parked her Lexus. "We have to walk from here and it's going to be a serious hike since the bridge over the river washed out and hasn't been replaced."

"Then I hope you brought something else to wear and boots. You won't get far in that skirt and those high-heeled shoes."

"I have other clothes in the trunk."

"And a blanket?"

She laughed, sliding out of the car. "Yes, in case I break down in the boonies. But, I don't need one to change my clothes."

"Then, don't complain because these rocks hurt your backside." He followed her to the rear of the vehicle.

A blush scorched her cheeks when he reached for her. "We don't have time for this, Rowindache."

"We make time for ourselves, *Vaslattel*." He drew her against him.

She tilted her head, moistening suddenly dry lips. "And if I refuse?"

"Are you?"

"No." She surrendered to his kiss, threading her fingers in his hair. He lifted his head, and she gasped when he cupped her breasts, his thumbs gently rubbing her nipples through her shirt and bra. "Let me get that blanket."

"Only if you hurry, my own. I have a yen to ride a witch in the moonlight."

———

Two hours later, they'd dressed. She wore heavy blue jeans, two shirts, a jacket and low-heeled hiking boots. She collected her backpack and tested the flashlight she kept in a box of supplies. Headlights from Rebekah's S.U.V. swept the area. The younger woman pulled up beside Astra's late model car, parking and sliding out of the rig before allowing Freya out of the back seat.

Astra petted the big black dog. "Any problems?"

"Meteor called Brigid, but she hadn't been able to contact her cousin when I left. They'll keep trying and send him as soon as possible."

"We won't wait for that or him, Rebekah. Get your flashlight."

"I'll create a witch-light."

"No *magick* until we find the one we seek." Rowdy eyed the night sky and trees before turning toward the path. "We don't want to draw attention to our activities."

"Hughondear should have thought of that before he sent your sword, pistols and pack." Rebekah opened the rear compartment, removing the blade still in its sheath. "He said to remember that silver always wounds or kills a shifter if your potions and nostrums fail."

"There aren't any shifters in Monte Cristo." Astra glanced at each of the *healers*. "What aren't you telling me?"

"That your father has probably learned by now this lawman is alive, that his wounds haven't killed him and has sent minions to rectify the situation." Rowdy adjusted the straps of the scabbard. "We may face a battle. Do you still want to seek trouble, or shall we return to the ranch and wait for a better day to die?"

"Even if you're less than sewer sludge, I never considered you a coward, Rowindache." Astra lifted her chin and started for the woods, Freya at her side. "Come or stay behind. The choice is yours."

30

WHILE ASTRA REFERRED TO THE ROAD AS A TRAIL, IT WAS WIDER than many of the paths he'd ridden in the past, wider than most wagon tracks. Granted, he'd also forded plenty of rivers back in those days. The crossings often required his horse swim through the water, but tonight a wide log provided access from one side to the other of this river and none of them got wet, not even the dog.

He glanced at his mate who'd taken over leading their group and strode slightly in front of him, enjoying the way the snug jeans outlined the flare of her rounded hips and the curve of her backside. Hard to believe the witch ready to confront demons and save an innocent was the same woman who'd rolled on a blanket with him for almost two hours. She'd moaned at his touch, his kisses, and screamed in pleasure when he'd had her with his mouth before finally taking her.

She flicked a quick glance over her shoulder and narrowed her dark blue gaze. "I know what you're thinking, Rowindache. This isn't the time or the place, so stop."

"I will if you promise to wear those pants with your other boots when we're safe."

She flushed and glared this time. He chuckled, caught up with her, and took her hand, pulling her close. He lowered his voice. "And nothing else, my own."

"All you think about is sex."

He kissed the side of her neck. "I'm making up for lost years and lives, *Vaslattel*."

A few hours later, faint streaks of dawn lightened the winter sky as they approached an assortment of ramshackle cabins, some obviously more derelict than others. Rowdy glanced up and down the dirt main street. No signs of human life and from the looks of things, there hadn't been any in quite some time. "Who lived here and what happened?"

"Not a lot anymore." Rebekah stopped beside him, carrying a large red bundle that she'd called a 'first responder, first aid kit'. "In the late 1800s and early 1900s, it was a mining town, but eventually the money ran out because there wasn't enough silver or lead to make the costs worthwhile."

"River flooding that damaged the railroad several times didn't help either." Astra petted the large, black dog beside her, then started toward the first cabin. "Now, we trust Freya to find Special Agent Newsome. My vision brought us this far. Let's go."

Rowdy nodded, listening intently. He didn't hear anything which was suspicious in itself. There should have been small animals moving in the underbrush near the buildings even if the early morning birds often remained silent until the sun actually rose. Yet, he felt more than saw predators approaching. A bullet would stop most of the local wildlife, but it wouldn't do much to a shifter. Reaching over his shoulder, he drew his sword from the scabbard. The motion caught his mate's attention before she returned her attention to the dog and the search.

The dog at her side, Astra scanned the inside of another cabin but didn't see anyone hiding in the shadows. Across the street, she saw Rebekah using a flashlight to mirror her actions, searching for the federal agent in an old store. Meanwhile, Rowdy continued to stand sentinel in the street, obviously on guard. He felt some sort of tension, although she didn't see any threats in the area. The law enforcement officer had to be somewhere nearby. Astra knew that much, but she didn't know precisely where. She'd searched half the shacks on this side of the street, but she'd only disturbed a pair of raccoons, a few owls and a couple rats.

Freya growled, pawing at a cedar board, trying to force her way into the remains of what undoubtedly was a wood or storage shed of some kind back in the day. The building didn't seem large enough for anyone to live there. Astra joined the large black dog, peering through cracks between the handmade cedar boards in what once must have been a solid wall. She'd nearly passed by the small building, thinking it wouldn't hide a grown man, but the dog's actions showed the canine had different ideas.

Astra spotted a huddled shape near the back wall. She took a moment to pet Freya, a quick reward, and then gestured for her companions to join her. "He's here."

"Remain on guard. Something or someone stalks us." Rowdy passed over his sword. "Prepare yourself."

Astra nodded, grasping the hilt. She stepped further into the road as he pulled away the boards and created a bigger opening, one large enough to admit him.

He turned to eye her; his dark gaze softer than a kiss. "Take care of yourself and my son."

"You mean my daughter." Astra managed what she hoped was a confident smile and watched him enter the shack.

Rebekah followed the other *healer* into the tiny room. Silence for a moment, then the younger woman spoke. "He's barely alive. Try to get a signal on your cell phone and tell Meteor to send help."

Since there weren't any cell towers near the ghost town overshadowed by the Cascade Mountains, all of them knew actually using her smart phone wouldn't work, but there wasn't any point in saying so. Instead, Astra called on her *magick*, using the *talipenlace* as a focus, and sent a text to her sister's phone. A response came in moments.

"Done," Astra called. "Help's on the way."

"Great. I'll assist Rowdy while you defend us."

Astra took a deep breath and leaned the sword against the wall of the shack. She removed herbs, salt, candles and a bottle of purified water from her pack, then drew the *athame* from the sheath in her boot. She'd cast a circle of protection around them and hope she could hold off their enemies until their allies arrived. Rain misted her face, and she shivered in the winter cold. Gray clouds piled on the horizon, and she knew the weather would worsen as the morning progressed. A fire first, then the circle of herbs and salt. The words would come when she lit the candles.

She began the work. While she built a small campfire, she visualized the invisible dome she'd use to cover the small cabin and the dirt track in front of it. Freya, her escort, Astra walked in a clockwise circle around the tiny building, laying down the salt and sprinkling rosemary, sage and rye. Finally, she placed the white candles in position and lit them.

"As above, so below, Lord and Lady guide my shield of powers. Protect us against evil and keep out harm in these upcoming hours. My shield, my domain, my space to hold and defend those who depend on me. No demons, dark entities or negative energies may breech this security and as I will it, so mote it be."

———

Her children slept, safely protected by Trina and Gard. *Time to go*, Meteor thought, lingering in the doorway to watch her youngest sleep, the little girl curled under the patchwork, handmade quilt. She glanced up the hallway at the sound of footsteps and nodded at her sister who held a small bag. "Are you finished with the fire-stones?"

Venus inclined her head in agreement. "Yes. I wish I could go with you."

"The only way I can leave them is because I know you're here to watch over them." Meteor led the way toward her sister's bedroom. "Astra needs our help and I don't know how long it will take law enforcement to arrive, or if they'll even come."

"I'll keep calling Agent Roberts until he answers."

"Good. I'm counting on you." Walking across the room, Meteor stripped off her sweater, tossing it toward the queen-size bed. She finished undressing as her sister opened the doors to the adjoining balcony. Standing naked on the deck, she stretched out her arms and began the shift from woman to bird form. In moments, she became a bald eagle perched on the railing and lowered her head long enough to take the bag Venus held.

Eagles usually hunted between sunrise and noon, so if anyone saw her flying near the old ghost town, it'd be accepted as perfectly natural. Of course, she had to admit that throwing flaming rocks at shapeshifters was abnormal, but a witch did what a witch had to do. As dawn continued to lighten the sky, she neared the remnants of Monte Cristo.

Even before she was close enough to see the battle, she heard the clash of blade upon blade. Latham Sellers, six foot of muscular menace in his three-piece, pinstriped suit, white shirt, and tie, swung a sword at Astra. She blocked the blow and countered with one of her own. Meanwhile, Freya fought three large wolves behind him.

As Meteor watched, she saw more wolves leaping into the fray. Behind her, she heard the distinctive cry often attributed to a bald eagle, but she knew it was a red-tailed hawk. The other bird dove at the wolves and one reared up, trying to bite the gray and black mottled hawk. She hastily remembered the drawstring sack she carried and shook it open, so the fire-stones started to fall, bursting into flames when they hit the shifters.

The hawk screamed again as it veered close enough to strike at the largest male wolf. The bird continued to distract the wolf from the ongoing battle with the dog. Meteor flew closer and dropped the last of the rocks on the pack, saving two to throw in Latham's face. Then she soared near the woods, changing forms as she landed on the ground.

Her gift was 'freedom of shape' and unlike these wolves, it only took her a few minutes to flow from bird to animal. Now a wolf, she charged into battle, hitting the alpha male in the shoulder and sending him flying away from Freya. Blood dripped from the huge, black, mixed-breed's shoulder and she dragged her hindquarters, more raw meat, exposed tissues like jelly at this point. Mortally wounded, but she wasn't ready to give up, not when her mistress still fought.

Dimly, Meteor was aware that the hawk had flown a short distance away and used the same tactics she did, gaining sufficient space to alter his shape. Then he was back, and she recognized Jed Corbett in wolf form. The two of them fought the shifters together while they continued to protect Freya. The English bull-mastiff, Bernese Mountain Dog and Rottweiler, wolf-cross whimpered, collapsing on the ground, blood pooling underneath her.

The sword battle raged. Blow upon blow and there wasn't anything fair about the fight. They intended to kill each other. Latham raised his blade, obviously intending an overhead attack, but Astra was too experienced to tolerate that. Stepping to the side, she evaded him and swung at his foremost leg. She nicked his calf, but he didn't falter, stabbing at her ribs. She redirected that attack, pushing his sword out of the way with hers, then countered, striking at his arm.

Meteor lunged at a dark colored wolf, teeth closing on his neck. She bit hard, barely missing the artery in his throat. She heard a distinctive thumping and recognized it as an incoming helicopter. She wouldn't kill this shifter, not yet. She shook him hard, then hurled him away from the fight zone. She felt more than heard the whine of a bullet and knew someone in the chopper overhead had decided to take part in the struggle. She nosed Freya, gave the dying dog a quick lick of sympathy, then turned and raced for the cover of the woods, aware that Jed followed her.

In the cover of the evergreens, she spun around to check on her sister. Sword lowered, Astra knelt beside Freya in an obvious attempt to comfort her pet before the animal died. Latham Sellers followed the shifters into the trees, intending to escape from law enforcement. He paused to look back. Before Meteor could howl a warning, he hurled his heavy, short sword at her sister's unprotected back. The blade sank deep and she collapsed on top of her dog.

———

Soul deep agony lanced through him and in that moment, he realized his mate was dying. Unlike what his friends faced if they lost their soul-matched witches, her death wouldn't kill him, but he'd face the rest of this life without her and his unborn child. Rowdy leaped to his feet. "No!"

He left the injured federal agent with Rebekah and pushed through the boards of the shack. The spell of protection she'd cast had already started to dissolve, part of the dome melting away into the ground while the rest floated into the cloudy sky. He saw Agent Fletcher Gaines kneeling beside her and the dog, calling for others to come and help from the large metal flying contraption.

Rowdy hurried to her side, spotting the silver chased blade buried in her back. "Who did this?"

"Not important." She drew a ragged breath. "Save Freya."

"After you and my son." He turned her onto her side, measuring the wound and the blood soaking her jacket with his gaze. "I've told you since we met again. I take care of what's mine."

"Sorry I failed you." A tear slid down her waxen cheek. "So sorry, Rowind—"

He kissed her, his lips brushing her ear. "You didn't fail me, my own."

"Meant to do better." She gasped for breath. "This time. This life."

"You will." He placed his hand over what he thought of as her 'soul-eye' in the center of her forehead. "Rest now. I'll take care of you. All of you." He turned his attention to the other man. "Your agent is in that building with Rebekah Corbett. We've bandaged his injuries. Go help him and send her to aid me."

"She's dying." Fletcher rose to his feet, mud on his clothes and blood on his hands. "I tried shooting at those wolves from the chopper, but I never saw the man who threw that sword at her. I'm sorry. She was trying to protect you."

"She did protect us." Rowdy smoothed the sunset red hair back from her face. "She did her job. Go do yours and send me her friend."

Alone with her, he waited to pull the sword from her back. If she hadn't worn three layers, two shirts and a heavy denim jacket, the blade would have gone deeper. Yes, she was badly injured, but he didn't doubt he could heal her. He glanced up as Rebekah joined him. "She sleeps. We'll bandage her and take her home."

"And Freya?"

"Sleeps as well." Rowdy glanced toward the evergreens. "Your sister mourns in those trees. She and Thojedescar need clothes before they can aid us. Send him to steal those of the shifters. Let them return to Corbettstown naked and cold in their shame since we won this battle, and they lost."

"As you say, *siblerbro*."

Rebekah faded away on her mission as Special Agent Wardrow Roberts arrived. "Gaines told me what he saw, that she was trying to defend you while you took care of Agent Newsome. Why didn't you call us earlier?"

"Because none of us knew if this was real or simply someone flapping their gums." Rowdy glanced at the shack and the crew of men and women entering it. "Go do your business and leave us to ours."

"I'm sorry for your loss."

"You have no idea what your words mean. Leave me with what's mine."

"I'll send the medics here to help her. We'll take her with us when we go." Wardrow Roberts turned toward the shack. "And the dog too."

"No. They're mine and I will look after them."

31

Jed Corbett reached for Meteor's hand, but she stepped away, refusing to let him comfort her. At least, she'd accepted the garments he'd taken from the defeated shifters. She'd hurriedly dressed in a tight green thermal top that clung to full breasts, revealing she didn't wear a bra, topping it with a blue-checked flannel shirt. Sloppy jeans barely stayed up, even with the belt she'd buckled on the tightest notch. She brushed past him and hustled toward the dirt street where Rowdy still held her older sister.

Meteor paused while he opened the circle, he'd cast to keep the law enforcement officers from seeing them and Jed followed her inside. Still ignoring him, she asked, "What do you want me to do?"

"Hold her while I remove this blade." Rowdy glanced at Rebekah, who sorted through the huge red first-aid kit she'd brought along. "I'll cut the jacket and shirts out of the way first. Be prepared to staunch the bleeding."

"I will." Rebekah drew on a pair of surgical gloves, then found a large bandage. "I'm ready when you are."

Jed grimaced when he saw the gleaming gray dagger Rowdy held. "I can't help if you're using that. Shifters and silver don't mix. Besides, dead women don't bleed."

"She's not dead yet. I put her into stasis so we could move her."

Rowdy carefully slit the coat from collar to hem, easing it away from the sword still lodged between Astra's shoulder blades. "I'll wrap the sword in her jacket. When I can leave her, I will return the blade to its owner and he will pay for what he did with appropriate interest."

"That works. Let me know if you need an alibi." Jed barely saw his friend nod, before he clipped the shirts halfway down and the entire nylon bra strap, revealing her skin and the sword embedded in her back.

Thick gauze pad ready, Rebekah met Rowdy's gaze, signifying she was prepared for the next step. Surprisingly, the blade hadn't penetrated as deeply as the *healers* obviously feared since Astra wore a turtleneck and sweatshirt under her denim jacket.

Rowdy took a deep breath, then grasped the hilt. He pulled out the short sword and dark blood oozed from the injury. "Good, it didn't strike an artery and missed her spine as well as her lungs."

Meteor held her sister closer, more tightly, their hair mingling together. "How do you know?"

"The color of the blood and the way it flows." Rowdy wrapped the sword in the remains of Astra's coat. "We'll bandage her and head for home. Thojedescar, carry the dog while I carry my mate. Sisters, you need to scout for enemies. Rebekah, will you guard us and fight if need be? Some *healers* can't take lives."

"As Meteor tells me, 'A *healer* can put bodies together and certainly knows how to take them apart.' I'll defend you to the last, *siblerbros*."

"Then, take my sword." Rowdy gestured to it when Rebekah finished her work, tucking Astra's bra inside the plastic box used as a kit for medical supplies. He slipped the enemy's blade into his own scabbard before adjusting Astra's shirts over the thick bandage, then gathered her into his arms. A flick of his hand continued to keep his spell around them, warding them from the law enforcement officers and medical crew who'd arrived in the helicopter while he led the way toward the surrounding forest.

Jed admired not only the healing *magick*, but also the defensive arts his friend used. They melted into the trees, finding the path from the ghost town to the trail head and the parking lot. He'd have left the uninjured shifters to attack their prey, but he wasn't in charge of the group sent by his uncle. He'd tracked them long enough to know they'd fled, running home with their wolf tails between their proverbial legs, injured and healthy alike. However, he wasn't sharing that with his *laspowima* or her *healer* sister. Protecting their older sister would provide the two women with a purpose they desperately needed at this moment.

———

She'd been watching for vehicles for the past three hours while she prepared breakfast, fed the children, and then encouraged them to watch a holiday movie. Later, they could write letters to the Holly King and let him know what they wanted for *Yule*. Now, she cleaned the kitchen and stared out the windows, praying her sisters would return soon. Hugh had gone off to mend fences and work around the barns since he couldn't stand waiting much more than she could.

Suddenly, a swirl of dust brightened the morning, and she recognized Rebekah's Ford Explorer coming up the drive. Bamse yelped at the back door while his older brother growled and joined him. Venus opened the door and followed the two black dogs when they raced toward the S.U.V. Jed Corbett opened the passenger door, strode around to the rear of the rig. In moments, he hefted Freya's limp frame into his arms. Escorted by her whimpering sons, he headed to the house.

"What happened?" Venus looked around the yard but didn't see any strangers who posed a threat. Still, she rested her hand on the hilt of her sword. "Who did this?"

"Some of the pack almost killed her. I don't know who sent them, but I'm betting on Frank Corbett," Rebekah said. "They wouldn't fight without his permission."

Venus nodded agreement. "That makes sense."

"We'll take her to the work-room and I'll get started healing her." Rebekah passed over her keys, then collected her emergency first aid kit. "Will you have my rig cleaned? We don't want to be tracked."

Venus nodded and watched the younger woman jog after Jed Corbett. Before she could call for Gard or Trina, her older sister's expensive, late model car pulled into the gravel parking area. Oddly enough, Astra wasn't driving. Meteor was behind the steering wheel.

Dread swept through Venus and she stalked to the back door of the Lexus, yanking it open before Rowdy could. She froze when she saw Astra's still, silent body in his arms. "What happened?"

"She sacrificed herself to keep him and Rebekah safe while they healed that federal agent." Meteor slid out from the driver's seat, switching off the motor. "Latham was with the shifters and he attacked her. She'd all but defeated him in a duel when the cops and the other feds arrived and started shooting. As he was leaving, Latham hurled his sword at her and struck Astra from behind."

"Is she—?"

"Asleep." Still holding their elder sister, Rowdy glanced past them to Hugh, who'd just arrived. "Take her for a moment."

"Gladly."

Venus watched the men ease the broken, injured woman from one set of arms to the other, keeping a blanket wrapped around her. "Where is Latham?"

"Either in Corbettstown, or on his way back to Olympia," Meteor said. "He'll have to wait for pay-back. Astra comes first."

"And even then, my vengeance overrides yours, little sister." Rowdy gently took Astra, cradling her body in a warm embrace. "This isn't the first time he's attacked your sister or arranged my murder and hers in our past lives. I will be the one to return his sword to the heart he won't have for long, and I'll send his remains to the dracklegons for disposal, so he'll never ambush us again."

"If he waits to attack, you can have him." Venus kept her hand on the hilt of her own sword. "If he comes when you're busy with my sister, then he's mine to kill."

Tears filled Meteor's blue eyes, threatening to spill onto her cheeks. Venus put her vengeful plans on hold. She hugged the sister she had left. "Come on. I made your favorite French toast for breakfast. It isn't as good as yours, but you can take a shower, put on your own clothes and eat something. While you look after the children, Hugh and I will set up defenses."

"I'm sorry I couldn't do more to save her."

"You did plenty." Venus guided Meteor toward the porch and the back door. "If you hadn't gone when you did with the fire-stones, I'm sure Latham and the rogue shifters would have succeeded in carrying out Frank Corbett's and our father's evil designs. If Jed hadn't insisted on following and fighting with you, who knows what would have happened? Rowdy could be healing more than Astra and Freya."

"The war queen is right." Hugh followed them. "The next time we battle, they'll face all of us and we'll be the winners. None of us will be injured in the fray."

"I hope you're right," Meteor said.

"I know I am."

Venus glanced over her shoulder at him. He sounded extremely confident, but both of them knew he lied in an attempt to comfort her sister. War and battles came without guarantees.

———

Pain washed over her in red waves, and she gasped for air. Her back ached and dimly she recalled Freya lying wounded and helpless beneath her. "My dog—"

"Rebekah restores her." Rowdy's low, gravelly voice sounded close to her ear. "Rest and let me look after you."

"It hurts. Everything hurts."

"Yes, I know. Journey among the stars until I call you back, *Vaslattel*."

She considered the idea for a few moments, wondering if she wanted to follow the suggestion. It was broad daylight, so she didn't see any stars right now. Instead, she saw Hugh stride by Rowindache's side as they walked up the steps and into Estelle's house. The men headed for the upstairs workroom, where they did *magick* rites. Her foster mother's scream cut the morning and Astra decided she definitely didn't want to join the rest of the Jamison family, much less listen to another of Estelle's or Diana's lectures.

She floated toward the sky, unsurprised when Freya loped to meet her. "Come along, puppy-girl. Let's find someplace else to visit."

The big, black dog wagged her tail and Astra took that as a sign of agreement. They'd stroll the star-paths for a few hours, or possibly even a day or two, or perhaps a week. Let Rowdy deal with the fall-out from the shifter attack in Monte Cristo. He was the first to tell her when she didn't measure up to his standards. He'd see how it felt to be unfairly criticized for sins he hadn't committed, for opting to fulfill his duties as a *High Healer* and doing what he thought was right regardless of the cost to others.

"I'm so tired of being told what I can and can't do. I hate having some man order me to treat others with the respect he thinks is due them, to allow my sisters and their *Chosen* to decide their paths without interference when I know they still need my help. And he doesn't like the way I intervene in my clients' lives and ensure they have the outcomes they've earned for crimes they've committed. He can try telling the Elder Witches what to do."

Freya seemed to enjoy the conversation by the way she pressed closer. Astra petted the dog and the two of them moved on, past the ranch house and into the early morning clouds shrouding the hills.

———

Tuesday afternoon, Meteor sat beside the queen-size bed where her older sister continued to sleep. She wasn't the only one who hadn't spoken or moved since the healing spells cast by Rowdy and Rebekah. Freya rested between her two adult sons; the three dogs crammed together on a comfy pet cushion close to the windows.

Every once in a while, either Bamse or Ivor whined and licked their mother's head.

Meteor glanced at the door as it opened and Diana entered, carrying a tray that held a bowl of soup, a sandwich, and a cup of tea. "What do you want?"

"To give you a break. I'll sit with her until supper."

"I'm okay. I should have done more to guard her. The least I can do is stay here until she wakes."

"It may be a few more days."

"What makes you say that?"

"Because I've seen this response before after a serious trauma." Diana put the tray on the nightstand, then drew up another chair. "Your sister has the power to walk the astral paths, doesn't she? Can't she be in more than one place at a time? Apparently, she's taken her dog with her."

"Is that what's happened? She's gone walk-about? How do we get her back?"

"Drink your tea. We wait until Rowindache has the strength to go after her. When he does, we need to watch over his body as well."

"All right, I'm going to find him and have a talk with him." Meteor rose to her feet. "Why didn't he tell us before this could be a result of her injuries? Granted, her boss had the 'second chair' lawyer take over the case for the client she was defending in court, but she's expected to return to work within another day or two. She'd be the first to say the law is what matters. It's what she loves."

"Estelle contacted the coven and arranged for a competent substitute. Your sister needs time to recover even when she's back with us."

"I don't trust either of you." Meteor crossed to the door. "I know Astra doesn't either. We were expendable when we were children and as far as the two of you are concerned, we still are. I'm not Venus, who allows her heart to lead her. I've made that mistake too many times in too many lives and learned better."

"At some point, we need to talk about the past, but not now." Diana picked up the teacup. "I can wait until you're ready."

"You'll wait a long time."

"I already have. It doesn't bother me as much as it bothers you."

"Obviously." Meteor closed the door and stormed down the hall. Fury laced through her, and she wanted to go back and scream at the woman who'd given birth to her. It wouldn't do any good, wouldn't save her elder sister, and it'd be a total waste of time. *Take a breath*, she told herself.

Breathe and think. Every problem has a solution, and the solution is within the problem. I'll find it. I'll find Astra too.

32

Rocking J Ranch ~ Tuesday, November 27th, 2018

VENUS DECIDED NOT TO SEND THE BOYS TO THE PRIVATE SCHOOL operated by the coven for a few days until she knew it was safe for them to return to class. They didn't seem to mind staying home with their younger sister, or at least they hadn't complained this morning. In the middle of creating peanut butter and strawberry jam sandwiches for lunch, Venus glanced toward the stairs when she heard the clatter of footsteps. She frowned as Meteor hurried into the kitchen. "Is Astra awake?"

"No, and she won't be for a while. She's not here, and neither is Freya. Both of their souls have disappeared." Meteor glared at Hugh, who stood by the counter with a cup of coffee. "Where is Rowdy?"

"I'm here." He entered the room from the adjacent bathroom. Long black hair speckled with gray tied in a ponytail with a leather thong, he wore his usual suede shirt, brown pants and low-heeled boots. He'd obviously had time to shower and shave and appeared alert. "What's wrong? You said Astra hasn't awakened yet. That doesn't make sense. Her wounds are nearly healed. Rebekah did an amazing job with the hellhound. She should be romping with her sons by now."

"Diana says they've gone on an astral journey." Meteor planted her fists on curving hips. "Fetch them back. Now!"

"How can he?" Venus turned from the counter, leaving the knife in the jar of crunchy peanut butter. "Our mother told me that Astra serves *Hecate*, the *Goddess* of Death, and the crossroads. What does Rowdy have to do with that?"

"He travels the star-paths too. He can bring her home to us."

"I can, but I shouldn't have to leave here." Rowdy took the cup of coffee Hugh offered. "When I finished mending her injuries, I called for her to return. She might still be sleeping, but she ought to be on her way back, not ignoring me. We're bonded, and she does as I wish."

"Are you really that stupid?" Venus looked him up and down, folding her arms. "Do you actually think she'll obey you or any man?"

"You're right, little sister." Rowdy drained the cup, then put it in the sink. "She's been a High Judge longer than a mere lawyer in this life, and she likes twisting the promises she makes. She knows better than to play these games with me, but she enjoys thwarting me. I'll leave right now. Holt, I trust you to look after my body while I'm gone. Depending on where she's gone, this may take a day or more."

Worry filled Meteor's face. "Where is she?"

"I have no idea." Rowdy shrugged. "As Venus pointed out, Astra can cross between *Life* and *Death*. She may be walking among the stars, or in *Liminfovia*, or even have gone to the *Land of the Dead*."

"Summerland?" Meteor caught her breath. "But you saved her. She's not dead."

"The *Land of the Dead* is different from where we go when we actually die," Hugh said gently. "It's where people end up when they travel through a *Time Portal*. You sent the marshal's brother there with his affianced."

"But, you told me you closed that portal when you and Rowdy rode through it." Venus looked at Hugh, then at Rowdy, narrowing her eyes. "Did you lie to me?"

"Never." Hugh's tone remained calm. "I'd never bear false witness, *Laspowima*, not to you or anyone. I hold to my honor."

"Because of her powers as one of *Hecate's* priestesses, my *vaslattel* doesn't have to use a portal to go to a previous *Time* or *Space*." Rowdy started for the staircase. "Since I'm following her tracks, I won't have to either. I can travel through the eternal star-paths."

"How long will it take to bring her home?" Meteor demanded.

"I have no idea. The sooner I leave, the sooner we'll return. I'll send the dog back when I find her, and you'll know we're on our way."

Venus measured the controlled anger in Rowdy's dark eyes. "How do you know Freya will obey and not attack you the way Bamse did?"

"I'm the one who controls the hounds of hell and your sister better not make the same mistake twice."

Hugh whistled softly, then started for the stairs after his long-time friend. "I hope you both understand about being careful what you wish for. Rowdy will bring her back, but your sister won't be happy when he catches up with her."

Venus lifted her chin. "If she doesn't care for the consequences of her actions, then she'd better stop being such a twit."

"What she said." Meteor nodded agreement. "Astra deserves to pay for scaring us half to death. I've been blaming myself for three whole days, thinking I got her killed."

Venus went to her sister and drew her into a warm hug. "I'm right there with you. I was afraid Rowdy's spells didn't work, that he wasn't able to save her in time. To discover she's in the middle of a snit is totally annoying and I'll tell her so when she's home."

Hugh chuckled. "You won't have to lecture her. Leave that to Rowdy. It's his job to join his *Chosen* on her path, regardless of where it leads."

"We'll allow him the privilege of scolding her the first time. After that, it's our turn." Venus glanced at the slices of bread on the counter. "Help me out here, Meteor. Our daughter's favorite princess movie will end in ten minutes. She and her brothers will be ready for lunch even if it's not quite ready for them."

———

Junction City, Washington Territory ~ Tuesday, November 27th, 1888

Escorted by her dog, Astra wandered slowly down the boardwalk bordering the main street of the small western town. Snow on their shingled roofs, the cedar shake buildings came in all sizes, from small cabins to one and two-story businesses. Raucous piano music poured from the batwing doors of the saloon. She carefully side-stepped around the two loggers enmeshed in a rough and tumble fight, rolling and punching each other in a foot of snow on the frozen road. In a moment, the marshal's brother would show up and kick butt. She suppressed the urge to laugh. Everything here reminded her of an old western movie.

She kept walking, drifting toward the graveyard on the east side of town. Because she and Freya traveled what her mate referred to as the star-paths, they actually weren't visible to most of the people who lived here. An exception was Nina Armstrong, the *Seer*. Another was the tall, dark-haired, translucent man who still paced around the cemetery near one of the most recent graves.

"What's keeping you, Tom Corbett?" Astra heaved a sigh. "You should be going to either *Liminfovia* or *Summerland*. Take your pick and move on."

"Where's your sister?" Wearing the same dark suit he'd obviously died in, he raked a hand through his hair, glowering at her. "I'm not going anywhere until Mary comes."

"I've already told you more than once. She said I was needed here and then vanished. Your life in these times is done. Go find her elsewhere or wait to join her when she's born a hundred years from now."

"I have to tell her who killed us before I go, or I'll forget when I come around again."

"I'll tell her when I go home." Astra petted Freya when the large, black dog pressed close, giving a gentle wag of her tail. "Your uncle murdered her, then you."

"But she thinks it was me and I'd never hurt her. He took my body and pretended to be me."

"I know. You've told me that a dozen times since I arrived. Like I said, I'll tell her she can trust you, although considering that you have three kids in the future, I'd say she already does to a certain degree."

"Three?" He stopped, stood and stared. "How can we have three when Mary was only having our second? My uncle swore to kill us before we had more children and he gave away Edwin to Mary's former fiancé."

"Yes and Hughondear brought him through a *Time-Gate* to us in the future."

"My prince lives with you?"

"With my youngest sister, the war-queen who guards your two wizard sons and your witchling daughter."

"So, my uncle loses." A smile slowly creased Tom's face, landing in the night-dark eyes. "I can accept that. What would be even better is if he's defeated here and now."

"He will be. Mary's sisters are staying at the hotel and they plan to burn Corbett's Town around his wolfish ears. They'll attack as soon as they have enough silver bullets."

"And the children? Most in the pack are innocent."

"They will be saved. The *Seer* plans to start an orphanage for them and in this era, Mary's sisters will raise them."

"And what about you? When do you return home?"

"As soon as I finish my work. I need to convince the woman who is me in this life that she needs to be careful or she'll be killed, murdered by the man who did his best to slay me. If he succeeds in killing her, our youngest sister will be the next victim. Their deaths would leave your uncle free to slaughter more innocents."

"If someone mortally injured you, how did you survive?"

"Rowindache, my *capostrol* sent me to walk the star-paths while he healed me and Freya."

"So, both my old friends live and flourish in your world." Relief eased the tension etched on Tom's rugged features, relaxing the tautness in the broad shoulders. "And they saved Edwin too. Now, I truly can leave and find Mary in *Summerland* until it's time for us to join you in our next lives."

"There will be difficulties."

"In each and every life, problems must be solved." Tom Corbett faded away, only his laughter remaining.

"Men." Astra heaved a sigh. "Come along, Freya. Let's go shopping before we head to the hotel and try talking to my stubborn self again."

Granted, she couldn't buy anything, but it was still fun to explore the mercantile and smell all of the spices. Maybe young children would visit and enjoy peppermint sticks, gifts from Susanne Prescott, the store-keeper while their parents bought supplies. Astra glanced around the graveyard once more, wondering what happened to it in her own time. There were very few headstones. Wooden crosses marked most of the snow-covered graves. Perhaps she and Rowindache could find the cemetery and bring flowers to honor those who'd passed.

Disturbed snow and footprints were the only signs of the brawl in front of the saloon. Music continued to play, and she smiled when her middle sister from this life stepped outside to join her. Although she was as much a ghost as her soul-matched wizard, Mary didn't seem as stressed or upset by her untimely death. She'd taken time to visit the mercantile and studied the latest fashion plates, modeling her garments after them.

She wore a light blue flowered dress with a drooping set of deep folds down the back that caused the skirt to hang straight from the hips. The overskirt swooped up and revealed the matching underskirt. The back was gathered in several low-hanging puffs, and unlike other women in town, Mary didn't wear a bustle which would make her derriere absolutely humongous. Her red hair was neatly confined in a bun under an ivory and blue hat decked out with artificial flowers, feathers, lace and beads. A few loose red tendrils escaped, teasing her forehead and neck.

Astra flicked a glance at the saloon. "I thought old-time ladies didn't visit such places."

"I didn't when I was alive, but now it doesn't matter." Mary twirled an insubstantial parasol. "I love music and Tom promised to buy me a spinet as soon as he could find a way to bring it to Corbett's Town from Seattle. His uncle had a major hissy fit when he heard."

"Why? What business was it of his?"

"Like most shifters, he didn't care for high-pitched sounds." Mary tilted her head to one side, showing off pearl earrings. "Or me or my sons for that matter."

"Then what Tom told me won't come as a surprise. He said his uncle killed both of you."

"It's impossible. I know my husband and I saw him that day. He was in a rage." Tears filled the sky-blue eyes and splashed onto a gloved hand. "He shoved me, then threw me—"

"He swears it wasn't him." Not for the first time, Astra wished she could embrace her sister, but the words would have to provide the comfort she couldn't. "In our next lives, our mother and aunt vow the soul-binding they placed on him prevents him from doing you or your children harm. However, our demon-father has many minions, including Tom's uncle. It comes as no surprise that he stole your mate's shape to murder you and your unborn child."

"I sent my baby to *Summerland* already." Mary's hand tightened on the handle of the umbrella. "I'll go find him and his father there, but first give me your word that you'll look after Edwin."

"In our next life, you already are and so is our youngest sister, but I'll do my part to take care of the younglings. So, will our mates." Astra tried again to touch her sister's arm, but failed, only grasping air. "As for your witch sisters in this life, they plan to wreak vengeance."

"Remind them to be careful so they don't end up like me."

"I will." Astra drew out her cell phone, turned it on, and found a picture of Latham Sellers. "What's his name in this life? He did his best to kill me a few days ago and they must look out for him too."

"That's Leander Selby, one of the Corbett's Town deputies." Mary shuddered. "He's vicious. He encouraged several of the boys to bully Edwin until Tom whipped him in three different fist fights."

"Well, he hasn't learned his lesson yet, but I'll warn myself and our youngest sib again. Now that I have a name, they may listen."

"All you can do is your best. Blessed be, Satiranika, until we meet in our next lives."

"Blessed be." Astra waited until the other woman melted away. A cold winter breeze brushed her face, bringing sudden tears to sting her eyes. She took a deep breath before she started toward the general store again. She'd miss her sister, and oddly enough, the brother by the soul-mating ceremony. She had one more task to complete.

She gestured for Freya to wait under the awning at the corner of the building and conjured up a meaty bone for the large black dog. The treat wasn't real, but then again, neither of them were either. Inside the store, she scanned the mercantile, closing the door behind her. Susanne Prescott, a tall, sturdy blond woman stood behind the long counter at the back of the room, tallying an order.

Coffee, spices, and tinned food filled the shelves behind her. Along the right-hand wall, bolts of bright calico lined another counter. Pants, shirts, overalls, and other clothes as well as pairs of boots filled the shelves. The hardware was through the back, but the tools bored Astra since she'd already checked out the new wood-stoves, axes, saws, shovels, hammers and store-bought nails.

Kegs and barrels of sugar, molasses, and flour sat around the room, including the stereotypical cracker and pickle ones. Baskets of pumpkins, apples and eggs showed to advantage in one bay window at the front of the store. The second displayed a selection of ladies' hats and a ready-made scarlet walking dress, one of Astra's favorite colors. She lingered by it, wishing she could stroke the material and see if the velvet was as soft as it looked.

The door opened, banging against the frame, and Susanne looked up from the order in front of her, heading around the end of the counter. "Darn that wind."

"Sorry, ma'am. It's me, not the wind." Rowdy gestured, and the door swung closed.

"I don't believe it." Astra gaped at him, then shook her head. "What are you doing here, Rowindache?"

A muscle twitched in his jaw and he swept her with a scathing dark gaze. "I told you I'd give you a loose rein unless you tried to balk, buck my plans, or buffalo me. When I *Call* you, *Vaslattel*, you come."

33

Junction City, Washington Territory ~ Tuesday, November 27th, 1888

ASTRA LIFTED HER CHIN AND MET HIM GLARE FOR GLARE. "IT MAY come as a shock, Rowindache, but as the saying goes, 'you aren't the boss of me,' and I do as I please."

"I'll let you 'please' me when we return home, *Vaslattel*." He enjoyed the blush that swept into her cheeks. He wouldn't tell her that he was both glad and grateful to see her alive and well enough to sass him. When he entered the bedroom, she'd worn a white nightgown and lay perfectly still in the wide bed, unmoving under the blankets, hardly breathing, her face a pale mask. "Let's go."

"I still have business here."

"Whatever it is, we'll do it together and then we go."

"Fine." She stalked past him. Tight blue jeans outlined the flare of her rounded hips and the curve of her backside. A curtain of sunset red hair hung down her back, obscuring the denim jacket and the two shirts she wore. "I still don't know why you bothered to come after me."

"Because you're mine and when you don't obey me, you should

expect me to rein in my witch. Even if you're not an easy ride, I can handle you."

Another toss of her head, another glare from dark blue eyes. "You couldn't handle me if I came with instructions."

"I've made you 'come' before and I will again." He didn't resist the temptation and aimed a swat at her rump as she sashayed past him. It wasn't a surprise when he barely made contact—after all neither of them was all that corporeal—but she still jumped. Not much, just enough to amuse him. "So, where are we going?"

"The hotel. Since they'd already died in this incarnation, I have to tell Nina Armstrong, who is the Seer that I've sent Meteor and Jed to Summerland. Then, I'll convince my former self to watch out for Latham before he kills her and Venus."

"And she's undoubtedly as pigheaded as you are."

"Thanks a lot." Astra stopped outside the mercantile and looked around. "Where's Freya?"

"I sent her home." He put his hand on her shoulder, a whisper of a touch. "Her pups need her, and your sisters needed to know I found you."

"Well, aren't you all that and a bucket of chips?" She turned and strolled past the newspaper office, then glanced across the street and crossed, her boots not leaving prints in the snow. At the hotel, she led the way upstairs to one of the most expensive rooms, elaborately furnished with a large brass bed, a bureau, a wardrobe, and a fireplace.

A red-headed woman in her early thirties wearing a dark blue dress sat in a chair at the table, pouring a cup of tea. The older witch stopped for a moment, then resumed the action. "I hadn't seen you since this morning. I thought you'd left. Who is he?"

"You know who he is, Satiranika," Astra said, her tone even. "Our soul-matched mate. He came to find me and we're leaving soon."

"Show her the picture of your murderer." Rowdy placed his hands on her shoulders, offering the comfort of his light touch for support. "Let her choose whether she and your sister die, although I remember you saying that you or rather, she, killed him before he slew her in this life."

The woman lifted a dagger, obviously ready to cast a Death spell. "You're the one who dies, Mage."

"No, you don't touch him." Astra took a step forward, ready to protect and fight, even herself. "As I told our demon-father, Rowin-dache is mine to do with as I please. I choose what happens to him, how long I keep him, when I finish with him. You don't have a say. If you try anything, I will end you even if it ends me."

Utter silence while the woman studied them. Then, she lowered the dagger and placed it neatly beside the plate of cookies and teapot. "You love him that much?"

"I don't love him at all." Astra stiffened. "I just don't share what's mine."

"I see." The other witch laughed. "And I do see more than you think or know. All right, '*Miss Who I'll Be*' show me the man who hunts us. I promise to protect the little sister I have left."

"And yourself," Astra said. "Don't let Leander Selby annihilate either of you again as he's done before. When I sent Matiranika and Thojedescar to *Summerland* to join their unborn son, I promised you'd destroy their murderer. They named his uncle."

"Aren't those two men our demon-father's minions?"

"Yes, but unlike them, he awaits us in the future, and we will deal with him there. I don't know if you'll find him here."

"If you do, take care." Rowdy nudged Astra's back gently. "Show her the picture on that gadget you always carry. Our time here is done. We must depart before anyone in our world realizes you've been out of your body for three days."

———

Rocking J Ranch ~ Tuesday, November 27th, 2018

Astra yawned, stretched, rolling her shoulders, and slowly sat up against the pillows. It was wonderful to be back in her body. She hadn't realized how much she missed it. Moonlight streamed in the windows. She still switched on the lamp on the nightstand. Across the room, she saw a large pet bed where her dogs had obviously slept, but it was vacant now. Someone must have let out the three huge hellhounds. She shifted under the covers again, then pushed the blankets aside to rise and head for the adjacent bathroom.

She needed a shower and looked forward to using the large walk-in stall she'd installed here at the ranch. She slipped out of the thin, white nightshirt, tossing it on the tile floor. She turned on the taps and tested the water temperature at the faucet before she pulled up the lever. The warm spray cascaded down from the center rain-shower head. It felt like a tropical waterfall on her hair and skin. She glanced over her shoulder as the glass door opened and Rowdy joined her.

She admired his broad shoulders, wiry frame and lean hips. His dark hair swung free, and she smiled at him. "Would you believe me if I said I hadn't expected you?"

"Maybe." He brushed her lips with his, then framed her face with calloused hands. "Have you ever been with anyone in this room?"

She tilted her head, laughing at him. "I've always bathed by myself here."

"Not today." The water coursed down his back as he kissed the hollow in her throat, slowly moving toward her breasts. "We have time for you to surrender everything, *Vaslattel*. Yield to me."

"In your dreams." She wound her arms around his neck, gasping when his hand cupped her. One finger eased inside her. "I thought—"

"Too much. You think too much of ways to torment me." His thumb rocked into her while a second finger joined the first and both slid in and out of her, starting a new pattern. "Now, think of me, only me and what I do to you."

She moaned, pressing closer. She nipped his ear. "Take me. Do it now."

He lifted her, and she felt the tiled wall against her back. She wrapped her legs around his lean hips. Then, he drove inside her. She clung to him, meeting the fierce strokes. "Didn't you say I had to please you when we returned home?"

"You are." His hands tightened on her derriere. "Satisfy me, *Vaslattel*. Scream for me. Say you want only me and promise you're mine."

"You demand everything." She panted for breath, rising and falling as he went deeper. She couldn't resist him and unfortunately, she feared he knew it. She gripped his shoulders. "I hate—"

"No, you don't." His mouth claimed hers with fiery passion. He lifted his head moments later. "Be honest, Satiranika. Say the words of your heart."

Water gushed down on them and she felt the negativity wash away, cleansing them in more than one way. She stared into the dark *magick* of his eyes and before she stopped it, the truth escaped. "I love you, Rowindache. I'm yours and I love you."

He smiled, increasing the pace of his movements. "And you're mine. My queen, my heart and my soul."

She arched, bucked against him in the last frenzy before she flew among the stars. He followed in a few more thrusts. Afterwards, between kisses, they washed each other, which led to another, slower bout of love-making in the shower. Drying one another with huge, warmed towels ended their time in the bathroom and she taught him to use the hair blower.

Eventually, she found herself lying in bed, naked in his arms. "You didn't say you loved me."

"You're my heart." He stroked her hair. "Of course, I love you, but that doesn't mean you rule me, *Vaslattel*."

"But, I'm your queen."

"Yes."

She shivered when he kissed her forehead, her eyebrows. "That means you serve me."

"Very well." He chuckled. "Just remember, this was your idea, my own. I'd have let you rest longer."

"What?" Her jaw dropped when he released her, to throw the covers aside and slide downwards. "I didn't say I wanted—"

She stopped talking, unable to speak, when he parted her legs and his mouth claimed her. He stroked upward with his tongue, exploring the folds of skin with soft strokes before diving deep. He kept lapping, licking and finally drew the small bud into his mouth and sucked. She fell apart, screaming his name.

When she returned to herself, he rested most of his weight on his elbows, gazing down at her. He lowered his head, trailed kisses to her breasts, then teased a nipple with his lips. She felt him probe, then slide into her.

She rose to meet his first stroke. "What do you think this proves?"

"That you should repeat your promises." He pulled back, lifting his head, then slid inside her again. Another set of long steady strokes before he alternated with shorter ones, then began the lengthy, deep ones again. "Say the words again, from your heart this time. Who are you?"

"I, Satiranika, first daughter—"

Her reward was a long kiss, one where his tongue explored her mouth and the motion of his lean hips started again. She arched against him, meeting him kiss for kiss, thrust for thrust. His gravelly voice repeated the questions he'd asked at *Samhain*, demanding answers she gave willingly this time.

"—eldest of the *Trecesalty*, born to Dianaranika and Jarvesel, thirteenth witch in the *Ranika relkinam* give myself, soul, mind and body to—"

A whirlpool of emotions overwhelmed her while the powerful strokes continued. Through it, she heard him encourage, insist on the promises. "I, Satiranika take Rowindache as my *capostrol*, his *vaslattel* now and always, through all my lives—".

"Finish it with me. Say all the words."

She met the movement of his hips with hers and the oath continued between kisses. "I follow my *capostrol's* ways for three eternities—"

"As I keep my *vaslattel* for three eternities."

His hips rocked into hers. He lowered his head and his mouth captured hers, his tongue plunging deep. She followed where he led in a dance that took both of them beyond the stars, each thrust taking them farther and farther until they exploded together.

Later, she rested against him, her head nestled on his chest while she listened to his heartbeat, toying with one of his nipples. "I thought things would change once I admitted my feelings, but you don't intend to have me as a *laspowima*, do you?"

"You're my *vaslattel*." He feathered a kiss over her lips. "We've exchanged vows twice during a *Sex Magick* mating. You'll have this lifetime and the next to prove you're worthy of being my *laspowima*. For now, you're the captive witch I've claimed."

She rolled on top of him, admiration filling her voice. "I liked the way you took me the first time against the door at *Samhain*. You don't make allowances or crawl to me because you don't fear me. You renounced me as a *laspowima* and you meant it."

"Truth-speaking honors both of us." He smoothed his hands over her back to the curve of her hips. "What's your point, *Vaslattel*?"

"That it's my turn to ride a wizard." She shifted, slowly easing onto him, catching her breath when he slipped inside her. "Keep up if you can."

"Not a problem for me, but I want to hear your vows again. And for you to say you love me again."

"You can want, *Capostrol*, but it doesn't mean it will happen." She gasped when he cupped her breasts, thumbs teasing her sensitive nipples. "At least, not now. Not yet."

"As long as you say the words before dawn. Now, ride me, *Vaslattel*."

"I'll do that." She rose, then slid down again, repeating the motion again as he rocked inside her. "I've repeated the vows twice. If you weren't listening, that's your issue, not mine."

"I like the way you make those promises." He drew her to him, and she surrendered to his kiss. "I'll hear them again before my son draws breath."

"You mean my daughter."

———

When he woke early the next morning, weak sunlight trickled in the windows. He saw her packing clothes into a wheeled suitcase. She'd already dressed for travel in one of her favorite striped tunics over blue leggings and high-heeled boots. "I've got to get back to Seattle. My co-counsel will be overwhelmed if he has to start the defense on that attempted murder trial tomorrow. Are you coming with Rebekah and me, or staying here?"

"Questions and not demands, *Vaslattel*." Tossing the blankets aside, he rose and went to her. "I like that. Where do you see us living?"

"I don't know, but I'm pretty sure you won't be happy in a city and I really want to raise my daughter near her aunts and cousins."

"And if it's my son?"

She shrugged. "He'll need his family too."

He slid his hands around her neck, tipped up her dimpled chin and kissed her. She swayed nearer. He drew her against him. "There's enough land here for me to build a house for us and we have time."

"Lots of it. Nothing but time." She heaved a sigh, nestling closer. "Do I design the home I want, or do you?"

"We do it together."

"Together. I like the sound of that, Rowindache."

"We're partners, Satiranika. From this day forward, we do what pleases the other and we do it together."

"Thanks to you, I'll live with that and so will our children."

THE END

———

Turn the page for a preview of the Seventh book in the *Liberty Valley* series, *Kitchen Witch!*

———

Keep up with Josie Malone and subscribe to her newsletter!
https://sendfox.com/josiemaloneauthor

———

Don't miss out on your next favorite book!

Join the Satin Romance mailing list
www.satinromance.com/mail.html

KITCHEN WITCH

"Turn your troubles over to the Goddess and let Her help."

— METEOR JAMISON, SHAPE-SHIFTER,
ENTREPRENEUR, AND HEREDITARY WITCH

ONE

Eagleville, Washington ~ Wednesday, November 28th, 2018

AT FOUR A.M, IT WAS STILL DARK WHEN METEOR JAMISON PARKED her van behind the two-story building on the corner of one of the main streets in town. She'd painted a giant mural of fantastic creatures that included unicorns, centaurs, and winged horses frolicking on the structure as well as huge letters spelling out Captivating Catering. She'd started the company with three of her college friends five years before and while they worked hard, it was worth it.

Her day usually started before dawn. Mentally, she began running through the list of tasks she needed to accomplish before the first customers arrived to order pastries and their breakfast espressos. She'd start by checking the walk-in refrigerator where she'd find loaves of bread, croissants and doughnuts waiting to be baked. Lizzie Drake, the head chef would have prepped the items on the lunch menu but sandwiches, quiches and two large tureens of soup always required finishing.

Still tallying the waiting work, Meteor unlocked the back door and entered the large commercial kitchen. She headed for the main bank of switches and turned on the fluorescent lights and then her favorite classic country music station before glancing around the room. The steel counters gleamed and so did the tile floor. Obviously, Daphne Hollister had finished her day by meticulously cleaning the establishment when she closed up yesterday. Meteor walked through the kitchen into the small restaurant area, admiring the pristine tables, chairs, and booths. Framed pictures of elves, fairies, satyrs and fantastic creatures courtesy of Lizzie and her friends brightened the cream walls

I'm so lucky to have such wonderful partners, Meteor thought, not for the first time as she returned to the kitchen. She turned on the commercial ovens, and the giant coffee pot on the way to look at the whiteboard outside the office and the list of upcoming events. Two birthday parties, a wedding and a baby shower this weekend. *They covered for me big-time while we waited for Astra to heal from her injuries and then return from that walk among the stars.*

For a moment, she remembered her sisters and the witchy work awaiting them before the winter solstice. The three of them had to deal with the evil that still stalked the streets of Corbettstown in eastern Liberty Valley, but the shape-shifting pack had run rampant during the forty-plus years Frank Corbett served as alpha. No, he didn't 'serve' the members, she decided. He ruled like a tyrant, and he needed to be stopped before there was more bloodshed.

As three hereditary witches destined to lead their people, she and her sisters had a duty to protect the innocents who'd followed them to this realm from their home in *Trilunon* so long ago. She remembered what Venus, their youngest sister proclaimed a few days before. "We're the *Trecesalty*, the three queens who stand together. As it was once, as it will be now and forever." "I'm the matriarch who protects the land, the sea and the air, along with their inhabitants," Meteor whispered softly, "and those include my children and my sisters." She took a deep breath, dreading the upcoming battle.

In four days, she and her soul-matched mate, Jed Corbett would confront Frank Corbett, the older shape-shifter and let him know that things were about to change in Liberty Valley. For a moment, she wondered if Jed feared the fight as much as she did. Probably not. He'd been a soldier-warrior long before they went through the soul-binding rite and male shape-shifters enjoyed wrestling with one another even in mock, rough and tumble battles. She'd certainly seen enough of that with their two sons during the past month after Edwin's arrival from 1888.

When she opened the walk-in refrigerator, she saw tall, upright carts with trays of cookies waiting to be baked. Obviously, Brigid Dawson, her apprentice, a younger kitchen witch had spent the weekend here instead of shopping holiday sales, or celebrating with her family, or saving a federal agent from angry shifters, the way Meteor had with her sisters. What happened? How had Brigid's family put the fun back in 'dysfunctional'?

Breakfast rolls baking and the baguettes for sandwiches in the other oven, Meteor brought out the first cart of cookies. The doorbell sounded at the front of the building, and she glanced at her watch. She didn't open for another three hours, but someone might not have received their order since the hours had undoubtedly been somewhat erratic for the past two days.

When she unlocked the front door, she saw the two F.B.I. agents from Friday night standing on the sidewalk outside. The older one, a tall, stocky man, stepped forward, opening a black billfold, and revealing a badge. "Ms. Jamison, I don't know if you remember me or not. I'm Wardrow Roberts." He gestured to his companion, a younger mixed-race man with close-cropped black hair. "This is Agent Fletcher Gaines."

"I know. I remember you." Meteor wouldn't tell Gaines that he was a hell of a marksman, especially when it came to shooting from a moving helicopter. He'd only wounded the wolves she fought on Saturday morning. If he'd been armed with silver rounds, he'd have killed them. "Did you find your missing agent?"

"Yes." Concern swept into Wardrow Roberts' face. "I don't know who your sister's client was, but the information she received was correct. She died trying to save Special Agent Newsome. He and Agent Endicott are still in the hospital, but they're both expected to fully recover. Your brother-in-law—"

"Your info is incorrect." Meteor glanced swiftly at the younger agent. "Astra's fine and will be back in court this afternoon."

"That's not true. She had a sword in her back and was bleeding out." Fletcher Gaines took a step forward. "I've seen people die in combat. She couldn't have survived an injury like that, not when she was taken away before receiving medical treatment."

Meteor shrugged. "I don't know what you saw, but both my sisters are fine. So are my cousins. So are all the women I know." She deliberately looked at her watch. "I have cookies baking, and I need to get back to work. There's a lot of prep to do before the breakfast rush. So, if that's all—"

"We'd like to speak to your brother-in-law about the incident Saturday morning and find out who assaulted your sister," Wardrow Roberts said. "Where do we find him?"

"I have no idea, and I still need to finish the bagels. But I do know what my sister would tell you."

"What's that?" Fletcher Gaines asked eagerly.

"Get a warrant." Meteor closed the door, locked it, and retraced her steps to the kitchen in time to hear the timers on the ovens buzz.

Two hours later, while she created gourmet breakfast sandwiches on the bread Brigid baked, the doorbell at the front door of the store jangled. Meteor went to greet what must be a new delivery person. Not everyone knew where to park or where she accepted supplies. It wasn't a truck driver or a customer wanting cookies, or to order a cake, or to arrange an event. This time it was Hilda and Erik Armstrong.

Meteor took a deep breath, hoping her dread didn't show. She hated hurting others, but Kyle Morgan and Nina Armstrong simply weren't safe in this day and time, not when the Corbett wolves saw them as prey. The couple had a better chance of survival in Liberty

Valley of 1888. It was why she and her witchy sisters sent them through a *Time Portal* to the days of yesteryear. She certainly couldn't admit that, so she opted to hide the truth when she opened the door. "Hi. Have you heard anything from Nina or Kyle?"

"Not from law enforcement or the detectives we've hired." Erik stood six foot, six in his socks. A giant blond, he always dressed in cowboy style like the Hollywood stuntman he'd been in his younger days. He carried a medium-sized, wooden, steamer trunk with metal trim. "Hilda found this in the museum at the Bar M. She says that Nina left it for you and your sisters. Where do you want it?"

"Upstairs in my apartment." Meteor hugged the taller blonde woman. "I'm so sorry. I know you miss them. I wish there was something I could do to help you."

"It's all right." Hilda smiled, faint amusement slipping into her face. "I know this will sound absolutely strange and my big brother thinks I'm ready for the looney-bin—"

"I haven't said that."

"I see it in your eyes when I talk about them." Hilda lifted her chin. "Nina came to the Bar M for weeks to take photography classes with Will Dawson. He taught her to use the antique cameras in the museum. She never was in the storage area where I keep the vintage clothes."

"Just because you didn't see her doesn't mean she wasn't there."

"She wasn't." Hilda gestured to the steamer trunk on his shoulder. "I know that even if no one in my family ever believes me. If they have me locked up in an insane asylum, I expect you and your sisters to rescue me, Meteor Jamison."

"We will." Meteor looked at the trunk. "What did you find?"

"I didn't remember seeing it before, but I must have. When I opened it, I found a red walking dress, button-up shoes, and a 'fascinator' style hat. They were very carefully wrapped with a tag addressed to Astra. There's an ornate dagger in a sheath for Venus and for you, an assortment of recipes in a bundle of sheet music for a spinet piano."

"How did she know I had one?" Meteor glanced at Erik. "I hate to agree with a man about anything, but your cousin was never upstairs in my apartment, and I don't recall mentioning it to her."

"I don't know." Hilda's smile widened. "I think I'll opt for Shakespeare and Nina's favorite quote, 'There are more things in heaven and earth, Horatio, than are dreamt of in your philosophy.' She left that in a note for me in another place she never went to when she came to the Bar M."

"Really?" Erik glowered at his sister. "Where was that?"

"The closed off wing of the house where the original Kyle Morgan, his wife, Antonina and their children lived. Nobody ever called her that here, but it was Nina's full name."

While Erik and Hilda squabbled about their cousin, Meteor led the way to the door that hid the staircase to her apartment. They might not entirely believe it, but now she knew she and her sisters had been right to save the young couple who'd obviously lived a full life in Liberty Valley. Nina had left them a message letting them know *magick* worked, and they'd used it appropriately, at least this time. Who was to know what would happen in the days, months, and years to come? Foretelling the future wasn't one of their talents although Venus still spoke of an upcoming war, and Astra *Saw* the outcomes when people tried to harm innocents.

An hour later, Meteor was back in the kitchen, packing the neatly assembled holiday turkey sandwiches into individual cardboard cartons so they'd be ready for the lunch crowd. She heard the buzzer at the back door and the jangle of the warning windchimes when it opened to reveal Lizzie Blake, the chef who created fabulous meals. She opted for tattoos that covered nearly every inch of her small body, most of which had something to do with dragons. She'd dyed her light blonde hair in varying shades of crimson and green, decorated with multi-colored ribbons. Purple, pink and electric blue makeup used as a fantastic fairy mask emphasized her large eyes, forehead, and the top of her cheeks.

As usual, she'd dressed for attention and to make tips when she worked the front counter, choosing a steam punk outfit, a skirt and fitted vest in rich, embroidered pewter gray taffeta. A cream stretch blouse with full sleeves matched the ivory and cream attached petticoat with layers of different ruffled lace. The skirt had a slight 'V' line shape in the front and dipped down longer at the back. The hem had been decorated with a pleated ruffled row of taffeta.

"Wow, you're styling today. What's the occasion?" Meteor laid out more slices of bread on the counter. "Hot date?"

"A major party tonight and I don't have time to go home and change." Lizzie paused at the end of the counter to check the two soup containers. "Jed Corbett is already here to pick up lunch for the logging crew."

"That doesn't make sense." Meteor spread a thin layer of cranberry sauce on the bread. "Those guys burn a lot of calories, and they prefer the he-man burgers and fries from the Cross Cut Tavern to what they call our 'yuppie' fare. Are you sure you saw him?"

"Yes. He parked in front of me on the street and was getting out of the Corbett Logging truck when he saw me." Lizzie replaced the lid. "Time to open up. I'll let him in the front door. I'll call back his order."

"Sounds good." It still didn't make a lot of sense, Meteor thought. She didn't know why he'd come to visit or why Lizzie hadn't mentioned his companion, Gard Devlin who always rode along with him. "I'll touch base with Jed later. Maybe he wanted to talk to me about the kids."

"Could be." Lizzie kept walking. "When Tolliver gets here, have him help set up the showcases before he begins making mochas."

"You've got it." Meteor glanced toward the back entrance when the stocky, short man in jeans and a sweatshirt entered. He must have heard Lizzie's request, because he nodded agreement and picked up the first tray of thickly frosted maple bars, carrying them toward the the dining area. Half satyr, he'd enjoyed October when he didn't have to disguise his pointed ears, or horns, or furry legs and hooves. Now, he suppressed his true nature when strangers were around.

A steady flow of customers kept all of them busy and Meteor didn't have time to think about anything except work. When they closed, she helped Daphne clean the dining room. Lizzie and Brigid prepped for the next day, scouring the kitchen between mixing new batches of cookies, setting bread to rise, and stirring up cake batter.

Just before sunset, while she washed the glass front door, Meteor spotted the older blue pickup taking a premier spot adjacent to the building. Jed Corbett slid out of the driver's seat. At six foot six, he towered above her by ten inches. Thick coal black hair curled around his ruggedly handsome face. A nose broken in one of his many brawls saved him from looking insipid. He could have been a cover model or an actor if a director wanted a rugged, he-man type. Today, he wore faded chopped off jeans, a red plaid shirt that jarred with the bright orange suspenders and corked boots, not a fashion statement, but he always sent excitement racing through her.

Gard Devlin, a brawny, brown-haired private investigator hired to protect him followed Jed. Luckily the other man had grown up in a logging town in Oregon, so he knew what to do with a bulldozer, part of the reason Jed was able to get him a job at Corbett Logging. Gard had dressed for cat-skinning success. His unbuttoned blue flannel shirt revealed a green tee that clung to muscled arms, wide shoulders, and a broad chest. Faded jeans encased long legs and battered boots.

The two men sauntered around the building to the back door and buzzed for entry. Meteor went to meet them. When she opened the door, Jed's slow smile warmed her to the heart, but she hoped that didn't show. She tilted her head and met his night-dark gaze. "We're closed."

"Good." He feathered a thumb over her lips. "Then, you can come look at that cottage your mom intends to rent to my cousin, Junior and his wife, Cherry."

"I'm busy and Diana's real estate shenanigans aren't my concern."

"Yes, they are, sweetheart." Jed chuckled, a deep dark sound.

"Bring your witchling to help you cleanse and ward the place while your mom and Rowdy sever Junior and Cherry's ties to my uncle's pack and connect them to us. Cherry wants to help guard you and our younglings, so they don't end up as a feast for the Corbettstown pack."

THANK YOU FOR READING

———

Did you enjoy this book?

We invite you to leave a review at your favorite book site, such as Goodreads, Amazon, Barnes & Noble, etc.

DID YOU KNOW THAT LEAVING A REVIEW...

- Helps other readers find books they may enjoy.
- Gives you a chance to let your voice be heard.
- Gives authors recognition for their hard work.
- Doesn't have to be long. A sentence or two about why you liked the book will do.

ABOUT THE AUTHOR

Josie Malone lives and works at her family's riding stable in Washington State. She's taught children to ride and know about horses for so long that she often discovers she's taught three generations of their families. Her life experiences span adventures from dealing cards in a casino, attending graduate school to get her Masters in Teaching degree, being a substitute teacher, and serving in the Army Reserve - all leading to her second career as a published author. Visit her at her website, www.josiemalone.com to learn about her books.

Subscribe to Josie's Newsletter:
https://sendfox.com/josiemaloneauthor

Contact Josie at:
josiemaloneauthor@outlook.com

www.josiemalone.com

facebook.com/JosieMaloneAuthor

twitter.com/josmaloneauthor

instagram.com/josiemaloneauthor

amazon.com/Josie-Malone/e/B006HC9VMI

ALSO BY JOSIE MALONE

Baker City Hearts and Haunts

My Sweet Haunt

More Than A Spirit

Family Skeletons

Ghost of the Past (coming soon!)

Kindred Spirits (coming Soon!)

———

Liberty Valley Love

A Man's World

Cowboy Spell

The Marshal's Lady

Hero Spell

A Trail Through Time

Time In Between

Kitchen Witch (Coming Soon!)